Praise for the series

'It's addictively brilliant! The protagonist is vivid and sympathetic – and I love both the story and the world Adrian has created. It's meticulously thought out and utterly believable'
John Gwynne

'A classically brilliant fantasy writer, a pusher of boundaries, a great storyteller'
Paul Cornell

'This is a satisfying read, a story you can really lose yourself in'
SFX

'A clever, compelling page-turner . . . a cracking sequel to *The Tiger and the Wolf*'
Sci-Fi and Fantasy Reviews

'Equally deft in the realms of science fiction and fantasy adventure, Adrian Tchaikovsky knows how to take you to a place, no matter the setting . . . Maniye Many Tracks is a fascinating character; layered, strong, torn, constantly developing and hugely empathetic'
SciFiNow

'Tchaikovsky has woven a richly textured world, brimming with difference and complexity'
SFReader

The Bear and the Serpent

Adrian Tchaikovsky was born in Woodhall Spa, Lincoln-shire, before heading off to Reading to study psychology and zoology. For reasons unclear even to himself, he subsequently ended up in law. He has worked as a legal executive in both Reading and Leeds, where he now lives. Married, he is a keen live role-player and occasional amateur actor. He has also trained in stage fighting, and keeps no exotic or dangerous pets of any kind – possibly excepting his son. He's the author of the critically acclaimed Shadows of the Apt series and the Echoes of the Fall Series, as well as *Guns of the Dawn* and *Children of Time* – which won the 30th Anniversary Arthur C. Clarke Award for Best Science Fiction Novel.

www.shadowsoftheapt.com

By Adrian Tchaikovsky

Shadows of the Apt
Empire in Black and Gold
Dragonfly Falling
Blood of the Mantis
Salute the Dark
The Scarab Path
The Sea Watch
Heirs of the Blade
The Air War
War Master's Gate
Seal of the Worm

Echoes of the Fall
The Tiger and the Wolf
The Bear and the Serpent

Other novels
Guns of the Dawn
Children of Time

ADRIAN
TCHAIKOVSKY

The Bear and the Serpent

Echoes of the Fall:
Book Two

PAN BOOKS

First published 2017 by Macmillan

This paperback edition published 2017 by Pan Books
an imprint of Pan Macmillan
20 New Wharf Road, London N1 9RR
Associated companies throughout the world
www.panmacmillan.com

ISBN 978-1-5098-3025-1

1 3 5 7 9 8 6 4 2

A CIP catalogue record for this book is available from the British Library.

Map artwork by Michael Czajkowski

Typeset by Ellipsis, Glasgow
Printed and bound by CPI Group (UK) Ltd, Croydon CR0 4YY

Visit www.panmacmillan.com to read more about all our books
and to buy them. You will also find features, author interviews and
news of any author events, and you can sign up for e-newsletters
so that you're always first to hear about our new releases.

*To the Storm Wolves, the Millenese
and all those other imaginary societies
that have welcomed me in the past.*

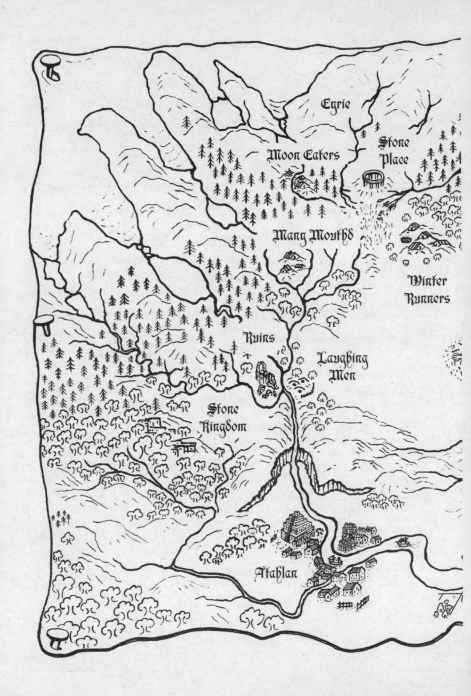

A Brief History of Recent Events

Maniye, daughter of two peoples

Maniye's life was once dominated by fear of three men. Akrit Stone River, her father, was the chief of the Winter Runners – one of the tribes of the Wolf. Kalameshli Takes Iron was their priest, the Wolf's voice. He was master of the magic of iron, and constantly sought to punish her for any infractions he could find. Lastly, Broken Axe was a lone hunter of fearsome reputation. And when Akrit tired of Maniye's mother, he gave Broken Axe the task of her murder.

Maniye's mother was queen of the Tiger people, captured in war. Maniye therefore has two souls and can take the shape of both tiger and wolf. This is unlike the rest of her people who can Step only into the form of the wolf. When she found out her father intended to use her to subjugate the Tiger and become High Chief of the Wolf, she fled into the wilderness. She left with the old Serpent priest – Hesprec Essen Skese – whom she freed to spite Kalameshli. Broken Axe was sent to pursue them across the northern wilderlands, but they found sanctuary in the home of the Bear, Loud Thunder.

Asmander, Champion of the South

Also travelling the north was Asmander, a Champion from the southern Sun River Nation. His goal was to recruit the legendary 'Iron Wolves' for his friend and prince, Tecuman. The south was, and still is, on the point of civil war between the young Tecuman and his twin sister. And foreign mercenaries are valued there as the loyalty of local warriors remains suspect. Asmander arrived accompanied by the Dragon pirate Venat, his slave. Shyri, a girl of the Laughing Man tribe – who had been dogging his steps for her own reasons – also formed part of his party.

As a Champion, Asmander Steps not only into a crocodile, the shape of his people, but also to the sickle-clawed Running Lizard, swift and deadly. After Hesprec's intervention, he can also take the shape of a bat-winged reptile. These are great souls from an age before humans walked the land.

Events at the Stone Place

At winter's end Loud Thunder was summoned by his cousin Lone Mountain to the Stone Place, the sacred heart of the Crown of the World. He was called by his Mother, shaman ruler of the Bear. She had sensed the same doom coming to the land that Hesprec had come north to investigate.

Keeping ahead of Broken Axe, Maniye and Hesprec travelled with Thunder to the Stone Place. Here, the wise of all the northern tribes had gathered. Kalameshli and Akrit were already present, but so were the Tiger. Chased by her father, Maniye found shelter with the Tiger priestess Aritchaka, thence travelling west to the Shining Halls where the Tiger holds court.

Asmander and his comrades had also been at the Stone Place and witnessed Akrit's pursuit of Maniye. For their own reasons they set out in pursuit and met Hesprec. As a native of their own land, his priestly authority was enough to recruit their aid to help Maniye.

Maniye on the run

In the Shining Halls Maniye discovered the secret the world has been keeping from her. Her mother Joalpey is not dead and Broken Axe is not her enemy. Against Akrit's orders Broken Axe had set Joalpey free because of his own personal code. However, the Shining Halls did not offer the homecoming Maniye had hoped. Despite doing her best to become a fitting daughter for the queen, Joalpey could not overlook the Wolf blood within her and they came into conflict. Maniye had to flee her mother even as she had her father.

Fleeing the Tiger, they ran into the jaws of the Wolf. Hesprec was caught, and died shortly after Maniye rescued him. The news of his death released Asmander from his oath of fealty to him, and he reverted to his original mission. In the midst of a battle between Tiger, Wolf and the newly arrived Loud Thunder, he delivered Maniye to her father to secure the Iron Wolves for his prince.

Maniye found herself caught between Akrit and Kalameshli. Her father wanted her death, but Kalameshli begged she could still be of use. Through this encounter Maniye divined she was Kalameshli's daughter, not Akrit's. In his cruelties towards her, he'd aimed to drive the Tiger from her and make her a true Wolf, safe from his god.

Asmander, torn by guilt, suffered a change of heart. He rescued both Maniye and Broken Axe and took them to a camp of the Horse. Here they were reunited with Hesprec – now in the body of a young girl. He had been reborn in a new skin, as is the way of the Serpent. By then, Maniye was losing control of her two souls, and their antipathy was driving her mad.

Maniye's transformation

With Akrit and the Tiger both coming for Maniye, she conceived a desperate plan with Hesprec – based on what she understood of Asmander's Champion status. At a ritual site nearby, Hesprec sent Maniye on a vision quest into the Godsland. Their goal was to find a Champion to adopt her. She fought her own souls across the land of all the clawed and fanged gods. Bringing both the tiger and wolf within her to heel, she was visited at last by a great beast from the deep past, equal parts bear, wolf and tiger: a Champion.

While she was questing, her friends fought both Tiger and Wolf to keep her safe. And Venat, whom Asmander freed before the fight, returned to save his former master. Broken Axe faced Akrit in single combat and fell. However, this won Maniye enough time to emerge in the vast form of the Champion of the north. She fought and defeated Akrit with the aid of Kalameshli – choosing his daughter over his chief at the last minute.

Maniye the Champion had become a force to be reckoned with and the Crown of the World was not ready. Half the tribes feared her influence and half wanted to control her. A few hunters and outcasts offered themselves to her service, and these she took as her warband. Then she escaped the demands of the north by travelling south with Asmander, to serve as his Iron Wolves.

The Bear and the Serpent

1

Maniye the wolf ghosted through the tall grass beneath a Plains half-moon bellied out like a pale orange sail. A moon in foreign skies, but all moons were the same moon; the Wolf's moon.

Her nose and ears told her where the others were, as they wove their own tracks between the stiff, saw-edged blades. Spear Catcher was closest, padding along a little behind her, wanting to make himself useful. On her other side, keeping level, was Tiamesh, a young woman a little too eager to win a hunter's name. The rest – some half dozen of her Iron Wolves – were spread out to left and right, approaching the camp from downwind. The scent of lion came to them, raw and harsh in the nostrils, but no tang of wolf crept out to trouble the Lions.

The night air of the Plains was full of unfamiliar sounds: insects; birds; distantly she heard a high whickering sound that might be the Laughing Men. She hoped not. She was going to be busy enough with the Lion raiders.

She had come south from the Crown of the World – from the lands where she had become something Other to those she had been born amongst. She had been Tiger; she had been Wolf: the world had cared for neither, and both her father's and her mother's people had done their best to kill her. Their best had not been good enough.

A new soul had made its den within her, which was neither Tiger or Wolf or Bear or Hyena but something of all of them, and the world had looked at her differently. She had become like something out of the stories. A hero to some, a Champion; a wonder, a thing foretold. It made her a threat, also. When the young and the disaffected came to her and sought to join her warband – a warband she did not know she had, until they invented it for her – she knew she would have to lead them somewhere. Otherwise she would become a rival. Tiger, Wolf or Bear, nobody wished to share territory with somebody who was strong and would not bow her head.

And so she had gone south, following the invitation of a man who had been her travelling companion, and then her betrayer, and at last a friend of sorts. She had answered the call of the young southerner, Asmander, and travelled downriver on the boats of the Horse Society to their great village of villages, that they called Where the Fords Meet. Asmander himself had gone further south still, to his 'prince', as he called the man, because for Maniye to bring her warband into the southern lands unbidden might be misinterpreted. They were the Iron Wolves, after all. In the south, apparently, they were legend.

Maniye wore no iron. Her people were the outcasts and the misfits and the discontented. In the north they had been looked upon as nothing but trouble. Perhaps to southern eyes there would be a glamour about them.

Asmander had promised to send word back – but his word had fallen into the paws of the Lion. Up ahead she could see the light of the Lion's fire. Their camp was a rock, an angled slab of stone that rose from a sea of grass like an island. The wind had given Maniye a gift: her approach brought her towards the shadow side, rather than the flat face where the Lions had set their fire. This close, she could hear the Lions speaking, the voices of their boisterous young men.

Now she paused, sinking down into the grass so that she could just see the jut of the rock like a curve of starless dark, limned by the leaping dance of the unseen flames. Spear Catcher crept beside her; he was an old man, but he moved as silently as any she'd known; a man with his own ghosts, certainly, but they were none of them free of those.

She Stepped back onto human hands and feet. A small girl – *still* a small girl despite it all – skin the colour of tanned leather, hair cut short and ragged about her ears. She wore a cuirass of bronze scales, a knife of the same metal at her belt. Nobody from any land would look on her and say *Champion* at first sight.

And yet there was something that this new soul had brought her. Hesprec, the Serpent priestess, had claimed this girl had a *promise* to her. A promise of great things, she had said.

Spear Catcher shook off his wolf shape too – with him it was just like that, a twitch of the hackles becoming a shudder of the shoulders, as though he was shaking himself dry. He had walked the Crown of the World for more than forty years, had Spear Catcher, and yet here he was in her company; there his hearth-wife was, back at Where the Fords Meet, neither of them with the folly of youth in their eyes but neither with anything to keep them in the north.

'Where are the Twins?' Maniye whispered.

'No sign. In trouble.' Spear Catcher was almost bald, his face grooved and lined by age, and grooved even deeper by the puckered scar across his cheek and ear that had burdened him with his name. 'I'll scout for them.'

'Hold.' She had a sense of movement around them, as though the Champion was keeping watch and listening on her behalf. The rest of her raiding party had stopped, holding their places in the concealing grass.

Then there was a flurry of motion above them: Maniye had her knife out, and Spear Catcher his hatchet, both about to strike. When the raven that swooped on them turned into a man, he almost became a dead one.

There would be no use cursing Feeds on Rags, even if Maniye could raise her voice; he would only forget the words a moment later. He was no youth either – ten years Maniye's senior at least, though he acted like a mad boy half the time. He

3

was the only person who had ever lied about his name to Maniye, which seemed a terrible thing to her, but perhaps was standard behaviour back in the Eyrie where he had grown up. Half his face was painted with curving, sharp-edged tattoos, a turbulent night from which his left eye stared like a berserk moon. He was grinning, of course; he was almost always grinning. Whenever he stopped, Maniye started worrying.

'Speak,' she whispered.

Feeds on Rags – or the man who claimed that name – bobbed his head animatedly. 'Found our missing messenger. Keeping him warm by the fire, they are.'

'They're eating him?' Spear Catcher growled.

'Not till they're finished with what they found in his baskets,' the Raven man told them, and not for the first time Maniye wished he knew how to get to the point the straight way. 'Happy with their guest's generosity.'

Maniye was about to question that, but a more urgent thought occurred to her. 'Where's Sathewe? Don't tell me you left her there?'

'Wouldn't come,' Feeds on Rags told her, his expression shifting to exaggerated misery. 'Was going to prise the prisoner from—'

Maniye cut him off with a hiss. Feeds on Rags and the Coyote girl Sathewe worked as a team, mostly on the basis that they could cause more trouble together than either could alone. Neither of them had the common sense of a baby. It was only in this way that they were twins, yet the name had stuck.

'Go find her,' Maniye spat at the Raven. 'Get her out, or you'll have her death on you.'

For a second she saw the real man behind the bluster: the man who realized he had got it wrong yet *again*. He Stepped in a frenzy of flapping wings, lifting into the night.

Maniye opened her mouth, but Feeds on Rags was back with them almost instantly, both eyes wide.

4

'More friends!' blurted from his human mouth, and over her questions he gabbled, 'Not Lions – from behind.'

Maniye bared her teeth, knowing what he meant instantly: that someone had pulled the same trick on her as she had been blithely using against the Lions. Had she been in the Crown of the World it would never have worked. Here, there were too many strange smells.

Spear Catcher was Stepped and gone instantly, rounding up the raiders without being asked, so that by the time the new-comers made themselves known, Maniye had all her Iron Wolves at her back.

The newcomers slunk out of the grass and out of the dark-ness. For a moment she thought they were the Laughing Men after all, but these were different – familiar, almost. There was more than a little wolf about them.

They had large ears, eyes that were so dark as to be bottom-less, and their hides were mottled, looking muddy in the moon-light. There were more than a dozen of them, and they made a loose crescent before the wolves, jaws hanging open and panting a little. The presence of the Lions was like a stone at the back of Maniye's mind.

Plains Dogs; she knew them. A tribe of the Wolf fallen from favour, driven from the Crown of the World in the old days, to find a new totem and a new way of life.

The leader of the Dogs Stepped then: she saw a man with skin more copper-red than hers, less so than the Lions or the Laughing Men. There was something of the north in his high cheekbones and his piercing eyes, but his hair was long and gleaming dark, bound into a hundred little plaits. He wore a cuirass and skirt of layered leather and there was a sickle-bladed weapon in his hand.

He hunched closer, then closer still, eyes flicking between her and the fire-lined rock that rose behind her. She Stepped for him, met him halfway, knife in hand and ready to fight.

'Lion-hunter,' he said very softly. When she nodded, his eyes skittered across the crouching forms of her wolves and he told her, 'Find other prey, little foreign girl.'

'We claim one of the Horse whom they have taken,' she said.

He shrugged, a fluid gesture. 'You are far from home, small hunter. These are not your wars.'

True enough. The feuding of the Plains tribes was a knot that all of history had been tying. 'Take all the Lions you wish, but I shall have what I've come for,' she said.

He grinned at that. 'Or we shall take you and the Lions both. Do you think we cannot do it?'

'I think you cannot,' she said, quite seriously. He must have seen the Champion in her even before she Stepped, for the mockery was already draining from him.

She brought the Champion to her. Maybe the Lions would see, but she needed to bring this dog to heel before he started a fight that would raise all the Plains. She Stepped, bulking out until she was huge as a bear, yet with the sleek hunting lines of a tiger and the muzzle of a wolf. When she called the Champion's soul to the fore she was a monstrous hunting beast from an age before human feet ever graced these lands, a killer out of deep time. The Plains Dog, who had been looking down on her, was craning his neck back. He would not be calling her 'little' again. When she had Stepped, he was between her forepaws, almost between her jaws.

His people – they had Stepped, some of them, with bows and spears, and others had fallen back, or rushed forward until their nerve failed. The leader of the Dogs just crouched there, looking up, and there was a wonder in his face that she had seen from others. He was a man who could look on the Champion without fear; a man with a large soul.

He stood slowly, shaking his head. 'Oh, we would be *honoured* if you would hunt the Lion with us.'

Then there was a high girl's cry from up on the rock – *Sathewe!* The Coyote girl's luck had run out again, as it so often did.

Maniye met the Plains Dog leader's gaze and dipped her head in agreement. Then he had Stepped and was dashing off through the grass, his people following.

She turned and took in the looming height of the rock, letting moon and fire tell its secrets to her: four man-heights tall and rounded, no easy handholds for human fingers.

'Go after them; Spear Catcher is leader,' she told her raiders. They could not follow the way that she would go.

She looked up at the rock. At its apex, at its edge, there was a bulge that she had already marked. There would be the Lion's lookout, supposedly watching the moon-touched grasslands for just such an attack as this. His attention was back towards the fire, though, watching his fellows having a good time. And the Lion were roaring, just as Feeds had predicted. The Horse messenger's baggage had plainly contained something to keep them entertained. Maniye had an idea what that was.

But now to make her entrance. She rolled her shoulders, stretched her spine, and then Stepped into her mother's shape, into the tiger that was the lion's cousin. No lion could climb as she could climb; only the leopard, so she had heard, and she had never seen one, nor met the Leopard's secretive and dark-auspiced people.

The rock was old: she dug her claws into its history, the marks of the rains that came to the Plains once or twice a year, the gouges of horn and claw, the cracks where the mice and the lizards hid. The rock's past was a ladder that she climbed, flowing up the stone face of it like a shadow.

Of course, it was possible to be *too* good at this, she thought. A little embarrassing to arrive on her own. The Champion would no doubt impress the Lion greatly, so much so that their leader might fancy her pelt for a cloak. She doubted she could hold them all off alone.

These were all young men, this band of Lions. That was their way, she heard: each Lion village had many strong women hunters, and a few men who ruled them and grew fat off their

7

labours. Excess sons and nephews and cousins were thrown out to bedevil the rest of the Plains, wandering until they either met their dooms or went home for a reckoning with their ageing uncles. It seemed a wasteful way to live, to Maniye, but then she knew the stories the Plains people told about the terrible savages at the Crown of the World. Everyone was everyone else's monster.

Besides, was she not taking her own band of unwanted hunters out to find their fates? Her mentor Broken Axe had done the same, when he was young. It was just that the Lions had made the practice a deeper part of their story.

It turned out one of the Lions was still alert, just not the sentry she was creeping up towards. A human yell turned into a deep, full-throated roar that she virtually felt through the rock itself. The yelping and yipping of the Plains Dogs rose in reply, and then she heard Spear Catcher's spine-chilling howl, all the bitter frustration of an ageing man with little to show for his years, caught in a wolf's clear voice.

The lookout above her started. Already on four feet, he turned and roared his own defiance, and she slithered up the last few yards of stone and fell upon him.

He must have caught her movement from the corner of his eye, because he rounded on her even as she struck. For a moment she was just swatting at him: a little tiger in the fire-shadow of a heavy-set lion. Then the Champion shouldered its way forward impatiently, and she thrust herself up on her hind legs like a bear, one set of claws scooping the startled Lion out of the way and off the rock entirely.

She bellowed. The voice of the Champion was a cry out of time, like no beast ever heard by human ears.

There were a dozen of the enemy there, half of them burly men in skins and leather and stiff linen armour, the rest already taken to their fighting forms, shoulders bristling with new-grown manes, baring their long fangs at her. And though they shied from her at first sight, they were ready for the fight at the

8

second. Enemies of the Lion often called them cowards, willing to fight only when they knew they could win. Yet these homeless youths looked like they would dare anything; they had nothing left to lose.

She lumbered forwards, using the slope of the rock to pick up speed. She saw the long-boned man in their midst, a noose about his neck to keep him human – that was the Horse messenger. Only in the moment before her charge hit home did she locate Sathewe – the skinny Coyote girl corralled against the fire by one of the Lions, but not restrained, in no immediate danger.

While the handful in front of her retreated, another leapt at her flank, raking at her with his claws. He connected with her thick hide and the bronze beneath kept him from drawing blood. His weight dragged at her, though, and she rolled to that side, forcing him to leap clear. The Lions in front of her took that as an opportunity, but she was ready for them, meeting them with jaws agape and bellowing, sending them twisting away.

Then the Plains Dogs and her Wolves were in the camp, and the knot confronting her disintegrated into individual beasts seeking individual fights. Maniye took a moment to catch her breath, and a starved-thin coyote scampered up to her on stick legs, the curve of the animal's panting mouth contriving to suggest laughter – Sathewe, no doubt already spinning a tale out of the adventure.

She made her way towards the Horse prisoner, and those ahead of her looked elsewhere to easier targets. Around her she could watch sidelong as Lion fought Dog. The Plains Dogs were a third the size of a grown lion: they fought two, three on one to even the odds, Stepping between human and animal from moment to moment, each taking a turn to nip at the enemy's heels and to strike with a blade. She saw instantly that they would not have had the numbers to be anything more than a nuisance on their own, despite their leader's bravado – a quick run through the camp and then away before the Lions could band together to tear into them.

Or perhaps not: the Lions were slower than she had expected, some still by the fire, and one or two – still human – looking almost bewildered. A litter of clay jars at their feet betrayed them: the Horse messenger had not been taken for the word he was bringing. The Sun River Kingdom of the south had many treasures, so she was told, but amongst the most prized was their beer.

The fighting was swift and savage, but quarter was given. There were times and places when the Plains people killed each other without qualm, but today those who ran were left to run.

A Lion challenged her – perhaps he was the leader, for he was the biggest beast there, his mane dark enough to be black in the firelight. He swatted at her muzzle, then tried to hook his paws about her head so he could bite. He was perhaps not used to meeting a bigger predator than himself. She took the sting of his claws – dangerously close to her eye – then reared up out of his reach, slamming her forepaws down at him in a move she had learned from the Bear Loud Thunder. He flinched out of the way, saving his bones, but she caught him with a sideways swipe anyway, drawing stark lines across his pelt.

Across the fire, Spear Catcher was bowled over by a beast twice his size and she saw the savage jaws lunge in at him. A moment later the biter recoiled, shaking his heavy head. The Lion's teeth were bronze, but Spear Catcher was a true Iron Wolf. Then the young she-wolf Tiamesh had leapt onto the Lion's back, biting furiously at his shoulder before springing away. Spear Catcher got back to his feet. Everything about his stance said, *I'm too old for this.*

One of the Lion was dead – had taken human shape to shout a warning or a command, perhaps, and an arrow had found his eye. One of the Dogs was down as well, still kicking, but curled into a brindled ball about his guts in a way that told Maniye he was unlikely to be kicking for long. For the rest, the Lions were already deserting their camp site, leaping down from the rock to lose themselves in the night and the sea of grass.

10

She Stepped beside the Horse man and cut the rope about his neck, then the bonds that held his hands behind him.

The leader of the Plains Dogs came trotting up, eventually, to find her with her raiders. Maniye's people had got away without anything worse than scratches, and Tiamesh had a torn ear that she was holding a wad of wool to. At Maniye's back, Sathewe and Feeds on Rags were whispering together, plotting mischief as always.

'Champion.' In his human form the Dog leader was grinning. 'Come guest with us.'

'I think your home is far from here.'

'Even so, you are welcome.'

'We are guests of the Horse,' she told him. 'We must return their man. Some day, perhaps, we will be your guests.' There was a certain way of talking that they had in the south – especially further south along the river. Maniye was trying to master it, though the words felt awkward in her mouth.

The Dog leader took that with good grace. It had not escaped Maniye that, had things been different, she could have been trying to recover the Horse man from *him*, rather than the Lions. They called her north savage and harsh, but here in the Plains everyone seemed to be at war with everyone all the time. Except the Horse, who warred with no one and always had friends, like Maniye's Wolves, to fight on their behalf.

'You are a sign,' the Dog told her softly.

She frowned. 'What manner of sign?'

He shrugged. 'Our wise women say to me, watch for signs in your travels. Here before me, I see what no man has seen in all the days. Is that not a sign?'

'A sign of what?' she pressed. She was remembering what Loud Thunder, the Bear, had said before she left. His Mother-chief had been seeking signs, too. Hesprec of the Serpent had travelled all the north in search of them. Why was the world so taken up with portents?

11

'The wise women say bad things are coming.' He shrugged. 'Who knows how wise they are? But I will tell them I have seen you. Perhaps they will know what you mean.' He spoke as if she was something he had dreamt, and with enough sincerity that for a moment she felt unreal to herself.

2

Maniye and her people had come to Where the Fords Meet on Horse boats down the Sand Pearl river. Here, where the river died, the Horse had made their stronghold. Having turned their back on the infighting of the Plains, they made themselves as hard to attack as possible. The Sand Pearl was a valiant flood when it left the north, broad enough for the flat-bottomed barges of the Horse, cutting straight and true on its southward course away from the highlands that birthed it. Unlike the Tsotec, that greater watercourse that the true south clung to, the Sand Pearl lost faith in itself as it crossed the Plains, spending itself into the dry earth until it foundered in a maze of marshy channels.

Here the Horse dwelled in a great scattered village of huts and walkways propped on stilts above the water. Here they grew food on floating mats of vegetation. Any attack on the Horse would meet with that treacherous ground; any bold raiders would have to wade and wallow and punt whilst the arrows of the Horse rained down on them. The Horse were the best archers Maniye knew. She had seen their children practising with little bows shaped from the timber they floated down from the north.

We have that timber, and make few bows. The Wolf, the Tiger, the other people of the Crown of the World fought in their Stepped shapes, and carried blades of bronze and iron to strengthen their teeth and claws. The people of the Horse fought on two legs, and took every advantage they could.

Dawn was close enough to lighten the sky, when Maniye and her Wolves returned to Where the Fords Meet. In their midst, the messenger was Stepped, a lone mount escorted by predators, with a coyote trailing behind them and a crow spreading his dark wings overhead.

She bulked out into the Champion's bear-huge form to enter the domain of the Horse. She felt guilty as she did it; the only other Champion she knew had told her it was not to be used to amuse the idly curious. Still, she was already part of a legend. What harm if she built on it?

That Alladai would see her was in her mind. She liked Alladai. She respected Alladai. She would not admit to anyone that the tall, clean-limbed Horse man whose boats had brought her south featured sometimes in her dreams. She was the leader of the Iron Wolves, after all. Such fancies were not part of her role.

Still, she hoped he saw.

The rest of her followers were here, a score in all. Aside from the Twins they were all born within the Jaws of the Wolf. What she had come seeking with them was breathing space, a time to let the Crown of the World grow used to the idea of what she was. What her followers sought varied, but they all sought something. Nobody undertook a journey like this if they had a settled place in the world. Spear Catcher and his wife were running from lives of ill luck and failed chances, children they had outlived and kin turned against them. Tiamesh saw this as a way of earning a name. Surely nobody could travel so far from home and still come back unchanged.

The rest of her band got up and took notice as she led her raiders over the high wooden roads of Where the Fords Meet. Some had been lazing in the sun that they were all still growing accustomed to. Others had been wrestling with some of the Horse, teaching and learning in equal measure. Chief amongst

14

these – the man she had left in charge while she hunted – was Moon Eye, a tall and broad-shouldered hunter falling between her and Spear Catcher in years, who had followed her for his own reasons. She had been in two minds, when he came to her, just as she had when Feeds on Rags had told her his real name. Moon Eye was slow of speech, patient, even dull; a man who retreated from fights and arguments that his strength would surely win. She would happily leave him in charge of the rowdy juniors who made up her followers when they were lounging about in the midst of the Horse village, but never in a fight. Moon Eye was a blade without a hilt, and he knew it. He was a man who shied from anger as if it was a plague, because he knew it might infect him.

She abandoned the rescued Horse messenger to his people and plunged in amongst her own, still holding the Champion's shape. They ran alongside her on four feet, or brushed their hands briefly against her pelt, renewing their fealty. Then she was human again, and apart from Sathewe, the smallest of them there.

Here were all her hunters, her warriors, but she didn't see any of the talkers. Moon Eye nodded towards one of the odd little roofless rooms dotted here and there, which the Horse used for meeting places. In the north, anywhere without a roof was outside, because that was where the rain happened. She had not seen rain in this land, but the Horse said it was so fierce when it came here, that inside and outside were barely different.

She had brought more than a warband south; there were three priests in the group. One she was repatriating to her home; one was a traveller from the north seeking the counsel of the wise ones of the Sun River Nation; one was her father.

Kalameshli Takes Iron sat brooding while the others talked. He was a man who had lived his life in the Wolf's Shadow. His lore was the Wolf's lore – he knew the secrets of iron, rituals of passage, the balance of power between the Wolf tribes and the other powers of the north. None of it was wisdom that would

15

carry him far round here. He was lost, more than any of the rest of them, and she could tell that every new thing struck him like an arrow. Of them all, he least wanted to be here, but if he was in the north, and not standing in her shadow, then the Tiger would kill him. Looking at his sullen, sour old face, Maniye sometimes wondered whether she should have saved him at all. He seemed a man who had outlived his time.

Back in the Crown of the World, when he had talked, others listened. Here others talked, and she thought he was doing his best not to listen to what they had to say.

Hesprec was talking. Maniye had heard her voice as she approached – the rhythms she had first heard from an old, old man's lips, now in the voice of a girl younger than she was. The Serpent had their own ways, and time could not kill them, but only renewed them in a different skin.

She found Hesprec sitting cross-legged, animatedly lecturing two old women of the Horse and the third priest that Maniye had brought with her from the north. And Kalameshli too, though the old Wolf never seemed to care what was said, so long as it was not said behind his back where he could not hear it.

Hesprec had gone north seeking wisdom, where Kalameshli had tried to sacrifice her to the Wolf. Others had been more forthcoming though; everywhere Hesprec travelled she had gathered prophecies and left warnings in her wake. Now she retold the stories of the north for the Horse women, and they nodded solemnly.

They too had heard of portents of disaster, but what could be done? Something terrible approached, but none could say from where. Would some tribe of the Plains rise to prominence in a tide of blood? Would there be a resurgence of the Rat cult, the gnawers of bones? Always Hesprec shook her head. 'It is as if,' she would say, 'what is coming is so far beyond our experience that we cannot see it. It comes from a direction we do not even have a name for.'

16

All very ominous, if not useful, thought Maniye.

The other priest there, the third who had come south with them, was a man with a painted face: grey with a stark white band across his eyes. The sight of it never failed to spark a twitch of fear in Maniye's stomach, as though here was the likeness of some ancient terror that history had forgotten, but that was still remembered somewhere in her soul. His name was Grey Herald and he was not of her warband. He was of the Eyrie, of the Owl; his purpose in coming south was never explicitly stated. He conferred often with Hesprec, deferring to the young southern girl with an automatic respect that Hesprec returned. Just as his face made Maniye afraid, so did his presence. He brought back all those fireside tales of How We Came to These Lands, which were born out of a terror – a people fleeing for their very existence. The Owl and the Serpent had been separated for centuries by all the miles that lay between the Tsotec and the Crown of the World. They had only one thing in common, and that was when their distant ancestors – or perhaps it was their gods – had banded together with one other to face a terrible ancient foe. Seeing the Owl now at Hesprec's side sent a shiver down Maniye's spine.

The Serpent girl glanced up and grinned brightly as Maniye approached, breaking off from what she was saying, standing smoothly from her cross-legged seat. 'I see success in your face,' she noted.

Maniye nodded. 'One Horse trader will not be food for Lions. I thought they'd be fiercer.'

'These things are known: the Lion is fiercest when there are no enemies,' Hesprec said sagely, and the Horse elders chuckled. 'And here is your Horse come to thank you.'

Maniye started around, seeing Alladai striding over. 'He is not my Horse,' she said hastily. Hesprec was grinning – when Maniye had known the Serpent as an old man, there had been no teeth between those pale and withered lips. That grin was entirely new.

17

'You could find worse steeds,' Hesprec murmured in her ear as Alladai neared.

'You are a thousand years old!' Maniye hissed.

'New skin, new bones,' the dark girl replied. 'The body knows what it wants. Sometimes the old should listen to the wisdom of youth.'

'The blessings of my hand-father for bringing back our foolish kinsman!' Alladai declared. He and his kin had sheltered Maniye when she had nothing, and she hoped sometimes that there had been more to it than simple guest-right.

The thought made her realize that she might be leaving the Horse soon enough, bringing a stab of sadness. The Horse sang a lot and loved their drums and their reed pipes. They did not live to fight or even to hunt, and life at Where the Fords Meet seemed to happen in some other world where all the chases and skirmishes and fear that had disfigured her existence were forgotten.

'Your man was lucky.' She wanted to talk to Alladai like a friend, to joke and grin and pretend there was no distance between them. If she had been older, perhaps she could have done so. Instead she felt her youth made her role as leader precarious. Her words clung to formality even as she tried to deliver a different message with her eyes.

'He was a fool.' Alladai flourished his hands, a gesture of exasperation. 'It will be a long time before he is trusted with something of importance again.' He shifted footing awkwardly. 'While you hunted, we had word from our scouts. The southern Champion is coming.'

Maniye felt the awaited disappointment alight on her shoulders. Asmander had returned from his prince to fetch the Iron Wolves. She had begun to hope he might take more days still – everyone said how the southerners loved to talk.

'I want to stay here with your people.' She got the words out quickly before they could clog her throat. 'You are the most open-handed hosts in the world. No guest could ask for better. Yet I can't.'

'No guest is so welcome as the one who comes back,' Alladai told her.

She had almost let herself forget why she had come south, spending time at peace amongst the Horse. But this morning Asmander had come back from seeing how the land lay in the south. She saw him stride into Where the Fords Meet with the dawn and knew it was the end of her pleasant interlude.

Asmander was a lean, dark youth. He smiled as much as Alladai but it seldom seemed to touch the core of him. The Champion's soul within him gave him a strong, alien presence, more than his frame could account for. It had little patience with the rituals and considerations of life in the Sun River Nation, she felt, and yet Asmander was always happiest when the Champion was riding him and he could pretend to share in its freedom.

Maniye understood that now. She had an old soul inside her, just as he did: a creature from a time when human niceties and customs had yet to trouble the world. She gathered her people about a fire and told them they would be moving on. One or two looked as though they would rather have stayed but most were glad: Where the Fords Meet was a half-world to them, neither north nor south. They had been promised . . . perhaps none of them was quite sure what had been promised. Something *other*. A new world where the mistakes and the blame of the old would not count; somewhere they could tell their story from the start. Somewhere these errant children of the Wolf would be seen as something mythical and special.

Kalameshli Takes Iron scowled and ground his teeth. He did not like being amongst the Horse. He had already decided he would like the Riverlands no better. Well, enough of him. He was old enough to make his own mistakes.

Only one of their party would not follow her south. Grey

Herald had never been her follower, just a man who shared a road. His painted mask of a face was unreadable. The Owl and the Serpent had been close confidants in the oldest stories. He had heard Hesprec's warnings of a great storm coming, and his own lore had brought him to the Plains, where he had work to do.

'They remember,' Hesprec said of the Owl. 'Better than us, some things.'

Asmander was keen to be going. He had been closed-mouthed, but Maniye could see the tension in him. She could see whatever he had found to the south was preying on him.

'Tell me,' she asked Asmander, when they were picking their way south of Where the Fords Meet. 'Your chief, he's where you left him?' Hesprec leant close to them, listening in.

'Tecuman, my Kasra,' Asmander named his leader. Maniye did not understand just what a Kasra was, save that it meant chief of something far larger than a tribe of her homeland. The Kasra of the Sun River Nation ruled a land as great as all the Crown of the World, save that it was stretched out down the course of the river they called the Tsotec. Each Kasra was the eldest child of the last – something that was alien to the Wolf, although not to Maniye's mother's tribe, the Tiger. The last Kasra's children had been twins, barely a heartbeat between them, and now the old man had died and the Nation was split in half. Asmander was pledged to Tecuman, the boy, and yet Maniye had seen his face twist in anguish when he spoke of the girl, too. He had grown up with them both, when titles and Champions were burdens none of them had to bear.

'So your Kasra, what's wrong with him?' she demanded, because plainly something was. 'He's not at this stone place of yours any more?'

'He is at Tsokawan,' Asmander told her. She knew she would forget the foreign name the moment he stopped talking of it.

'So?'

'Tecumet is coming there too, with her soldiers.' From which

20

she deduced that Tecumet was the name the sister had taken since the father's death. And 'soldiers' were warriors, Alladai had told her, who always remained warriors, and weren't just hunters who fought when the season came.

'There will be war,' Asmander explained hollowly. 'I was too long in the north, bringing you. It has already started.'

3

Loud Thunder would have gone with Maniye, if he could. Offered a choice, he would have taken up his axe and his fleece armour and set out into the world. Maniye, whom Broken Axe had named 'Many Tracks', was as good a star to follow as any. They had shared a cave all winter – and anyone who can live with a wintering bear must be doing something right.

Instead, he was slogging west from the lands of the Bear, and not just roaming the wilds with his dogs, but travelling with his kin. Perhaps for the Wolf or the Deer that was a thing to take joy in, but the Bear did not delight much in each other's company. He was the largest of his kin, a huge, shaggy-bearded man in a robe made from many sheepskins stitched together, and as a bear even larger. A slap or a cuff with his paw was just enough to keep discipline amongst the others, but, since Mother had made him a great man amongst his kin, every stone underfoot, every slope to climb, every shower of rain was implicitly his fault.

It would not be like this if I were Many Tracks' follower, he decided. Loud Thunder had done it before, just taken off south with a band who were mad with youth and lust for adventure. He, Broken Axe and the rest had sold the strength of their arms on the Plains. They had done bad things, wild things. They had died, many of them, but they had died free. And what would any of them have said, his past comrades, if someone had come to them and told them what their life must be? Would Broken Axe have bowed his head? No. Peace Speaker would have found some way to weasel out of it. And Storm Born . . . well, he had always been crazy.

Storm Born was dead now, almost certainly. And Peace Speaker had died on the Plains when his words had deserted him. Broken Axe had perished right here at the Crown of World – because Loud Thunder had been wounded too badly to stay by his side. Of all those mad-eyed youngsters who had gone looking for their fortunes, Loud Thunder might be the only one still alive.

But he would still rather have travelled again than have his Mother load this destiny upon him, and go before all the world to stutter and mumble as though he was one of the wise.

His Mother had come to him – the Mother of all his kin, the great strong woman who was chief and priestess to the Bear. Loud Thunder had reached for all the defiance his huge frame could muster and it had not been enough. He was to be the war leader of the Bear, because apparently there was a war coming. Against who, nobody yet knew. But he must train his fellows, he must have weapons made. And he must travel to the Stone Place, and go before the other tribes and unite them. By saying . . . what? What could bring all those feuding people together, apart from a distrust of him?

He had a cousin – everyone in the Bear was his cousin – called Lone Mountain, a warrior and a speaker of fine words. He had travelled and knew more than this cold high corner of the world. What's more, he had been ready to become war leader all his life – to take up this mantle. So why not him? Thunder knew this would rankle with Lone Mountain. But Mother would not be questioned.

Some dozen of the Bear were in his party. The Bear were never many, but each of them cast a long, wide shadow. A dozen was a lot of Bear. With them was Mother, a looming presence to make even Loud Thunder feel small.

23

'If you are going yourself, why don't you speak?' he had asked her. No need to say how much more keenly the wise would listen to the Bear's Mother, rather than to Loud Thunder, the Bear's most surly cub. And she gave no answer, either. It seemed to Thunder that nine parts in ten of Mother's rule of the Bear lay in letting the silences lengthen and refusing to explain herself.

Loud Thunder had met a man once, from the south. And then he had met a girl, in whose body that man had been reborn. Hesprec was that southerner's name, Hesprec of the Serpent. The way Hesprec had told it, the Serpent lived on secrets and wisdom too. The Serpent was in the ground everywhere. Anyone could follow the back of the Serpent, no matter what tribe they were born to. The Serpent had built the oldest kingdom; the Serpent had held back the Plague People; the Serpent taught the secrets found in the earth. The Serpent helped people.

Sometimes – and always when he was very, very sure Mother would not see him – he scratched out a spiral on a flat stone, closed his eyes, and tried to feel the Serpent. Once or twice he had felt something shift in the earth, as though deep-buried coils were coursing there. So far he had received no guidance or enlightenment, but Loud Thunder was a patient man. His people generally were.

They were travelling on four feet through the cold forests, heading south and west along the slope and fall of the land, letting their bear natures find the easiest paths. Alongside Loud Thunder his dogs trotted, drawing a sled of cured fish and meat, of bagged nuts and seeds. Currently, Yoff and Yaff were in the harness, the elder dog keeping the younger in line, while Husker, the youngest but the biggest, loped alongside, or dashed off between the trees to investigate new smells.

His cousin Lone Mountain was ahead, a great brown-black bear trudging along with uncomplaining endurance. He was only a little smaller than Thunder, and he was pointedly in the lead, where Thunder should be. Probably the two of them would fight at some point, but Loud Thunder was actually looking forward to that. A little cuffing and bellowing would relieve some of the animosity that had grown up between them.

There was smoke on the wind, and Lone Mountain was abruptly a man, his great slope-shouldered body wrapped in hide under a robe of fine green cloth. Adorned with shell and stone ornaments, a necklace of hooked teeth, trinkets and oddments he traded for with the Horse, he looked every inch the war leader, a thick-hafted spear in his hand and a maul slung over his back.

Loud Thunder Stepped as well: he was perhaps a few fingers' breadths shorter than Lone Mountain, but broader and more powerful. His weapon was a copper-headed axe a lesser man could barely have lifted in two hands. As with all his gear, when he was Stepped it became a part of him – the metal of its blade became his fangs and claws, as the fleece and skins he wore strengthened his hide when he was a bear.

'What now?' he grunted. For a moment he thought that they were all too late, that this invisible, unknowable war was already upon them. Instead, though, his eyes picked out a trailing band of figures moving through the woods.

'I think Boar,' Mountain told him. 'We are south enough to be in their lands. There will be villages near.'

'Boar lands mean Wolf lands.' Loud Thunder frowned. 'The Winter Runners, is it?'

Lone Mountain nodded; he always knew these things. 'Your friend's people.'

'Not any more.' Maniye had been born to the Winter Runner tribe, but her current status put her outside such kinship. 'So what do these want?'

'They are here because of us.' Mother's voice made them both jump. She stood behind them, a vast cloaked figure with her hood up. She was not of a size with Loud Thunder, but there was something to her, a gravity and a presence, that made her seem larger: more akin to mountains than either human or bear. Mother's face was stern, her mouth like a crack in weathered rocks, her eyes like caves.

'They will fight us?' Lone Mountain hefted his spear.

'No, talk only.' Mother drew in a deep breath. 'They are here because the world is ending.'

And . . . ? But Loud Thunder could not ask, only wait for the Boar to reach them, knowing that he would have to speak to them, and that he would have only his ignorance to speak about.

The Boar approached cautiously through the trees. In the lead was an older man, short and stocky as the Boar tended to be, and wearing a long dark robe, open at the front. Despite the cold, his bare chest gleamed, rough with wiry grey hair. The wooden mask pushed up to the top of his head jutted with twisted tusks. Beneath it, his face was closed and secret and old. His staff was topped with a spray of feathers, and a little shiver went through Loud Thunder. Not just a Boar, but the Boar's priest, a man who had opened himself to the unseen.

The others behind him were of all ages: a young girl with a babe in her arms, women older than the priest, strong youngsters fit to be warriors or hunters, a child surely no more than ten who could have been either gender.

'You're going to the Stone Place,' the Boar priest accused.

'Yes.' Loud Thunder nodded, trying to keep matters amiable.

'This is not the time to go to the Stone Place,' he was told.

'Still, that is where we are going.' *This is why Mother left this to me; she would have had to work at being mysterious. I just say what little I know, and it sounds mysterious because I know so little.*

'You will stir up the great spirits, the Boar says.'

'Perhaps they need stirring.' It sounded trite to Loud Thunder even as he said it, but apparently the Boar had heard something different in the words. Something gleamed in the old priest's eyes.

'There is a storm coming, the Boar says.'

26

Loud Thunder resisted the temptation to look into the real sky; that was not what was being spoken of. Probably. 'The world is changing,' he pronounced. It was, after all, the one thing Mother had said.

And the Boar took that as some great promise by the world. 'We will travel with you,' the priest announced, for all that they would surely slow everybody's progress to a crawl. And yet Mother continued to say nothing, letting Thunder have the burden of all today's bad decisions.

'Of course you will,' he decided, more to annoy his fellows than for any sound reason, because if they were fool enough to make him war leader then he would make them understand just what a poor choice he was. *Why not the Boar sharing our road? Just you watch, I will find even worse!*

When they were moving again, he began to think. All the villages of the Boar and the Deer around here paid tribute to the Wolf – as it was across much of the Crown of the World. Were the Boar looking to break free of the Wolf? And where would that leave him when the Wolf spoke to him? The world might be changing, but change wasn't likely to leave everyone happy.

Except Loud Thunder didn't feel that was the sort of change Mother anticipated. She saw on the horizon not the sort of change a man might himself bring about, but the sort of change he could only hope to survive.

★★★

His name was Sees More and he was born on the back of the Seal, as they said.

Those who cowered from the elemental temper of the sea behind mountains were referred to by the people of the Seal as Inlanders. The sea was a terror to them. The storms and the waters would have their due. When the Inlanders thought of the Wetback and the Pebble Dweller and the Wave Dancer tribes, they shuddered. A life by the open ocean was the stuff of nightmares. Even to the Seal it was something to be respected – many of them died on the sea, seal shape or not.

Sometimes the wise of the Seal travelled beyond the mountains, using ways few others cared to learn. They came across the Bear, who traded for fish. They travelled to the far Stone Place, but not every year. They had their own sacred places on the strand, wooden henges and stone monuments worked by the hands of the sea. They were not as bound to the spirits of the land as were the others.

Sees More of the Wetbacks was not a young man. He had lived with the sea four decades, all his life. He had learned to swim as a boy, and then again as a seal. He had grown up with the shark and the shoal, laughing at the Inlanders and their fears.

He had been away from his home for five days and four nights, following the schools. Let the younger hunters keep the shore and the hearthsmoke in sight when they fished. It was a point of pride for the veterans of the Wetbacks to range further afield. He had gone south down the coast to cast his nets. He had Stepped and taken the ropes in his mouth, and trawled the fish from the deep waters, where the sun was but a memory. On other years he had gone north under the ice, where life stretched from air-hole to air-hole. *One day*, he always said, *I shall travel so far I shall reach the shining land, where all the women are beautiful and nobody needs to work or hunt, and I shan't come back.* When he said this, his mate and children would complain, and he would laugh.

The sea had been kind to him; his lines had been heavy when he hauled them from the water, and while they had been trailing, he had been filling his nets as well. Now he was a man again, even though the sea called to him to dive into its endless waters. He was a man with a narrow boat made with the hide of his dumb brothers, a boat full of fish. Now he would return home and show the young men what a real fisherman was capable of.

But when the village of the Wetbacks came in sight, the smoke he saw was not the smoke of their cooking fires.

He paddled in slowly, knowing this could be raiders. The Wolf perhaps, though they had not come in living memory; or the

Bear, though they only raided during the worst of winters. He didn't know who else it could be. Living in their world of sea and ice, what else could threaten the people of the Seal?

The beach was disturbed: marks up high showed a boat had come in at high tide. A huge boat, or was it perhaps . . . ? Sees More's heart was stuttering in his chest as he took in what had happened.

The houses of whale skin and bone were cut apart. Some had been burned, but the fires had not been systematic. Boats had been destroyed too, separated out into their composite pieces. One boat's bone and hide sections had been laid out by size with the exacting patience of a child. Some of the bodies had been served the same way, hide and meat and blubber and bone.

There were many bodies. All had died while Stepped, which meant that when the threat had come the Wetbacks must surely have plunged into the sea for escape. Yet not all had made it. Seal shapes were scattered all the way up the long beach to the bluffs as though, when they faced the ocean, the very water had terrified them. On those that had not been butchered he saw marks as though they had been pierced by spears infinitely sharp.

By now Sees More was shaking, collapsing to his knees. But he looked. He forced himself to bear witness to this massacre.

They were laid out like the others: his kin, his family. Behind those seal faces were human faces he knew. In his mind he heard the voices that had laughed with him, the people he took joy in. They had Stepped and been killed, and then something had sifted through the parts and pieces of their bodies. The overall impression was not one of wrath or hate or anger, but of dreadful, distant curiosity.

There were no children there, who could not have Stepped. They had been taken or driven into the sea.

At last he could keep the cry inside no longer. Sees More threw back his head and screamed. He yelled. He beat at the stones of the beach and hurled handfuls of them into the sea. He had no way to deal with what he had found, no way to get past the enormity of what had been done.

Later he searched further afield and found some who had got away and yet not escaped the terrible hand of What Had Come From The Sea, and the sickness in him only grew and grew. He found them, but they did not know him and could not tell him who had done this to them, only stare at him with round, agonized eyes and then flee into the water to vanish beneath the waves. The day after, he met with some few who had seen a little of the ending of it, from far enough away that the shadow of the newcomers had not fallen on them and destroyed them. He heard what little they could stammer out. A terror had come from the sea, a thing that walked on two legs like a man, but whose *inside* had been hollow and wrong. This, Sees More heard again and again, and he struggled to understand. Its insides had been hollow? He questioned them, but time and again, their memory of the sight got the better of them, and fright rid them of words. All Sees More learned was that terror had slaughtered his kin and taken the children, and picked through the pieces of their lives.

He was left with one thought: *I am cut from the sea now; I must go Inland. I must find someone who will understand.*

4

Leading Maniye's warband south from Where the Fords Meet, Asmander's head was filled with problems. No use telling himself not to think of them: they crowded so closely within his skull there was no escaping them. He could only envy Maniye. Would she trade her brutal upbringing and the hateful old Wolf priest for the maze Asmander had to navigate? It would be a poor exchange for her, he reckoned.

As they followed the Horse's trail towards his home, Plainsmen came to stare: hunters of the Lion or gatherers of the Boar. They saw Maniye and they saw Asmander – two Champions of different tribes – and swiftly melted away. Whatever trouble was afoot was none of theirs.

To be a Champion was to host more souls than most, and take more forms. Asmander's fighting shape was the one they called the Running Lizard: the savage, bipedal reptile with crescent claws that flinched from neither hunt nor fight. The priest Hesprec had gifted him another: a leather-winged creature with a stabbing beak that struck terror into those who saw it, and was always nagging him to let it into the sky.

But now he felt the need for his first shape, the shape of his people. For now he wanted to leave his humanity behind. The world of his people was built of a million complexities: loyalties and obligations, family, friends, honour, all pulling different ways. When he reached the river his homeland was built around, he wanted just to become Old Crocodile and slough into the waters of the Tsotec, where he could know only hunger and calm.

When Asmander had left for the north, Tecuman and his sister had been at odds, both determined that they must be the Kasra. Normally it would be for the Serpent to decide, but the priests were split too. Such a rift, with no clear solution, spelled disaster for the nation. There were a hundred stories of terrible things to come. People had spoken of the Rat cult, the Stranglers and the Pale Shadow – all the terrors from the old stories. If such times were ahead, the Sun River Nation would need the best possible leader. And yet there was no way to choose: as children, Tecumander and Tecuma had come with all the virtues in the world. Asmander had known and loved them both. He understood full well why the priests could not choose between them.

Tecumander and Tecuma were no more, of course. When their father had left them orphaned and adult, they had grown into their new names: Tecuman and Tecumet, twin Kasra of a nation that could have only one.

When Asmander left for the north, Tecumet had held the capital of Atahlan, while Tecuman ruled from Tsokawan, the fortress that commanded the rich lands of the estuary. Between them stretched the whole length of the Tsotec's head. Enough space, surely, to allow diplomacy to prevail.

Except that all the coils of the Serpent had not sufficed to find a straight path out of this. None of the priesthood wanted war, of course, and yet there were priests who were determined that the boy should inherit, and others equally passionate over the girl's right. The clan chiefs supporting either side had shaken their spears. Such situations were a breeding ground for fatal misunderstandings, opportunist raids, the rebirth of old feuds. While Asmander had been in the cold north gathering Iron Wolves for Tecuman's bodyguard, the River Lords had gathered up their soldiers and mustered for war.

Asmander had left the Wolves at Where the Fords Meet and run ahead with Shyri and Venat, to make sure that a warband of barbaric northerners would be welcomed as guests when they came, rather than repulsed as raiders. What he had found was that a great force was already on its way downriver from Atahlan. Asmander's father, Asman, had expressed frustration that he had not just brought the Wolves straight south – did he not know they were on the brink of war? Well of course Asmander had not known, but there was no use trying excuses with old Asman. His father's expression of disappointment had been the most familiar sign of home Asmander had seen.

He glanced at Maniye, wondering if he could talk of such things, Champion to Champion, underachieving son to abused daughter. But he was bringing her to his home for the first time, the greatest nation of the world. He wanted her to see it with wide eyes, and not know all the cracks that ran through it. He kept his complaints about his father to himself.

After being dismissed by his father he had gone to find the two who had come south with him, Venat and Shyri.

'So we go east to the islands,' Venat had said promptly. 'I've unfinished business there. You should come too. Plenty of fighting. You'd do well there.'

Asmander had just given him a glower.

'Oh, look at the sulky one!' Venat's worst mockery was still easier than that look in old Asman's eyes. 'You can't want to stay here?'

'This is my place.' He had wanted to petition Venat for the man's strength and bloody-handed ruthlessness. He had known better than to ask, though. Venat was a man of the Dragon, and he had been Asmander's unwilling companion in the north. He had chosen service to the Champion over death, and probably regretted the choice many times over. Now he was free. He had walked this far with Asmander only because it was the road to the islands of his home.

And still Asmander wanted him to stay. Surely there was

33

some argument that might sway the man. But Venat prized only bloodshed and violence, and even those only on his own terms. He was a soldier for no man.

'The Dragon will have been called,' Asmander had cautioned him. 'You are still subjects of the Kasra, even if you are the worst and most unruly.'

The quick rejoinder had not come, instead just a long breath as Venat considered. 'There is nothing here that can command the Dragon,' had been his eventual response. 'If we come, it will be to pick over the bones. Ask *her*,' nodding at their other fellow traveller.

Shyri was a Plains woman, copper-skinned and swift and just as vicious as Venat when the mood took her. She was of the Laughing Men, carrion eaters whose creed was that they would one day rule the world over a mountain of corpses. Or so she said. She also spent much time mocking Asmander.

'What about you, Laughing Girl?' Venat had asked her. 'You'll come bait the Dragon with me? I have wives to claim.'

'If there is a woman so blind and mad as to want you, old man, I have no wish to meet her. I like this river place.' Seeing Asmander's expression, she smiled sweetly at him. 'I want to see what your father makes of the Iron Wolves and their Champion girl. I want to see him swallow his tongue with anger.'

'My father will be pleased his son has accomplished the task that was set him,' Asmander had told her, but deep inside he thought she probably had the right of it. Now he looked at the warband that was trailing him – the grey-pelts, the Wolf-iron, the savage customs.

'I hope my father does swallow his tongue,' he told the world at large, despite the looks it earned him. The sentiment made him feel better than he had in a long time.

***

Kalameshli Takes Iron was in one of his moods where nothing was good enough for him. He was in such a mood more often than not. When they had been guests of the Horse, he had com-

34

plained about that. He had looked about their settlement – larger than any Wolf village and the centre of a network of travellers who journeyed to every land there was – and found nothing but fault. Where the Horse were simpler than the Wolf he called them primitive; where they were more complex he used the word decadent.

Maniye had realized that she did not have to listen to him. She had just got up and walked away. All her life Kalameshli had been a figure of fear, the Wolf's great priest, the master of iron. He had taken on another unwelcome mantle when she had discovered that it was his old loins, and not Akrit Stone River's, that had fathered her. All of this authority he had tried to put into his voice, to browbeat her into acknowledging the supremacy of the Wolf – himself. That was why she had walked away. At first he had ordered her, then he had urged her, and at last he had come begging after her, and that had shown her exactly how things stood between them.

'Who will advise you?' he had almost spat. 'That little River girl?' meaning Hesprec.

'Always.' She had watched the anger flare on his lined face, watched it surge back and forth because it had nowhere to go. It could not leap over to her any more.

'I made a mistake,' Maniye said to Hesprec the night after. Most of her own people were sleeping, save for Tiamesh on watch. Maniye and the Serpent girl huddled close to the fire, for the great open stretches of the Plains robbed the world of heat soon after the sun went down.

Hesprec waited, the firelight dancing in her eyes.

'I should not have brought Takes Iron with us.' Maniye rubbed her face, feeling her souls shift and twitch inside her, wanting to sleep and yet unable.

'Why did you?' The expression on the dark girl's face suggested that she was well aware of the answer, but wanted Maniye to speak it herself. The Serpent was many things, but direct was not one of them.

35

'If I left him behind . . . he would have spoken against me to the Wolf.' There was nothing in Maniye's intonation to indicate whether she meant the tribe or the god.

'And they would listen?'

She shrugged. 'And my mother would have killed him.' The words came from her unbidden, unexpected. Hesprec was still watching her, bobbing her head slightly in encouragement.

'I should have let her kill him,' Maniye hissed in a small, fierce voice. 'I shouldn't have protected him.'

'For you, she stayed her hand.' Hesprec said softly.

Maniye gave a little broken laugh. 'What a show of a mother's love!' She clamped her lips together, fearful of waking the others.

Hesprec sighed. When it was plain that Maniye had no more words, she said: 'Do you know how the Serpent lost his legs?'

'I . . .' With the Serpent, nothing was unconnected, but Maniye could not see the link. 'What legs?'

'There is a story: once, the Serpent had four legs, like the other beasts. The story can be very long and laden with detail, but I will speak it briefly for you. In those days, the people of these lands had nothing, and knew nothing, and lived like their mute siblings in the forests and on the plains. But Serpent found a crack in the earth, and twisted and twisted until he came to a great place of secrets, for all secrets worth knowing are buried deep. There Serpent met four great spirits, each more terrifying and ill-favoured than the last, but each guarding a trove of secrets that would bring ease and ambition to those who lived in the world above.'

Maniye nodded, still trying to find a path from the story to her own difficulties.

'Each of these spirits offered to teach Serpent its secrets,' Hesprec explained, 'but there would be a price. Each would tear a limb from Serpent's body in return.'

'So Serpent is wise because it traded its limbs for the spirits' secrets,' Maniye concluded.

'Would that it were so simple. Serpent did not know whether any of them could be trusted at all, but he agreed to the trade anyway. And three of the spirits were wicked. They tore away Serpent's limbs and gnawed on the bones, and guarded their secrets still. Only one kept its word. All the wisdom of the Serpent is just one part in four of what still waits to be discovered.'

Maniye frowned, having lost her train of thought. 'But then . . . but what . . . I don't understand,' she admitted.

'Sometimes good things arise out of bad. All we have of wisdom was born in treachery and betrayal, pain and loss. Is that fourth part of the secrets of the earth something to cast aside because it was bought at such cost? No.' Hesprec put a hand on her arm. 'You came into this world from terrible deeds – Stone River and Takes Iron's deeds. But that is what *made* you. Like Serpent, you can still come from that dark place with something of value.' Her teeth gleamed in the firelight as she smiled. 'So why did you save Takes Iron?'

'Because . . . because I had thought he hated me all those years, and he didn't. He just wasn't good at showing it.'

'Perhaps he still isn't.' Hesprec cocked her head to one side, birdlike. 'These things are known: give to a comrade a comrade's honour; to a parent, a child's obedience. Or that is what they say on the River. You owed him a comrade's debt, and paid it. I do not think you owe him more.'

Soon after, they came to Chumatla, which was a village atop a lake. On the other side of the open water was a busy riot of trees and foliage cut through with a hundred silver streams, extending as far as they could see to the south and the east. This was the estuary. Here the River Tsotec, backbone of the Sun River Nation, broke apart into a shifting skein of channels as it fought its way to the sea. Whole peoples lived within its bounds, nominally ruled by the Sun River Nation from its fortress at Tsokawan. Here, at Chumatla, they came north to trade with the Horse and with each other.

37

Maniye and her warband stepped out over the water with trepidation. The homes of the lake dwellers seemed fragile and temporary. Maniye took to her tiger shape, and the rest became wolves: nobody wanted to end up in the water wearing a hauberk of iron or bronze.

There were plenty of Asmander's kin amongst the lake people, dark lean men and women with closed faces. They watched the newcomers narrowly, or else sloughed off the rafts and walkways into the water, Stepping to long, scaled shapes to vanish into the lake. She spotted a couple of heavy-set men with sand-coloured skin and blue-grey hair and knew them for people of the Dragon, just as Asmander's friend had been. Beyond these, there were plenty of others who were dark as the River Lords but who belonged to no tribe she knew: small people; broad and paunchy people; men and women whose skin gleamed with vivid painted patterns. These were the people of the estuary forests, she guessed – those who lived within the Shadow of the Sun River Nation.

Asmander had been quiet all the journey, keeping himself apart and speaking to none but Hesprec, but now he hissed and was pouring out over the raft's side into the water, human to Old Crocodile in an eyeblink. For a moment the Wolves formed a defensive ring, waiting for the attack, but then the same reptile surfaced ahead of them, powering out of the water to land on two human feet before a copper-skinned Plains woman of Maniye's acquaintance.

Shyri stepped back, making a great show of wringing out her clothing from the splash. Asmander was questioning her urgently, and after a little more clowning the Laughing Men huntress was giving him some report. Impatiently he turned to beckon Maniye and her company over.

Picking their way from raft to raft was a far slower way of travelling, but nobody suggested swimming over. The water was criss-crossed with the trail of scaly backs, and the northerners had no way to tell if all of them had a human mind behind those fearsome jaws.

'We are in time, but we must hurry,' Asmander explained, when they were with him. 'Tecumet's soldiers are camped at the edge of the estuary. Her speakers are at Tecuman's court, demanding that he kneel to her.'

'So he needs to show them some extra teeth,' Maniye divined. 'Our teeth.'

'And mine. I can't be away from him now. He needs me.' The personal urgency in his voice took her aback.

'Lead then, we'll follow. Just find us a dry path.'

He set a brisk pace over the rafts, and the locals were quick to give him room.

Shyri fell into step familiarly with Maniye, leaning close to speak into her ear.

'Just wait till you meet his father, Northern Girl. He's even worse than yours.'

***

'Your sister holds great love for you.' The thread of cold in the whip-lean woman's voice belied the words. 'She wishes for nothing more than that you and she should be friends once more. But she cannot permit this continuing affront to her authority. Know this, Tecuman: every day you refuse to bow before the Daybreak Throne, the laws and traditions that hold the Sun River Nation together are lessened; everything your father built is lessened. Love you as she might, she cannot ignore it.'

Tecuman shifted slightly on his stone seat, but said nothing. The Kasra did not address petitioners directly. That small motion spoke of how young he was. The rest was swallowed up by the Kasra's regalia. The golden mask that hid his face was counterfeit, made by estuary craftsmen after the old Kasra died, for Tecumet held the original. The robes of green, russet and silver were older, the colours the Kasra wore when he brought his court to Tsokawan. They had been in storage for a generation, and they filled the air with the faint scent of perfume and rot.

'The Kasra makes the same demands of his rebellious sister, who sits unworthy upon the Daybreak Throne.' The voice was that of Asman, the boy-Kasra's chief adviser. 'If you ask why the workers stir unsettled in the fields, why the fishermen draw up empty nets, why the wise see omens in the flight of birds, you have only to look towards Atahlan. The Kasra values greatly his sister's regard, but they cannot be reconciled so long as she lays claim to a title and a privilege that is not hers.'

Tecumet's emissary was a Serpent priestess, Esumit Aras Talien. When Tecuman had been a child in Atahlan, Esumit had been a teacher to the royal children. She was a compact, dark young woman now, but in their youth she had been a strong-framed old man never slow to chastise with voice or hand. He – she, now – must surely have been sent in order to arouse memories of meek obedience behind the gleaming mask.

'Do not make a fight of this, Tecuman,' she said now. 'Your sister will give you all honour if you pledge yourself to her cause, but she has come with more spears than you have in all Tsokawan, more than you can defend yourself from. Do not let this end in blood.'

'Where shall the wounded point, when they are asked who gifted them their wounds?' Asman demanded. He was a shorter man than his son Asmander, the Champion, not as lean as he had been, and his hair grey as slate. He had a voice fit for a Kasra, though: it filled the vaulted court of Tsokawan and resounded from the carved walls. Now he strode to look Esumit straight in the eye. 'Who shall the spirits of the dead curse, before the river draws them down? She who brought the battle, not he who defends his own. And when you count soldiers, you forget that the estuary holds a hundred thousand you cannot see.'

The powerfully built woman at Esumit's shoulder tensed, staring at Asman, who blithely ignored her. Tecumet had sent one of her own Champions to add weight to her arguments, and she was plainly itching for a fight.

Esumit herself was unimpressed. She directed her own words at the golden mask. 'How many have come at your call, Tecuman? How many of the Hidden Ones or the Mud Feet or the Salt Eaters? Do the Dragon serve you still, or do they just make free with all those you can neither control nor protect?' Real sincerity was in her voice. 'I beg you, go and prostrate yourself before her, seek her forgiveness and it will be given.'

'The Kasra—' started Asman, but Esumit cut him off sharply.

'I have looked into the secret depths of the earth! I have asked the Serpent whose back is strongest, to carry the burdens of state. I have asked whose hand is the steadiest, to guide this nation through the dangers that we all see approaching. It has always been Tecumet. There is no shame in—'

Asman was itching to interrupt, but instead a new voice broke out, strung taut with emotion: Tecuman's.

'And all my life I have known it was me!' he shouted, standing now with his fists clenched. 'The priests of the estuary told me it was I who must be Kasra. How can they be wrong and you be right? Why does the Serpent have two heads?'

In formal court the Kasra did not speak, but Tecuman was pushed past the point of endurance. As if his breach of protocol signalled the end of all laws, Tecumet's Champion pushed past Esumit, almost shouldering Asman in the chest to stand before the boy-Kasra.

She was called Izel: low-born and nobody's idea of a beauty. She would never have come near any Kasra's court save that the Champion had come to her, just as it had come to Asmander.

'The words that were given you are just wind,' she called out, and when Esumit plucked at her shoulder, she shrugged the Serpent off. 'You are nothing but what your sister names you. She names you brother for now. Do not make her name you something more.'

Tecuman had dropped back into his seat, trying to gather his dignity about him. His shoulders twitched when Izel glowered at him, as though he was trying to dig his way through the back of the throne.

'You forget your place,' Asman intoned, but the woman was having none of it.

'My place is here, doing what must be done for the nation. Where is your Champion, Kasra of the rivermouth? Is he gone to ride the Horse, like they say? Is he dead in the cold north?' And she took another step, and everyone there saw she was mad enough to do it: to attack Tecuman in his own court and shatter a century of careful etiquette because she saw a chance to cut all this short.

But then there were footsteps beyond the room, echoing through the halls of Tsokawan; the click of claws and the scrape of metal.

Shyri was their herald: a high-shouldered beast slinking in with a flash of spotted hide and the hideous cackle of the Laughing Men. Behind her was Asmander, stalking in his Champion's shape, and with him many foreigners, a whole war-band of them. Some were lean grey beasts and others walked on two legs, clad in coats of leather and dull metal. These were the Iron Wolves, and at their head was a small girl – so small, so young, and yet none looked on her without knowing that she was just as much a Champion as Asmander or Izel.

Asman alone showed no surprise. 'Here is a sign you should take back to Tecumet the pretender,' he announced. 'Go tell her who has come at her brother's call. Go tell of the strength that the rightful Kasra can command.'

It seemed that Izel would not step down, for a moment. Her face flashed hatred for Tecuman, and most especially for the newly arrived Asmander. The Champion looked so large in her human face it seemed impossible she could hold to her shape – she must explode in a flurry of killing claws at any moment. But Esumit's hand on her shoulder leached the fury from her, heart-beat by heartbeat, and the Serpent priestess bowed pleasantly to

42

the masked boy on the throne, and to old Asman himself. When she departed she appeared not at all daunted by Tecuman's new allies.

5

As Maniye's warband had passed beneath the shadow of
Tsokawan's walls, Maniye had been reminded of the Shining
Halls where the Tiger held sway. There was a similarity to the
way the stone had been worked, and a kindred reluctance to
leave any wall uncarved. Just like the Tiger Queen's court, every
detail of the walls marched towards the throne. The images were
of rivers and fish, boats and crocodiles and serpents, but Maniye
saw in one the echo of the other. It threw her off-balance to
think that the ideas conceived here had crept north over time,
through the Plains into the very Crown of the World, taking so
long to get there that nobody remembered where they had come
from. Tsokawan was greater than the Tiger Queen's temple-
palace, though, reaching high enough that the stone claws of its
peak seemed ready to pluck the sun from the sky, dominating all
the land around it.

She was acutely aware that she was in a land of different
spirits and different gods: the Serpent, Old Crocodile and the
Dragon and all the other totems of the south. She did not know
whether a Kasra was a priest who mediated with spirits, or
whether even the ruler of the Sun River Nation was just another
frightened soul in the greater darkness of the world.

Now she stood in front of the young Kasra, however, she
wondered whether he was anything more than just a metal face
and a fancy robe, for Tecuman barely moved at all as his new

warband was presented to him. Did he nod, after the middle-aged River man finished his speech? Or was that the shadows of the throne room shifting? Impossible to tell.

Asmander's father, Asman, seemed simple enough, except that he was talking in place of his chief. He talked, and everyone there, all the southerners, seemed to accept that his words came from that golden mask. While Tecuman sat, and did nothing.

The strong-looking woman with the angry face and the Serpent priestess – Maniye could see the bright scale tattoos tracking across her brow like a headband – had listened and gone away unsatisfied. They were still within the fortress, under guest-right, but soon they would return to tell Tecumet of all they had seen.

'That girl was a Champion,' Maniye observed to Asmander. 'You looked like you were going to kill her. And she looked like she was going to kill you.'

'These things are known,' he agreed solemnly.

They had retreated from Tecuman's audience chamber to a low-ceilinged hall where food and drink was brought for the Wolves. Now they picked over the unfamiliar meats and dishes, tasting and comparing – the fish and fruits immediate favourites – while Kalameshli scowled and declared everything to be rotten or ill-prepared, a bad guest in every particular. Around them, the walls seethed with carving: animals and people and little spaces of odd small abstract shapes arranged in regular vertical lines.

'Did you know the priestess, the thin woman?' Maniye asked Hesprec, who was sitting on a stone bench, her face without expression.

At the question she opened one eye and nodded. 'An old friend.'

'That is a shame,' Asmander pointed out. 'She is siding with our enemy.'

'I don't understand why there *is* an enemy,' Maniye complained. 'Aren't you Serpent people all-wise? How can there be some saying one thing and some saying another?'

'Nobody is infinitely wise,' Hesprec muttered evasively. 'These things are also known: sometimes wisdom lies in admitting ignorance. When I left to hunt portents, Old Tecuman was still alive and none of this had happened.'

'Will you speak out?' Asmander began.

'What if it isn't for your boy there? Do you really want to commit another coil of the Serpent to this knot?'

'Will you find out *why* the Serpent is tying itself in knots?' Asmander asked more sharply. 'The priesthood's word would calm these waters, one way or the other. But suddenly the Serpent has two heads, and there is no agreement, and . . .' He reined himself back, plainly ready for some stern reprimand at talking to a priestess in such a way. His tone had caught the attention of the Wolves, who were quiet, waiting to see if this would become their problem. Kalameshli's eyes were narrow and thoughtful, scenting weakness.

'What can be done, I shall do.' Hesprec's nose wrinkled. 'I return to the River reeking of prophecy, and everyone is too busy wrestling with each other to listen.' Hesprec had not been afraid in the pit of the Wolf, waiting to have her throat cut, but now, Maniye thought, she had found something to fear. 'It is time I told the Serpent's heads that I have returned, much may they joy in it. Maniye, perhaps you would accompany me?'

That was an unexpected invitation. Asmander looked thrown – presumably he had expected the honour himself. Kalameshli's expression found new levels of sourness.

'Spear Catcher,' she told the warrior, 'you lead while I speak to Serpents.' *Don't do anything stupid while I'm out of the room.*

Maniye had half imagined to find the people of the Serpent Stepped and twining about one another, exchanging wisdom somehow from the rub of scale on scale. Instead she saw two women and a man lying sidelong on benches, picking jadedly at little round fruits and drinking something blood-coloured from clay bowls. The rainbow marks of the Serpent tracked their cheeks and brows, and they had scarves covering their heads even here, humble before the unseen sky. All three stared at Hesprec as she entered, seeking familiarity in the young girl's strange features.

'I know Esumit, and I know Therumit Essen Fiel, of course,' Hesprec announced, addressing first one woman then the other. Her eyes then lit on the man, broad-shouldered and just starting to run to fat, a fighter who no longer fought. 'Matsur, is that you?'

For a moment none of them was sure who had come calling for them. Esumit smiled first. 'Have these eyes lasted long enough to see Hesprec Essen Skese once more?'

'Some shadow of me,' Hesprec agreed, and then they were all on their feet, touching fingers in little hesitant contacts.

There were four of the Serpent here at Tsokawan, and each well known to the others. Maniye had another moment of vertigo, thinking on it: they were few, and they lived many lives, shedding faces and bodies while the mind within went on and on in an endless undulating progress. Of course they were all old friends: who else did they share that awful span of time with, save each other? Hesprec seemed younger even than Maniye, Esumit a lean woman in the prime of her youth, Matsur ageing and Therumit almost as old as Hesprec had appeared in his previous body. Her face was creased and re-creased with lines, her skin paper-thin and faded almost to white.

'For all the joy I take in seeing you again, I could wish you had come next season,' Esumit observed drily. 'Give Tecuman hope, you give the country war.'

'It will not come to that,' Matsur murmured, although his words lacked certainty.

Hesprec held up her hands. 'Is it even two years since I put the Tsotec at my back, and this is what I return to?' Bizarre, to see so young a girl castigate her elders, and to see shame touch them at her words.

'You spoke of omens before you left,' Esumit observed. 'None doubted your truths. A great doom will fall upon us and destroy all we've worked for. We need a great leader to endure. The temple in Atahlan is unanimous: Tecumet is that leader.'

She nodded tiredly as Matsur raised a hand. 'Here in the Tsotec's mouth we see these omens, and then speak for Tecuman. And so we have talked and talked, calming the ripples of the Kasra's death. The Sun River Nation has never known twin heirs.'

'And we were all fools to let this play out without making a choice long before,' Therumit's cracked voice put in. 'We should have strangled one at birth.'

Maniye stared at her, and then at them all, because nobody was leaping up to denounce the words.

'The girl, the boy, it wouldn't matter, and we'd not be in this ridiculous position now,' the old woman spat. '*Twins*,' she added, in tones of the utmost disgust.

'Or if one had shown some great flaw or vice before now,' Matsur added. His voice was gentle and rich, as though there was a song in it somewhere, trying to break free. 'The Serpent's path cannot be seen.'

'These omens are not unique to the River,' Hesprec said tiredly. 'That is the news I bring you. The wise of the north, the Plains people, the Horse Society, the Owl, they all see some small part of the same great doom. This is not a threat to the Sun River Nation. This is a threat to all the world.'

The other Serpents digested this unhappily.

'If the world is to be saved, how else but by the efforts of the Sun River Nation?' Esumit pointed out. 'Where else have we poured out our wisdom and knowledge, but here? This is our second kingdom, a worthy successor for our first.'

'A shadow of it,' Therumit muttered. 'If we had the power we once had . . .'

'If, if, if,' Esumit chided. 'We cannot eat *if*, nor can we wield it as a rod.' At last she glanced at Maniye, weighing her.

'Hesprec, I am glad to see you again, but your friend does not see us at our best.'

Hesprec's smile lasted until she was out of sight of the other Serpents. Then it became a thoughtful frown.

'Sometimes it helps, to be away for a time,' she mused. 'If you live with a child, you do not realize how he grows day to day. Only seeing him year to year brings home how much things have changed . . .'

'Something has changed?' Maniye prompted.

'Something is wrong.'

'You spoke to many in the Crown of the World about what they foresaw.' Maniye felt her way through a subject she did not really understand. 'You must have more wisdom than these others, who haven't stepped away from this river of yours in – what? – many lifetimes? Can *you* not just say, *he* is chief, or *she* is chief? Surely you know the most, now.'

Hesprec laughed at that, a young girl's unguarded amusement. 'Oh, I wonder if I could try that with them! But the portents of the north didn't care who was Kasra on the River. And I fear that my fellows care for nothing more. Their horizons are the banks of the Tsotec, no wider than that.' She grimaced. 'Tecuman, Tecumet, born within a breath of each other. I remember it. Alike as two stones, none could tell between them. And now we have to choose and we cannot agree. Ridiculous.' She shook her head, a child mimicking adult concern. 'Tell me how the north would cut this knot, O Champion?'

Maniye opened her mouth a few times, wondering what value her opinion could possibly hold. 'We would never have tied it,' she said at last. 'We have no great leader of all the north.' And then she thought again and said, 'But if it were High Chief of the Wolves, say, and two challengers came who were strong, then probably they'd fight. Tooth and claw, knife and axe. And then one would win and one would lose, and that would be that.'

She smiled at Hesprec, feeling that she'd passed a test, but the Serpent looked solemn.

'Some things are the same the world over,' the priestess declared. 'But where your Wolf chiefs might shed each other's blood, in the Sun River Nation they are civilized. They fight with armies and the blood of hundreds.' Abruptly the priestess leant back against the wall, her fingers clutching at the carving there, the stone fishermen and their boats, as though they might be washed away any moment. 'Do you know how it was, when first we came to the River?'

'When?'

'Fifty lifetimes ago.' There was something ghostly and distant in Hesprec's voice, as though a spirit spoke through her. 'Before my first birth, in times that even we only know about from stories.' She shook her head. 'We were fleeing the fall of our great kingdom, which was older still. Running from the Pale Shadow People and their faces like white fire.' Her voice fell into ritual cadences, a tale told so often that the edges of its meaning had rubbed away. 'We crossed the desert and came to the river, where a hundred clans of the River Lords fought amongst themselves, each making a meagre stretch of bank their whole world. Like the Plains peoples, they were, but worse. They knew only hunger and feuding, revenge and the taste of blood. And we taught them, and we brought them together before the Daybreak Throne. We gave them learning, writing, showed them how to grow new life in the dry land, how to borrow from good years to weather the bad. We built the greatest nation we could, here on the river. And what will happen if it goes to war against itself? If the river runs bright with burning boats? How long before the chiefs decide that their loyalties go no further than their clans, and everything falls?'

'So what will you do?' Maniye asked her.

'The wrong thing.' Hesprec shook her head. 'Soon enough, the only choices we have will be between wrong things.'

'Was . . . the old woman priestess, was she serious about . . . strangling children?'

The Serpent girl took a deep breath. 'Ah, Therumit. She was always a hard one. But if we had known, back then, how many lives might be lost out of the birth of twins . . . ?' She shook her head. 'The Serpent's back can be crooked. Be glad you do not have to walk it.'

They returned to the warband, many of whom were sleeping off their meal. Amelak, Spear Catcher's wife, was darning clothes – she had become something of a mother to them all. Feeds on Rags and Sathewe were playing some sort of nonsense game with stones on the floor, as absorbed as children. Kalameshli sat stiffly on one of the benches, refusing to let his guard down. His eyes lit on Hesprec with a lifetime of suspicion. *Foreign gods, foreign ways*, his expression said. Maniye found her way to her own bed, and sleep.

She woke in the depths of the night to find Spear Catcher standing over her, his hand on her shoulder.

'What is it?' she asked, sitting up. Around her, some of her people still slept, but others were awake, and others still were missing.

Spear Catcher was nervous and would not look her in the eye. He seemed at war with himself, only just loyal enough to warn her that something was amiss, unable to be drawn further.

She drew a cloak about her – the river days were hot, but their nights were almost as cold as home. Stepping to her wolf shape, she scented smoke on the air. For a moment she wondered if there had been an attack by Tecumet, but no: there was another scent beneath the burning wood, something of the north and of the Wolf.

She went through to another chamber, up a flight of steps and into a room whose windows gave onto the clear and cloudless sky of the south. There, with rough rocks, Kalameshli had made a crude, open-jawed idol with the fire lit between its teeth. It was not the iron-toothed effigy in the Winter Runners' village. It was a small, sad thing, and if she had not guessed what Kalameshli was about, she would not have recognized it. Here, in the heartland of foreign gods, he was making sacrifice to the Wolf, dragging his indifferent deity in to be his crutch and his rod.

'What, now?' she demanded of him. She was used to seeing him by firelight. Back in the village, his temple had been his forge. He had made magic there, breeding iron out of earth and wolf-wood. Now he stood on hostile ground, a lean and scarred old man. He had painted his face with red and black, but the work was crude and hurried. She imagined his fingers jabbing and darting across his weathered features, hasty lest his nerve go before he had finished.

He had an iron dagger heating in the fire. It was that scent that had drawn Maniye here.

'We have travelled through strange lands, where they do things wrong. Differently. Wrong.' His lips twitched back from his crooked teeth. 'We live amongst people who do not hunt and have crooked souls.' He fixed Maniye with his gaze and her own uncertainties let him in; for a moment he was the terrible priest of memory, the giver of the law.

Around him there were a handful of her warband. Spear Catcher had followed her in, and she noticed some of her younger followers, those like Tiamesh who had earned no hunter's name to give them strength.

'We have come to an evil place,' Kalameshli went on. 'This River Nation, this hot land of black men where they trust each other so little that they must call foreigners to guard themselves. This land where the people worship *serpents*. If we are to carry our Wolf with us in this land, we must be marked. We must carry him on our skin.' He plucked the dagger from the fire just as the leather of its hilt began to smoke.

'Many Tracks, you are the Wolf's Champion,' he told her. The unspoken words were: *and I am the Wolf's priest.* 'You must be first.' The dagger trembled in his hand, ever so slightly: nerves perhaps, or just age. He needed to join the shreds of his old authority back together, and for that she had to submit.

She shook her head.

'How will Wolf aid you, if you do not bear his mark? How will he know you for his own?' Takes Iron snapped.

'All my life you've said that Wolf doesn't help; the Wolf tests us. Why would Wolf suddenly change his ways and aid us?' she asked flatly. She was thinking of all the running she had done, to get out of this man's shadow. The Wolf had not helped her then; the Wolf had watched her and grinned. Now she had survived, she *had* the Wolf's approval. If she had stumbled and fallen, those jaws would have been waiting for her.

'I am the voice of the Wolf here!' Takes Iron was trying to work up a righteous fury, but she detected a plaintive, whining tone to his voice.

'Old man, the Wolf may whisper in your ear, but I have seen him.' The words came from her unplanned, the Champion rising up to breathe through her mouth. 'When I became what I am, Hesprec sent me to the gods' own land. I stood before the Wolf, then, and I stood before the Tiger. The Wolf knows me, and a little distance will not let him forget me. Keep your dagger and your fire. You are only alive because of me. I will not bow to you now.'

Kalameshli's face twisted. 'Obey your father!'

Only when the words were out did Maniye recall that this was not common knowledge. Because she did not wish it known; because priests did not sire children. Now the others were staring at Kalameshli, his hold on them slipping away. She looked from face to face and found no love or respect for Takes Iron the man there. All he had was his status as Takes Iron the priest, and now he had confessed his failure even there. The Wolf was death and winter, and devoured children rather than bringing more into the world. For all he spoke for the Wolf, his voice had become faint in their ears.

'Come,' Maniye told them, and turned away, Stepping into her own wolf shape as she did so. *Let Takes Iron remember who leads whom.* For a heartbeat she was not sure that her authority over them had prevailed, rather than the hooks of the Wolf that Kalameshli had been intent on forging, but then she heard the click of their claws, and knew they were hers, and not the old priest's. For now, at least.

The next morning, the faint, disagreeable smell of smoke was still in the air, even to her human nose. Or perhaps it was just her human imagination.

As they dressed and ate breakfast, she noticed her warband were watching her carefully, too. They had taken her side last night, but balance of power was a fluid thing. They were all a long way from home.

Later that morning, Asmander came to find her, looking part-sullen, part-embarrassed. Shyri was skulking along in his shadow, inordinately amused with herself as usual.

'What?' Maniye asked at the youth's expression. 'Are we not welcome, suddenly?' After so long a journey south it would be maddening to be heading straight back north again. Although she would not refuse the Horse Society's hospitality if it were offered . . .

'It's not that. I have to ask you something,' the River Champion said. The words seemed bitter in his mouth.

'For yourself or your chief?'

'I need you to disobey my father.'

Maniye's eyebrows went up at that. 'I . . . don't really know about your father. Am I supposed to be doing what he says? He hasn't said for me to do anything yet.'

'He has a plan: when Esumit goes back to her mistress, there will be an embassy with her. My father will stand before Tecumet and argue the strength of her brother's claim. I am to stand with him, to show the strength of Tsokawan. He wants you, too.'

She shrugged. 'Why?'

'Because,' Shyri broke in, 'if Asman the elder is to wave his parts in someone's face, he wants them to be as big as possible. Even if he's pretending they're the Kasra's parts.'

Asmander gave her a pained look. 'Must you?'

'What is it you people say? "These things are known": I laugh at what is funny.'

'Asmander,' Maniye broke in. 'What is this to me?'

'My father has asked for you,' the River Champion told her. 'But I want you to say no. He is not your master. He doesn't hold your name.'

Maniye took a deep breath. 'Do you River People ever make sense?'

Shyri snickered.

Something real and desperate flashed briefly in Asmander's eyes. 'Tecuman has two Champions now,' he explained. 'Just like his sister. And I fear for him. I do not want him stripped of both of us, no matter how grand the errand. I must go. You can stay.'

'I'll stay, then. I'll keep my warband close by his side.'

'Thank you.' Asmander clasped her upper arm, a brief squeeze that she pulled back from uncomfortably. Apparently it was something entirely appropriate for him, though, some comradely gesture, Champion to Champion.

Champion to Champion. That was a strange thought.

'I will go with you, of course,' Shyri decided.

'You will not.'

'I will, and your father will settle for me if he can't have his northerner,' she declared. 'Show this Kasra-girl you have the Plains at your back, why not?'

Asmander was frowning, ready to dismiss the idea out of hand because it was hers, but the sense got through to him a moment later and he nodded reluctantly. 'Why not?' he agreed.

'It'll be like old times,' Shyri said. 'Except you let your slave go.'

'Venater,' Maniye recalled. 'No, Venat. What happened to him?' She had been expecting the big, angry man to turn up at some point, although she hadn't exactly been looking forward to it.

'He went home,' Asmander told her. 'He went to cut throats.'

6

Venat was coming home.

At the estuary's edge, he had parted company with Asmander, who had been his keeper and then his liberator. The youth would go on to step within the open jaws of his father; Venat had more pressing business than watching two crocodiles tear at each other.

The people of the Dragon held a knot of islands at the seaward edge of the estuary, where the eastern horizon gave onto the endless ocean. Venat remembered watching storms stalk over the sea at night when he was young. He remembered roaring at the clouds to challenge the thunder.

Little had changed with him, really. He would take on the weather or the Sun River Nation or his own people. He was never one to shirk a fight.

He had made good time crossing the tangled fastness of the estuary. Where a human form was less than ideal, he had slid through the channels and slithered over the mud as a great lizard with scales like black pebbles. He had hunted fish and deer, snakes and capybara, eaten what he wished and left the rest. He had been moving fast to reach the isles of the Dragon.

The Black Teeth were the largest of the four clans of the Dragon. Venat had been born into their number, just another bloody-nosed boy-child fighting his peers. Later he became a raider, then a leader, then others of the Black Teeth had ganged up against him and he had gone away to trouble other shores, plaguing the River Lords and their docile subjects.

The trip north with Asmander had put him in mind of home. He had seen the Wolf and the Tiger tear at each other, and it had made him oddly nostalgic. It was about time he fought for something, he had decided.

He had never thought Asmander would set him free to do it.

He tried not to think about that.

Now he had reached the shore of the Black Teeth's home. It was time to see how things had gone in his absence.

He clawed out of the waves as a great lizard; he stood on the beach as a man, powerful and scarred, sand-skinned, lantern-jawed, wearing a coat of sharp-barbed sharkskin and carrying a greenstone club. Venat had come home, and somebody would regret it soon enough. Possibly himself.

His people practised just enough agriculture to fall back on. The fertile parts of the island were fiercely contested, seeded by slaves and women and those of his people too weak to fight and too timid to flee.

Venat had come back to the beach of his childhood after all this time. Further inland there was the Whale Seat, where the chief of the Black Teeth – whoever that was these days – would be lording it. Venat remembered the Whale Seat, made of curving bones as tall as two men together. It had looked comfortable, and he might have had it, too, had he not overplayed his hand and been forced into exile.

But there was always tomorrow for that heap of whalebone. Right now he had humbler ambitions. Not far inland was the low hall in whose shadow he had been born. It had once been his to command. Shark Hilt, it was called and, now he was back on home ground with his name intact, Venat rather fancied making it his again.

He spotted workers in the fields and decided to grab one and ask a few pointed questions about who sat in the big seat up at

Shark Hilt. Before he was close enough, though, he caught sight of a familiar face.

The man was Uzmet. He and Venat had grown up together. There had been a time when he had stood at Venat's shoulder and been counted amongst his people. Then Venat had grown too powerful and his rivals had grown too generous, so that men like Uzmet had found other hearths more to their liking.

Crouched in the saw-edged grass overlooking the fields, Venat watched him narrowly. Uzmet was skirting the edge of the field, shouting at some of the workers. He yanked on the tight leather collar of a slave, and then moved on to cuff one of the women. She Stepped instantly, whip-like tail lashing as she bared curved teeth. Uzmet was almost twice her size when he took his own lizard form, but she faced him down for a few more moments, hissing and rising up on her hind legs. Then she had Stepped back, on her knees, fists clenched but head bowed. Uzmet slapped her across the face hard, and then turned and ran straight into Venat.

The look on Uzmet's face was worth the whole journey north and back.

Venat struck him across the temple with the pommel of his club. The man fell; what struck the ground was a dragon, a fighting lizard of the islands. Venat was ready for him, though, dropping on the writhing, clawing creature and grasping for its twisting neck. Uzmet was still half stunned, his tail lashing a weal across Venat's shoulders, one claw hooking painfully into his attacker's thigh. Then Venat's fingers had gripped Uzmet's throat, digging like iron into the thin scales there, choking and clutching until what was beneath him was a man, not a beast.

He smashed a broad fist into Uzmet's face twice – harder than necessary, to be honest – and then had a thong about the man's neck, dragging it tight to stop the man Stepping back. That done, he hit Uzmet a few more times, because it felt good to do it, and then hauled the man away to where they could have a private conversation.

The answers he beat and choked from the man pleased him

greatly. The alliance that had driven him out was long shattered, his foes dead or exiled just as he had been. Only one remained to claim Shark Hilt: not the man Venat would have picked as the strongest or the most dangerous, but evidently the most patient.

When he had learned all he wanted, he grinned a yellow grin at Uzmet.

'I'm back,' he said. 'You're mine now.' He loosened the cord about the man's neck and stepped back, waiting. For a long time Uzmet stared up at him from the eye that was not swollen shut. Then the man spat out a tooth and nodded, because this was how the Dragon ordered their affairs.

Venat went back to the field, with Uzmet limping bloody and bowed behind him. They were watching for him, those women and weaklings and slaves. He saw from their faces that more than a few had recognized him, and they had told the rest.

'I'm back!' he yelled at them all. 'You're mine now!' And then he was marching for Shark Hilt because he had enemies to kill.

Haraket was lord of Shark Hilt, and probably he dreamt of unseating the current chief of the Black Teeth. That was the way of the Dragon, after all – Haraket must know he had underlings already measuring their feet against his shoes.

He had fought mightily to get where he was. He had seen off many rivals; killed some, driven others away. Now he sat on a stone throne decorated with pearls from the Salt Islands and the skin of some luckless River Lord, and helped himself to all his domain had to offer.

The longhouse of Shark Hilt was of sealskin stretched over timbers and pegged down into the ground; only in its centre could a man stand upright, and so the warriors of the Black Teeth crouched under the sloping walls, gnawing and gulping, while their women passed in and out with food and drink. Smoky brands gave a hazy yellow light to it all, but when Haraket's eyes passed over the throng assembled there, he could be forgiven for not marking every face. Venat was counting on it, crouching under the eaves where the shadows fell most thickly.

He had sat upon that throne in his time. Now, looking at the lord of Shark Hilt, Venat wondered if he was seeing himself as he might have been. He had returned to these islands a different man, seen too much to simply go back to being another Dragon warlord. The throne now appeared to him to be crude and ugly, as though someone had plucked out the eyes he had been born with, and given him Riverland sight instead.

There was a certain path for those who rose to lead the Dragon. That fierce struggle of youth all too often turned into complacency. So it had been with Haraket, Venat saw. Everything in Shark Hilt's shadow was his for the taking. He ate the best food, had his pick of the plunder when his followers went raiding, called whatever woman he wanted to his bed. Why else strive for dominion, if not to enjoy all that life could offer? That had always been the Dragon philosophy.

Venat found the doctrine wanting. The thought was like a thorn in him. Part of him wanted to pluck it out, to return to the man he had been, who had known only strength and the reach of his arms. But he could not unlearn what he had learned – nor, really, did he want to.

Haraket had always been a strong big man. Years without a challenger had made him fat, and had shrunk him. Not physically, but in his head; Venat could look on him and see little more than an overgrown child, wilful and selfish.

A score of Haraket's men were returned from raiding: their canoes were beached on the shore and their plunder piled up in the hall. The voyage was esteemed a grand success, the warriors cheered for the great wealth they had brought back. Venat's eyes saw half a dozen women, a few boys, a meagre pile of pearls and shells. Compared to the wealth of the River Lords, it was nothing. How many had died for it, or had their lives destroyed for it? And how long before the Hook Jaw or the Dark Eye tribes made their own raid, and took it all back? Venat's childhood had been a constant round of such raids, which had seemed to the boy glorious, the pinnacle of manly ambition.

When Haraket had first become chief, he had been generosity personified, so Uzmet had claimed. It had not lasted, and these days little bounty trickled down to those below him. Many of the raiders would already be wondering how strong Haraket still was. Leadership amongst the Dragon was a bloom that was sweet while it lasted, yet never lasted long. Venat began to wonder if Uzmet's nerve had failed, but at last the man pushed his way into the longhouse. The rumble and belch of the crowd died down at the sight of the vivid tapestry of bruises that puffed out his face. A quiet fell on the hall of the Shark Hilt, until even the prisoners were silent.

'Who've you lost a fight with?' Haraket demanded.

'I come with a challenge,' Uzmet spat through thick lips.

'You?' Haraket levered himself to his feet, already reaching for his stone blade. 'You challenge me?'

'No. I am sent.' Uzmet's fists were clenched, waiting for the first blade or club to strike him down. 'I am sent to say you are not fit to track your filth on the sands of this island. I am sent to say that one comes who you thought shackled and gone forever.'

Venat had mouthed the words along with him; it had taken him long enough to pound them into the mind of his messenger.

'Shackled . . .' Everyone marked the uncertainty that crossed Haraket's face. 'How was he shackled?'

Uzmet straightened up, some vestige of pride returning to him. 'They took his name from him and bound him with it, but now he is free.' And, having said all, he dropped to his knee to await his fate.

Haraket went very still, eyes narrow. '*He* went upriver with a child's name and died,' he spat.

'He is outside, waiting for you,' Uzmet said, and sincerely, since that was what he believed.

'Lies,' Haraket breathed. Venat could see clearly that he wanted not at all to go outside, and the sight was curiously nostalgic. *Ah, did I leave that much of a mess behind me?* The lord of Shark Hilt was in a bind now though. He must know that enough of his followers had begun to chafe under his rule. Fear of a spectre, fear of a name, would be all the encouragement they needed.

The lord of Shark Hilt growled, deep in his throat. 'I'll have your hide, Uzmet. I'll flay it off you while you're still alive.' But Uzmet just stood still, resigned to his fate. Venat might not have Serpent priests and their rituals to bind Uzmet as he himself had been bound to Asmander, but the Dragon had their own way. He had made Uzmet crawl on his human belly before him. He had held the man's head in his stinking lizard jaws and called upon the Dragon to witness Uzmet's capitulation. What life Uzmet lived was Venat's to own. Each breath the man took was a gift.

Haraket saw that in the man's eyes; he saw truth there.

Around the longhouse, in the smoke and gloom, hands were finding hilts. Weapons of greenstone and wood and shark-tooth were waking in their owners' hands as the chief faltered.

But then the lord of Shark Hilt found his heart, and he snarled and gestured sharply to his warriors, the score or so who were there. He Stepped, sloughing forwards into the long, lead-scaled reptile that was the Dragon, and shouldered his way past Uzmet. He rammed through the sealhide flap of the longhouse and emerged into the relative cool of the evening, claws raking at the earth. Haraket was a man gone to seed, but as a lizard he was powerful still.

His men came out with him in a loose mob, some human, some Stepped. Nothing in the ways of the Dragon said a chief had to meet his challenger one on one.

Haraket twisted his body, raising himself until he was up on his hind legs and tail, croaking out a bellow of defiance at the darkening sky. Around him, his people were watching in all directions save one, and Venat noted which of them stayed close

to Haraket, and which had already started to distance themselves.

The one way they did not look, of course, was back to the
longhouse, where Venat stood in the door with his stone *meret*
blade in hand.

Now Haraket had found his human feet again, emboldened
by the lack of an enemy. 'I knew you were lying!' he cried out to
the sea and the horizon. 'He's gone, dead, with a child's name on
him still! And now I'll take your skin—' and he turned and
found himself looking Venat in the eye. His voice withered to a
little hoarse whisper.

For a long moment they faced each other, and the world
around them held its breath. Venat had his arms spread, as
though about to clasp his enemy to him, or offer his chest to the
knife. Haraket was clenched in about himself, crippled by shock.

Then: 'Kill him, kill him,' hissed from his lips, even as he
stumbled back a step.

Venat tensed, waiting to see if the seeds he had sown would
sprout now. A good number of Haraket's followers seemed to be
drifting away, holding themselves aloof from the fight. The rest,
who had been ready to shed blood for their chief, were looking
at their comrades and weighing their chances.

Nobody killed Venat.

After forcing Uzmet's submission, Venat had taken a day to
go amongst the women in the fields and speak to them. He had
given them messages and made promises and sent them
amongst the men. They had carried his words into the ears of
those who were already tired of Haraket. The people of the
Dragon were ruled by their men under the sun, but the wise
man knew that the moon and the night belonged to women.
Men who forgot that never held power long.

The lord of Shark Hilt – in the last moments when that was
still the case – saw that he was alone. He could have Stepped
then; he could have gone for Venat with his blade; he could even
have trusted to his heels and hoped to take a canoe into exile.

What he did was hesitate, unable to comprehend just how swiftly his world had been brought down.

Venat lunged at him, Stepping halfway so that his lizard body slammed Haraket to the ground. He felt the bite of his enemy's blade then, digging shallowly at his scale-armoured ribs, but his teeth were already gouging at human flesh, tearing into his enemy's face. Then Haraket was a dragon too, and the pair of them reared up, clasped in each other's talons, biting furiously. Perhaps Haraket was slightly larger, but he was wounded already and still off balance in his mind. Venat bore him writhing to the ground, tail whipping, and got his teeth into Haraket's sinuous neck. This was where his mute brothers the dragon lizards would have abandoned the fight, the victor made plain to all. He was no animal, though; he was a man and he knew when he had to kill.

He sawed deep into Haraket's reptile throat and felt the salt blood bloom.

After, when it was done, he strode over to the pearl-dotted seat, and none stood in his way. The people of the Black Teeth crouched in the longhouse and watched him, waiting to see what he would do. Others would already be running all over the island with the news; the other houses of the Black Teeth would know soon enough.

So Venat sat there, lord of Shark Hilt once more, and thought about the wide, wide world he had seen, and about the future.

7

The Stones, or the Stone Place, that was how they knew it across the Crown of the World. And they did all know it – every tribe and totem of them.

Loud Thunder stood at the edge of the stone ring, now; to step inside would be to bend the attention of the world to himself, and he was not ready for that yet. The circle stood at the centre of an island that had been made by human hands, heaped up in the midst of a marsh. The waters of the Crown of the World came here, it seemed to him, to mingle and converse amidst the half-liquid earth, around the roots of the sawgrass and the stunted, poison-berried bushes. His mind followed them: seeping away to streams, to rivers, and at last south and to the sea.

Nobody built stone circles like this now. All those places in the Crown of the World where the spirits gathered – the great forces of the sky and the earth – had been found and marked long ago. The stones weighed them down and fixed them in place. Still, it amused Loud Thunder to consider how he might go about reproducing the Stone Place. The logistics of it – the transport of the earth and the great stones, how to float them across the marsh, how to raise them up . . . He could see his way to all of it and, if his Mother had asked that of him, he would have leapt at the chance. Far easier to build an island and raise a few vast monoliths than to do *this*.

They were all here on the island. Just the thought of it quickened his breath with anxiety. The Horse and the Coyote and the Raven had carried word to every corner of the Crown of the World. This was not the great gathering of the wise that marked the equinoxes, where priests came to sacrifice and to petition and to watch each other suspiciously. This time they had come for *him*.

They were waiting, too. Night had fallen, and someone had built a grand mound of tinder and wood in the circle's heart. And now Loud Thunder stood here with a brand in his hand and they watched him, and waited for him to step in. If he held off any longer, they would start to disappear into the dark.

The Boar were out there – the old priest who had travelled with him, and at least two others, painted and masked. There were Deer wearing antler headdresses, still and silent in the darkness. There were Eyriemen and Coyote. There were many from the tribes of the Wolf, still strong despite having no great chief to unify them. And there were the Tiger, so Loud Thunder had heard. His own eyes could not confirm it, but the Tiger always did take night as their own. Only the Seal were absent, and they seldom joined their voices to anybody else's. Besides, they were mad; anybody living with the terrible, hungry sea every day would have to be.

In the face of that massed scrutiny, Loud Thunder took the first, the greatest step, and entered the circle. Without ceremony he crossed to the centre and carefully put the brand to the tinder. The fire-maker had done the job well, and flames leapt swiftly through the gaps within, so that the blaze mounted quickly. Its light fell across the great bulk of Loud Thunder, then spread until it reached out between the stones to the many gathered there. He saw their faces: the stern, the painted, the scarred, the hooded, those who would brave the journey to the Stone Place to know what the Bear had to say.

He stared at them mutely. He wanted to look back at Mother and the rest, but he knew there would be no help there. He had tried to prepare some clever words, but they had all fallen out of his mind the instant the fire caught.

For a moment that was all there was ever going to be: a big man made bigger by his awkward silence, standing by a fire and being stared at by all the priests in the world. Then inspiration came: he swore he felt the ground shiver, and the words creep into him through his feet.

'There was a man, a southerner, who came to us last year,' he told them. The first few words were too quiet – he had a tendency to mumble – but then he made good on his name, drawing deep breaths and letting his voice boom so that he struck echoes from the stones themselves.

'He was of the Serpent and he came seeking news of what messages the gods had given you, the Wise.' Of course, when Loud Thunder had last seen Hesprec, he had not been a *he* at all, but no need to complicate matters. 'Yes, we have stories of Serpent; yes, they are not happy ones. Still, he came. He came because his own people had been telling each other stories of a . . .' He faltered for a moment. *A darkness*, he had wanted to say, but darkness meant different things to different people. 'A bad thing,' he went on, weakly. 'A terrible thing, like a great cloud that swallows the sun.' Had Hesprec ever said that? Probably not. 'He spoke to many here. He spoke to my Mother,' Loud Thunder went on. 'She too has had warning that hard times are coming. As have many of you.'

So far, so good. They were not exactly hanging on his every word; they were not walking away. The Boar and the Deer were very still; the Wolf were restless. Amongst the Eyriemen, one had stood as though to begin the great exodus that would leave Loud Thunder alone and unlistened-to. Surely that was Yellow Claw, their Eagle Champion, whom many of the Eyrie would follow. But then another had put a hand on the man's arm, guiding him back down, and one of the Eyrie was stepping forward.

A woman – that was the first surprise, for the Eyrie kept a close guard about its women, forbidding them to leave, or even to Step. Here was not just a female face, though: painted grey with a white bar across her eyes – one of the Owl. Her dark hair was cut back close to her skull and that, along with the paint, gave her a look like death might wear, if it was a woman. When she spoke, the night was silent for her.

'I see all that is under the moon,' she declared – her voice was so strong that Loud Thunder briefly considered just going, letting her take over. 'The moon has brought us warnings, just as this man says.' Her own eyes were fixed on nothing, and Loud Thunder wondered if she was blind. 'Who can deny the omens of the last five years, how they have grown worse and worse?'

There was a lot of grumbling and muttering from around the circle. At last, one of the Wolf came forward, a stocky, crease-faced man of the Moon Eaters, demanding, 'Did you call us here to tell us what we already knew?'

Now the moment of truth. 'The Bear has seen a doom coming, like a cloud. We are strong, in the Bear, but we are not strong enough to fight this.' Loud Thunder took a deep breath. 'The Owl has seen a doom coming,' he went on hoarsely. 'But though the Eyrie's people are masters of the air, they cannot stand alone against what is to come.' Yellow Claw most definitely didn't like the sound of that, but now it was said. Loud Thunder wondered philosophically just how many enemies he could make before the end of this ordeal. He had intended to name all the tribes at this point, but had a dread of forgetting one, so he just said, 'You have all seen this thing coming. And none of you can stop it alone.'

He had thought through a whole train of reasoning that would lead them to his conclusion, none of which he could now remember. However, a new voice spared him the need to.

'So the Bear comes down from its highlands and tells us we should band together?'

Loud Thunder had assumed that having to stand and shout in front of a crowd of priests would be the worst of it; now he took the time to correct himself. *This* was the worst of it.

The Tiger had made itself known, and it was presenting him with a familiar face. She was a priestess, Aritchaka. He knew her because she had tried to kill his friend, Maniye Many Tracks.

Aritchaka entered the circle, and a shudder went through everyone there. The fire flickered and danced across the bronze scales of her coat and the stones on either side of her. She was a graceful, elegant woman. She could stand motionless, hands by her sides, and still threaten violence. For a moment, Thunder thought he saw all that dancing firelight come together to make a single vast shape that stood over and around her, staring down at him with forbidding, narrow-pupilled eyes.

'The Bear has kept to its high places for too long,' she told him, head tilted a little to look him in the eye. 'You think to raise a shadow, and bring everyone here together in fear of it?'

'And if there is already a shadow?' Loud Thunder tried.

For a moment some easy dismissal hovered on Aritchaka's lips, but it died, and she shook her head, almost despairingly. 'Loud Thunder, the Tiger knows you. Not as a friend, but it knows you, and your Mother also. Has there ever been a season when some priest somewhere did not cry doom? No. Is there any surprise that all those voices should align some season, to make it sound as though a great doom is coming? No.'

'But—'

'Let us say you are right.' She took one step further into the circle and laid a hand on the closest stone, her eyes boring into him. 'When they raised these stones in the long-ago times, they say the people of twenty tribes worked side by side. Have you heard that story, Loud Thunder?'

He nodded, a little hope kindling in his heart. He never did see these things coming.

She smiled back at him, but her expression cut like a knife. 'Do you think, by bringing us here, that you will bring those days as well? Do you think your talk of terrors will bring us meekly into your shadow, Cave Dweller? If a doom is coming then the Tiger will fight it, but do you think that even the end of the world will see us share a roof with the Wolf?'

Loud Thunder opened his mouth, but the reply he had been hoping for failed to occur to him.

'You know their crimes against us,' Aritchaka said, almost pleasantly. 'We are owed.'

'*You* are owed?' The voice came from amidst the Wolf priests, who had drawn closer to one another as the Tiger spoke. 'There are plenty living who remember when the Tiger stretched its shadow out, and what came of that.' This was some young firebrand out of the Many Mouths. 'How many of our souls did you eat, how many of our people did you kill, a thumb's width at a time?'

'And how many of our children have burned in the Wolf's jaws since then?' the old Boar priest grunted out. 'When the Shadow Eaters were strong, they took our people and ate our ghosts. Now the Wolf are strong they make thralls of us and give us to the fire.' His people stood with the Deer now, another distinct and antagonistic faction. Only the Coyote were still scattered, and they were plainly not going to be joining anyone any time soon.

Then more voices were raised and other complaints made, some quiet, some louder. Yellow Claw shouted, though he did not step into the circle. The Wolf were furious, retelling tales of When the Tiger ruled. Now there were people pushing between the stones, taking that single step forward that would let the world mark them. These were priests, protected by their calling, but tempers were flaring; the passions of younger and more warlike men were tearing rents in their wisdom. Through it all, Aritchaka, her piece said, just stared at him. Her face was not devoid of sympathy but it changed nothing.

Loud Thunder looked helplessly towards Mother, but her face was unreadable, her eyes fixed expectantly on him. Behind her, Lone Mountain's expression showed clearly, *I would have done this better*, a sentiment Thunder could only agree with.

71

And again he felt something. A slight shifting in the earth, perhaps, that only he could detect. It was as if he had asked, *What can I say to make this right?* and the universe had whispered him an answer, some piece of ancient learning saved for this moment alone.

'I am very strong!' his voice boomed out and stilled them all. 'Look at me!' He jabbed a fist at himself. 'Who here is as strong as I? Who would match themselves against these arms? These shoulders? Would any here wrestle me? Any of you?' He stared about the ring, at the youths and old men and women, and was unsurprised to find he had no challengers. For a moment, Aritchaka held his eye, but if sheer strength hung in the balance, she could not have matched him.

'I,' he declared grandly, desperately, 'am the strongest man in the Crown of the World. In all of the world!' He beat his fists once against his chest and glowered at them defiantly. 'What do you have to say about that?'

There was a little laughter: some snickering from the Eyrie, smirking from a Coyote man and woman sitting outside the ring of stones.

'When this doom comes,' he told them, more quietly, 'I will put my strength against it, to hold it back, but even my strength will not be enough. No man alone is strong enough.'

Aritchaka shifted, about to say that this changed nothing, and he cut her off.

'I am strongest. The Bear is strongest. Any fool can see that. I invite you to come to our lands – to send your strongest. None will be as strong as me.'

He had more to say, to bring them round to where he wanted them, but just as Aritchaka had run ahead of him before, now another voice spoke.

'I am a great teller of tales.' It was the Coyote man, stepping into the circle at last with a nervous glance at the dark sky above. 'I am Two Heads Talking, and there is no man who ever told a tale as I can. While I speak, you might think stone was

72

water, summer was winter. I will go to the lands of the Bear, and I will tell my tales. Who would dare to match their tongue to mine?'

And something that had been clenched within Loud Thunder abruptly released, because it was perfect. Of course the Bear were strongest: they were biggest. His challenge of strength was ill-considered. But stories, though: everyone thought they could tell a good story, though so few really could. Already there were murmurs and mutters about the circle as challengers for Two Heads Talking's crown made themselves known.

'In my tribe we have a hunter who runs faster than any you ever knew,' said a whip-lean woman of the Deer. She was watching Two Heads as she said it, and Loud Thunder guessed they knew each other, and she trusted him enough to follow his lead. The Coyote travelled everywhere, after all, and spoke to everyone.

Then someone – he could not even say who – was boasting about what a good shot their niece was, and after that there was some business from the Boar about catching fish, and someone else talking over it about riddles, and Loud Thunder knew it was time to speak.

'So, we all hate each other,' he boomed out, quieting them. 'But we all run and wrestle and hunt and fish and tell long stories, and we all think we're the best at all these things. Except for wrestling. Surely nobody thinks they're better than me at that.' And now the laughter was back, creeping cautiously into the circle, but they were at least no longer laughing *at* him.

'The doom is coming,' he told them simply. 'But we have hated each other a long time. The Tiger is right to say it. The Boar is right to say it. So I do not say to you: come and set your troubles aside; stand together like brothers, like sisters. I say instead: come and we shall call you our guests. Guests of the Bear – who would have ever thought it? And we shall find out who runs the fastest race, and whose eye is keenest, and whether Two Heads Talking can truly talk as well as he claims. And perhaps from that, we shall know each other better. I say this; the Mother of the Bear says this, through me. Send your chosen to us, and we will pledge them guest-right, and they can show the world what they are best at. For we will need all skill and strength and cunning, if we are to face what is coming.'

8

The fortress of Tsokawan broke through the treetops of the estuary, spires threatening the sky like rigid bone fingers. The blue and cloudless sky didn't care though, Asmander thought. Sometimes it felt as if he was the only one who really worried for Tecuman. Others just saw the mask and the regalia; they feared or they coveted, but they did not really understand that there was a man under all that. Asmander knew that man – that barely-more-than-a-boy, as Asmander himself was barely more than a boy. *But we grow up fast, all of us.* Maniye came into his thoughts then, running out the last years of her childhood with half the north chasing her. *I suppose it could have been worse for us, Tecuman.*

Tsokawan was the stone fist of the River Lords here at the estuary. Yes, it was defendable, but it was built beyond the simple need to keep enemies out. It was the anchor that stopped the estuary peoples drifting into feuding and outright rebellion.

And now Tecumet had brought soldiers to Tsokawan, something never done before. How would that look to all the peoples of the estuary? Asmander was not so naive as to think they were all blissfully happy under the rule of his people, no matter if they had profited greatly from it. How long before they felt freedom outweighed peace? How long before the Hidden People and the Milk Tears and the Crest Bearers started to twist in the grip of the Kasra? How long before the *Dragon* . . .

He wished with all his bitter heart that Venat was with him. And yet if he saw the old pirate now, what could he possibly think? Surely Venat's reappearance, at the head of a warband of the Dragon, would spark the fragmenting of the estuary.

So he looked out across the water towards Tsokawan, his mind a knot of fear and doubt.

By his side, his father brooded, leaning on the rail and no doubt thinking through how their embassy to Tecumet might progress. Asman had no eyes for the spires of Tsokawan. He was doubtless cataloguing the defences of this, Tecumet's barge: the archers, the spearmen, the Stepped soldiers who coursed through the water with lazy sweeps of their scaled tails. Would he turn to his son, when they returned to the fortress, and order an attack? Would his mind have cut apart this vessel until he had seen the perfect way to breach it?

'This is normal, to keep guests waiting?' Shyri asked. She was making her boredom very obvious, prowling about the deck in both shapes, heckling the guards, kicking at the gilded ornamentation. The soldiers watched her constantly and she played games with them. She would transform herself into a pretty Plains girl, blinking coyly at them from under her lashes, then she would be a high-shouldered, spotted hyena baring its hideous, bone-crushing teeth, laughing at them. They did not know what to make of her.

'Tecumet claims the Daybreak Throne,' Asman told her shortly. 'So: we wait for her to show us how grand a Kasra she is.' Asman did not like Shyri, which to Asmander was one of the pleasures of having her along.

'Or perhaps she is flustered by having her childhood lover board her?' Shyri leant back against the rail, speaking quite loud enough to be heard by anyone who cared to listen.

Asmander awaited the angry rejoinder from his father, but old Asman's face was closed, leading to the inevitable thought, *He cannot think it, surely?* 'What foolishness is this?' he demanded, on his silent father's behalf.

Shyri grinned at him, opportunist hunter from head to toe, and one that had scented weakness. 'When we were in the Stone People ruin, wasn't it? You told me how good a Kasra your boy Tecuman would make, and just the same for Tecumet. Didn't you all grow up together, the three of you?'

'Yes,' as curt as his father. And of course, because the Blue-green Reach was a strong clan and Asman a clever clan head, Asmander had grown up at Atahlan, a companion to the royal twins. They were almost of an age, and the three of them had run riot through the palace grounds, and often further. They had been irrepressible, inseparable.

Later, older, he had felt of them as more than family, more than future rulers. He had loved them both, that pure bond of youth that feels at the time as though it will last forever.

I don't know if I can go through with this. Let my father not call me to speak, please.

He had closed his eyes and, opening them, found Shyri right before him. Her grin was gone. 'These things are known,' he got out. 'The Laughing Men talk too much, and nothing to the purpose. I am Tecuman's Champion. Tecumet is my enemy.' It was hard to say, far harder than he had anticipated.

Shyri made a doubting noise, but she stepped back. 'What about that other Champion, Angry Girl? She was one of your little warband?'

'Izel? No.' Izel was low-born, brought to Atahlan only after the Champion had possessed her. And he and Tecuman had not been kind to the awkward, defensive girl back then. They had mocked her mercilessly, in fact. So had Tecumet, a little, but she had cultivated the girl, too – a ration of kindness that had bought Izel twice over.

I will have to fight Izel before this is over. I will have to kill her, if I can. He had considered that before: everything could come down to the blood of Champions being shed. *Or will it be Maniye? And will I fight Tchoche?* For Tecumet had two Champions as well, one of the River, one of the Stone Kingdoms.

77

Even as he thought it, Asman was pointing out a new boat drawing up to the bank: men and women were getting out of it, ruddy-skinned and armoured in heavy bronze, no doubt glad to be off the water. Stone Kingdom soldiers, mercenaries from the high places west of Atahlan, they had always made a good living out of disputes along the river. How many of them would make their fortunes out of a civil war?

'Let me tell you what you don't want to hear,' Shyri started, looking out at all the boats the river was busy with, at all the fires and tents on the bank where Tecumet's forces were disembarking. She did not finish the thought, though, just grimacing and looking away. Asmander found that oddly touching, that even the carrion-eater felt his feelings were not fair game today.

'I know,' he agreed, 'they have more than we do. But we have walls. And we have the true Kasra.'

He put as much faith as he could into the words but they sounded hollow in his ears.

Then a young woman was approaching, her face tracked with rainbow scales: Esumit, the Serpent priestess.

'Asman of the Bluegreen Reach,' she stated, 'Tecumet Kasra invites you into her presence.'

Asmander's father nodded once, brief but cordial, and then the three of them were being ushered towards the stern of the barge where a great edifice of awnings had been put up, the travelling palace of Tecumet Kasra.

The Daybreak Throne in Atahlan was a vast stone covered with beaten gold and inscribed with centuries of history, sequential panels showing the deeds of heroes of legend and half-remembered scenes from the Serpent's lost Oldest Kingdom. There were houses that would have been crushed beneath the weight of that throne – and not the mean huts of peasants either. Here on her barge, though, Tecumet sat in the coils of the Serpent: a chair of gilded wood worked into the loops and curves of a snake's body. Rearing over her, the carved head looked down on every supplicant with eyes of sapphire.

She wore a new mask, Asmander saw. It was wrought into features that were part human, part reptilian, and angry, frowning and snarling, the line of the mouth showing sharp teeth all the way up to her ears. A war mask: the intent was unmistakable. Her robes were red, a purer, bloodier red than any cloth he had ever seen. In her hands, which were heavy with rings and bracelets, she held a rod and a toothed sword, both of gold and precious stones. She was so still, so serene on her seat, that he wondered if she was there at all. *This is how people feel before Tecuman*, he knew. *This is how everyone feels except me.* And he wanted to reach out, to speak to her of the younger days they had shared, but to do so would have been unforgivable.

Even Shyri was subdued, lurking in the shadows at the back in her human shape.

Tecumet's Champions flanked her throne. Izel stared at Asmander with cold loathing whilst on the other side Tchoche gave him an easy nod. Tchoche, the Stone Kingdom Champion, was a heavy-set man, his pale face leaping out of the shaded gloom. He looked slow and complacent and lazy, and was none of these things.

Esumit was speaker for the Kasra here: no clan chief but an actual priestess, words from the mouth of the Serpent. 'Asman of the Bluegreen Reach, you stand before Tecumet Kasra, rightful claimant of the Daybreak Throne. Can it be you are here to kneel?'

It was a bold opener, but Asman just smiled slightly and spread his hands. 'These things are known: wise is the Serpent, whose words are to be heeded. But there are snakes back at Tsokawan who whisper other messages in my ear. Who am I to believe?'

A brief tic of frustration touched Esumit's face and was gone. 'What purpose can you have, then, to seek this audience? Know that Tecumet will smile on any who recognize her right. You have your own share of wisdom, Asman. Your clan has ever been strong along the river. May it always remain so.'

The threat, unspoken, hung in the air.

Izel shifted forward, ever so slightly, and Asmander braced himself. *Is this to be it? Will someone say, 'Let the Champions fight,' right now?* He felt his own other soul rise within him, the fierce and timeless essence of the Champion. It would relish the battle. It could never see why humans made their lives so complicated.

With that, he found his own mouth open, the words backed up against his teeth: *Let's just fight. Her and me, or Tchoche and me, or both of them against me. Let's fight, and shed blood, and let who wins decide who is Kasra.* His father would be enraged, but once the words were said, who could take them back?

Tecumet moved, leaning forward ever so slightly, and Esumit stepped back to hear her murmur. The priestess's face twitched with emotions swiftly hidden, and she said something back, a whisper only the Kasra could hear. But, whatever Tecumet wished, she would have. Now the rod tapped against the throne, and Esumit was nodding resignedly.

'Asman of the Bluegreen Reach,' she announced, 'Tecumet Kasra appreciates your coming to speak for her brother, for all her brother has set himself in rebellion against the Daybreak Throne. You and yours are honoured guests for as long as you choose to remain with us, and free to leave as soon as you wish. You doubtless have words from the pretender Tecuman, and the Kasra shall hear these in due course. However, for now she wishes to speak alone with your son.'

Asmander had thought that Tecumet's 'alone' would be qualified: once Asman and Shyri had gone, he had assumed one or both of Tecumet's Champions would remain to safeguard his good behaviour. He had assumed Esumit would continue to make pronouncements on behalf of the Kasra. After all, to be Kasra was to have all the life of the Riverlands invested in a human body: the recognition of the Serpent, the fierce hunger of Old Crocodile, all the wisdoms and cunnings of the estuary people, even the bloody-mindedness of the Dragon. The Kasra

80

stood between the great spirits of the world and the mere humans who dwelled in it. Of course the Kasra required a mouthpiece: her words were laden with power.

And yet they all left, though it was plain they did not want to. The Champions were ordered out, though Izel's angry glance suggested she would not be far. Esumit bowed and backed away. Servants absented themselves with the ease of long practice until Tecumet Kasra's cloth-walled domain was ceded to her and to Asmander, closed off to prying eyes.

Asmander had felt a knot tighten in him, all through this. He stood before that metal face, that impenetrable barrier of regalia, and waited to be judged.

But instead, those ring-cluttered hands set aside the sword and the rod, and then they lifted to the fierce war-mask and fought with it a little until it slid aside and revealed a young woman's face, barely more than a girl's.

She was just as Asmander remembered: almost the image of her brother, the pair of them flawless in his eyes. Her eyes were the orange of fired clay, her cheekbones were sharp, her chin delicate. Her hair had been bound back but now she let it spring out, tugging loose the gold braid that had penned it in. Asmander's heart leapt with it, marvelling again at how beautiful she was, seeing at the same time the girl he knew and the brother who shared those features.

Through all this her face had been expressionless, a second mask, and he felt that his own was the same, not a spark of recognition in either of them. But at last a human look came into her eyes: a little afraid, a little sad, even a little mischievous. He remembered how she had always loved setting him and Tecuman against each other, just as he had goaded the pair of them in his turn.

'I don't think your father has anything to say to me,' she told him: the voice of the Kasra, or one of them. She sounded just the same as she had when neither sibling was trying to fill their father's shoes.

'No.' An unforgivable betrayal, but right there Asmander found that he didn't care what his father wanted or thought. 'I don't know why he's come, Te. Except that he thinks others love his voice as much as he does.' Asa and Te, their names for each other from way back then. Asa, Teca and Te.

She giggled, then put a hand to her mouth to stifle the sound. Long ago it had been a joke they made about old Asman, that he would talk to rocks if only he could hear the echo.

Then she was speaking quickly. 'If there is anything you can say to Tecuman—' and then raising her hands against his protests, 'I know, I know, you're loyal to your clan and your father and the Kasra they've both chosen. I know you, Asa. I *know* how you are with loyalty, and I weep every day that your father chose my brother and not me, because I want you by my side, as *my* Champion, But I can't have you. And now, for reasons that nobody in a generation's time will ever understand, I am about to go to war against my brother. I am about to storm Tsokawan and have the Stone People bring down its walls, and destroy generations of what we've built around the estuary for – for what? Because we must have a Kasra. Because . . . terrible things.'

And he had to smile, because that was another childhood joke. When you ran out of any other consequences, when hyperbole had been exhausted . . . terrible things. The difference was that now the terrible things really *were* coming.

'I'll give him whatever he wants,' Tecumet said urgently. 'All honours, riches, command of armies. I would give anything to have him by my side, and you, all three of us together again. But every priest in Atahlan is adamant it must be me – and yes, I know that around the estuary they say the opposite, but what am I supposed to *do*?'

'Does the Kasra not speak in you like a soul?' Asmander asked. 'The Champion is in me and it cuts everything down to simple matters. *Fight*, it says. Izel would say the same.'

'You think that fighting Izel would solve anything?'

'She wants to fight me. If you order it so, I will fight Izel. Let that decide it. No other blood need be shed.' He saw in her eyes just what she thought of the idea, and went on, 'If you are Kasra, then all the blood of the Tsotec is yours to shed. And sometimes it must be the blood of friends.' Where all this wisdom was coming from, he couldn't say: perhaps the Champion itself. 'Yes, Izel will die or I will die. And Tecuman need not, nor anyone else.'

That was the end of his audience, and now he was on deck again. The advance of night had swallowed the outlines of Tsokawan, but he could see its fires. They looked small and brave and always on the point of being extinguished.

His father was below, and Asmander knew he was speaking to other clan chiefs, people he had known when the old Kasra lived, but who had chosen the other side afterwards. Was he winning any over with promises of riches and reward? Seeing the numbers that Tecumet had brought, Asmander thought that would be a hard deal to broker. Although, if anyone could, it was old Asman.

Shyri was at his shoulder: he could not say how he knew it, unless there was some particular quality of silence she brought with her; perhaps the silence of one laughing on the inside.

'So, has she made you her rug?' the Laughing Girl asked.

Asmander had no idea what that was supposed to mean.

'Has she cut your guts out with her words, and made you into a thing to rest her feet on?' Shyri clarified with some relish. There was a nasty edge to her voice beyond the mere mockery.

'I am still in possession of my guts,' he informed her with dignity.

She smirked. 'And I thought you and she had been renewing your old friendships.' The salacious twist she gave the words was finally too much for him.

'What do the Plains know about such things, who never touch another human being save to cut their throats?' he snapped.

'We know not to fool ourselves with too many stupid words,' she replied hotly. 'It's plain to these eyes that she—' Abruptly Shyri stopped. 'What was that?'

Asmander opened his mouth, about to get another jab in, but then he heard it too, drifting across the water. A warning cry, but no voice of the Riverlands: a wolf call of the Crown of the World. There was only one band of northerners anywhere near the estuary right now. If one of Maniye's people was calling the alarm then Tecuman must be in danger.

Asmander cursed and then he was over the rail, Stepping into the long, ridged shape of a crocodile even as he met the water, thrashing his tail as he fought his way towards the trees of the estuary, knowing he would be too late.

9

Earlier that day, Moon Eye came to Maniye and told her that his spirit was coming. She had been expecting it; he had been walking off by himself all day, snapping at anybody who got too close except Sathewe. This would be the third time since he joined her warband that he would accept a collar, for fear of what would happen otherwise.

She did not know precisely what had happened before she had known him, when his spirit had come and he was unmuzzled. He had come from the Moon Eaters, who were more secretive than most of the Wolf, and who did not give names like his lightly. The blood Moon Eye had shed remained buried in his past, the details not volunteered.

It was angry, his spirit. Sometimes it came to him in a fight, and then he rode it and it fed upon his enemies with savage abandon. But sometimes it grew bored – perhaps there was a full moon, perhaps too long had passed since Moon Eye had tasted blood. Then the spirit would force itself into him like a second soul; it rode him, and he would do its bloody will.

So, as sunset approached they put a rope about his neck and bound his arms behind him, and he was set out of the way, in one of the storerooms of Tsokawan, with none near him save Sathewe. The Coyote girl could walk brazenly before the angry spirit and it would not harm her. None could say why.

As the world darkened outside, the gloom within Tsokawan

swelled and grew. Servants of the River Lord padded barefoot through its halls, lighting clay lamps pierced with holes, so that each cast its light out in a scattered constellation. They fascinated Maniye, and she tried to work out whether the patterns were random, or if they really were echoes of the night sky in miniature.

Tsokawan was a huge stone maze, and most of it was dark despite the lamps. She Stepped and trusted to her wolf's senses to find the way. Moon Eye was seven rooms away but she could hear him. She padded closer, slunk to the doorway and looked in as he gnashed and strained against the ropes, foaming and thrashing. Sathewe sat with a hand on his brow as though she was a line stretched taut, holding the real soul of Moon Eye to this world while the angry spirit racked his body. In the morning, Maniye knew, he would be weak and shaken, and even though he would have shed not a drop of friends' blood, guilt would ride him just as the spirit had.

In the morning, too, Sathewe would find an excuse to creep up behind Maniye and start suggesting names she might have earned. She was very keen on Moon Tamer at the moment, which made Maniye shake her head in exasperation.

But who did I think would follow me on this road? Only the mad and the broken. She wondered what this great chief of the River would make of his vaunted Iron Wolves if he knew what misfits they all were: young fools like Tiamesh, old fools like Spear Catcher, mad Coyote girls . . . and then there was the Crow. Feeds on Rags, they all called him, but he had confessed the true name the Eyrie had given him. *Feeds on Dreams*, they had cried as they threw him from the heights forever. Dream Eater, because he ate the hopes and desires of others; whatever he touched turned to ash.

Yet she had taken him. As well as Moon Eye and the rest. She had taken them all. Was hers such a life that she could turn them away for such pasts? She had only turned away those who tried to bind her to a tribe, to a people, to a hearth. To run with Maniye Many Tracks was to sever all ties.

She should sleep, she knew, but her body was filled with wakeful energy. She had left Tiamesh keeping watch on four paws at the threshold of their chamber. Now Maniye herself patrolled the echoing halls of the River Lords' citadel, a small grey wolf where no wolf should be. When she came across servants – lighting lamps or cleaning – they stopped still and watched her pass almost superstitiously. They knew her: one of the Kasra's magical northern monsters.

She considered what she might do if she rounded a corner and found one of them in their other form: tooth to tooth with Old Crocodile. That led to the thought that the southerners spent their time on two feet, far more than any northerner. Probably, if the Wolf tribes had tried to claim dominion over the waters, they would have done so with human hands, while Crocodile's children had conquered the land with the same approach. She wondered if this need to set aside the shapes of their souls had made them what they were, had given them their complexity. Or was it all part of the Serpent dream, trying to recreate that lost kingdom they were always talking about . . .

Having the run of Tsokawan led her thoughts to strange places, with the alien architecture and carvings meeting her eyes every corner she turned. What was left of that kingdom, and who were the Pale Shadow People Hesprec had spoken of? Did they still rule in the Serpent's old halls, and how far south? Did raiding parties cross the dry lands between there and the River, or had the Serpent cut themselves off from those lost lands forever . . . ?

She stopped. Abruptly all the needless human questions were gone from her mind because her wolf nose smelled blood.

The darkness around her, which had been no different to the forests of the north, was abruptly oppressive, the shadows hiding all manner of unknown southern monsters. She was a tiger in an instant, seeing the gloom shift as her eyes did. She tracked the scent down on soft paws through a quiet relieved only by Moon Eye's cries.

There was no body, but the blood did not lie. Someone had died here, and there was a window nearby from which the body had been taken . . . She got her forepaws up onto the sill, seeing a few smears of dark there, looking out at midnight water.

A wolf again, and her nose told the story: there had been men here, several. One had come from inside, and died. Others had entered here, rid themselves of the corpse and gone deeper into Tsokawan. How many? Several – too many unfamiliar southern scents merging into one another. How recently? Surely not so very many heatbeats.

She was on their trail, following the tracks they left in the air, even if the stone retained no mark. And what purpose would they have, to come here by stealth and murder any who saw them? Asmander's warning was loud in her mind. He had done well to keep her back here. Tecumet had been sending emissaries of a very different nature back the other way, with a personal message for her brother.

Maniye upped her pace. She had no idea where Tecuman slept. All she could do was assume the assassins knew more than she did, and let them lead her to him. And be in time to save him, or so she hoped. The trail led her up stair after stair, climbing through the galleries of Tsokawan.

Here was another corpse – one of the lamp-lighters, and thrown hurriedly into a side-room, for anyone with a keen nose or good eyes to discover. The attackers were aware time was against them, determined but not subtle.

She heard a noise from ahead – a scuffle, a clatter, a hiss. She was a tiger without thinking, her footfalls silent, slinking about the next corner to see a scene from a nightmare.

There were at least half a dozen men there, and they were killing two southern soldiers, men in armour of corrugated hide. One was scrabbling at the jaws of a monstrous lizard that had him by the throat – a breed of reptile Maniye had seen before.

The other was . . . he seemed to be standing, bent back, clutching at his neck and strangling all on his own. Maniye bared her fangs at the sight, thoroughly unnerved, until the shadows moved and she saw there was another assailant there, a lean man and stark naked, his skin shifting in pattern and shade to match the stones around him. Even the carvings wrote themselves in blurry, unfinished detail across his bare abdomen.

Beyond them . . . was it the Kasra's chamber? Surely it must . be. And in the scant moments that had let her tiger eyes take in these details, the bodies of the guards were discarded on the floor and the killers were filing in.

She had no time to decide what the Kasra was worth to her: that mask and robe and the ephemeral concept of having come here to serve. She had in her heart two questions.

What would the Champion do?

What would Broken Axe do?

The same answer to both.

She was running forwards as a wolf. The click of her claws alerted them so that a few – some Riverlanders and the man she couldn't properly see – were already looking back. She saw eyes widen, but not in alarm: she was a very small wolf.

When she sprang, she was a tiger, and the tiger was bigger. When she landed amongst them she was the Champion.

That huge shape left precious little room in the doorway for any of them. She scattered them, feeling a stone blade bite briefly at her hide. Her forefeet came down hard on one man, crushing bone, and her jaws caught a second. She had a brief sense of him: terrified, scrabbling frantically at the fangs of this whatever-it-was before she had shaken him hard and cast him aside. If he lived, so; if he died in human form then she had thrown his ghost far enough that it could not haunt her.

She burst past them into the chamber beyond. There was space there for her to be what she had become. The room was heavy with drapes, divided and subdivided into a maze of false-walled chambers. Somewhere in there must be Tecuman, or everyone here was wasting their time and blood.

She rounded, turning to catch one man about to put a spear in her. Her bellowing roar froze him in his tracks and he fell back; they all did. Five of them left at least. She looked for desperation on their faces: all chance at stealth lost. She did not see it. They were hard, determined men, and they obviously felt they had time to make an end of this.

Where was the man she couldn't see? Gone, lost against the draperies. The others were edging around: four Riverland warriors, dark-skinned and armed with short-hafted spears and knives, and the fifth a younger, paler man of the Dragon, some errant cousin of the absent Venat.

She roared again, testing their courage: enough that fear alone wouldn't win her the battle.

She became a wolf, and even as she did she caught the scent of someone close and getting closer – the unseen man, his skin shifting through all the patterns of the rich cloth as he tried to flank her. She threw back her head and howled, that long, lonely cry of the Crown of the World.

Then the half-seen assassin was on her, the dark blade of his flint knife the only clear thing about him. She found her human feet and the training the Tiger had given her, letting his thrust slip past her, striking at his face with her elbow and then cutting a line of bronze across him with her own blade, a flesh wound only but she had marred his camouflage with the stain of his blood.

A Riverlands youth stepped out from between the hangings, wearing a robe of black and silver open down the front. If not for that, he might have been a servant. Even with it, he could just have been an official, some noble's second son. Except these were plainly the would-be-Kasra's chambers, which made him—

They went for him – one of the Riverlanders and the Dragon man, slipping past her left and right. She Stepped to the Champion's bulk, pushing them away just by being there. Her cuffing paw caught the Dragon, but he was a stone-scaled lizard before her claws could eviscerate him. The River man she just barged aside with her shoulder, knocking him down only to find a crocodile at her feet, long jaws gaping.

The Champion lived to fight, to test its strength until the day that strength was not enough. Maniye felt herself fighting its desires, because what the Champion was not good at was protecting someone else. It acknowledged no allies in all the world, for everything it knew was lost in the far reaches of time.

There were too many of them, not enough of her. They would kill the boy. He was just standing there, not even Stepped, a useless streak of flesh in a ridiculously ornate robe. She backed him into a corner, roaring at her adversaries. They flinched away when she faced them, but she couldn't face all of them at once. *Where were the Kasra's other guards? Where were all the other occupants of Tsokawan?* She was left with the unwelcome certainty that either this little warband was not alone, or on seeing his sister's host Tecuman's own people had decided to turn traitor.

A spear darted at her and she swatted it away, just as another found her from the other side. The shallow spark of pain showed even the Champion was not proof against death. And if she rushed out to chase them about the shifting confines of the room, then she could not protect her charge.

Why couldn't the boy just have sent us out to kill his sister? That would have been so much easier!

Only one choice then: forwards, no matter what.

She lunged, raking with her claws, the vast gape of her bear-like jaws forcing them to give ground. Then she was human, jumping back, laying hands on the gaping Tecuman and throwing him in front of her as though offering him up to his enemies.

She let the Champion overtake her again, covering the boy-Kasra with her shadow. She had him in her jaws moments later, feeling him as just a small parcel of flesh and bones that a flex of her muscles would crush. And forwards she went.

91

She took them shoulder-on. A spear splintered against the dense slabs of her muscles. Most of them scattered, but at least one fell underfoot and regretted it. She rammed past them into the antechamber, back the way she'd come, the Kasra writhing and crying out in her jaws.

She went down, and badly. The stairs were meant for the delicate feet of men, not her huge paws. She skidded and scraped all the way, and with the assassins frantically trying to keep pace. Ahead of her the tangled architecture of Tsokawan opened out, and she let the Champion's nose track her own wolf scent back to the source, pushing through the passageways and halls as though she was squeezing through thick vegetation, the space between the stone walls barely open enough to admit her.

Then there were men ahead: River Lord soldiers. She thought they must be loyal, part of the Tsokawan warband, but they heard the shouts of the assassins behind her and it brought them to the fight. Plainly Tecumet had been very determined that her brother die this night.

They fell back a few steps when they saw her coming, but they lacked nothing of courage. Moments later they had their spears set, ready to receive her.

This is going to hurt, she knew. And a heartbeat later, *I can't*. The Champion was goading her to it, but she couldn't bring any flesh and blood of hers straight onto those sharp stone points. It just wasn't in her. She was caught between them and the killers on her trail.

Then her allies arrived, summoned by her wolf's cry of just a minute ago.

Spear Catcher leapt as a wolf but was a man when he struck the back of one of the soldiers, bringing the man down and stabbing at him. One of her younger hunters, Ukamey, came next, biting at another man's legs, trying to hamstring him. Feeds on Rags was behind them, throwing stones and hopping from foot to foot. Abruptly the spear-points were away from her face and Maniye surged forwards, swatting them aside. She ran, and her pack were behind her, or at least a handful of them, those whom her howl had roused.

She had only the faintest idea where she was going, and every sense was telling her of other armed men moving close by. Could she risk a few breaths to gather her wits? How close behind were the enemy?

She skidded to a halt, turning with difficulty in the cramped space. There were no spears and knives at her heels, only wolves. Probably she had only a handful of breaths until the killers caught up.

She Stepped, dropping Tecuman Kasra to the floor like an old toy. He cried out when he hit the ground, clutching at skin already mottled by the dents of her teeth, cut and bloody in places. His expression was incredulous, unable to grasp what was going on around him.

'Listen to me,' Maniye told him swiftly, 'there are killers all over Tsokawan. Do you know who is loyal?'

He gaped at her, mouth starting to form words, names, but finishing none of them. She read a lot of fear in his eyes, but there was something behind them that was thinking, and its conclusions were not encouraging. Who was absolutely loyal? Perhaps only the absent Asmander.

'What about the Serpent?' she demanded. 'The priests?'

'No,' Tecuman said. 'This – perhaps this is *their* work. Perhaps they have decided that my sister . . .'

'Then what?' Maniye asked. She was surprised how shaken she felt by that last revelation. Surely *Hesprec* would save them? And yet Hesprec had made no choice at all as to who should rule the River, and the Serpent – the great and wise Serpent – could not make up its great and wise mind.

'They're coming,' Spear Catcher said, his scarred face set. 'Sounds a fair few of them.'

'My throne,' Tecuman whispered. She couldn't tell if he meant his ambitions or the throne room itself. Neither seemed likely to bring him much joy right then and there. She looked

93

into his face and saw . . . a boy. For all that he was older than she, he was a boy. She wondered if he had ever made a decision or done anything for himself, ever in his life.

'We get out,' she decided. 'We come back when we know what's what. For now this place is a grave if we stay in it.' She looked the young Kasra up and down. 'Can you run?'

Then the hunters were upon them, the same killers who had survived the Kasra's chamber, and reinforced by more.

'Get help!' Maniye shouted at Feeds on Rags, and then at Tecuman: 'Get behind me!' Then she was the Champion once more and the time for words was done. She stood before the killers, barring the way with the sheer bulk of her body, roaring defiance in their faces and hoping that someone would come soon.

The River warriors clustered together, short spears levelled, but wary. The little weapons they had brought would see them in range of her teeth and claws soon enough. If they had brought the weapons of the soldiers outside then surely they could have driven forwards and skewered her, but who crept into an enemy citadel with a ten-foot spear?

Then the Dragon man came forwards, Stepping into a lizard that was bigger than his human form, powerful and armoured. He was still dwarfed by the Champion but he attacked anyway, snapping at her with hook teeth she knew to be poisoned, letting her claws rake across his hard scales without flinching.

'The boy's running,' came Spear Catcher's voice, but she had precious little time to listen. The Dragon was trying to get his jaws in her, and she slapped him aside, bouncing his long body off the wall. By then the spears were coming, jabbing for her eyes and mouth. She gave ground, and then more ground, and then the walls opened up around her and she backed into a grand chamber, full of the scent of outside. *Out, need to get out.*

But her attackers were spreading around her, penning her in. She saw Spear Catcher go for one, shying back as a wolf but then coming up under the spear as a man, his knife jabbing. On her other side, young Ukamey tried the same, but he was slower or his opponent swifter, and the stone point found him and pinned him screaming to the floor.

Where was Tecuman? But he was still close: she could smell the incense and the oil of him. He was too frightened to run far from his protectors, even when they could no longer protect him.

She snarled and swiped, feeling them gather their courage to take her down.

There had been a sound through all of this, something she had grown so used to she had shut it out. It beat its way back into her mind now. Why? Because it was getting closer. It was the agonized voice of a madman.

'Help is here!' came Feeds on Rags' triumphant voice as he Stepped. Maniye wanted to demand *What have you done?*, but turning human even for an instant would get her killed. Besides, she already knew.

Moon Eye was in their midst in the next heartbeat, wide-eyed and teeth bared. He Stepped from man to wolf to man more swiftly than any other she had known, the angry spirit riding him relentlessly. He cut at Maniye's face with his hatchet, but he hacked at the Riverlanders too, splintering a spear-shaft against the stone flags and laying open a man's arm. And he howled. Wolf or man, it made no change to his voice. The very presence of him was like a great hammer hurled into the midst of the fight. Maniye's people had seen him with the fit upon him; they knew to move aside. The Riverlanders tried to meet him, and he lunged past the points of their spears and came up with his jaws already digging for their bellies. Then he was a man again, picking up one of his foes and slamming the man into the wall, strong as a bear while the spirit drove him on.

One of them drove a spear at him: the tip sliced into Moon Eye's arm and he almost ran up it, driving his axe into his attacker's face and then tearing the man open with wolf teeth. He howled again and the assassins fell back from him, and fell over themselves to do it. They saw the spirit in him now, and knew it was death. Surely the whole fortress must be awake, but Maniye could not say if it was filled with friends or with enemies. The outside air beckoned.

Maniye became a woman just long enough to tug on Tecuman's arm, and then she was a tiger chasing the breeze for a sight of the outside world, straining for the sight of moonlight, not knowing who, if anyone, was following.

10

'So, has Mother said just how wrong you got everything?' Lone Mountain was doing his best to sound sympathetic, but it wasn't quite working. A little amusement – at Loud Thunder's expense – was leaking out around the edges.

'Not since we came back from the Stones.' Loud Thunder sat on his rock and stared out at the forest, and most particularly did not look at the other Bear. He thought wistfully of his cave and his cabin, which seemed so far away, but which he could surely reach in a few days of determined travel. At the foot of the rock, his dogs sat and gazed mournfully at him, aware that he was unhappy, but unable to understand. Loud Thunder felt a keen kinship with them on that point. *What was I supposed to say, if not that?*

'And the others?' Mountain pressed.

'Not speaking to me either.' Because the Bear were a private people. They did not like visitors. And he, Loud Thunder, was most private of all, because most of the time he did not even visit others of the Bear. The Bear had no villages like other people, nor even kept much track of borders. They were scattered across the highlands in caves and huts where lived either a family or a solitary man or woman. There, each kept the great treasure of the Cave Dwellers, which was their solitude. And now all of the Crown of the World had been given guest-right in the Bear's Shadow. Nobody was pleased with Loud Thunder.

'What would you have done then, if you're so clever?' He was so weighed down by his own culpability that a mean surliness was all he could manage.

'It wasn't up to me,' Lone Mountain pointed out smugly. 'It was up to you.'

Thunder opened his mouth to ask what Mother's grand plan had been, then. He couldn't quite get the words out though. You did not speak out against Mother. Nobody did.

'They won't come,' was all he could come up with.

'They're already here.'

'The Coyote don't count.' A pair of that wandering people had travelled back with them, taking very early advantage of Loud Thunder's impromptu invitation. Two Heads Talking was one, and the other his mate, Quiet When Loud. But he was right: the Coyote didn't count. Of all the Crown of the World's people, they had come and gone from the realm of the Bear with impunity, trading goods and news and knowing where the borders of the Bear's hospitality were laid out. If only Coyote showed up, then Loud Thunder had both won and lost. He would avoid his own people's ire, but would have failed in his task.

'Mother wants the tribes to sit up and listen. What if bringing them here is the only way?' At Lone Mountain's expression he scowled. 'I will go. You like talking, so when I am gone, you can talk to them. You'll get it right.'

There was a tight, dissatisfied look on Lone Mountain's face. 'You won't leave,' was all he said. 'She told you to do a job, and you'll do it. Badly, as we all know. But you won't *not* do it.' For a moment his expression had the embers of his old anger behind it, but then he shrugged and the ill feeling went away. 'Go speak to the Coyote, Thunder. They have wise heads on them.'

Where Mother lived, that was the closest the Bear had to a community. There were seven, eight families at any one time, gathered here in the highlands above where the Wolf held sway, where dwellings had been carved from the cliffs. Many of the caves remained empty, but a single glance in any direction would reveal some dozen or more of the huge, shambling people. That in itself should warn off any casual visitors.

The Coyote had set up their little tent a diplomatic distance from any house of the Bear. That made Thunder like them more: he was someone who appreciated the importance of putting space between himself and others. He wondered how long they would stay. A few cloudless nights would test how well that tent of theirs kept the warmth in. Probably they would get little welcome if they came scratching at cave-mouths when it froze. Not unless someone had taken that extra step and made them a guest.

He had a sinking feeling that they were *his* guests, because he had thrown open the homes of his people to any vagrant or wanderer who wished to come. He guessed that his people would make that his problem. It was thoughts like these that kept him warm as he stomped towards the tent, his dogs trotting briskly at his heels.

The two Coyote lay side by side before their fire, and abruptly the smell of roasting hare was in his nostrils, his mouth awash with saliva. He picked up his pace without meaning to, and the Coyote man looked up at him with a wary smile.

'Will you not sit and join us?' he asked softly. A half-dozen skinned rabbits were propped on skewers beside him, awaiting the flames: far more than the two of them might need.

Loud Thunder grimaced, pride and hunger warring in him. 'You are our guests. I can't take your food.' He frowned as he said it, trying to work out if the words actually made any sense.

'I won't tell any gods if you don't. Please?'

Reluctantly, Thunder took a place at the fire, feeling awkward and outsized and in the wrong place: normal, then, for when he was around other people.

Two Heads Talking was a compact-framed figure, his buckskins thrown open before the fire to expose a chest patchy with wiry grey. His hair was bound back, his iron-coloured beard cut close to his chin. Quiet When Loud was younger by maybe ten years, Thunder guessed, her own hair cropped to the nape of her neck, softer and more good humoured than her mate. As he sat down – and with no idea where the knowledge might have come from – Thunder was abruptly convinced she was with child. It was something about the way she held herself, and something about the way Two Heads watched her.

'The gods look at you and scratch their heads,' Two Heads Talking went on, not looking at him, eyes only for the colour of the cooking rabbit. 'What are you at, Loud Thunder?'

Thunder snorted dismissively. 'Nothing. It won't matter. No one else will come.' Voicing it, he felt a vast relief at the words. It lasted until he saw Two Heads' expression.

'Oh, they'll come. Loud Thunder has asked it.'

'They don't even know who Loud Thunder is.'

The two Coyote exchanged looks. 'Most, maybe, but one or two here and there, the older ones, the wiser ones, they might. The strongest of the Bear, they'll say. The Bear warrior who went south and came back. Broken Axe's brother in battle.'

'Axe is dead.'

'Yes.' A shadow passed over their Coyote faces, shrouding the secrets they kept there. 'He is. We're poorer for it.'

'That, we agree on,' Thunder said with feeling. The first rabbit was out of the fire now, another already in its place. Two Heads quartered it nimbly with a sliver of flint, gave one piece to Thunder and threw another for the dogs to squabble over.

'Everybody hates the Wolf,' Two Heads murmured, fanning at his portion to cool it. 'Everyone hates the Tiger too. And the Eyriemen hate everyone – and, let's be honest, nobody much likes them. They will come as your guests, will they?'

'No,' Thunder mumbled about a mouthful of rabbit.

'Yes,' Quiet When Loud put in unexpectedly. She waggled her eyebrows at his surprised look.

'Nobody likes the Bear much either,' Two Heads pointed out.

'You keep to yourselves, except when the winters are worst, when you turn up and take what you want. But you know what? They maybe respect you a little. You can respect someone you don't like, you know that? And though the Tiger and the Wolf and the rest, they don't respect each other, they know how strong the Bear are. They will come here, because who wouldn't? Such an invitation comes once a lifetime, or less. They will come here, some few of each, but will they leave their hatreds at your borders? Nobody will want to break guest-bond with the Bear, but they hate each other *so* much.'

'And you?' Thunder grunted.

'We hate no one, surely you know that?' Two Heads gave him an appraising look.

'No room in Coyote's belly for hate,' Quiet When Loud agreed. 'You know that story?'

Thunder thought he probably had at one time, but he wasn't in the mood for stories right then. 'I thought it would be like priests at the Stone Place. They hate each other, but they talk and they listen.'

'If that is how it will be, you must make it happen. Or all their hates together will make a river no man can stop when it flows.'

The very next day more guests came, a ragged tail of them shuffling their way into Bear heartlands. In the past, those who came from outside did so fearfully. The Bear were unpredictable and their wrath was terrifying. But here they were, and they came not as trespassers but as guests.

And they came with music and noise. Loud Thunder had honestly not thought he could look more foolish in the eyes of his people, but here were the guests he had invited to their hearths: the old Boar priest and a score of his people – men, women, squalling piglet children coming in procession with dried-bean rattles and low, mournful hooting horns. The priest himself – and Thunder was struggling to remember what the old man was actually called – had a staff with discs of bronze about the head that clattered and rang as he walked. And of course by then the dogs were about, startled and excited by the noise, and the serene, slumbering quiet of the Bear was in pieces from here to the horizon.

And Loud Thunder had to go and greet his guests, of course. He felt every glowering eye of the Bear on him: a score or more from near and far, louring out of cave mouths and looming from the trees.

The old Boar stopped before him and pushed up his tusked mask. 'Greetings to Loud Thunder. Greetings to the Bear. We accept your invitation.' He was solemn and straight-faced, but a girl of no more than ten chose that moment to brandish a rattle ferociously at Loud Thunder's knees, and he was abruptly close to panicked laughter.

'The Bear welcomes you,' Thunder said loudly, knowing that the Bear did no such thing. 'Our homes are yours.' *But best pitch your own tents like the Coyote, if you know what's good for you.* He felt, more than saw, the other Bears slowly approaching, sullen and hostile. This would go down in the stories as Loud Thunder's Terrible Year.

And then the old priest – Gnarl Hide was his name, Thunder recalled with a start – was gesturing impatiently at some of his people, and they were coming forward, each holding up a heavy-looking jar.

'We are proud to be guests of the Bear, who so seldom shares his fire,' Gnarl Hide stated. 'As guests, we bring gifts.'

Loud Thunder eyed the jars uncertainly: who knew what the Boar considered good gifts? He heard a huffing and a rumbling from between the trees, though, from other Bears who had Stepped and whose keener noses had brought them forward.

He broke the wax that sealed one jar, and saw the treasure within. The Boar had brought honey: more honey than Loud Thunder had ever seen before.

He could feel the awareness of its scent rippling out between the trees. Abruptly there were far more of his people drifting

102

close. All peoples valued honey. No taste was better: medicine, food and wealth all in one. And here were the Boar with an inestimable hoard of it.

He wanted to turn to his people then, and say, *You see?* They were coming closer – not accepting, not grateful, but it would be hard to hold up hostility in the face of rich gifts like this.

That night turned into something almost joyous. Not a true celebration: the Bear saved those for midwinter and no outsider would ever be let in for them. Still, there was mead and meat, and the Boars danced their dances, some of which were funny and some of which were just strange. Two Heads Talking told a long story about a man who forgot his spear – only it hadn't been his actual *spear*, Loud Thunder realized later, but his . . . well . . . Lone Mountain had been in his element: laughing louder and talking more than anyone, comparing trinkets and travel with their guests. Loud Thunder had just sat back and let the relief wash over him.

And then the Boar had fallen quiet, as though the cold of winter had descended, because a new band of visitors had come to the highlands. Gnarl Hide and his people were abruptly gathering together, the children in their midst, and more Bears were appearing, loping alongside a ragged train of travellers who came on four feet.

Wolves. At first Loud Thunder thought it just was the Swift Backs, the Wolves who lived at the feet of the foothills, at the edge of the Tiger's Shadow. And there were Swift Backs amongst these new visitors, but they were towards the back, slinking along like Coyote's elder brother. The bulk of the newcomers were Moon Eaters, who were another matter altogether.

The next morning Thunder awoke to a dry mouth and a dry head. He drained a bucket of water and then went wandering to refill it, the dogs meandering in his wake. There was a stillness to the air, the sky stark white from horizon to horizon. A handful of others were awake and about already, shambling about without hurry, on two feet or four. Loud Thunder felt a curious sense of well-being, as if everything was going to be all right after all.

Then a change seemed to run through the world all around him, like the wind turning. It was like nothing he had ever experienced before: nothing physical was different, but it was as though every soul and spirit in the world had shuddered. Abruptly all that well-being was gone, for no reason he could name.

His eye was drawn upslope, towards the grandest of the caves, its mouth flanked by sheaths of bones and tusks and antlers. Mother stood in its mouth, human, but so close to Stepping that the bear shape was practically about her shoulders like a cloak. She was looking east, her face a blank mask. The sight of her struck fear into him, because he saw fear in her. He would not have believed that anything could make her afraid.

Then there was a fleet shape darting between the trees towards him. At first he thought it was just another dog, but it was too small, too lean. A Coyote, rushing in from the east, where Mother had been looking with such uncharacteristic fear.

The skinny animal shied away from his own dogs, then Stepped and Quiet When Loud crouched in front of him, breathing heavily. 'You have to come,' she got out.

'What is it?'

'A new visitor.'

'A guest?'

'I don't know.' Quiet When Loud stood. 'My mate is with him. He is hurt, near dead. He has come a long way.'

'From the south?' For a moment Loud Thunder was thinking of the Serpent, Hesprec, but of course Hesprec was not a *he* any more.

'From the sea,' the Coyote told him flatly. 'One of the Seal. We had only a few words from him but . . . something has happened to the Wetbacks.'

★

'His name is Sees More,' said Two Heads Talking. 'We had that from him, and not much else. But there will be more.' The Coyote man looked like a stranger, grave and tense and shorn of all good humour.

They had brought the Seal to Mother's home: a single nod from her had been enough to order it. There was something between her and Two Heads, some common understanding denied the rest of them, as though they knew what the newcomer would have to say.

The Bear and the Seal were uneasy neighbours, even with mountains between them. In good years there was some trade – the more enterprising of the Bear, such as Lone Mountain, making the crossing to exchange the land's bounty for the sea's. Bad years saw a different kind of visit: hungry Bears coming down from the peaks to drive the Seal into the sea, and take what they needed. If the Seal tried to resist, then seal meat was better than fish. The Seal very seldom made the return journey for any reason: they had the sea and needed nothing else.

But here was Sees More of the Wetbacks, and he had suffered much to come to them. He was thin as a Coyote, his skin almost grey, his fingers so bloodless that most likely he would lose some. When he slept he was never still: he twitched and shivered and kicked, as though fighting a current that sought to drag him away from them.

When he woke, his eyes stared at nothing for a long, long time, lips drawn back from his teeth in frantic defiance. It was a long time before he could be made to understand where he was. Loud Thunder was already wanting to dismiss him as some madman who had chosen to walk into the wilds to die – save that surely a Seal would vanish into the sea, not trouble the land with his ghost? That shift in the world was still in his mind: too strange and unsettling to be dismissed. *When we tell stories of this, I will say, That is the moment things changed. That is when it began.*

As well as Mother and the two Coyote, a handful of others

had come: Lone Mountain, Gnarl Hide, a few of the more curious of the Bear. When Sees More spoke, he had an attentive audience.

He told them that the Wetbacks no longer existed. Where the Wetbacks had lived was not a place for humans any more. His words fell into the horrified silence of his listeners. When he stopped, as though desperate for another voice to spare him, there were none. What words could meet so swift an extinction of a whole tribe?

And so he had no option but to continue, his cracked voice stumbling and choking over the details. He told of how he had found so many of his people dead, the bodies so precisely arrayed, so unnervingly *investigated*. Sees More fought for words but the horror leaked out of his voice to hang heavy within the cave.

He had found those who fled and his voice broke when he tried to speak of them. A doom had fallen on them. They had been unmade, not his people any more, no words, no understanding of what they were. Mute, he called them. They had been made mute, but it was more than just their voices that had been stilled. Their very souls had been smothered inside them.

'But what was it?' urged Loud Thunder. 'What *did* this?'

'They came out of the sea,' and it was dreadful to hear one of the *Seal* say those words with such terror. 'They rode a beast that howled with the voices of spirits.'

'Who did?' Lone Mountain demanded. He was trying to sound angry, but Loud Thunder could see he was afraid, and trying to cover it.

'They had man's shape, my people said, but they were hollow,' Sees More whispered. 'There was nothing within them, no soul at all. My people looked once on them and knew they were not of our world: nothing more than pale shells in the shape of people. So my people, my family, they fled for the water, which had always been safe for us, but . . . Where they looked, and where they pointed: death. Death like an arrow in the heart, invisible death. They killed whatever they gazed upon.'

'There have always been reasons to fear the sea,' Two Heads said softly.

Loud Thunder knew the same stories as everyone else. He knew where the sea had come from, and what it had been put in place to protect them from, back in the far dawn of time, in the earliest stories.

Nobody was saying the name, of what all the people of the world had fled, in those stories.

'So is this . . . *it*?' Thunder's eyes sought out his Mother, hoping for any answer other than the obvious one.

For a long moment she was silent. This was not indecision, but she had felt the change in the world just as he had. It was no time for hasty words.

'We must know more,' she said at last. The Bear were not hasty, least of all their Mother.

'I will go,' Loud Thunder said determinedly. *At last something I can do!* 'I will take the high passes and go to the coast. I will see what has happened there. Or what is happening there.' He felt a prick of fear as he said the words, but at the same time he would be off on his own and doing something he understood. Surely that was better.

'You will not,' his Mother told him flatly. 'You will have guests to welcome.'

'But this is more important—' he started, and a sharp look from her silenced him. One did not argue with Mother.

'You think these are separate things?' she asked him in a low growl. 'There are others who know the passes far better than you. You cannot carry the world on your shoulders.' Then she added mildly, 'Even you.'

Her eyes were already straying towards Lone Mountain when he said, 'Then I will go.' And he had travelled to the sea before to trade with the Seal. He knew where all their villages were and knew their ways. He was by far the better choice.

Loud Thunder was struck by a sudden sense of scale. *How much of this has she foreseen, felt out like a blind man in a forest? And what if any of those guesses were wrong?* He looked at Lone Mountain, his comrade and his rival, and felt the fear inside increase now that he was not going himself.

11

Venat slept on the pearl-studded throne of Shark Hilt.

He slumbered Stepped, a long, heavy reptile with dull-black pebble scales, coiled about the seat with his whip tail tracing a sinuous curve over the floor. Around him was scattered the wealth of his newly conquered fiefdom: coins of the Riverland, shells of the Salt Islands, pearls from the sea and amber from the north.

An assassin would have to step very carefully indeed to avoid some errant trinket crunching underfoot and the Dragon slept far more lightly than a man would, even drunk and sated.

This was the dream. This was what he had warmed himself with, travelling in the north. A chief of the Dragon takes and then enjoys. As a boy he had known that. As a man he had done it, and then been betrayed, and now he had come back and done it once more. Shark Hilt was his for as long as he could hold it.

And if a quiet part of his mind whispered, *And then what?* he did his best to ignore it. He was of the Dragon. They were not supposed to have *quiet* parts. They sneered at all the ways the River Lords had chosen to cripple themselves, all those customs and laws to keep a man from pursuing his desires. Strength was all, and what was strength if not put to use.

The night just gone, with Haraket dead and his name forgotten, had been wild. Venat had pushed Shark Hilt hard with his demands, and those who had scowled, he'd fought. No deaths, but plenty of bloody noses and torn hides, plenty still recovering from the venom of his bite. He'd taken joy in it, beating down the young men who didn't know it wasn't their time yet; mastering the old men who knew they'd never get another turn at challenging. They'd liked it too, he decided. They could be sure their new chief was the hard bastard they remembered. You knew where you were with a vicious brawler in charge. That was the Dragon way.

And he woke, opening one narrow eye to look out at the hall at Shark Hilt. There the treasures, heaped and scattered like sand after a storm. There the people, just as wildly strewn, sleeping off fermented yams and stolen River beer and the thin, clear head-destroying *kass* they made from seaweed and shark blood. He Stepped and sat more easily, leaning on the seat and feeling the pearls dig into his skin.

We are the Dragon, he said to himself. *We are the last people made in the world, because all the others were wanting. We are the scourge so that none sleep easy. We are the jaws of night so that all might fear. We are the strongest of all the peoples, the fiercest, unmastered since the dawn of time.* Those words and words like them echoed to him all the way from his childhood, over and over. After reciting these words there would be dancing and drinking and boasting again, and one of the few men who'd lived to be old would put on the wooden mask of the Dragon, trailing its streamers of red and yellow cloth which were the fire and devastation that came in the Dragon's wake. He'd put on the mask and become the priest, and the children would run around in his wake, brandishing their sticks and acting out the raids and murders that the legends of the Dragon were full of.

We are the Dragon, the strongest, the fiercest, unmastered since the dawn of time.

The words rang hollow. A rage was building in him: he wanted to storm across the hall at Shark Hilt and kick and slap at those complacent, sleeping people. He wanted to Step, to claw and bite and fill his mouth with blood. He wanted to do these things because that was how he had always solved his problems. But what, truly, was the focus of his anger?

Was it the people before him? No. It was him, he was the problem.

He could not just let this be: he could not just be the boy who believed in *We are the Dragon*. They had thrown him out; he had met the River boy, Asmander, and had ventured to the bloody north and back. He had seen too much and too many different ways.

And so he looked within his mind and saw his true enemy. He looked into those yellow eyes and knew his foe was the Dragon itself. *We are the Dragon?* he demanded of his god. *And what have we made, with our strength? What has our ferocity achieved? And how is it we call ourselves unmastered when we are Riverlands thralls in all but name? We raid, we kill, we fight, but we do so in their shadow, like children who fear their parent's hand.*

He shifted on the seat. The pearls and studs of it bit at him: more comfortable to drape himself across it in the armoured shape of a lizard than as a man. They might be valuable, but they made the throne impossible to *sit* in, and wasn't that the whole bloody problem right there? *We are the Dragon, we make such a show of how fierce we are that we're our own worst enemies.*

The anger that had been bubbling in him was suddenly more than he could contain. He slid from the throne and snatched up his *meret*, the greenstone blade that had travelled so far with him. Turning, with a single blow he sundered the throne in two.

That woke them all up. Men leapt to their feet fumbling for weapons, half blind with stale drunkenness; they Stepped and lunged at nothing, whipping each other with their tails, clawing at the walls. Women woke and fell back to the corners, Stepping or shielding their heads. At the last, they looked at Venat, and saw what he'd done, and a few even raised a cheer. A little pointless destruction for the Dragon, that was all they thought

111

it was. Their new chief breaking something just because he could.

Venat stared at them bleakly, and then he stormed out into the pale morning, grinding his teeth.

Three days was all it took to exhaust his capacity to enjoy the pleasures of Shark Hilt. He slept with those women he chose, he fought those men he disliked. He ate rare meat brought to him by slaves and let the pearls run through his fingers. And he tried to slough off that skin he had grown, in his travels with Asmander. He tried to remember why he had wanted this, and forget all the other things he'd learned.

In the end, what was there? He would have to keep moving, or he would become a fat, failed man like Haraket. He had begun to goad his underlings already, not setting them against each other but just giving them reason to hate him.

And then word came that Gupmet, chief of all the Black Teeth, wished to meet his new underling. Venat's heart leapt at the news, because what else could it mean? Gupmet had heard that Haraket was dead. The name of Venat was being whispered about the Whale Seat itself. And of course, if Venat wished to keep moving, then it was in that direction he would move. He had already considered it: find a handful of discontented chiefs, broker a fragile alliance and then, when Gupmet was overthrown, take the Whale Seat for himself over the bodies of his erstwhile allies.

He was not summoned to the seat itself, of course. No man would be such a fool, and nor would Gupmet come to Shark Hilt unless it was with a score of canoes filled with raiders. Instead the slave messenger named an island, little more than a spit of sand with clear waters all around. Each of them would bring a precise number of fighters, and they would talk.

Venat showed a big grin to his people, after the messenger was done. His expression showed them how concerned Gupmet must be about the new lord of Shark Hilt, to call such a meeting.

And yet, when he picked his men and had them paddle him to the island, his mind could not content itself with its own dreams. What was the Whale Seat but another uncomfortable place to sit?

Gupmet's people had set up a tent – no more than a couple of poles and a blanket to keep the sun off. Venat sat, facing the chief of the Black Teeth, who had a woman at his elbow: too young to be the man's mother, too old to be a concubine. Venat stared at her suspiciously, then at the chief. Gupmet was an older man than he, older than most of the Dragon ever got, yet still strong. His eyes were narrow and cunning.

They talked. They did not honour Haraket's name by mentioning him, nor did Gupmet bring up Venat's years of exile. Instead Venat decided to mention it of his own accord: where he had gone, what he had seen. The Laughing Men, the Stone Place, the Tiger and the Wolf. Gupmet nodded and made the occasional wry comment, and the woman leant in at his shoulder and murmured to him.

At last, the chief of the Black Teeth rested his hands on his knees, sitting there cross-legged out of the sun, and made his offer to his new subordinate. Venat had to smile at it. If he were Gupmet, he could never have thought of such a way to deal with a threat like himself. He could say no, of course. He could try to fight, he could make his play for the Whale Seat. He might even win.

Or he could be the warlord of the Dragon. The Kasra – a Kasra – had called for warriors to fight on the River. Gupmet wanted to send them, not out of obedience but because all that chaos and destruction would be wasted if the Dragon were not there to take advantage of it. And the leader of that band would be above all other chiefs of the Dragon, second only to Gupmet. And yet – he would also be away from the isles, of course, rather than standing behind Gupmet with a knife. At least, for now.

There would be raiding and treasure and blood, all the things the Dragon loved. But rather than be swayed by this, Venat looked again at the woman, the only woman of the Dragon he had ever set eyes on with overt power. He saw how Gupmet narrowed his eyes and stared at his enemy, and yet all the time he listened to a woman's advice. Venat wanted the Dragon to become something more than the lightning – the thing that starts the fire and makes a noise, and then is gone as if it never was. And simultaneously Venat knew that he was not the man who would ever achieve it. Yet here was Gupmet, holder of the Whale Seat these many years, and not so shallow that listening to a woman would break his pride. Perhaps Gupmet *would* reforge the Dragon. Venat's reasons for saying yes were complex and many, but the woman at Gupmet's elbow was one of them.

***

Once, long ago, there were three brothers.

Grey Herald travelled by night, and on the wing. Below him the moonlit grasslands of the Plains thronged with dangers, but he was above them, seeing all, hearing all. No creature knew more of the night than an owl, and though he had been born to the north, the night travelled everywhere. The same moon shone on the icy peaks as on the river, and on everything in between. He had a whole world to search, though, on a quest for something only known through myth.

In the Other Lands dwelt all the People once. But there were some amongst them for whom all forms and souls were not enough and, in seeking more, they grew less and less, until they had no souls at all.

When the sun was high, he rested. He made his camp in the shadow of rocks, or with Horse Society caravans when he spotted them, or by waterholes. The Plains people approached him often, sometimes in numbers and with spears and arrows at the ready. He showed them his face, grey-painted with a pale band across the eyes, and they recoiled. There were few who could look on that mask and not know fear, for it was the face of their enemies, the soulless ones, the Plague People.

And they consorted with monsters that had come into the world,

114

and that sought to devour all the People, all the mute brothers, every living thing. And so they were called a plague.

Most of them turned away from him, but some went to find priests, for they could see Grey Herald was a priest and, as such, it would be ill fortune to raise a hand against him.

In truth he had not known whether they would respect his role, or if priests died as easily as anyone else out here. In the north they told tales of the Plains tribes and their constant infighting, how they held nothing sacred and could not be trusted. Grey Herald suspected that the Plains people told very similar stories of their northern neighbours. And of course there was plenty of traffic between them: the southern reaches of the north, the northern edge of the Plains, there were plenty there who held kinship in both directions, whose families had been canny with the gods, picking and choosing as the seasons best advised.

Then the three brothers, seeing that the Plague People blotted out the sun like stormclouds and left nothing but bare earth in their wake, knew they must lead the People to a new home where the soulless could not follow, and they petitioned the sun to lead them to a land where they might be safe.

When the priests came to his camp, he asked them questions. Not about their dreams or the omens they had seen – the Serpent priestess Hesprec had already added these to the great stock of such warnings she had collected from the River to the far northern cold. Instead he asked them about their own old tales, their legends, seeking word of night terrors, of soundless voices speaking vast distances across the sky.

And the sun bent low and red to the earth, and those People who yet lived followed that light into another place that is These Lands That Are Ours. But the Plague People were hungry yet, and they came after, determined that they should devour the People unto the very last.

And most of the time even the priests did not know what he sought – or at least they feigned not to know. For there were things the Plains people did not want to speak of, secrets they would not barter with a strange northern priest. And for all his pedigree, Grey Herald had little sway with them. He could only hope that they saw the truth of his mission and how urgent it was.

And as the last of the People crossed from the Other Lands to the Lands That Are Ours, the three brothers turned at last to face the coming storm. And they fought from sunset to sunrise, and stood against all the monsters that the Plague People had allied themselves with.

But sometimes there was someone, some matriarch of the Laughing Men, some grey-maned Lion priest or ancient Boar crone of surpassing ugliness, and they remembered the oldest stories. They knew the old fears – not just the story of the Plague Peoples but the stories that came after.

In the north, only the Eyrie remembered, and they gave the stories little credence, for Grey Herald's people had dwelled amongst them for many generations without seeking to rule them, and familiarity breeds contempt.

In the south, the stories were often told, but they were day-light stories, for the Serpent had long served those lands as guardians, priests with wisdom that reached back to the oldest days. The Serpent had always been the first and the eldest, and they knew secrets they had never shared with their brothers. Grey Herald could only hope they knew what they were doing.

And on the next morning, the sun arose with such a fierce fire that it scorched the land away, all that stood between the Other Lands and Our Lands. And the sea rushed in, so deep, so wide that even the monsters of the Plague People could not cross it.

But the Plains had different tales, and less happy. Not the Serpent's wisdom nor the Owl's relative obscurity, but a name that had shadowed the Plains with fear in those far-off days. The peoples who had spread out across those tall-grass lands had been fleeing a terror that came in the dark of the moon and took from them: lives, children, dreams. But that was long ago, and

116

few now even remembered the stories. Those stories did not have the comforting shapes of myth. They taught no lessons and they had no endings. They were just warnings of something that came out of the dark, screaming in a voice nobody could hear.

And as Grey Herald travelled, winging his way across the Plains, he began to hear other tales: not just dust-dry ancient memories, but more recent warnings. *These are places we do not go*, they said.

And the three brothers who had fought the Plague People during that long night were burned by the sun as well, so that none of them would ever again be true creatures of the day, but they must travel the moon's road, or else find a path within the dark earth itself. That was the price they paid for calling down the force of the sun against their enemies.

The Plains people told of the abandoned places of the Aurochs, who had fallen into silence when they had tried to enslave their own totem. They spoke of the closed forts of the Horn-Bearers, who had armoured themselves against the world so far that at last none of them ventured out beyond their thick walls, and the Rat crept into their places and ate their stores and drove them mad and picked their bones. And these tales were terrors enough, but they were not what Grey Herald was listening for.

But sometimes they spoke of other places that they did not go, and that they warned their children about. High mesas haunted by terrible spirits, lands watched over by shadowy wings. Places where an ancient horror slept, which must not be woken until the end of the world. For sometimes, when the worst threatened, an ancient horror was just what you needed.

And Grey Herald listened, and he nodded, and he knew he had found what he sought.

And the three brothers, and all their children who came after them, kept the secrets of the Other Lands and formed brave societies to teach them, lest they be needed again. And they painted their faces

117

in the colours of their enemies, and each of the three remembered who had stood beside him in that battle: the Serpent, and the Owl, and the Bat.

12

For a warm land, sunrise by the river was surprisingly cold. They had taken themselves well away from the water, but still a damp pervaded everything, settling out of the cool night air so that they awoke sodden and freezing even as the sun bloodied the horizon.

Maniye shook herself and Stepped, but the damp had crept into all of her forms, as though it had soaked through to her souls. The others were just the same, cursing and stretching in the early grey light. She realized she was not sure just who had made it out, and who had stayed behind to cover the escape. They had run and run through unfamiliar country, to get clear of the assassins, and once convinced of their own safety, then they had dropped where they were. Someone – she hoped – had kept watch. She herself had slept soundly after so much Stepping and fighting and carrying the Kasra around. It was enough to wear down even a Champion.

They were amongst the trees, drawn up on an island that seemed made mostly of roots, while the water rippled on all sides. Where the sky was darkest, she thought she saw the true river there. Without going to investigate, she could not be sure.

She took stock of her warband, what fragment of it had come with her.

She had Tiamesh, she saw: the young huntress was tending to bindings about one arm, where some weapon had gashed her.

Maniye padded over on wolf feet and nudged the woman with her muzzle, just a brief brush of recognition before she moved on.

Feeds on Rags was next. The Crow looked unharmed, his head cocking left and right as he looked around him in that Eyrie fashion: first one eye then the other, two views of everything. He had a bright, brittle smile on him that she didn't trust.

She Stepped, prodded him in the shoulder. 'Sathewe?'

That killed his grin, at least for the moment. 'Not here,' was all he said. He hadn't seen where the Coyote girl had got to after he went to her for help.

'And by *help* you meant Moon Eye?'

His expression was blank. 'Yes. He helped. I thought he helped.'

She remembered the fighting in Tsokawan, and Moon Eye's mad intervention. The angry spirit had been riding him, but perhaps it had seen the southerners as its first prey, drawn to their difference.

Feeds on Rags' head twitched, the eye in the painted half of his face tracking something new. She turned and Moon Eye was there, shouldering his way between the trees as a dark, heavy-shouldered wolf. Maniye tensed, but the angry spirit had left him, enough time or enough blood sending it back to wherever it dwelled when asleep.

As she watched, the wolf became the man, bruised and black-eyed. 'I had a moon dream,' the man slurred.

'You did,' Maniye confirmed, reaching up to put a hand on his shoulder, feeling the slight tremble to him.

'What . . . ?' There was an animal in his eyes, still, but it was in pain. 'There's blood in my mouth.'

'Our enemies' blood.' *I hope.* But no sense loading him with guilt when they didn't know.

'What now?' Feeds on Rags asked the question as though he was wondering what they might break their fast with.

Maniye shook her head. 'I don't know. Find dry land, maybe.'

'No, I mean "What now?" about *him*.'

For a moment Maniye did not know what he meant, and then she felt a sudden inner lurch as she realized, *But of course, we're missing someone important.* Feeds on Rags meant that their little band was five, not four.

She had taken it for a log or a root, just another piece of the tangled undergrowth of the estuary. Now the rough-barked log opened an eye and she met its yellow gaze, feeling as though she were snout to snout with Old Crocodile himself.

It was not a large crocodile – Asmander made a bigger one when he chose that shape, and she had seen plenty of more impressive beasts on the banks of the Tsotec. Still, given the opportunity to study such a beast, she had to admit she wasn't fond of them. There was something implacable and alien in that cracked-looking back and the saw-edged tail that trailed off into the water. And the bristling line of its jaws ended in a disconcerting curve. Old Crocodile was always laughing.

Then it Stepped, and in its place was the boy who called himself Kasra – or whom the rest called Kasra. Maniye had barely heard him speak yet.

His human eyes were wide with fear. He wore only that thin robe, its fine fabric fouled now, soaking wet and drooping. It clung to a frame thin as a coyote's, and she remembered how he had looked enthroned, the heavy clothes of state making a far bigger man of him, the mask hiding his expression.

For a moment she could not even remember his actual name, and something in her rebelled at calling him 'Kasra', for all the title was foreign and meaningless to her. The wolf and the tiger and the Champion, all that was northern in her, rose up and said, *What use is he? Leave him for the carrion eaters.*

What duty she owed to this southern boy might not have survived that. Nor might her wary friendship with Asmander, which had never been very strong. What saved him was that he had Stepped, for the night. Ripped from his comforts and his people, cast out into a nightscape that might be as unfamiliar to

121

him as to his rescuers, he had the wit to sleep Stepped, a water shape in this watery place. That meant there was a mind there she could give a grudging nod of respect to.

There was precious little in his face to respect, right then. He stared at her as though he had no idea who she was, and when the others shifted and moved, he had the same wide, frightened regard for all of them.

'Tell me, do you know this place?' Maniye asked him. She had to ask twice before she had his attention.

'It is the estuary,' he got out between his teeth.

She rolled her eyes. 'What is it you River People say? "These things are known"? Asmander told me the estuary is very big. Do you know it? Have you hunted in it before? You grew up here, didn't you?'

'I was raised in Atahlan,' he told her.

Maniye had no idea where that was, but apparently it wasn't here. 'We'd better get you back to your people,' she decided, because the sooner she could do that, the sooner he wasn't her problem. 'Back to Asmander?'

'Asmander . . .' Tecuman's eyes widened further, something Maniye hadn't thought possible, as he remembered the events of the previous day. 'He went to my sister!'

She nodded; she was supposed to have gone as well . . . 'It was a trick. They invited him for parley so he would be out of the way.'

'He was ever Tecumet's playmate,' Tecuman spat, ignoring her offered alibi.

'These southerners . . .' Tiamesh murmured, shaking her head. 'Crooked and cruel, the lot of them.'

Maniye would have liked to agree, but she remembered her own childhood with something less than fondness, the hard hands of her father and Kalameshli looming large. And the Tiger hadn't been much more welcoming, in the end. So perhaps people were the same the world over.

Tecuman had gathered the thin, slimy-looking folds of his

robe about him, as though clutching for an echo of his former grandeur. She wondered if he would stick a leaf to his face and poke eyeholes in it.

'You came to Tsokawan to be my protectors,' he declared. His shaky voice undermined the authority he was trying for.

'I reckon we did all right at that,' Tiamesh pointed out.

'You shall be rewarded,' Tecuman tried. 'When I am returned to Tsokawan, you shall have wealth, mates, land. When I am Kasra at Atahlan—'

'Let's work on the nose before thinking about the tail,' Maniye told him. 'You don't hunt. Do you fight?' A look at him and she shook her head. 'You don't fight. What do you do, Tecuman?'

His jaw twitched and she saw his thoughts: here, now, this small and disrespectful band was all he had. They were all the Sun River Nation he had left to command, and they weren't even his kin.

He lowered his head, hiding his face for a moment, and when he looked up again, he had donned a new expression. 'I rule,' he told her. 'That is what they made of me. Others fight and hunt for me, and I rule. And the Serpent says a terrible thing is coming to the River and to the world, and some of the Serpent say that I am the nation's best chance of surviving. And I believe them.'

She nodded slowly. It wasn't much, but it was his soul talking truth, not just his face speaking words. She held her doubts back and nodded. 'Well, then,' she asked him. 'Who do you trust?'

In the end it seemed Tecuman could trust pitifully few. Asmander, he said – and even then there was doubt in his voice. Old Asman had sunk so much into supporting his claim that the Bluegreen Reach clan was surely still his if he could get to them. But Asmander and his father had been on Tecumet's barge when the attack happened. If they were not dead by now, they must surely be imprisoned. Tecumet had planned this well.

'But you're lord of the whole estuary or something, aren't you?' Maniye asked him.

His expression said it all: so long as he sat enthroned in Tsokawan he was. A fugitive commanded few loyalties. The hierarchies of the Sun River Nation were more delicate than they appeared.

'Betrayed,' the youth spat, and it was hard to argue with him. Maniye asked him who had arranged for Asman and his son to go to Tecumet, but he didn't know. He had simply been informed at third-hand that it was his will.

'I will give the traitors to Old Crocodile,' he swore. 'I will empty their veins into the river.' But the threats rang empty, delivered while raving half naked on the shore.

'We get you back to Tsokawan,' Maniye decided, stumbling a little over the name. 'There are . . . will they know you, even?'

'Of course they will know me!'

She rounded on him, because from her point of view he had no weight to throw around right now. '*Who* will? You're just a mask and fancy clothes and a big chair. Who are you? Who knows you?'

'There are . . .' He stammered, for a moment unable to even substantiate his own existence. 'Servants, some of the clan heads, they know my face. They will know me.'

'And of your sister's people?'

'Yes. Those who knew me in Atahlan, before my father . . . Before I was Kasra.'

Were you ever Kasra? Maniye had the feeling that more of his enemies would know him than his friends. Again she felt the temptation to abandon the youth right here. But then what? Track all the way back north? Then what would she tell Alladai, returning so soon? That she had cast aside her duty, however lightly that duty rested on her.

She had already decided that the Sun River Nation and all its ways had been put in the world to vex her, but there was no helping that. If she ever got the chance she would complain to

Asmander about it. He was always an appreciative audience for misery.

Feeds on Rags got aloft and spotted the spires of Tsokawan, but he was terrible for giving directions, and even worse for losing his way when landmarks were out of sight. Instead, they headed for the clearest, most open water they could see, then followed the channel, going against the current where a current could be found. Tsokawan was visible from the river, and whenever the Crow got them utterly turned around, that was their compass. There was a dryish path to be had, jumping and hopping from island to island, root to root. The water was murky and cluttered with leaves, broken branches and clots of mud. Only Feeds on Rags delighted in it, because he could snatch fish from the sightless depths with unerring accuracy. Raw fish was no great meal to human tongues, but it went down readily enough for wolves, and more so for crows, crocodiles and tigers.

Gradually the gleam of the sun through the trees intensified, and they saw it was not reflecting off pools and channels, but the great widening expanse of the river itself, and beyond it rising the dark shape of Tsokawan. Out on the water were the big boats of Tecumet's fleet, and there were tents and fires on the bank beyond, but it seemed Maniye's band had a clear run to the fortress.

With the prospect of being reunited with her warband, Maniye let her guard down and made a break for it at top speed. She was human, then tiger, then human as she kept her balance over the root-strung and patchy ground. Tecuman was at her shoulder, and the other two Wolves behind. Only Feeds on Rags was out of position, looking for fish again, and she soon had cause to be thankful he was.

'Monsters!' he cried out, leaping back from the water – in his panic he had forgotten the word for crocodiles.

As if his shout had called them into being, suddenly she saw ripples in the water all around them. She shoved Tecuman backwards as the first scaled snout slid out of the water. A second rugged back broke the surface to her left, and then a third beyond it, and then there was a man standing up dry from the water, a spear held loosely in one hand.

'Ulsenaser!' said Tecuman. It sounded like a nonsense word, but then Maniye realized it was this man's name.

In a ragged crescent before them, in and out of the trees, stood a half-dozen Riverlanders where before had been logs and drifting debris. Men and women both, they wore dark hide armour in ridged and uneven plates – the skin of their totem. Most had spears, though a couple had the stone-toothed sword that Asmander favoured. One, hanging wisely back, carried a bow that was almost as tall as she was.

'It is Ulsen now, lord,' said their leader, and there was enough respect in his voice that Maniye thought for a moment he might be a friend. But then he said, 'Your sister wishes you to visit her.'

'And has she decided to bow the knee, that I should stand before her? Will she swear herself forever in my service and hail me as the true Kasra? No? Then what profit would come from such a meeting?' Tecuman spat.

Ulsen nodded. 'That you would come to no harm, for she wishes you none. Lord, I remember you at Atahlan. I think of you fondly still. But you are not the Kasra.'

Tecuman drew himself up, pulling his robe close as he clutched for dignity. 'Does your father yet live, Ulsen?'

Maniye remembered the business with the southerners and their names – how the child had a child's name until . . . until the father died, or until . . . ? Asmander had never been explicit about it, even when he had given back an adult name to his Dragon friend.

Ulsen looked unhappy. 'He was torn as our land is torn, lord. He has taken himself away from the court to live in retirement. I lead my family now.'

'He would die of shame if he knew what you are doing,' Tecuman hissed at him.

Ulsen took a deep breath. 'Please, Tecuman, look where you

126

stand, and with whom. The whole River is against you now, but you can yet live and be honoured.'

Tecuman laughed. It was a terrible, broken sound. 'Tell that to the men my sister sent last night with blades in their hands! Tell that to your own men, who came here hunting a fool. My eyes are open, Ulsen.'

Ulsen's face was all innocence, but Maniye saw him shift his grip on his spear, and took it as her signal. Perhaps he really did think Tecuman would be spared. But if so he was surely misinformed.

Even as the first words of a reply were out of Ulsen's mouth – what words she didn't hear – she had Stepped and gone for him.

When she loomed before him as the Champion, a great wall of hair and hide and fangs, Ulsen froze and his followers did too. The archer at the back let fly with an arrow, but the string had been only half back and the shaft just tangled in her pelt. Then she was on them, knocking Ulsen flat and bellowing at the others, sowing as much chaos as she could.

Moon Eye darted past her on the left, lunging forward and then skittering back from a spear thrust. Then Feeds on Rags was in the spearman's face, flapping with his great black wings, calling out, *Death! Death!* and stabbing with a dagger-like beak. It was enough to give Moon Eye an opening and he ripped into his enemy's leg below the skirt of his armour.

A pair of jaws opened up before Maniye, snapping at her feet, and she slapped them with her claws, driving the crocodile away. Ulsen's people were Stepping now, but they were scattered, confused, and she attacked them wherever she found them, whatever shape they were in. Tiamesh and Moon Eye harried their flanks, snarling and snapping.

Teeth grazed her, lunging up from below and trying for her belly. Instantly she was a tiger, leaping over them, and then she turned with knife in hand and found Ulsen and his spear. His thrust was too hurried, too soon, and she knocked the shaft away, knowing this would be her only opening. She darted in as he tried to back away, cut him shallowly and made him Step again. She leapt as a tiger and had bulked out into the Champion as he whipped round, His tail stung her ribs and he lunged at her, but even the gape of his jaws was not enough. She hooked a fistful of claws underneath him and flipped him over, trying to bury her teeth in his underside.

The scales there were still tough, and he writhed out of her jaws, his own teeth worrying at one of her forelegs. They Stepped at the same time, both to human, he to get clear of her, and she to drive her knife into him.

Ulsen gasped and fell back, sitting down in the murky water as the red ran down him. Maniye shoved him away, and he became a reptile again, writhing in a darkening stain of its own blood. She looked around, hoping desperately that Tecuman was still with her.

He was there, Stepped, a smallish crocodile drawn up on a sandbank, mouth wide to threaten all the world. She knew it was him because Feeds on Rags was sitting on his back like an omen of doom.

By that time Ulsen's people had taken enough, and they were falling back. Moon Eye had put an axe in one, and Tiamesh had left deep toothmarks in another. Ulsen himself was dying, or perhaps already dead and still twitching. The open water between them and Tsokawan beckoned.

But it was a trap, she knew. This would hardly be the only hunting party with some old friend of Tecuman's at its head. Tecumet had missed her chance to kill her brother overnight, but she was going to do her best to stop him reclaiming his seat of power.

'Deeper into the trees,' she said, pointing. 'Away from the stone fort. They'll be everywhere near it.' And the boy-Kasra was human once more, staring at Ulsen's scaled corpse. His eyes flicked once to the jagged dark shape of Tsokawan against the morning sky, but he didn't argue. Another mark in his favour.

Feeds on Rags had hopped off and Maniye caught his attention by waving her fingers in front of his beak. He fixed her with one eye and she told him, 'Get to the stone fort, find out who's left there. Find someone who you can lead to us.'

The Crow Stepped, nodding sagely in the way that told Maniye he had no idea what he was doing. 'Who? How? Where?' he asked.

'We will be . . . you'll have to find us. And just . . . just find someone who can make decisions. Spear Catcher. Anyone. But go now, and be thankful none of these Rivermen fly.'

13

That morning, the sky was thick with wings, the scream of hawks, the harsh *Death! Death!* of crows. The Eyrie had come to the lands of the Bear.

They had not flown all the way – they would have outstripped all others if they had, and arrived earlier than the knowledge of their invitation. On the ground was a train of Eyriemen: warriors taking their turn as guards, a line of evil-eyed goats as walking provisions, and of course the women. The Eyrie had strong thoughts on a woman's place in the world. The air was not that place.

Loud Thunder watched them come in, the shadows of their Stepped shapes flitting over him back and forth. The men of the Eyrie lived in a high land, and the trails to it were few and guarded. Hard to assault, but hard to make a living in, too: there was a reason the Eyriemen were raiders all across the Crown of the World. They came out of the sky on screaming wings to take lambs and kids and calves. And children. Hawk was a cruel god, cruellest of all to his own people.

The men of the Eyrie mined pride, so they said – the only thing they had in abundant supply up on their bare heights. On human feet they still strode as though they were looking down on everyone else from a great height. They wore armour of bone and their faces were half painted, with one eye staring madly out from a knot of jagged tattoos. Their women kept their faces downturned, their long hair looped about their necks, wearing halters to keep them from Stepping. Loud Thunder shook his head at the thought. Pity the man who tried to keep a she-bear from going where she wanted. The few decisions that troubled the Bear were made by Mother and the other women.

He guessed the women of the Eyrie didn't get to make many decisions. There were stories about them, of course. Everyone knew the story about Hawk's first wife, who found him such a cruel lover that she tried seven times to fly from him, until at last he bound her to her human shape.

Towards the rear of the Eyrie train, though, came a woman riding. A Horse Society man led the beast and she sat sideways in the saddle, cradling her heavy belly. She wore a cloak of feathers dyed many colours, and the long coil of her hair was bound with gold wire. And yet it was about her throat still, making her its prisoner. She was plainly someone important, yet in the Eyrie that made her valuable property and no more. Loud Thunder had no idea who she was or why she had come on such a journey.

Following her, bringing up the rear save for a couple of foot-dragging spearmen, were a pair of collared thralls carrying . . . *something* between them. It was draped with woollen blankets, but where those left off Loud Thunder could see slats as though the burden was a cage. A small cage, fit for a child or small animal. A sacrifice? A gift for their hosts? Knowing them, Thunder didn't think so.

There was a great blast of wind as though the weather had suddenly turned. Everything around him was cast in shadow. He looked up, and the hawks and crows were scattering out of the sky, for something greater was coming. The bird descending on them could have borne a full-grown man away in its curved-dagger claws. Its hooked beak was like an axe blade, its wings swallowing the sun. The Champion of the Eyrie had arrived.

Loud Thunder took a step back as the great bird clutched at the ground, wings still spread. The giant eagle could have looked

131

a man in the eye, but Loud Thunder was more than head and shoulders above most men. As if frustrated by that, the eagle shrieked, the piercing sound echoing from the caves and the mountains, and clapped its wings once, forcing the Bear further away by the sheer bluster.

Any more of this, thought Loud Thunder, and I'll walk away – no way for a guest to behave. But then the bird was gone and in its place a man twice as haughty: Yellow Claw, a name well known across the Crown of the World.

Of course he would come, Loud Thunder considered glumly. He didn't like Yellow Claw but he dragged a smile onto his face as best he could and bade him welcome, standing there before the caves of his people.

The Eyrie's Champion looked at him, first in one eye and then the other. He had a wooden frame about his shoulders that was thick with feathers: wings even for when he was in human form. He wore ranks of bones down his chest for armour, and there were bronze knives at his belt. He did not look like a man who had come for any purpose related to peace. Still, he took a swallow of mead and a mouthful of meat when it was ritually offered, binding himself and his people to act as guests should. And he had come, was that not at least a little triumph for Loud Thunder to take joy in?

Watching the Eyrie make camp – watching their women make camp, anyway – Loud Thunder found he was too tense to take joy in anything. He had not thought it through. Too many people were here, of too many different tribes. Too many Bears, as well, for they had drifted in, singly and in small bands, when the news reached them. Now every hand's breadth of flat land within sight of Mother's cave was occupied by someone, and there were arguments and fights and accusations that apparently nobody but Loud Thunder could deal with. Someone had stolen someone else's blanket, or bowl, or sheep, or wife. And because Thunder had invited them, it was to him they brought all these petty grievances. He had a feeling that the arrival of this party from the Eyrie was unlikely to smooth the waters very much.

The woman with the gold in her hair was helped down from her mount by the Horse man. She smoothed her cloak down and then looked at Thunder. Her eyes met his briefly and he felt a shock of connection. They were Hawk eyes, and, like the men, she looked through her eyes one then the other. Eyriewomen did not paint their faces, but he felt that division anyway: each eye weighing him for a different purpose. She was not beautiful, this woman, but that one look nailed him to the spot: perhaps because none of the other Eyriewomen dared look beyond their feet.

Then there was a presence at his elbow, and Loud Thunder turned to see Yellow Claw staring at him narrowly. 'Kailovela, my mate,' the Eyrieman named her.

'Of course she is,' Loud Thunder mumbled, and quickly changed the subject. There was talk of what challenges the Eyrie would set for the other tribes, and the Eyrie Champion claimed there was some great secret that the Owl priests had brought – whatever was in that covered cage, apparently – and through it all, Loud Thunder kept thinking of Kailovela, terrified that his preoccupation would show on his face.

Over the next few days, more Wolves drifted in, and two bands of Deer. The first challenges were played out, though most were waiting for more emissaries to be sent. Loud Thunder had not put much thought into how games and contests would actually work. He had pictured everyone standing on a hillside, wrestling or running around. That was how these things were done, wasn't it? He was lucky to have Two Heads Talking slinking from camp to camp spreading good sense.

The Coyote had come to him and said, 'So, you're the great wrestler.'

Loud Thunder had shrugged: what point denying it?

'So you will throw all the others and call yourself the greatest in your own challenge?'

Another shrug: it had seemed the simplest way to do things.

'And will you race, when the Deer come?' Two Heads had pressed gently.

'Why would I?'

'Why would anyone wrestle you?'

Loud Thunder had flapped his mouth a bit over that. A moment before it had seemed absolutely plain why it would be a good thing for everyone to be thrown to the ground by the strongest son of the Bear. With five words, the Coyote had dug beneath all his assumptions until they fell in on themselves.

Two Heads had what Thunder thought of as a stealthy smile. It crept up on his face without you seeing it. 'There's no glory in winning your own game,' he had suggested. 'You call your challenge – give the glory to the man who matches himself best against you. Even more so if he beats you. Then all men will come to try your strength, because it is not you they have to beat, it's the others.'

So it was decided this would be how things would go. Therefore Two Heads Talking and his mate Quiet When Loud went amongst the other tribes as none but Coyote could, and soon everyone knew it.

The Tiger were last to come. They dwelled on the Bear's very doorstep, their Shining Halls weighing down the highlands, but came last, as though wanting to ensure all the other tribes and peoples assembled to watch their entrance.

They came grim-faced but splendid: tall, copper-skinned women with gleaming mail of bronze squares, plumed helms and cloaks of dark fur where the stripes smouldered like embers; men with scars on their cheeks and forearms, clutching bundles of javelins; fire-coated cats on soundless paws, the strength of earth harnessed to the grace of water. They were proud as the Eyrie, bloody-natured as the Wolf and, when they finally deigned

134

to appear, all the others stopped to watch. Within the living memory of the oldest, the Tiger's Shadow had covered most of the Crown of the World and many had learned about the terrors that came with the darkness. There were few who thought of the Tiger with love.

Not so long ago the Wolf had resisted them, and then the Crown of the World had discovered that, change the pelt from orange to grey, a tyrant is still a tyrant. There were even old stories of when the Bear had sought to dominate the north, although Loud Thunder could not even imagine such a thing. *But perhaps we were different then. Perhaps Bear slept less and raged more.*

Yet the Tiger had come, and all the peoples of the Crown of the World had sent their wise and their swift and their strong to come and clutter the Bear's land and irritate the Bear's people. So that was something.

And somewhere – the thought came to Loud Thunder out of a clear sky – somewhere Lone Mountain was travelling east past the mountains, because something bad had happened to the Wetbacks, or perhaps to all the Seal. Now Thunder had to try and bring all these people together for more than just the chance to throw each other to the ground and tell each other stories. They might be here for the chance to save their own skin.

That night, he saw the Owl's trophy.

Thunder had not seen any of the Owl Society when the Eyriemen had arrived. They were stealthy as the Tiger, secretive as the Serpent. They had stolen into the Eyrie camp with their grey faces and white-banded eyes, and now they had sent Two Heads Talking from camp to camp as though he was their thrall.

They had taken a cave as their own, twisting guest-right and the fear of their pale faces until the resident Bear had shambled out to seek a quieter hearth. Now three of the Owl clustered in there, a woman and two men. The men were bare-chested, while she wore but a twist of cloth across her breasts, no matter the cold. They had cloaks of black wool woven with silver-white patterns that could take forever to lead the eye nowhere.

Two Heads Talking went from fire to fire and spoke with Gnarl Hide the Boar, and with an old man of the Deer who wore the antlered mask of a priest. He spoke with Aritchaka, who led the Tiger, and he went amongst the iron-priests of the Wolf. He even came as a hesitant petitioner to Mother's cave. To all of these he said, 'The Owl has something you will wish to see, something you have never seen.' To a priest, no matter what tribe, those words were irresistible as honey.

And to Loud Thunder he said, 'There will be a space at the fire, a large space, enough for two men,' until the huge Bear grumbled and agreed to come along.

Loud Thunder expected to see the cage there, but the Owl always did things their own way. They were Eyrie and yet not Eyrie; the woman led them, and it seemed that her grey mask cut her off from the strictures of the Hawk. She had spoken at the Stone Place, Loud Thunder remembered. Her name was Seven Mending.

Now the Owl woman's eyes passed across each face, never settling or focusing on any. She was slender and unarmed, and Thunder could not imagine being frightened of her, save that when she turned to him, her eyes were closed, and the painted lids made them seem white through and through. For a moment, he was terrified beyond all reason.

'See,' she said, and the cave mouth was darkened by Yellow Claw, leading a small figure, cloaked and hooded.

They bring us a child? Thunder wondered uneasily, because everyone knew stories of how harsh the Eyrie was with children. Yellow Claw strode forwards, a thin, cruel smile on his face, yanking at the tether to drag his prize stumbling after him. The diminutive captive's hands were bound behind its back.

Thunder wasn't going to say anything in this august gathering, but his Mother asked, 'What is this?'

'Nobody knows,' the Owl woman said, and Yellow Claw got

his prisoner into the centre of them. Without warning, a knife was in his hand: bronze and sharp and shaped like a feather. At a nod from the Owl, he whipped the cloak away and stepped back.

A horrified murmur went through the gathered priests – Wolf and Tiger and Boar and all, united despite their enmity.

Loud Thunder saw a girl-child. *No*, he realized: he saw a woman of child's stature, as though she had been shrunk. She wore a woollen dress, some Eyrie girl's cast-off, but her face was ghostly pale and her features as alien as a southerner's: wrong chin, wrong brow, wrong everything. *Exotic*, he thought; attractive in a bizarre way . . . and then he saw further. The priests around him had seen it already, but they had the wisdom and the eyes.

The tiny woman turned her head, and Loud Thunder felt he was looking into her, as though she was made of ice and he could see a cavity within her skull. It was empty, and it ran deep: like a well, like a cave without end, like the space between the stars where even the gods couldn't live. Deep like a nightmare, and hungry. It was where the woman's soul should be, and Loud Thunder thought he felt it dragging at him, that emptiness that was desperate to be filled but never would be. It could consume all the world and still be lean and famished.

'It came to us from the sky two years ago,' the Owl said. 'It is a spirit, we think.'

'From the *sky*?' asked the Deer priestess.

At another nod, Yellow Claw reached out and cut the cords binding the spirit woman's arms. There was an expression on the hollow creature's face. It would have been some mix of shame and fear and hate had there not been that dreadful void behind it.

Yellow Claw yanked at the tether and the hollow thing pulled away, clutching at it. Sounds came from its mouth that were like words, but not words. At last he jabbed at the creature with his

137

knife, and it leapt away from him – and up, up to the end of the leash, up into the air.

It had not Stepped, but it flew, wings shimmering from its back. It cursed Yellow Claw and cursed all of them with nonsense sounds as it hovered up near the cave's ceiling, before the horrified eyes of the priests. The gaping emptiness within it dragged at their souls, jealous for what it could not have.

Loud Thunder did not sleep that night, and he reckoned the rest wouldn't either.

'Take me to the Eyrie camp,' he asked of Two Heads Talking the next morning.

The Coyote gave him a squinting look. 'You know where it is.'

Loud Thunder shuffled. 'If I go alone they will laugh at me.'

'And if you go with me . . . ?'

'Perhaps they will laugh at you instead. Just . . . I have seen you sit at every fire.'

Two Heads shrugged and grumbled, but at last he went with Thunder to where the Eyriemen had camped, a little further off than any others, aloof in all things. The welcome they received was cool and Yellow Claw watched him narrowly – sat atop a crag of rock, his own meagre little roost. He didn't descend to trouble his visitors. Instead, Loud Thunder sought out the Owl, finding them at their own fire, where their painted faces turned to him wordlessly.

'I wanted to . . .' His words trailed off and he fought with them, trying to make them do what he wanted. 'Your thing, last night – the spirit woman . . .'

Seven Mending, the priestess, rose. Her gaze passed through him; he still didn't know if she was blind or not. 'Men tell me they find her fair,' she stated.

Loud Thunder didn't know what to do with that so he made a polite noise in the back of his throat.

'So you want to see her once more, Son of the Bear,' the Owl prompted.

138

'It's not that,' he protested. 'But before you came, there was a man of the Seal, of the Wetback . . .'

She cocked her head sharply. 'So?'

'His people were attacked, he said. Those who came were . . . he said they were hollow, with no souls. Your spirit creature . . .'

Seven Mending gestured sharply, and at once one of the men came forward with a skin for Loud Thunder. Just snowmelt water, but it was an invitation. 'Share our fire,' she said. 'Tell us your tale.' And then, with another imperious flick of her fingers, 'Bring the keeper here. She'll want to know.'

Loud Thunder had assumed the spirit woman was purely the Owl's business, but it was Yellow Claw's mate, Kailovela, who came to hear him speak, guarding her belly and walking carefully. She glanced at Thunder for a long moment. He felt a sinking feeling inside him, because while she held his gaze he felt more than happy, and such feelings were just the sort of complication he didn't need. He gave the Owl a pained look – wasted on her – and asked, 'Why Yellow Claw's woman?'

'There is a magic she has, a generous soul,' said Seven Mending. 'From her youth she could tame beasts and quell arguments. That is why Yellow Claw claimed her. Even with the spirit woman, her touch, her voice make the creature biddable, as if she lends the thing some part of her soul to make it whole again. And Yellow Claw claims the spirit, anyway. It is his trophy.' There was disdain in her words, but only a little. The Champion of the Eyrie was not lightly criticized.

So Loud Thunder told them of Sees More's ragged words. 'A man's shape, but hollow,' he recounted. 'No soul within them, he said; shells in the shape of people.' He looked Kailovela in the eyes then, feeling the jolt of it as though she had stabbed him. 'But nothing of them being small, like yours.'

The three Owl priests were silent, their painted faces ghastly. Two Heads Talking had sunk into himself, looking ill.

'She speaks, sometimes.' Kailovela's eyes were full of the Owl's fire. 'She has no true words, but she speaks. Perhaps she's warning us. Or threatening us. Perhaps her kin are coming for her.'

'Or it was fleeing,' the Owl priestess murmured. 'Perhaps this spirit is the Daughter of the Spirit People and they must have her back.' Her hands were clasped together, and she was shaking slightly. There was not the least grain of belief in her voice, even as she tried to cast all these things as a familiar tale. *You know,* thought Loud Thunder. *You know, and nobody will say.*

He opened his mouth. He was Loud Thunder of the Bear, here in the shadow of his Mother. What should he not dare? And yet he could not say, *The Plague People*. He would not make it real by speaking the words.

14

Wolves were not suited to the estuary, that much became clear very quickly. Tiamesh and Moon Eye kept to their human shapes, scrabbling hand and foot from dry land to dry land, keeping a wary eye on the water. So far they had seen leeches, poisonous-looking insects, jagged-toothed fish, a selection of snakes and, of course, crocodiles. And whilst any of the last could have been spies for Tecumet, the estuary was well stocked with the River Lords' mute brothers as well.

Maniye's tiger loved the place, to her surprise. Let the others pad gingerly where roots or earth would hold them. The tiger slipped from water to land to water almost as easily as Old Crocodile himself. So she led them, and the creatures of the estuary gave her a wide berth.

Tecuman himself sometimes Stepped, when there was water to be crossed, or when he slipped into it, which was often. He held to his human shape as much as possible, though, and Maniye puzzled over that for a long time: they were in Old Crocodile's very jaws, so surely his shape would be protection and comfort. She came close to asking him several times, until she realized his soul's shape was not familiar to him. He had lived his life in stone halls, in robes, behind masks. Crawling on his belly through the palace of his father had probably not been encouraged.

What am I going to do with him? The sheer difference of the south was defeating her. A village chief in the Crown of the World led his people by example, but then he had only to worry about some hundreds, at most. She could not grasp the scale of the Sun River Nation, so many people standing on each other's shoulders that the man at the top need never get his feet wet.

Well, Tecuman was making up for that now, she judged. She wondered if anything she could do would help him survive this. She wondered whether she *should* help him. She could hear Kalameshli in her mind, telling her how the Wolf tested his people to make them strong. Hesprec had always said that the Serpent made people strong by teaching them and bringing them together. All fine words until one of them was cast away alone. Tecuman was the only native they had and he couldn't guide them or give them any help. He had no idea what could be eaten or where to find shelter. He was like a child.

If he had been all demands and spoiled complaints, she might have abandoned him, even so, but Tecuman was sunk into himself, following numbly along, with Moon Eye and Tiamesh staying close, keeping him moving. It was hardly useful, but at least he was no active hindrance.

Maniye had been expecting more hunting parties, and probably they were out there, but the estuary was big enough to lose a thousand Kasras. She was regretting sending Feeds on Rags away, even though she knew she needed to find what had happened to the rest of her people. A crow's-eye view would have been handy.

Then they finally saw more human faces – not hunters, but estuary-dwellers.

It was a single dwelling: a house built of sticks, set on poles over a fast-flowing channel so that the residents could presumably catch fish right out of their front door.

Maniye watched from cover, a tiger crouched in dappled shade at the edge of the water. She saw a mottle-skinned boy arrive at the house on a boat smaller than he was, heaving himself up onto the wooden walkway that circled the house, and dragging his little craft up with him. He was no River Lord – he lacked their spare leanness of body, and his skin was a skewbald motley of pale and dark, as though he was diseased.

She fell back to the others and told them what she'd seen.

'We could use something more than raw fish to eat,' Moon Eye stated. 'Especially since the Crow's not here to catch it for us.' Maniye had had some luck with fishing, but the others had not been able to land a single one. And Tecuman, who should have been best suited of all, had no idea how to go about it.

'Also, Chief Kasra here could use something other than that rag,' Tiamesh added. The fine robe that the Kasra had been sleeping in was now barely fit for use as a loincloth.

Maniye looked at the Riverlands youth. 'Well, these are your subjects, aren't they?'

He rolled his shoulders and wouldn't look at her. 'They will know who we are. They will have heard.'

'They won't know you—' she started, but then realized that any who had heard of the hunt wouldn't have to recognize the Kasra, only his exotic travelling companions. 'Well, it's just one house, so if one of them decides to paddle off to fetch your sister's people, we can stop them.' Maniye bared her teeth. 'Isn't there any loyalty on the river at *all*?'

Tecuman's face twisted, and she realized that he was on the point of weeping.

'We go in, we seek hospitality – you do understand host and guest here on the river?' Almost a plea, but at least Tecuman was nodding. 'Moon Eye will keep watch outside, and if any little fat boys start paddling off towards open water he'll give us some warning. What tribe are these, anyway?' She told Tecuman what she had seen.

'Milk Tear People,' he identified, which was something. When she asked him for anything more, he told her, 'Don't eat anything of theirs.'

'We're going there for *food* so you realize how useless that is?' Tiamesh snapped.

'They are alchemists, herbalists,' Tecuman tried to explain, using words that Maniye only vaguely understood. 'It is said that they can eat poison and sweat medicine, or the other way around.'

'What's their shape?' Moon Eye wanted to know.

'They are the Toad's get,' the Kasra explained, then blinked in surprise at the smirking this occasioned. Once he told them just how large and venomous the toads of the estuary were, they stopped laughing.

At last, hunger won out. They decided to approach over the water, which led to Tiamesh clinging gamely to Maniye's back. The thought, *Look at us, the invincible Iron Wolves*, came and went in Maniye's mind. But then they were across and scrambling up the far bank, looking up at the house on stilts. Who lived out in such a hostile place in just one house? Did the Milk Tear People hate each other that much, like Bears, or was this some renegade? How did you get thrown out of a tribe renowned for poisoning people?

Too many questions without answers. Their presence would be well advertised to those within by then, and so Maniye kept to her human form. The other two followed her lead, and so there came to the Milk Tear dwelling a soft River Lord youth and two women of the north, none of them many years past their childhoods. Only Tiamesh, with her hatchet, looked remotely like a threat, albeit a threat as bedraggled and miserable as could be.

'No rain in this cursed place,' she muttered in Maniye's ear, 'but so much water! It's as though all the rain there ever was fell years ago, and it's just sitting around.'

There was a door of wicker closed against them, and Maniye called out, unsure of the traditions, and guessing Tecuman wasn't going to be much help on that front. 'Greetings to your house! Travellers seek to share your fire.' She hadn't been sure if the estuary people would even have fires, given how damp everything was, but a thread of smoke was escaping the house's flat roof. It seemed more magical than sweating medicine.

The door swung open to reveal the boy she had seen before. Close to, he looked even more as though he had some illness that gave him pale, licheny-looking patches across his face, chest and sagging belly. His eyes were bulbous, his mouth wide, and he goggled at the visitors as though they had three heads each.

Maniye found herself acutely aware of the threshold of the house, as if a spirit sat above the door to guard it. Abruptly she knew exactly what sort of person might live on their own away from villages and neighbours. She swallowed nervously and made her voice as polite as she could to ask, 'Is your mother within?' What drove her to ask for a mother? Nothing she could name, but the word felt right in her mouth.

There was a croaking voice from further in and the boy backed up fast, leaving the way clear. It was as much of an invitation as they were likely to get.

Inside, the house was one room with a fire laid on stone in the centre, a pot boiling over it. Herbs and dried fish and less recognizable things hung from the rafters – reminding Maniye of the upper storeroom of her father's hall, where she had hidden so often. The boy retreated to one corner, where he joined a young girl like enough to be his sister. The air was dense with clashing fragrances, thick as water.

Across the fire from them was a great broad-bodied woman, large enough that Maniye wondered whether the floor would hold her. Sitting, her body bulged out like a half-full waterskin, and she wore a long stained dress that a lesser woman might have used as a tent. Her face was wide and crooked, the whites of her protuberant eyes gone red with blood. A disfiguring splotch of white, warty skin was splayed across her features.

A priestess. A sorceress. Maniye's mouth was abruptly very dry, before that blood-rimmed gaze.

'Mata,' Tecuman said, his voice shaking slightly. The word

meant nothing to the northerners, but apparently it was some honorific and the right thing to say.

'Do they not have doors where you come from?' the Milk Tear woman demanded, not angrily but as though all the world had ever been a disappointment to her. Tiamesh fumbled with the wicker panel, fighting it back into place, and the woman gave a great belch of a laugh. 'Oh, they don't? Dear me, think of that.'

'Mata—' Tecuman started again, but she silenced him with a single pudgy finger.

'Salt,' she demanded, and the girl brought forth a bowl with hard tablets of grey in it, waving it under Maniye's nose.

Maniye remembered Tecuman's warning, but this was host and guest. Even a token would seal that bargain, and it was taste or walk away. She took a finger-sized stick of the stuff and put it to her tongue, finding it was salted fish, strong-tasting and delicious, hard to the teeth but then melting on the tongue. Right then, it was perhaps the best thing she had ever tasted.

The Milk Tear woman shifted, and the whole house seemed to creak about her. 'Ah, well then,' she decided. 'You might as well sit, while you're at it.' She licked her lips with a tongue that seemed unreasonably long.

Tiamesh stayed crouching near the door but Maniye sat by the fire and pulled Tecuman down beside her. She could only hope there was no Riverland strangeness to host and guest in these lands, or that the boy would warn her if she put a foot wrong. 'We are travellers—' she started again, but that thick finger silenced her too.

'I know who you are,' their host told them. 'There's nothing like water for carrying bad news, don't they say? And so you are the false Kasra and his northerners, and I am Mata Embe, and this is my house.' *And my territory, and my law*, remained unsaid.

Tecuman had started to protest at that 'false', but once more she halted him. 'If that backside of yours is on a fancy chair somewhere, then you can argue with me. Until then, you're just

146

some boy who got told he was important some time long ago, and believed it until now. And that's three times. Once more and you're no guests of mine any longer.'

The Riverlands youth shut his mouth like a trap. Being polite to the Milk Tear People was obviously an art.

'Mata Embe, everything you say is true,' Maniye said finally, deciding that a little abject flattery was probably no bad thing, 'and here we are at your fire.'

'Hrrrrmp.' A sound from deep within the woman's thick throat. 'But not for long enough to share a meal with me or my apprentices. For the hunters will come back soon, calling, "Mata Embe, have you seen them?" and offering me gifts if I have news for them.'

How would Hesprec say it? 'One in our position might wonder what answer you would give,' she managed, feeling as though she was trying to choke herself with her own tongue.

Mata Embe chuckled. 'The same as I told them last time. Come back when the Serpent decides who the Kasra is.' Tecuman shifted, mouth opening, and this time she just looked at him. 'The estuary is full of voices. The wind asks why the Patient Ones are shaking spears at each other. The water brings us word from Tsokawan that we are to take up our knives and clubs and spill our blood in the river to decide which child gets to own a chair. The birds call to one another, "Since we cannot bow in two directions, why bow at all?"'

'And what do you say?' Tecuman demanded before Maniye could stop him. She expected an explosion, but Mata Embe settled back, apparently feeling it was a fair question.

'I? If the Serpent was not knotting itself about all this, I'd say bury ourselves in mud until there was one Kasra, or none at all. But the Serpent says bad times are coming, and we don't like fighting them. Nobody wins when a snake swallows a toad. I will not shelter you, false Kasra, because I do not want the anger of your sister like a knife at the bellies of my people. But I will give

147

you some little help, because you have some little chance to win, and then you will be grateful, and remember Mata Embe.'

Tecuman nodded convulsively. Whatever emotions were at war within him, he was wise enough to give none of them access to his tongue.

The girl and boy came forward then. They gave leaf-wrapped packages to Tecuman. Maniye hoped they would be food, but the first was a garment, a coarsely woven robe, that would be both too short and absurdly wide on Tecuman. She made Tecuman dress in it there and then, to forestall any argument.

'It is good,' pronounced Mata Embe, presumably not at the fit. Her eyes rolled until they rested on Maniye. 'And when you see that villain Hesprec Essen Skese, you tell him Mata Embe remembers him all too well.' And she chuckled again, low and filthy.

'Hesprec . . .' Maniye stared at her. 'Hesprec is . . . not as you remember.'

The Milk Tear woman studied her, and then blinked slowly, like a nod that never left her eyes. 'Shed his skin at last, has he? The river is never still.' There was a sadness in her voice, and Maniye tried to understand it: perhaps that an old, old acquaintance had gone where this woman would never follow.

But then Mata Embe clapped her hands together wetly. 'It's time for you to go, before more guests come to stretch my hospitality. And besides, you've a caller of your own.'

And when they got outside, there he was: Feeds on Rags, crouching at Moon Eye's side.

'Well?' Maniye demanded of him, when they'd forded the water again.

The Crow looked hurt, as though he was amazed she would doubt him. 'Yes, yes I found your followers. Yes they are safe, though watched. Yes, I found one who could creep out of their stone walls to come with me.'

'Sathewe,' Maniye guessed, with a sinking heart, because the

148

Coyote girl would hardly be able to rally the warband. Most likely nobody would even listen to her.

'No!' Feeds on Rags protested. 'You wanted someone important, and I did it. I!'

And so they followed him, trying to find dry paths where he simply flew, aware at every step that they were closing on Tsokawan, and that Tecumet's hunters might still be scouring these nearer reaches of the estuary.

But they found a slow channel, and beached in it a narrow boat. And in the boat, exactly the wrong person: a man who fitted her request exactly and yet whom she did not want to see.

'Why couldn't you get Spear Catcher?' she hissed, and Feeds on Rags looked at her, wounded.

The old man in the boat stirred, the paddle across his bony knees. 'So,' said Kalameshli Takes Iron.

Maniye approached him carefully, on human feet. 'Why did you come?' she asked him.

The Wolf priest looked at her without expression. 'You are the Wolf's Champion.'

'I am more than that.'

'You are the Wolf's Champion,' he repeated sternly, and she felt a phantom lash from childhood, from those years when his voice had carried fear with it. Then his face shifted and he said, 'And you are mine.' Not as Akrit Stone River had said it, back when he had lived, but just a blunt admission that she was his blood.

'What of the rest?' she demanded.

'Watched,' Kalameshli told her. He put a hand out, and reluctantly she helped him out of the boat while Tiamesh tied it off to an arching root. Standing on the nearest thing to dry land, Takes Iron looked about him, lip curled at the south's general failures of climate and terrain. 'All is confusion in their great stone hall. The River People run back and forth and talk too much. Their boy-chief is gone, some say dead.' He looked sidelong at Tecuman, plainly disappointed to find it was not so.

149

'Those Snakes who speak for the girl are all over that place with their people, arguing that the fortress should be given up to her. Your warband is . . . not quite under guard, not quite free to go. The River People argue about what part they played. They don't listen to *us*. They just talk and talk. Your people need you.'

Maniye nodded. 'We must bring Tecuman back to his seat.'

'No.' Kalameshli stared at the young Kasra with undisguised contempt. 'Bring him to have his throat cut, by all means. Bring him to win praise from his sister, if you care for such. He cannot even command his people. If he were a Wolf then another would be in his place, and he would be out in the wilds just like this, only there would not be all this *talking*. They can never say anything plain, on this river. Even the sister claims she did nothing, as though she was ashamed to take by strength, rather than the flapping of lips.'

'I came here to protect him. We all did,' Maniye told him flatly.

'Oaths to these people cannot bind you,' Kalameshli snapped. 'They use so many words that they drown all oaths and promises beneath them. How can you see their confusion and their words and think them worth your time? At least on the Plains they know how to live and how to die.'

He had complained every day they had been on the Plains, of course, but perhaps that had just been practising for the River.

'The one clear sight of the world they have,' Takes Iron went on, 'is to know the worth of a priest. Hence, I am free to come to you and tell you: give up the boy, abandon him to this cursed water, whatever you prefer. Come back to your people, who wait for you. Loyalty spent elsewhere is like piss into this river of theirs, carried away and forgotten.'

'Would Broken Axe have said so?' she challenged him.

He faced the name without flinching. 'Broken Axe went south but he came home. He knew there was no truth or faith in these lands.' And then he lunged forward, clutching at her shoulders.

He was old, but he was forge-strong still. She would have to Step to pull away.

'You are chosen by the Wolf,' he insisted. 'You are special, Many Tracks. But you are not special to these people. You don't belong here and the Wolf has no patience with their weaknesses.'

Maniye took a deep breath. 'Do you know what the south can do?' she asked him, her voice brittle. 'It can feed five times all the Winter Runners on half the land. It can put its words on stone, to be heard by others in different times and places. It can—'

Kalameshli released her as if she had burned him, and threw up his arms. 'This talk,' he choked out, 'you have their talk, their too-many-words. That Snake girl's venom is in you.'

'A priestess,' she reminded him, because the hospitality that let him run free had not been echoed in his past treatment of southern priests. 'A priestess, and older and wiser than you.'

He stepped back, his face set. 'I will not help you while you drag this weakness behind you.' A jabbing gesture towards Tecuman. 'Come back when you have found the Wolf's path, Many Tracks. Come back when you have found your strength.'

And he stepped into the boat, his dignity momentarily sabotaged as he clutched for balance. Then he was casting off, sculling away without a backwards glance.

15

Of course Shyri couldn't exactly just jump into the river after Asmander. She might laugh at his people and call them long-mouth, but that didn't mean she wanted to go swimming with them any time soon.

On the other hand, something was clearly going badly wrong and being on the boat of the enemy chief didn't seem to be a good idea.

But the problem with boats and exits . . .

She ran to another rail, trying to get a picture of the river around her. Things were not looking happy out there: too many ridged backs and thrashing tails for her liking. There were shouts and alarms all too audible from Tsokawan and, around her, Tecumet's people were waking up to the fact that something was happening.

Except some of them already know, Shyri decided. Of course Tecumet would send a few knives as a present for her brother. It was what Shyri would have done in her position, although she had started to think that the River Lords were unthinkably dense in that respect. Good to see some of them had sense. Shame it was the enemy rather than her own side.

Not that I have a side, she thought. But Asmander did, and that left her shackled to a great big weight dropped in the river, as far as she could see.

She skipped towards the back of the boat, aware that more

and more of the crew were paying attention to her. There were raised voices from elsewhere on board, and she thought she heard old Asman's tones. *Well, that canny old bastard can look after himself.* They would no doubt treat him with the respect due to someone worth keeping alive. Would they extend the same to a Plains woman in their midst? No, they would not.

At the back rail of the barge, uncomfortably aware that she was now very close to Tecumet's tent-thing – and hence tweaking the noses of all the guards just by being there – she took stock.

There was a lot of river out there. There were a lot of boats. Tecumet still had warriors arriving.

Just as she had the thought, someone shouted at her. Possibly they just wanted to get her further from Tecumet. Possibly they were demanding she surrender to the mercies of Old Crocodile. They might even have been warning her about the drop, because she was leaning out in order to get a good view. Whatever the intent, she took it as her cue to leave.

In another breath she was standing on the stern rail. Then a moment of perfect balance, before kicking off.

A flat-bottomed boat had been nosing towards the barge, laden with casks and sacks, and several of those were now in the river, displaced by a snarling hyena. The rowers yelled in surprise, and two of them went into the water as well, to come back at her with long, toothy jaws agape. Shyri wasn't standing still, though, and she had no intention of taking up an oar. There was another boat, a long canoe, gliding past on one side, and she Stepped to human for the jump, clung for a moment to the new vessel's hull as it heeled over alarmingly, and then Stepped back to run down its length, claws scrabbling and tearing rents in the hide hull.

She jumped again when she reached its pointed end, upsetting the canoe entirely but giving herself just enough purchase to clutch the wooden side of a bigger vessel. She was dragging a long tail of yells and complaints behind her, and the consensus

153

was plainly that someone should stop her. The crew of her current conveyance had just got to peering over the rail when she exploded up into their faces: a copper-skinned girl with a bronze knife in her teeth who turned into a spotted, cackling beast the moment she hit the deck.

She was running out of luck. There were soldiers on this boat with spears. After their initial shock, they came for her with a vengeance, because they had fought Plains people around here for generations, Laughing Men included. Shyri skittered back along the boat with a dozen River Lords on her heels, only to see another half-dozen clambering up from below decks ahead of her. She cursed all the gods of the south, and Asmander as well for good measure, and ended up on the rail again. Two or three of the soldiers instantly plunged into the river, Stepping as they fell, so that they would be ready for her.

Not in the plan, but that thought exaggerated just how much plan there was. The spears were coming in, and the odds of her keeping them all at bay with a knife whilst teetering on the ship's rail seemed poor.

In times like these she had to fall back on human nature. In this case, human nature meant that some fool woman with a boat full of fruit had decided that her delivery took precedence over whatever was going on. Shyri Stepped and leapt, landing on all fours with her teeth in a sack of mangos.

The fruit woman was game, Shyri had to give her that. Seeing her cargo under threat from – she must presumably have thought – Plains fruit raiders, she Stepped herself and lunged at Shyri, scaled body humping itself over the crates and boxes. And of course some concerned boatman was coming to help *her*, as though she was the one who needed it. But he was poling his little skiff, which told Shyri the one thing she desperately wanted to hear. *Near the shore.*

She got onto the little skiff, frantically scrambling for balance while fighting over the pole with its owner. Neither of them wanted to Step and relinquish it, so she took the man's arm and twisted it about his shoulder until he howled, then dumped him head-first into the murky water.

Poling a boat around was probably a skill that could be learned quickly, but not nearly quickly enough – and the bank wasn't far. Instead she jabbed the pole into the riverbed, bent it back and then let it help her final leap.

She ended up in the water, even so, and had ten heartbeats of frantic splashing and scrabbling, fully expecting a pair of jaws to close on her and drag her to her doom. Then she was on the bank.

All around her were tents and Riverlanders and spears and soldiers, and all the general clutter of the army that Tecumet had brought to the estuary. What had been mud and a few fisher-men's jetties was now a dense maze of Riverlanders, and at this moment every single one of them seemed fixated on the Laugh-ing Girl that had turned up in their midst.

But she laughed her people's derisive heckle at them, and then she was Stepped and running, dodging and weaving through them and leaving them behind, tracking chaos and alarm through their camp and heading towards the spires of Tsokawan.

Some entertaining chasing, hiding and arrow-dodging later, and she was running through the stone halls looking for Asmander. Nobody in the place seemed to know where he was, and all of them had better things to be doing than talking to a Plains stray. Shyri heard at least a dozen contradictory stories of what was going on, and the only connecting feature was Bad Things.

At last, by dint of going up and up until there was no more up to go, she found him. He was staring out of a narrow slit of a window in some finely draped bedchamber. There were guards on the door who had tried to stop her, but a gesture from the Champion had dissuaded them. Even so, their looks as they let her past were entirely suspicious.

She padded up behind him. He spared her barely a glance,

fists clenched and all the muscles of his back and arms knotted, a man holding himself together by sheer will. She felt she knew Asmander by now. They had gone to the north together, and he had taken enough blows there for her to see him opened up and bleeding. Now she read not his face but his body, which he was less skilled at keeping impassive.

'So,' she observed, 'you've got a plan.'

He rounded on her angrily and she faced him, arms folded and grinning a little – because when you were one of the Laughing Men you could always find something to grin at. 'This is your friend's room, isn't it? Tecumander?'

'Tecuman.' He bit off the word, killing the child's suffix. Everything that happened now revolved about the loss of that little sound. Asmander tried to stare her down but something shook him, something from deep inside, and he said, 'My friend, yes.'

What did the River Lords do with their grief and despair? Laughing Men learned to feed on such things. Comfort was for children, and not needing it was a badge of honour Shyri had awarded herself before her tenth year.

Right then she knew that Asmander was still a child, travel as he might. She felt a weakness in her: to tell him comforting things, to make the world easier for him. She shook it off and forced her grin wider, to show the world how little she cared. That was how the Laughing Men endured, after all. Care about as little as possible, because the world will destroy it and the gods are cruel.

'So what then?' She looked about exaggeratedly: *Tecuman's chamber? So where is Tecuman?* The mummery turned into a more serious examination. Blood had been spilled here. 'He's . . . ?'

'Gone,' Asmander said.

She looked at him narrowly, trying to work out what he actually believed. 'Gone beyond?'

'Gone,' he told her firmly.

She was about to say something like, *Poor Kasra with no Champion to guard him* – which would, in retrospect, probably have set his teeth at her throat. Then something fell into place and she said, 'What about the Wolf girl, Maniye Many Feet or whatever she calls herself?'

'Gone.' And there was a little spark of fire in him at last. Travelling with Asmander she had seen him pitch from a man who would take on an army singlehandedly to a man who couldn't defeat the darkness inside himself. She far preferred the former, and for a moment that Asmander was burning in his eyes.

She hooked a little stool with her foot and sat down on it. 'Longmouth, you're going to wear that word out. So tell me a story: what happened?'

Asmander was piecing together what he could.

There had been fighting within Tsokawan. Many were dead, some of Tecuman's people, some strangers who had surely been brought in by his sister. That a band of armed men had infiltrated the fortress with the aim of cutting royal throats was clear. What had actually happened was far less clear. There had been fighting in Tecuman's very chamber, but the Kasra's body was not to be found. The northerners had been up to their elbows in blood as well, and some claimed they had betrayed the Kasra – because they were strange and frightening and nobody knew them. Others said that they had simply gone mad.

Asmander hurried through the halls of Tsokawan with Shyri trotting at his heels, questioning everyone he came across, trying to stitch it into whole cloth.

Maniye's warband were in the rooms that had been set aside for them, and nobody was entirely sure whether they were prisoners or not. Right now, the question was being dodged by providing them with plenty of food and drink and hoping they didn't try to go anywhere.

The Wolves themselves obviously felt the changing tides around them. When Asmander intruded on them, he found

157

them all with weapons to hand, and hostile. They knew him better than they knew the other southerners, but they didn't like him much. In the end it was Shyri who tipped the balance in his favour. They liked her more than they liked him. *All savages together.*

Many Tracks was absent with a handful of others, which gave him some hope. One of their number was dead, too, and they had the body there, laid out with weapons on a bed of smashed furniture. He realized that they intended to burn him, and the old Wolf priest who Maniye hated so much was obviously going to do things the Wolf way, no matter how far they were from their own lands. Asmander guessed giving the body to the river wouldn't sit well with them.

He found Spear Catcher the next morning – the old hunter with that horribly scarred face that had apparently given him his name. He and his mate sat aside with Asmander and told him everything they had witnessed.

Maniye had called them, howling *Danger!* When they had found her, she had been fighting 'your people', meaning anyone from the south, as far as Asmander could guess. She had been protecting Tecuman. The Wolves had torn out more than one throat.

'She left,' Asmander summarized.

Spear Catcher nodded. 'The boy was with her. She took him away.' He gave Asmander a level look. 'These stone walls of yours don't work. They just make it hard to see where the enemy is.'

Shyri snickered, and Asmander couldn't find any argument.

He went to find the priests, any priests. Later that day, he found all of them, and more besides. A sizeable delegation had arrived from Tecumet, priests and Izel and all, with Asman himself striding along as if they were his escort and not his captors. And they talked, with Esumit pressing the case for Tecumet as Kasra,

158

and Matsur giving ground, but never conceding that Tecuman might not just walk in at any moment, inexplicably mislaid.

Sitting apart from the nail-pullingly polite talking was Hesprec Essen Skese, listening to every word and saying nothing. There was a saying about priests of the Serpent that Asmander knew well. *Always listen to the silent one.*

Aware of Shyri dogging his heels still, he sat beside the young girl, seeing her eyes flick to him: not old eyes, even – bright with the spark of a new youth, after so many other rebirths. How long had Hesprec's hand guided the Sun River Nation? How long Esumit and Matsur? And yet . . . this confusion.

'Have you come for my voice on Tecuman's behalf?' Hesprec asked softly.

Asmander shook his head. 'No fish in those waters, I know. But the Wolf Champion is your friend.'

Hesprec nodded slowly. 'So, not for him but for her? I must be moved by that, hmm?'

'I . . .' Asmander bit back all the things he wanted to say.

'The Serpent is working himself into knots,' Hesprec said quietly. 'And we must assume there is purpose in the pattern that his body writes, but we can see only a hand's span of his coils. And even now we are drifting further from one another. Far enough that some voices are not even here for me to hear.'

Asmander frowned, but it was true: the old woman, Therumit, had apparently given up on the whole business. 'I am sorry,' he told the young priestess. 'There are greater matters than . . .'

'You fear for your friend.'

'Yes.'

'And what of Many Tracks?'

Asmander looked into himself to see what he might find. 'I trust her,' he said at last. 'She will protect him, if she can.'

Hesprec nodded slowly. 'I hear the Crow has been and gone more than once, since all this happened.'

'The . . . ?'

159

'Did your time in the north teach you nothing, Son of Asman?'

Asmander glanced at his father, currently holding forth to Esumit. 'The . . . the Eyrieman? The man with the bird soul.'

'I heard he was gone, but I have seen him in Tsokawan since,' Hesprec said, her eyes on the debate, as though none of this was of any great importance. 'Who knows what his eyes have seen? To the others here, they are all "the northerners", but you and I can tell a Crow from a Wolf.'

Asmander stood very carefully, as though hoping not to startle the debaters. 'My father will have tasks for me.'

'No doubt,' Hesprec agreed. 'But your father loves his own voice, and so you might remain your own master for a little while longer.' She smiled at him. 'Tell Maniye that I have spoken to the Serpent on her behalf, to help her find her way.'

'And Tecuman.'

Hesprec's expression did not change. 'No fish in those waters, remember. Go cast your nets in the estuary.'

Finding the Crow was another quest suitable for a hero from the old tales and Asmander wasted much time scouring the high places where a bird might roost. When he finally caught sight of the odd little man with his half-painted face, what he felt was not relief but frustration, for Feeds was skulking along one of the narrow-windowed arcades of the fortress in the shadow of the old Wolf priest – the one who Many Tracks had such an angry history with, and yet had brought with her anyway. They were almost back with the rest of the warband before Asmander caught up with them, and the stare of the priest stopped him in his tracks. Asmander was not welcome. There was no concession for his having been Maniye's comrade in the north, no remembrance of his travelling south with them.

'Have you seen her?' he demanded. He felt the Champion shift in him, bucking against the walls the Wolf priest tried to put around him.

'What passes between the Wolf and his Champion is hidden from the likes of you,' the priest snapped. He had on a robe sewn with hundreds of little bones, the costume that presumably made him a figure of terror in the nightmares of northerners. To Asmander it made him seem the barbaric madman he probably was.

Behind the old man, the other Wolves were getting to their feet about their chamber. The whole place was smoky with fires, smelling of dog and sweat. They had made a northern hall out of this small space of Tsokawan.

Asmander had no idea how loyal they were to the priest, given Maniye's generally disparaging treatment of him. They would defend him against a southerner, though.

He stalked off again. Simply striking out into the great cluttered morass of the estuary was never a good plan, but it was all the plan he was left with. Shyri found him shortly afterwards, claws clicking as she trotted up to him. As always, her hyena face looked insufferably amused at all of his concerns.

'What?' he demanded of her.

She Stepped and stretched. 'Your father's looking for you.'

'I have no doubt of it,' he agreed. 'Are you his dog now?'

'Perhaps I am yours, since I bark to warn you. What's the plan, Longmouth?'

'I go and find Tecuman, wherever he's gone.'

'If he's with the Wolf girl?'

'All the better.'

'If he's in chains on his sister's boat?'

'Even then.'

'If he's dead?' And, to her credit, she wasn't grinning when she said it.

'Then I've failed as his Champion and I will probably do something rash.' Asmander tried a bright, brittle smile of his own. He suspected it ended up the sort of expression a skull wore.

'Do something rash anyway. He's not dead,' a new voice broke in.

Asmander spun around, a flint knife almost leaping into his hand. A man was squatting awkwardly in the square gap of a nearby window, where before there must have been a hunched black bird. The Crow cocked his head, looking at them through the tattoo-ringed eye.

'I'm not supposed to talk to you.'

Asmander said nothing, not wanting to scare the bird into sudden flight.

'But Many Tracks thought you were dead because of where you went before it all happened. I can talk to a dead man, can't I? Kalameshli can't mean I couldn't talk to a dead man.'

Asmander ground his teeth impatiently but managed to turn his frustration into an approving nod.

'So if I said,' the Crow went on, apparently navigating some internal northern etiquette, 'that I had seen Many Tracks in the estuary and they were heading away from this stone place to avoid the hunters, and that she had a River Lord youth with her who barely knows enough to Step when he's swimming, that couldn't be wrong, could it?'

'Take me to them,' Asmander snapped.

The Crow started. 'I can't. Takes Iron said. I don't want him as an enemy.'

'You're not even a Wolf!'

The northerner plucked at his clothes nervously. 'You'd be amazed at how much that makes me *more* want him not to be my enemy. I may be a fool, but I know that much. Listen. If you travel south you will find a hovel on stilts. It belongs to Mata Embe of the Milk Tear – a witch. Or whatever they call them round here. That was where they were. From there they were heading deeper in, further south. Nobody could think it wrong for me to tell a dead man that, surely.'

Abruptly he was a bird again, shaking its wings out, regarding them through one orange eye before casting itself off into the sky outside.

Asmander breathed the Serpent's blessing on all errant, half-mad Crows. 'It seems I have a better plan,' he announced.

'Let's go then,' Shyri agreed.

'No.'

'Seriously, you're going to—'

'You can't keep up with me,' he told her flatly. 'Not through the channels of the estuary. And I need you here.'

She folded her arms and frowned at him. 'So now you need me.'

'Because I can trust you.'

She laughed at that. 'You trust a child of the Laughing Men, Longmouth?'

'I do, yes.' He let his level expression sober her. 'Because you're from far away, and not one of us. So of everyone in this fortress, I know that *you* aren't in the pay of someone else.'

She snorted. 'Need me for what, though?'

'Something is rotten here,' he said, lowering his voice so she came close. 'My *soul* tells me something is wrong. The priests, fighting one another, or . . .'

'You want me to uncover the secrets of the Serpent?' she asked, amused.

'Keep your eyes open. Tecuman needs me, but this place needs someone to watch and listen. And I have no one better, so it will have to be you.'

She peered into his face as though hoping to see the Champion behind it. 'You are sick with loyalty,' she told him. 'You think I have the same disease.'

'Even so. Remember I trust you.'

She might have looked frightened, and not for herself. 'Go carefully, Longmouth.'

'Alas, I feel we're beyond that.'

163

16

Lone Mountain spared a thought for his cousin, Loud Thunder, who by now was probably drowning in guests, annoying the great men of a dozen tribes, getting under Mother's feet . . . It was worth a chuckle, as he woke in a snow hollow high in the mountains, a great bear on a hard journey with plenty of ground still to cover.

I would do it so much better. If he had been there, everyone would have been his friend already. Ancient enemies would be vying to sit next to him. Lone Mountain would trade and tell tales and make them all laugh. And then Loud Thunder would be here, on this lonely, dangerous, thankless quest into the unknown.

It would have suited them both down to the ground, Lone Mountain considered, breaking himself out of the snow and scenting the air. He had some food left, for there would be precious little hunting or foraging, even in the best passes.

He moved fast for a bear, loping with great heavy strides, scrabbling up where the rock rose ahead of him, skidding and scraping down the far side. He was no fleet wolf, no deer, but he carried his bulk without tiring, dawn to dusk, eating up the miles with an inexhaustible appetite.

He wondered, as he ran, just what Mother had seen, and how long ago? Why else choose Thunder (who so prized his solitude) to host, if she had not known that Lone Mountain (the talker, the traveller, the bear known far and wide) would be called on to travel? Some mornings he thought she had made a lucky guess, but on others he knew she saw more of the future than even the old Serpent from the south.

He thought about this, and how badly Loud Thunder must be suffering – both amusing and sorrowful to contemplate. He thought about the future of the tribe, and of all the Crown of the World. All of these things together did not quite quell his fear of what he might find on the road ahead.

Perhaps the Seal was mad, he considered. *A terror from the sea.* Lone Mountain had stood with the Seal and stared out at that endless, turbulent expanse. The sight of the ocean filled him with dread, and none but the Seal were mad enough to brave it. Out there where the land met the water, where the mist crept in and the gulls wheeled, out there he might meet . . . anything.

No soul was braver than a Bear's, but all of a sudden he felt his feet dragging. He thought of the Death that had come to the Wetbacks, soulless and unknowable. It was his very fitness for Loud Thunder's task back home that suddenly made him slow his feet, demanding: *Was it all for this: all my years, my travels, my words? All to die beyond the sight of my people?* And worse: *What of my soul? Will it haunt the lonely shore forever?*

And he feared, and the fear rode him like a great weight. But Mother was there, in his soul and in his memories: Mother, who had given him this task. In the end, Mother angry was more terrifying even than the unknown. So Lone Mountain forged on, downhill now, descending from the high passes towards the shores of the Seal.

★★★

Mother was speaking to the priests: sometimes it was Crown of Stars, the Moon Eater with his milk-blind eyes, or squat Gnarl Hide of the Boar; sometimes it was the fierce Tiger priestess Aritchaka. Most often she had the two Coyote at her fire, and no others. Two Heads Talking and Quiet When Loud would sit, attentive as children, or else Quiet would talk in the ear of her mate, and then he would outline their combined thoughts to Mother's towering bulk. They looked no more than a mouthful between them, the Coyotes, but Loud Thunder had learned to respect their wisdom more because it did not brag or call attention to itself.

Loud Thunder himself spent time with Kailovela.

Yellow Claw was a great challenger for games he thought he could win. He was a strong man, swift and fierce – even without wings he bested many who thought themselves secure in their titles. He was no gracious winner, either. He stalked from fire to fire with a dozen hunters of the Eyrie at his back and had little enough respect for his hosts, and none at all for anyone else. But he kept himself busy and away from his own camp.

Loud Thunder came asking to see the spirit woman again. He was their host, the man who had made such a remarkable invitation to all the Crown of the World. Blind-seeming Seven Mending stood up at his voice and guided him faultlessly to Kailovela's tent, where the hollow creature was kept.

It was a large tent – as it must be, for half was prison, and half was for Yellow Claw. In the middle, between two worlds, dwelled Kailovela. She was wary when he came in – not unreasonably, for he felt he filled its entire space, forcing her and the spirit to the very edges. He felt huge and clumsy. She bade him welcome nonetheless, although she would not look him in the eye.

'You have questions about her,' the Eyriewoman observed. Loud Thunder eyed the spirit creature, which was crouched on its haunches, freakish in its diminutive size, in its hungry hollowness. It was watching him keenly and the sight made his skin crawl.

But he could not lie. 'About you,' he said.

Kailovela drew in a deep breath and let it out, saying nothing. 'Yellow Claw made you his mate.'

'He is a great man of the Eyrie, and what his eye alights on

166

he will have.' Her fingers brushed the halter of her own hair, looped about her throat.

'You are lucky to have such a great man to guard your hearth,' he said. He had intended to be cunning, but he heard bitterness in his voice despite his best endeavours. In the back of his mind was a voice like Mother's telling him, *Stupid, stupid, get out before you become an even bigger fool.* 'A great man to father your child,' he added, with an awkward gesture at her belly.

A shudder went through her. 'It is not his,' she whispered.

'I . . .' But Thunder could not imagine how to answer this. He was rendered dumb.

She looked him right in the eye, her face full of anger and hurt. 'There was another, my mate.'

'He died.'

Her smile cut him. 'Yellow Claw challenged him and then gave him to the Hawk.'

'I am sorry.' He truly was, and he wondered how many other hands had taken her, only to have her taken from them in turn.

'I did not choose him either.' She looked him in the eye as though she could read his thoughts. 'And are you here, then, to challenge Yellow Claw?'

He wanted to. She was not inviting it, but he wanted to. There was something about her that drew him like honey. That she drew this reaction from strangers was something she was plainly aware of, and just as plainly would have rid herself of if she could.

'If you were my mate I would take you away from this nonsense to a place with only the sky and the forest.' The words fumbled out of his mouth without a plan. Her eyes went wide as he spoke, but then her mouth closed to a twitching line, fighting an unwanted smile.

'This "nonsense" is of your making,' she pointed out.

'I know. It's all the more nonsense for that,' he said. 'What . . .' He didn't want to ask, but he had to. 'What would you do, if there were no Yellow Claw?'

167

She said nothing. Her eyes strayed to the open tent flap, the pale sky visible outside.

He looked away then, and found himself face to face with the spirit woman. To his shock he discovered that for all the creature was no more than a husk, she wore an identical expression to Kailovela: trapped and yearning for freedom.

***

There were three who dared camp in the shadow of the mesa. Grey Herald had come here following nightmares. The Plains people were fierce, he knew that. Their history had been a paring down of peoples. The Plains were dotted with long-sealed fortresses, the footprints of vanished villages, skeletal remains of whole tribes. Plains people did not live in harmony with their gods, as he was used to in the Crown of the World – their prayers were more than half threat, their offerings born of hard bargaining. It took a lot to scare the Plains people.

And so Grey Herald had rooted out that fear and followed it like a road to this place.

The Bat Society: scarcely even a rumour; not heard of these many centuries. In the stories Bat was just the third brother, after Owl and Serpent. All were wise, all were brave. But everything he had heard on the Plains suggested the Bat had become – or always been – something darker before they had vanished from the world.

Grey Herald shook his head wearily as he circled above the speck of fire. Myths were lies that taught, so the Owl cried. Picking the lesson from the lie was ever a hard art, and the legends of How We Came Here were the oldest of all.

Grey Herald faltered, his troubled mind making his wings flounder against the wind and losing him twenty feet of height before he regained his composure. A strange thought, that: there was a time Before We Came Here, when the people lived in that other land. And in that land they would have had legends, still, heroes and gods and deeds and histories that were now not even dust. *That way lies madness,* he told himself and beat his wings a half-dozen times as though trying to escape from the vast, sad emptiness he had touched.

The Bat Society are dead, everyone knows that.

And yet there was a fire.

There were caves in the side of the mesa, craggy stone mouths harbouring darkness even his eyes could not pierce. He eyed them thoughtfully as he descended.

Three, then, sat before the flames.

He set down at a polite distance and Stepped, holding his arms out to show he did not come for war or raiding. His knives were prominent at his belt, because that was the Plains way. The locals liked to know their visitors kept their weapons openly; who would trust an unarmed man?

'Approach,' came a woman's voice, rough and soft at the edges. Grey Herald stepped forwards until the firelight caught him, and watched them studying the painting of his face.

There was a big Riverlands man there, tall and broad-shouldered, ridged scars down his bare chest. He was sitting with a stone-studded sword across his knees, replacing its missing teeth. River Lords were not seen so often out on the Plains, Grey Herald suspected. He guessed at a story of exile and disgrace for this warrior.

The woman who had spoken was of the Boar – a tribe who were at home on the Plains as much as in the north. She was stocky and strong-framed, and about her neck was a cord, hanging down past her breasts, strung with little masks: a priestess, then.

Tending a pot over the fire was a lean creature in garments that were mostly rags stitched together. He was of the Laughing Men, one of their much-abused menfolk keeping hearth for these two strangers. He had a wiry beard, long, silver hair and a thin hatchet of a face.

All three had ash smudged across their eyes in a crude band, stippled with fingermarks. It was the best sign yet that Grey Herald was on the right track.

They were all renegades, cut from their people. The River-lander had a child's name, a curse on him for some wrong against his people. The Laughing Man had fled the beatings of his mate. The Boar priestess had something hard and dead behind her eyes; she did not volunteer what had brought her there and Grey Herald didn't ask.

They had come here for a ritual, he discovered after much talking around the fact. He had never heard of it before: it was a Plains thing and little known even there. Thinking back, he could find odd fragments of lore he had been told that might have hinted at it, but he had not seen the pattern.

Each of these three carried ghosts that could not be washed away. Perhaps one had killed an enemy who had not Stepped in death, leaving a soul that clung to its killer. Perhaps one had betrayed a guest, or kin, breaking those bonds even the Plains people honoured. Looking at the Boar woman, Grey Herald wondered just what worse crimes there might be that clung to and twisted her soul.

They were here because, in the shadow of this mesa, such stains might be scrubbed clean. Not out of mercy, not out of forgiveness, but because here was a power that would devour even ghosts. Grey Herald thought of wounds gone bad, and how the sickness might be burned out or cut away.

He shared their fire. He was a priest, and they thought his presence might aid their purpose. That he was from a far, far place was even better. They were here seeking alienation from their pasts. He watched the Boar priestess paint them with ash and dark dust until their faces were like blurred reflections of his own. He watched as the Laughing Man took a slender knife and etched pictures into them that represented the wrongs they had done, the wrongs they had suffered. They submitted silently, biting back their curses behind clenched teeth, then did not wipe the blood away but let it crust over so that Herald could not see the meaning of the images beneath.

When they slept, he slept. They had eaten together and they

170

were his hosts, and he guessed none of them would further risk their souls by turning on him. They had taken his coming to their fire as a good omen, the first any of them had seen for a long, long time.

That night he woke to hear wings beating overhead – not the familiar sounds of the Eyrie but a leathery flapping he had never known before. He could have Stepped into his owl shape and seen more clearly what it was that blotted out the stars, but he sensed he was in the midst of a piece of very old magic. Step, show his soul, and he might become a part of it. Stay human and he could just watch and be safe.

In the morning, the Laughing Man was dead. His expression was broken and twisted, bulge-eyed, open-mouthed. His body was withered as though he had been out in the dry lands for days. The other two awoke knowing their ghosts were ripped from them and taken away just as the Laughing Man's soul had been taken. They were free to go home.

They left Grey Herald staring up at the mesa, at the high empty sockets of the caves.

***

Quiet When Loud came to find Loud Thunder in his tent the day after. He could see the trouble in her face when she Stepped.

'What have you done?' he growled. 'Or your mate, what trouble has he made?'

'Not us,' she said curtly. 'You come shout at these fools or someone'll get killed. The rest of your people won't stop it.'

'Of course they won't,' Thunder grumbled. Bear so seldom cared about anyone else's dealings. He saw that if he wanted people to care about this doom Mother foresaw, he should have started with his own kin.

He crawled out of the low tent flap and stood out in the chill air. 'Tell me.'

The stocky Coyote woman looked back over her shoulder. 'You thought you would bring all these enemies to one place and there'd be no knives drawn?'

171

'Who?'

'Some Wolf, some Tiger.'

'Wait.' He caught up with her. He could hear the sound of the fight already, but he made a show of her leading him there because he wanted a chance to talk, now she was here.

'You're . . . carrying.'

Her round face was a picture of bewilderment for a moment before she understood. 'I bear Two Heads Talking's child.' Her expression was wary. Thunder was more than twice her size and all of a sudden very close to be talking of such things.

'You Step.' Amongst the Bear it was not done: a mother-to-be would have other women all around her, ensuring she would not need to call upon the bear in her. Only when the birth neared would she Step, she-bear whelping human infant.

But apparently it was different with Coyote mothers. Until now this was a part of life of which Thunder had happily been ignorant. She walked him towards where the fight was going on.

As he approached the fight he learned more from Two Heads. A hunter of the Swift Backs named Stag Taker had gone to the camp of the Tiger and thrown down a knife. They had his father and mother's blood on his hands, he had told them: she in the fighting years ago, he in a recent raid. Stag Taker had not just challenged the Tiger as a tribe, either: he had challenged Aritchaka, their leader. He was a man with his first grey hairs and no living family. He did not fear the curse that came with killing a priest.

The fight had been on for some time before Loud Thunder came: both combatants were bloodied, and there was quite a gathering there to watch, especially from the Bear. It seemed that Thunder's people had finally found a part of hosting they could really enjoy.

He wanted to Step and just push in straight away, to cuff Stag Taker and Aritchaka both and separate them like unruly children. He wanted to stride in and shame them for breaking the bond of guest on host.

Except they had not. He listened to the talk amongst the onlookers: not a mention of such a breach. Everyone obviously felt this was what Loud Thunder had secretly intended by bringing the tribes here. This was to be a time of challenges, was it not? Well, Stag Taker had made his challenge. There was no insult.

Loud Thunder would have bellowed his rage at the sky, save that the gods were even less likely to heed him than the humans.

Stag Taker stepped to his human form, clad in a long shirt of iron. He held a hatchet in his left hand; his right was a bloody, chewed mess. There was a long cut across his brow that dripped blood into his eyes. For a moment Aritchaka menaced him as a cat, but he hacked at her and she became a lithe woman, swaying beneath the stroke. Her bronze knife played about his side, but she knew better than to try its strength against iron. She had a couple of shallow cuts on her arms, and the blood on her leg was from where Stag Taker had tried to get his teeth into her.

He hacked again, down and then back up as she gave each stroke just enough space to miss her. Her bronze cuirass had a ragged gash in it, the square plates askew where his axehead had dug.

Stag Taker drew the hatchet back for an overhead cut and the Tiger priestess Stepped and leapt, driving her forefeet into his chest and knocking him back with the weight of his own iron. She threw her weight against his left arm and her teeth went seeking his throat. Thunder saw the Wolf fumble the axe into his right hand and cut with it, but he had no grip and the weapon was lost. Stag Taker Stepped to a Wolf but she still had his throat, the strength of her jaws grinding against the iron there. He raked at her underbelly furiously but she shook him like a rat.

Then he was a man once more, his armour still holding, his thumb going for her eyes. Aritchaka Stepped with him, though, grappling at his throat, head leant back away from his clutching hand. Thunder missed the knifework, but abruptly there was a great release of blood and the Tiger priestess sprang away, Stepping once more to become a great striped cat crouched across the fighting circle. Stag Taker lurched to his feet, his whole hand clasped to the opened vessels in his neck. Then he dropped to one knee, and Thunder willed him to Step, to give his soul a chance to fly free and be reborn.

But something failed in the man, and he dropped forwards, face down. He died a man. A current of rage went through the Wolves gathered there. Loud Thunder felt only despair: this was the first, it would not be the last. All he had achieved was to give the tribes of the Crown of the World the opportunity to seek blood and vengeance on one another. His task had failed before it was begun.

Close by, someone sniggered. He turned to see Yellow Claw crouched, human, atop a rock. He was grinning broadly and his expression said clearly, *What did you think would happen?*

17

The estuary around Tsokawan had been crawling with River-men, mostly soldiers. Tecumet had emptied her boats into the trees and the channels, so that every time Maniye sighted the fortress she found a maze of spears and crocodile jaws in the way.

They had fallen back deeper into the estuary over the day, spending the night on a narrow island of dry land. Above, the trees strangled the moon. At her elbow, Moon Eye hummed a little dirge that never ended. Maniye wondered how far the angry spirit had gone when it left him.

The next day she let Tecuman take the lead, hoping some instinct would guide him to the fortress another way. They would have lost Moon Eye entirely had Tiamesh not nipped at Maniye's flank and drawn her attention to the man, who was almost out of sight in the morning mist. She Stepped and called to him, and for a moment he was just a dark wolf in a foreign land, paying her no heed. Then he was a big-framed Wolf man, uncertain and off-balance.

'What is it?' she asked him. At her feet, Tecuman dragged his scaled body up the bank and Stepped into a human shape, dry as a bone.

'I thought . . . we should go this way,' Moon Eye said.

Maniye closed some of the distance between them. 'Why?'

'It seemed right.' He was plainly searching through his own mind to find a reason. 'Last night . . .'

'Did the spirit come to you?'

'Last night I dreamt of a song,' Moon Eye told her slowly. 'I was following it, in this place. The song of a snake.'

Maniye frowned. *Why him and not me?* But Moon Eye's mind was like a cave, ever open, always with dangerous, unknowable depths. Perhaps the doorway the angry spirit used was an invitation to others.

She glanced at Tecuman. Here was where the boy's pride would be tested. He had been leading them a secret way to Tsokawan, he said. Maniye guessed he had been leading them nowhere, but clung to the idea because that was better than being a follower. She saw the battle on his face. Something won out over his pride, whether wisdom or curiosity. 'Lead,' he told Moon Eye, making the decision his. Maniye felt herself nod; again, another little sign the boy was willing to become a man. It was a path he would need to travel swiftly.

Moon Eye had no idea where to lead at first, but then it seemed something whispered in his ear and he found his path, picking a way through the estuary from dry island to island, now as wolf and now as man.

Tiamesh found the first ruin, leaping up a rise that was uneven and rough beneath Maniye's feet. It was worked stone, eaten away by water and roots. There was too little there for Maniye to guess what it had been – save that any building of stone in this place must have been a formidable challenge and therefore a significant structure. Maniye was put in mind of her approach to the Shining Halls of the Tiger. The power of her mother's people had been broken a generation before, and the retreat to their stronghold was marked by a trail of burned and fallen places behind them. Was this some similar remnant, a hundred years on?

Her suspicions were confirmed soon after. The route Moon

Eye led them through the jungle was full of stones. They lay half submerged, or rose up amongst the trees, grey-white stumps and stubs. Then Maniye came face to face with a statue, huge-eyed, outstretched arms ending in worn-down stumps, wide mouth crawling with stone serpents. Time had used it badly but there was an ugly power to it nonetheless. It looked a little like the carvings at Tsokawan, but only a little.

Tecuman's face had closed up. Maniye shot him a pointed glance.

'The Serpent has many heads,' was all he would say.

'Is this a trap?'

He didn't know; it was plain on his face. 'There was a cult here once, who walked the Serpent's path with murder. The Stranglers, they were . . .'

'Someone's out there,' Tiamesh murmured.

'What did you see?' Maniye demanded.

'Movement. A person. Pale cloth.' She nodded in the direction they were heading. 'I'll go hunting.'

'No.' Maniye looked at Tecuman again. 'What now, Kasra?'

The title brought him back to himself. 'The estuary is full of darkness,' he said faintly, 'from long ago, from yesterday. We go on, into the darkness.'

There was a tale Maniye knew from the Crown of the World where a young hunter was cast out of his tribe. The names and the reasons varied, but all those stories shared the same soul. The exile would wander, meet strangers, overcome challenges, and at last return to his village to call out the chief or whoever had wronged him. Usually he became chief himself, after that. As a child she had always wondered at it: why would the chiefs and the priests allow such a tale that challenged the way things were? She understood it now: no matter how the chiefs and the priests might want to keep every tomorrow the same as yesterday, sometimes the world called for change. Better to have that path safe in a story, than let that change rip all your laws and bonds when you could no longer hold it in.

And here was Tecuman, the boy-Kasra, cast out from his home and wandering in the company of exotic foreigners, heading into the darkness. And of course the Riverlanders would know that story. They would tell it differently but it would have the same shape.

Then Moon Eye stopped, because ahead was the stone place someone had built out here in the mud.

It had been raised and it had fallen, and the greenery had crept back over the years and tried to reclaim it. It had been grand and spectacular in its day, though, so that something of its grandeur still showed through the vines and moss and fungi, and the whole trees that sprouted from between its shifted stones. It had four walls, all sloping inwards and stepped, so that Maniye could run up its side with ease. Whatever had crowned it had fallen in, though, along with most of the wall that faced them, so that they looked through that broken, tree-lumpy breach into a dark, sunken interior where water ran and gurgled and the air was flecked with hanging clouds of flies.

Maniye could see Tsokawan in this place, but Tsokawan was greater and more elaborate, and somehow tamer. She could see the Shining Halls here, too – another more distant descendant, using lore taken north over how many lifetimes. The sense of *Old* made her legs weak.

And then, even as she thought the word, there was an old, old woman standing there at the breached wall. A woman whose skin had gone pale with age, her head wound with cloth, and rainbow tattoos tracking about her face. Maniye could not remember her name, but Tecuman ran forward, calling, 'Therumit! Therumit Essen Fiel! Do you know me? It is Tecuman, your Kasra!'

He splashed forwards, knee deep, then waist deep in the pool that separated them. Then he Stepped, then did so again, knee deep and human once more, while the Wolves raced about the pool's edge trying to keep up. All the while, old Therumit watched him approach with a stern and forbidding expression.

As he reached the first staggered stones of the ruin, Tecuman slowed. 'Do you not know me?' he asked. His smiled faltered. 'I am Tecuman.' A man who had gone before his people silent and masked, demanding recognition.

'We shall see.' Therumit's voice was without warmth. Abruptly she had turned and gone into the shadow of the broken walls.

Maniye and the others caught up. 'What is this?' she asked.

'The Serpent's will,' Tecuman said, and she heard his voice shake a little. He clambered up to follow after Therumit. Which meant the rest of them had to follow too.

The interior of the ruin had boasted several floors, but they were fallen in, one into another, leaving only dark shelves under the cant of the walls, and a drop into dark water choked with lianas and reaching roots. Maniye eyed the pool beneath uneasily, wondering if the sun ever touched it. Rivulets of water coursed their winding ways through the greenery and the maze of tumbled stone on all sides to converge at that sunken surface, lower than the water of the surrounding estuary. She thought of vast networks of rooms beneath, and what blind things might dwell there.

Therumit was at the far side of the pool, and plainly she expected them to edge around the jagged fringe of surviving stonework to reach her. Tecuman had stopped, looking up at walls that rose around them. Maniye could not make out much of the carving, but there were statues, stylized human figures with bulbous eyes and open mouths, clutching at serpents that encircled their wrists and waists and throats.

'The Stranglers built this place,' the Kasra said softly and, at her enquiring look, he just said, 'In the estuary, the Serpent has many heads.'

Therumit called back, 'Everyone knows the Strangling cult is long buried in time, young Kasra. But they built well and their ruins still hold power.'

'And what will you do with that power, Messenger?' Tecuman asked respectfully.

'Test you.'

He blinked. 'You have said the Serpent means for me to sit on the Daybreak Throne.'

Her pale dry face admitted nothing. 'You are a Kasra without a kingdom, and perhaps the Serpent says now: better a lesser ruler than a land divided.'

Tecuman's fists were clenched. 'But you *said*!'

Therumit gave him a look of contempt. 'Will you stamp? Will you go running to your father, as when you were a boy? Know that a doom is coming, a doom for all the world. How hard, then, to hold a nation together, to be responsible for saving all the peoples from the enemy that threatens? Too hard for you, perhaps. Perhaps it would be best you should not return to Tsokawan.'

Maniye remembered this woman talking offhandedly about killing Tecuman or his sister at birth, and stepped closer to the youth, Tiamesh and Moon Eye at her shoulder. Harming a priest would bring a curse down on her, but she felt she might brave it. She was a Champion, and Therumit reminded her of Kalameshli in all the wrong ways.

But then a humming took up – not Moon Eye, but exactly that sound he had been making the day before. It came from all around them, and something in the pitch and timbre of it sent fear through Maniye, reminding her for some reason of the white-eyed face paint of the Owl Society – something that scared her for reasons she could not explain.

And on the broken shelves above them, she saw figures, men and women, Riverlander and Milk Tear and others she could not name. They were filthy and thin, some naked, others in ragged loincloths or torn robes. Each had a stark red weal about their necks, as though a halter had been rubbing there for a long time. She remembered the word from a moment before. *The Stranglers.*

Tecuman drew a ragged breath. 'You said they were buried.'

'And the Serpent finds all buried things in time, even cast-off skins like this,' Therumit pronounced. 'The Nation is divided. Small wonder that some have sought succour in older ways. Small wonder their minds are open when other voices whisper.'

'Say the word,' Maniye murmured to Tecuman. 'We'll fight or run.' The Stranglers were on all sides but they looked weak and many were unarmed.

Tecuman shook his head. 'What does the Serpent want of me?' he demanded. Therumit had supported his claim; to run from her would be to run from the mantle of Kasra.

'Come here,' the priestess commanded him. 'Kneel.'

'No,' Maniye hissed, but Tecuman straightened, reaching for courage and finding it hiding somewhere inside himself. *At exactly the wrong time.* The Champion was rising in her, sensing her unease and wanting to fight. The humming of the cultists all around her was speeding her heart, making her human shape feel soft and vulnerable. She wanted claws. She wanted teeth.

Yet Tecuman stepped away from her and made his way to Therumit quite humbly.

'Test me,' he told her, looking her in the eye. 'I am the true Kasra of the Sun River Nation. You will see.'

18

The Serpent was moving within Tsokawan, but in such a tangle of coils that Hesprec could not tell which way: all she could see was the knot.

Esumit was telling the clan chiefs the boy was dead, while Tecumet was here with soldiers and boats and *power*. When she had passed onwards, Matsur would follow, step for step, and speak to those same matriarchs and patriarchs, telling them exactly the opposite, singing the praises of the living Tecuman.

Hesprec put her back against the cool stones and closed her eyes, trying to find the Serpent's will within the great heavy structure of the fortress. But if it was that easy, there wouldn't be all of this squabbling.

'All the way to the Crown of the World,' she told the small stone cell around her, a room deep in the maze of the servants' cellars, the floor slick with damp. The Serpent moved in the earth; the ardent priestess could seek guidance in buried places.

'Ardent, or desperate.' The words tasted old on her tongue. She imagined her own voice as it had been when she had been wrinkled and toothless. 'All the way to the Crown of the World, and this is what I come back to.'

She stood, decisively, eyes still shut. 'Do I care, the brother or the sister?' she remarked to her silent, buried god, shaking her head. 'But there are other things I care about, so . . . She placed her palms against the dank stones, fingers digging at the cracks between them. She stayed there for a long time, head bowed.

The Serpent shifted around her; she saw the gleam of its scales in her mind. In its movements she could divine death, atrocity, a terror from the long-ago.

Has it started already? She had a dreadful feeling that she was too late.

She shadowed Matsur as he shadowed Esumit, but she had no words for the clan chiefs, no pronouncements to make on the brother out in the estuary or the sister out on her barge. Hesprec was very aware of the eyes on her: a priestess of the Serpent who had yet to venture an opinion on the succession. Had she been interested in playing king-maker she was ideally placed.

She scowled at herself for thinking it, but the *reason* all this was happening was that they needed the *right* leader. What she had begun to think of as *her* great threat – as though her long pilgrimage in the north had given her some personal claim over it – was so overwhelming that the Sun River Nation must be given the very best of chances to survive it, and that meant the right Kasra on the Daybreak Throne.

She tried to ignore the crippling fear that might of course make the *wrong* decision.

Yet she sensed there was something more, to lead to this division. Why was Tecumet so self-evidently wondrous? Why did Matsur vouch for Tecuman even now, when he had been driven out of his own stronghold and might be no more than bones out in the estuary? Yet there was Matsur Chac Mosen still speaking the boy's name in praise, and Matsur was no fool . . .

So she shadowed Matsur until he had ceased to unpick Esumit's careful stitching. Then she followed him down to the windowless rooms beneath Tsokawan, where he knelt to his own prayers.

He had his eyes closed, but she knew he sensed the touch of her shadow as she darkened the door. He remained still for a long time, and Hesprec fancied he was gathering his strength to battle with her, word against word. She was patient, though, and if he had been drawing out his devotions in the hope she would go away, then . . . well, he knew her better than that.

At last Matsur sighed and shook his head, shifting about until he was sitting on the damp stone floor with his back to the wall. 'Hesprec Essen Skese,' he named her. 'I have been three lives here in the estuary, where you have seldom deigned to tread. Perhaps it is time we knew one another better again.'

She sat beside him, lowering herself gingerly out of respect for her aches and pains – clean forgetting about her bright new body.

'These things are known,' she began, 'none knows all the paths of the Serpent.'

Matsur nodded slowly. 'One might ask why, when you have returned home so full of news, you waste it here rather than taking it to Atahlan where more might hear it.'

'I have wondered just that,' Hesprec agreed. 'And yet we have so many Kasras here; a wealth; an overabundance.' As he sighed again, she added, 'Perhaps I should be speaking with Esumit, whose path has brought the girl to the Daybreak Throne.'

'But here you are.'

'Help me to understand, Matsur. Why are you still pressing the boy's claim, when you don't have the boy?'

Matsur was silent a long while, hands flat to the stones of the floor as he hunted out the presence of anyone nearby. At last he said, 'Because if the boy ascends to the Daybreak Throne he will do what we say.'

'Has there ever been a Kasra not advised by the Serpent?'

'Not the Serpent, *us*,' Matsur said flatly. 'Myself, Therumit. We of the estuary.'

Hesprec felt a worm of fear move in her, because the Serpent did not play *those* games and strangle itself in its own coils. *Am I in danger?* But even if there was some faction that sought to rule, she could not imagine violence between them.

184

Matsur tilted his head back until it rested against the wall. 'We have come across a secret, Hesprec, a terrible one. Only a handful of us know. It is crippling to know this thing, but it could change *everything*.'

'And this doom we see approaching this land. This is part of your secret?'

'Perhaps it is the key to defeating that doom. It could be the key to many things.' Matsur's voice shook, and Hesprec wondered how long the words had been bottled inside him, unable to escape. 'Hesprec, I know you are wise: you watch when it is time to watch, you strike when it is time to strike.'

'And *you* flatter.'

'Would you come into the estuary, if I asked?'

'Is it the Serpent's path that takes me there?' *I should not have to ask*, she considered, *but this is something new. Who is it that speaks to me, through Matsur's mouth?*

Even as she thought it, Matsur's reply was a passionate, 'It is! More than anything we have done these last five lives and more. It is . . . I will send to Therumit. I will tell her I have opened to you. And when you have seen what we have seen, you can go to Atahlan with your warnings and your travels, but with our secret too. And perhaps it will be you that leads us all on the Serpent's true path, when the doom comes.'

The vote of confidence was probably intended to reassure her, perhaps to recruit her. For Hesprec, all the words brought were an increase to her already turbulent disquiet.

Kalameshli Takes Iron prowled about the edges of his domain.

The warband, Spear Catcher and the others, seemed content. There was food and drink and, although there were southern soldiers keeping an eye on them, they were not overly worried. They had all decided the River People were soft.

And they *were* soft, but it was a softness that spread like a disease. Kalameshli had spent his long-ago childhood having the tenets of the Wolf beaten into him, and his adult years beating those same tenets into others. The Wolf did not make his people comfortable and complacent. The Wolf made them swift and strong through a life of running and fighting.

But here there was no need to hunt or protect what they had, and when Kalameshli spoke of the Wolf the others all nodded and looked solemn, but he could see the rot eating them from the inside out.

It was worse when he thought of *her*.

Of all the children he had whipped in his life, he had whipped her the hardest. Of all the unwilling students, she had been least willing. But she had been most important. He saved his greatest efforts for his own child.

That had been the project of his latter years: his daughter, got on a Tiger mother, and so vulnerable to outside influences right from her birth. He had worked so hard to force her to learn, to slap the Wolf into her. She could have been something great . . .

He paused then, for surely Maniye *was* something great – she was a Champion. Her people had never had a Champion before, or even realized they were lacking one. *But whose Champion is she?* That shape she took was not just a grand wolf – there was tiger and bear and other beasts rolled into that shape. And how had she come by such a transformation? Under the ministrations of the Serpent Hesprec.

Kalameshli had been forced to travel alongside Hesprec Essen Skese. He had seen his protégée, his daughter, choose the Serpent's advice over the words of the Wolf. He had seen his child swayed by that creature who looked like just a dark slip of a girl, yet had been an old man in the shadow of Kalameshli's knife not so long before.

And if only I had struck sooner! Maniye had made the rescue of Hesprec her first act of rebellion, the act that started to sever her from the Wolf.

And now, here we are . . . ' Half guests, half prisoners, far from home in this hot, dry, fish-smelling place. Maniye was out there

186

in the murk with that useless boy-chief, that weak child who was alive only because he stood on the shoulders of others.

Kalameshli Stepped and hunted through the halls and rooms of this huge stone tomb until his nose told him he had found somewhere private. There he built up the stones he had brought with him until he had something like a wolf's head – if he squinted and stretched his imagination. He set a fire within it, and heated a knife blade until he could smell the hot iron – Wolf's secret.

He had such plans for Maniye. There were rituals and ordeals for her. She needed to become iron's sister, so that she could carry it with her Stepped. How much more formidable would her Champion be then? But the chance was slipping between her fingers. Soon she would care for nothing but the whispering of this Serpent priestess; she would forget the Wolf and the north.

Kalameshli told the flames that *this* was what he cared for. It was not that his daughter was being taken from him. Priests had no offspring, only their god and their duties. He crouched before his little fire and stared into it, looking for a vision. What was the Wolf's way to free Maniye from the tightening coils about her?

There is only one way. The words came to his mind, and he did not know whether they were the Wolf's or his own. *Or perhaps we are in perfect agreement.*

He would cut away those coils with an iron knife. He remembered how he had first seen Hesprec: that pallid old man ready for the Wolf's jaws. *I drew your teeth then.* Since then, the Serpent had shed its skin and grown new fangs, but he – she – was young and small-framed, and went about Tsokawan alone.

Staring into the fire, Kalameshli was struck by the perfect pattern to it. Hesprec the Serpent had not escaped the Wolf; that had just been the start of a long hunt that would end here.

I will shed your blood in your own stronghold. And even if they kill me for it, I will have freed Maniye from you.

★

After he had scattered the ashes of his fire, he went in search of aid.

The warband would do what he wished, he knew. Without Maniye here to gainsay him, Spear Catcher and the rest knew the Wolf, and knew his priest. They were unsubtle, though. Unless Kalameshli planned full-scale war, he would need to hide his hand.

But there were a pair who came and went as they pleased, skulking unseen in every shadow and behind every chair. He had them sent for and sat them down before him, scowling at them ferociously to make them sure he had no time for their foolish jokes. Sathewe, the Coyote girl, and the addled Crow, Feeds on Rags. That he had to rely on such leavings was a bitter mark of how far he had fallen, but the Wolf tested a man many ways.

'There is a Serpent in this place,' he told them,

'There are many Serpents, O priest.' Rags was squinting at him from one eye, in that annoying way the Eyriemen had.

'You know the one,' Kalameshli snapped at him. 'The creature that came south with us.'

The pair exchanged glances. Yes, they knew.

'Set aside your mischief and watch her. Most of all, find her when she is alone.'

The Crow and the Coyote exchanged a troubled glance. But they were afraid of him, and so they would do what he said.

19

Lone Mountain had traded with the Wetbacks in better years than this. Of all his people, only he could come to their village without sending them fleeing for the water. They called him Great Coyote in jest, because he loved to talk trade and news; because he was a good guest. Of course, they called him Whale Eater too, because he had a Bear's appetite.

He would not be trading with the Wetbacks any more. Lone Mountain Stepped onto his two human feet and surveyed the ruin of the Seal village.

He remembered what Sees More had said, and here he found the proof. There were no bodies now, just bones that had been fought over by the fox and the gull. The houses of hide and whalebone had been treated just as the man had said, cut apart with no respect for the shape and craft of how they were made. Some of the skulls were divided in the same way.

Lone Mountain stood looking around at the devastation, knowing only that he was too late to learn any more truths from it. The keening of gulls overhead sounded the last lament for a people who had neither present nor future.

He cast his gaze past the shore at the waves, remembering what Sees More had said. *They came from the sea.* Facing that great expanse of water brought a shiver to Lone Mountain. He squared his shoulders and tried to stare it down, but the sea was endless, depths unknown, monsters undreamt of.

He thought he saw dots bobbing there, far out. Seals. Were they Stepped or just mute brothers? He wasn't about to swim out there to ask them their story.

The Wetbacks were only one tribe of the Seal, of course. Sees More had said some of his people had gone begging at other hearths. South along the coast were the Tide Born, another village he had traded with in past days, and so he Stepped and began lumbering along the shore, his thick hide and fat shielding him from the cold breath that came off the sea.

Bones; bones and ruin. Time had worn down the sharp edges of the horror Sees More had described. Gulls and crabs had cleaned away the gore, until this could be just one more place of death, and his tale just a madman's raving. Lone Mountain gripped his burgeoning fear and forced himself to master it.

That night he slept as a bear, huddled in a cleft between rocks with the sound of the sea in his ears. He slept poorly. Towards morning, when the moon was down and a pall of mist had rolled out from the shore towards the mountains, he heard other sounds across the great expanse of water: roaring and rumbling, as though from a beast made of equal parts rage and thunder. He huddled low and looked out: through the mist there were strange lights that owed nothing to any fires he understood.

He found the seals the next morning.

They were up on the beach, a score or so of them, lying on the sand in the early morning or else shrugging along through the breakers with their awkward slumping gait. Mountain was a bear when he came across them, and he expected them to all go slithering into the sea as he approached.

But they stayed where they were, staring at him with their big, round eyes. Some of them honked and called urgently, but not in fear of him. They watched him draw closer until he could have broken into a sudden run and taken them in his teeth. He came closer still, and they continued to stare, until he was spooked by them. By these seals that were not acting like seals.

Are they scared to go into the water? he wondered, but it was more than that. They were fixed on him, calling to him. *Are they trying to speak to me?*

Are they seals or Seals?

He Stepped, showing them his human face. 'What is it?' he asked of them. 'Tell me what?'

But they remained seals, even though they clustered close to him, the cacophony of their cries becoming nightmarish. Seal mouths gaped, seal throats shuddered as they forced the sounds out.

As though they were trying to speak.

Abruptly a terror swept through Lone Mountain and he recoiled from the babbling throng. He did not want to listen to those voices. He did not want to look into those liquid eyes, in case he saw a human awareness trapped in there that could not make itself known. He Stepped and he ran, leaving the desperate chorus of the seals behind him. He had come to find out, and yet he did not want to know.

He had always known his mute brothers *were* his brothers – the souls of his people reborn as animals, which would in due course be reborn as human once again. But humans could Step and speak, while their mute brothers could not. And there was no halfway point, no moment when the animal shape became a prison for the human soul.

He told himself again and again that it could not happen.

Late that day he came to the village of the Tide Born.

Unlike the Wetbacks' home, it had not been broken apart and dissected and carpeted with bones, but it seemed empty. The fires were cold ash, the boats were drawn up on the shore. In each hut were all the precious tools and toys and garments of a Seal tribe family. Yet of the Tide Born, there were none.

He found some dried fish there and chewed on it thoughtfully, staring out at the sea. Searching for answers, he just found more questions.

Stepping to carry on down the coast, he smelled smoke.

191

He let his bear nose lead him, tracking slowly between the huts of the Tide Born, then beyond them to where a jut of rocks had hidden the fire from his view. As he came round the side of the crag he found a bone spear-point pointing straight at his nose. It was a remarkably welcome sight, after all he had seen, to come eye-to-eye with some live Seal.

He Stepped, hands open to show them two things: that he meant them no harm; that he was easily too big and strong to be afraid of their little spear. Here at last was one little family of the Seal. It was a relief to see human faces after all this time. He saw one woman, one girl who must be on the very point of being tested, and three smaller children. All they had was their fire, and a sack of possessions. They looked half starved and weary almost to death.

'I am a traveller who has come far,' said Lone Mountain, keeping his voice soft and easy. 'I would welcome the chance to share your fire.' There was etiquette for this, amongst the Bears, and if he had been coming to a Seal village he would talk with various old women and strong hunters before they offered him guest-right, but this impoverished hearth had been stripped down to that one question.

The woman sized him up, and he saw her understand that, if he wanted to take what she had, she could not have stopped him. 'Share our fire,' she said. At least, as guest, he was bound not to harm his hosts.

He settled himself, shared a little food with them, let the silence set in as the children stared. The Seal woman was Salt Fire. She did not offer the names of the children, and Mountain was not even sure they were hers.

At last, judging the time right, he said, 'I come in search of the Tide Born.'

'As do we.' Salt Fire did not ask why a Bear had come so far. He had the sense she had learned so many terrible things in the recent past that she had ceased to ask new questions.

'You are Wetback?' he tried.

192

She shook her head. 'Tomorrow, we will go to them. We have nowhere else.'

A cold weight grew in Lone Mountain's stomach. 'Do not go to the Wetbacks.'

Salt Fire stared at him.

'I am come from their village. They do not dwell there any more. I had thought they came here, those . . . those that lived.'

She was trembling, ever so slightly. The others, the girl, the children, were utterly silent, watching him or watching nothing.

'Which tribe are you?' Lone Mountain prompted.

'I come from the Stone Breakers,' she said hollowly, and Mountain nodded. They were a larger Seal tribe, living on a bluff down the coast. They were his next hearth to call upon, though he had seldom gone so far south and knew few faces there.

'Tell me of the Stone Breakers,' he said.

She shook her head. 'There are no Stone Breakers.'

'Tell me.'

'A doom came from the sea and destroyed them, unmade them. A doom came to dwell in the village of the Stone Breakers and cast white shadows over their hearths.'

Lone Mountain grimaced. 'Please, just tell me what you saw.'

'I *am* telling you!' she snapped at him furiously. 'What do you think I'm doing? A white shadow is on my people's home. My people are dead or gone to the sea.'

'But who?'

'Hollow men. Hollow men hungry for souls.' And then the smallest child began to cry. Salt Fire took him to her and held him close.

The dark had come on by then, and the fire was guttering. Loud Thunder wondered about doing without it, but the children were shivering, so he went down the beach looking for driftwood left dry by the tide.

With five sticks under his arm he heard the sound from out across the sea, that same mournful howl as the night before.

Some beast was moving across the water, invisible in the dark. He heard the panicked cries of the children and the voice of Salt Fire trying to calm them.

Lone Mountain Stepped, and the night air had a reek on it, like something burnt and rotten at the same time. He growled, and on the face of the waters the beast growled back, a sound vast enough that his own little threat vanished into it. It sounded closer now.

The Seal children were crying out now, over and over, and Salt Fire as well. Mountain wanted to go to them but movement would draw the attention of the monster in the water. Lone Mountain felt fear in him and he fought it as a bear fights anything, mauling and cuffing and gnawing at it to bring it under his control.

In his ears, the growling was louder, and he saw some great low shape in the water, passing closer to shore with its rumbling, hungry bellow. He thought he saw men riding it, or things that wore the shapes of men.

The voices of the Seals were suddenly further away. He realized they were in the water now, because when danger threatened that was what Seals did. But the children . . . children couldn't Step. Children couldn't survive the cold sea. He heard the voice of a seal, calling and calling, and answered only by the echo. He heard no human voices, and thought of the greedy swell of the receding tide. He told himself, *One cry from the children and I will go, I will brave all the terrors of the sea.* But there was only that single animal call, the seal calling out in anguish that could no longer find words. It grew further and further, searching out to sea for something that would never be found.

And then the howling beast was growing further away, its work done. Lone Mountain ran back to the camp, but the fire was dead and Salt Fire and her children were gone. The rolling backs of the waves bore no bobbing heads or floating bodies. Lone Mountain was left only with the echo of a terror that had driven her to something unthinkable.

In the morning, Lone Mountain knew he had a choice. He could go home now, and tell Mother what he knew – or could guess. This would be the coward's option. Or he could go to the village of the Stone Breakers and see where these hollow men had made their home and cast their 'white shadow'. Every part of him, body and mind, recoiled from the idea. Every part except that part which made him Lone Mountain. His image of himself was of a man who dared, and so he would dare.

The Stone Breaker village was on a bluff that jutted out into the sea, with a broad beach either side for their boats. The village itself, with steep rock on three sides, was defendable enough to hold off raiders from Wolf or Tiger or Bear. With dense forest cloaking the mountain foothills close by, the Seal had built with wood as well as hide and bone, making something grander and more permanent than their cousins elsewhere. Within the bluff itself, the combined efforts of the high tide and the Stone Breakers themselves had carved out caves that gave swift access to the ocean. Lone Mountain wondered whether these had been their downfall in the end.

Salt Fire said a white shadow had fallen on the place. She had spoken no more than the truth. Lone Mountain peered from the shelter of the trees, trying to make sense of what he was seeing. There were walls of something pale that shimmered and gleamed in the sunlight. The whole village was surrounded by them. From the look of it, many of the huts within had been destroyed, and the remainder were hung and strung with more white, making a labyrinth of angles so that his eyes watered to look at it.

Abruptly it was clear to him, as if he had been staring long at a cloud and then suddenly seen it had the shape of a familiar beast. The white wall about the perimeter and within it the confusing riot of shapes taking a kind of rigid, alien order. He knew now what it meant.

But as to *who* had raised it . . . From the trees he could not see them well – within the whiteness they were just grey shadows. Some were walking on the beach, though, and he crept forwards with that surprising quiet bears have, to get a better look.

They had two legs and two arms, and faces with eyes and noses. When they opened their mouths, sounds came out as though they were trying to speak. They were clad in outlandish garments: some wore metal that looked like the Wolf's iron. Some carried rods as though they were priests. Some were pale as fishbellies and others dark as southerners. And they were hollow, quite hollow. Looking on them, Lone Mountain felt that he could peer into them, but not into that *inside* which contained bone and guts. He could tear them open with his claws and never uncover the void he saw in them. But he saw it nonetheless. They walked and they made sounds, but they had no souls. It was just as Sees More had said. He could almost feel that emptiness tugging at him.

Puppets, then; some mockery of people formed from magic. Except, as he crouched and watched, he heard them make their speech-noises, and listen to each other and reply, just as if they were talking. Lone Mountain knew the different voices and accents of Rivermen and Plains Men – even Stone People. This, though – this was not language.

Even so, looking at their encampment, Mountain felt he could read their intentions. They were making plans to change the land around them, to extend their white shadow over it. He needed to get closer. For all his fear was screaming at him, he needed to *understand*.

He was a bear, and these hollow men seemed fragile. Perhaps if he took one and tore into it as they had served the Wetbacks, he might understand then. He hunched, inching forwards, and there was a sound behind him, a very deliberate intake of breath made solely to draw his notice. A chill went through Lone Mountain and he wheeled swiftly.

A woman crouched there, sharp-featured and wearing a long

coat of deer hide studded with bronze. A true woman, with a soul and a shape to Step into – in contrast to the hollow creatures of the compound her humanity was blazingly evident. She had placed herself outside easy claw-reach, and she had knives in her hands in case that was not enough. Under each eye she bore two slanted scars.

Carefully, Thunder moved deeper into the trees, and she shadowed him, maintaining a precise distance. When Stepped, she cocked an eyebrow at him.

'I know you, Cave Dweller. You are Lone Mountain. You came to the Shining Halls once.'

He nodded. 'And you, Tiger?'

'Keheacha.'

They regarded each other silently for a moment, each trying to see into the mind of the other. At last Lone Mountain spoke.

'What do your people know of these creatures?'

'Rumours of something from the sea.' She shook her head. 'I must tell my queen: no more raiding the Stone Breakers. But if the Cave Dwellers have come to see, then there is more?'

'There are two dead villages, two dead tribes, north up the coast from here,' he confirmed to her. 'But nothing like this. This is the nest of the hollow men.'

'I spoke to a Coyote two days back. He came to trade with the Seal and was eating his own trail as fast as he could,' Keheacha revealed. 'He said they are the Plague People.' Her voice faltered on the name, just slightly.

'I think they *are* the Plague People,' Lone Mountain confirmed.

'But that means this is the end of the world,' the Tiger said.

He shrugged, because some things were too big to speculate about.

'You're quiet for a Cave Dweller,' Keheacha observed. 'Not quiet enough to hide from me, but quiet, still.'

'Is that an invitation?'

She gave a tense smile. 'I am of the Fire Shadow People, and night is my time. I will go to these Plague People and teach them that, tonight. What there is to know of them, I will know. Perhaps I will put a halter on one, and drag it back to the Shining Halls.'

'And if the hollow men try to stop you?'

'Then having a Cave Dweller at my back won't hurt,' she told him.

They waited until darkness drew in, expecting the hollow men to light their fires and set their watches. Instead, a pallid, unnatural light suffused the creatures' camp, spreading a cold glow across what had been the Stone Dwellers' bluff so that the white shadow walls they had thrown up were no less white under the stars.

Keheacha scowled, but she Stepped nonetheless, becoming a striped cat that was almost immediately lost in the shadows of the forest. She crept forwards, and Lone Mountain followed her scent.

The land from the edge of the trees to that pale shadow was rocky and uneven, and Keheacha slunk from shadow to shadow, creeping up the gradient from darkness to that steady, eerie glow. Mountain followed at a distance and to one side, wondering if she was using him as a distraction. What watch had the hollow men set?

He realized he had no idea what they could do to him. He did not understand what they had done to the Seal people, save that they had killed some, for reasons he could not guess. The fear, which leaguing with Keheacha had briefly dispelled, was back in his heart. He stared at the white shadow walls, seeing only darker shadows move behind them.

Then he saw a more familiar shadow, as the Tiger scout crawled on her belly between him and that light, and he followed her around, silent as he could. He wondered if the hollow men were blinded by their own lights.

Keheacha had stopped, and he saw her raise a paw and try it against the wall, finding it proof against her. Her claws snagged, and she fought briefly before she came free. Mountain was about to move in, when she was darting back, ducking into cover. He saw a mouth open in the white wall, and two hollow men come out.

One held a pale ball of light in his – no, her – hand. It was a hollow woman, dark like a Riverman but squatter, as though she had been formed from clay. Beside her was a man of similar build and hue. The hungry emptiness of them tugged at Lone Mountain's soul, even as far away as he was. It must be far worse for the Tiger.

Beyond them, the interior of their walled-off world was a blaze of that icy light.

He saw movement from Keheacha, creeping forward again. Whatever the powers of the hollow men were, they had not spotted her. Mountain heard their strangled nonsense voices.

Perhaps the Tiger was going to dart in, snatch one and haul the creature away in her jaws. The thought of having whatever was *inside* such a monster flood into his mouth made Lone Mountain feel sick. Surely everything about them would be poison.

But she was creeping forward; perhaps she did not care.

A moment later, the hollow creatures were moving away, obligingly putting distance between them and their white walls. They walked without caution as though they were proof against all the world. They were coming directly for Lone Mountain and the light the hollow woman bore was already falling on him. He felt it on his skin and in his soul, like sand under his eyelids.

And yet they did not see him. He was just another rock to them, and Keheacha was stalking behind them. Their babbling voices went on and on. He wondered if they had heard real human words once, and were trying to imitate them.

Then they were too close, and he saw the moment they registered the rock they walked towards had eyes and teeth.

Then their faces twisted, and their fear was not like their speech. He could understand it perfectly. He rose up onto his hind legs and bellowed at them, roaring defiantly at the unnatural absence in the heart of them,

Keheacha sprang, knocking them both down. She had her
teeth on the hollow woman's arm, clamped tight, so that the cold
light spilled from the creature's grip to rattle on the ground. The
hollow man stumbled up, and Mountain cuffed it, half expecting the creature to shatter but instead feeling the solid contact of
flesh.

There were alien cries from the white shadow, and more of
them were coming, but Keheacha had her hold and was hauling
it away despite the creature's struggles. Lone Mountain turned
to fight whatever was sent out after them from the camp,
whether hollow warrior or howling sea monster.

Something like a swift wind passed him, and he felt an
unseen hand pluck at his pelt. Keheacha screamed.

He whirled back towards her. He saw her as a tiger, letting go
her quarry and convulsing on her side, then she was a woman
clutching at her leg, which was laid open as though a sword had
sheared through the muscle there.

'Take the creature!' she yelled. 'Bring it to the Shining Halls!'
Lone Mountain was lumbering towards her, when something
stepped into the pool of chill light the hollow woman had
dropped.

It was another of their kind, but its face was one that Mountain knew. It was a grey face with dead white eyes. It was the
death mask of the Owl Society, in remembrance of their ancient
enemy.

Keheacha snarled at him, brandishing her knife, and Mountain saw another wound appear in her shoulder, splintering the
bronze and piercing the leather to tear out a chunk of her. She
yelled and drew back. Lone Mountain was backing up as well,
forced away by a palpable wave of dread. He could not have
done anything else in that moment. A great invisible wave was
rolling over him and he felt it eating into his mind. It had its
teeth in him, trying to devour everything that was Bear,

200

everything that was Lone Mountain. To stand before it would be to go mad with terror, to flee in the only directions left to him, into lands from which there was no return.

Keheacha was a tiger again, yowling, limping and stumbling. For a moment her proud soul was blazing in her eyes, furious and defiant. And then that power overcame her and something intangible left her, so that a wounded tiger hissed and spat before the hollow man, and nothing more. She bared her teeth furiously, and those featureless eyes saw only a beast when they looked on her.

Another wound opened spontaneously, punching in her ribs, and yet another still in her side. The animal that had been Keheacha gave out a long, high cry, and died.

That unreadable gaze turned on Lone Mountain, but he was retreating further and further. Although the soullessness of the creature reached for him, he was already loping for the treeline as fast as he could, because daring only went so far.

He was already past the first trees when something struck him a tremendous blow to the haunch, a spear-head of pain burying itself in his body and his soul. He let out a terrible bellow of hurt and fear, but he never slowed.

20

Stripped to the waist, Tecuman knelt before Therumit. His head was bowed and one hand flat to his temples, a show of hiding himself from the sky as the Serpent priests hid themselves.

'What's this then?' Tiamesh asked suspiciously. Whatever it was, her tone implied, it was un-Wolf-like.

Maniye's eyes were narrow as she tried to eavesdrop on the old priestess's words while she instructed Tecuman.

Moon Eye bared his teeth and hawked up a throatful of spittle, then thought better of it.

Whatever this place was, it had power. It was like the Stone Place back in the north, or the hill where . . . *That's it.* Maniye understood what was happening. She knew because she had been tested in the same way, though not for the same purpose.

Walk away; stay clear. That was her immediate response. No good would come of meddling in these matters, if she *could* even meddle. She was no priestess, and this was not her land.

But I am a Champion. It was supposed to mean something. Nobody had been around to tell her what her duties were. She had only the new soul within her to be guided by – its desires and urges. It was urging her to act, now. It thought that to run, to fight, to *oppose* was always the answer. Perhaps in the north it would have been, but here, in this half-drowned, half-parched country, things were so *complicated.*

In the end it was Therumit who decided her. Maniye knew

the Serpent priests commanded vast respect from the southerners, but she didn't *like* Therumit. And she was supposed to be Tecuman's guardian. She was supposed to go with him.

'You two keep watch,' she told her Wolves. 'Any of these scarnecks get close, you give me a shake.' *And I don't know if that will help, but what else can I say?*

Moon Eye gave a questioning grunt and she just shook her head. It was beyond her to explain it.

As Therumit's voice whispered in the Kasra's ear, telling him of the land he would walk in, so Maniye sat and put her back against the dank, moss-slick stones, and searched within herself for the path that would take her to the Godsland.

And if the Serpent is listening and hasn't forgotten me, then trace a path to where I need to go to earn my thanks. She thought about the way that sounded, and added, *Remember how I saved Hesprec?* That deed had been paid for already. But, when you're in another tribe's shadow, no harm in reminding their chief how you helped them once.

She closed her eyes and tried to still her body, letting the tide of her heart lift her like a boat and carry her to that dark place. She built a picture of how it had looked: the tall hills each with their gods, the Wolf and all those lesser wolf-like gods, the Tiger and its cats. And somewhere, beyond that country she had seen, the gods stretched on, less and less like her totems until, somewhere, there would be . . .

Not a hill, but a pool. Not her uplands but a landscape like the estuary, where the play of fireflies against the all-shrouding canopy stood in for the stars she had seen before.

All around her was a great, watchful silence, and she knew the eyes of many gods were fixed on her. Some vast bulk shifted in the dark of a nearby pool, and she saw a shiny dome of shell as great as a house breach the surface. A head rose on a snake-like neck and gaped at her, the edges of its hooked beak sharp and savage enough to sever day from night.

She backed away from it, almost falling into another pool as

203

she did so. She turned to find another pair of beady, hostile eyes watching from the waterline.

They didn't look like crocodiles, though they were armoured in scales.

She knew she could not Step; here in the Godsland she could only go on her two human feet, her souls walking in her shadow like an invisible entourage.

A thought struck her. All the beasts here were gods, but the Champion was special, not bound by the same laws. The daring of her idea rose in her and she called quickly, letting her voice sound in the ears of the surly reptilian gods.

'Come,' she tried again, hoping that it was not bound to the north, as the Wolf and the Tiger were. 'Come, surely a Champion goes where it wills?'

She felt his breath on the back of her neck as he stepped out of her shadow. His flank pushed her aside slightly as he came to stand before her, a reminder of the vast strength he had.

She looked into his great eyes where the light of the fireflies collected. He stood before her vaster than a bear, as padfoot-silent as a tiger, more ferocious than any wolf. What was she thinking? Would he pick her up in his mouth like a cub?

But the Champion valued action and boldness, and so she took hold of his great shaggy hide and hauled herself up until she sat astride his shoulders, as though he were a horse.

From that vantage she scanned the gloomy world around them, hoping for inspiration . . . For a moment her eyes tricked her into seeing a rainbow gleam, as though some long, sinuous and many-coloured body was reflected in a chain of pools leading off towards the horizon.

'There,' she told her soul, and felt his body tense beneath her, muscles like iron sliding over each other as he bunched to spring.

And then he was running, and she let out a great whoop of joy without meaning it, unable to keep the feeling within her.

How she would miss this when she woke, for no living human being ever rode such a beast in the daylight world.

The land fled past them on all sides: murky pools and the shadows of the estuary's trees, night piled on night by the overarching canopy. Then she saw Tecuman ahead. It must be him; no other being here took human shape. He stood at the edge of a lake vast enough that all she could see past its shore was the fireflies reflected in rippling water. She had expected to find the boy cowering, but he was straight-backed and proud, gazing on the depthless water as though it was some great source of pride. And she realized that he saw this land differently: it was his land, the home of his gods. She only found it hostile because she did not belong.

Tecuman was waiting, staring out across the water, and when the Champion hung its muzzle over his shoulder, he did not see them. His hands moved and she saw gold and pearls and amber glint there, to slip through his fingers and strike ripples from the water.

An offering, she realized. He had conjured these things from his mind because that was the proper form for his god.

She had heard of other offerings to Old Crocodile. After all, the Wolf liked a meal of human flesh once in a while, so why not the long-mouthed god of the river?

Why not, indeed?

She froze. The voice came to her mind and plainly not to Tecuman's for he continued to stare off across the dark expanse of the water. She felt the Champion's hackles rise and it backed away, head low and baring its teeth at something in the darkness.

She let her eyes feel their way, until she saw that what she had taken for a ridge of the bank was a vast body, half in and half out of the water. She could have lain comfortably – briefly! – along the inside of its jaws, and its eyes glimmered with their own greenish light.

Why do you come here, little stranger? Old Crocodile's voice was deep and rich, constantly on the point of an avuncular chuckle.

Maniye made a vague motion towards the oblivious Tecuman. 'To help him.'

Old Crocodile made a low, croaky noise in the great bladder of his throat. *Come down, little stranger. Let the earth know you.*

'Why?' she asked, not at all happy to get closer to those teeth.

For this is my home, and you place yourself above me. His head shifted a little on the muddy ground, watching her through one half-closed eye. *Do you know no respect, at your hearth?*

She slipped down unhappily, wondering how fast crocodile gods could move. Could she could claim guest-right from him? And how, given the only food they could share was probably herself?

What do they call you, little stranger? The great creature's voice was soft and pleasant.

'Many Tracks.'

Old Crocodile gave that croaky rumble again: a laugh. *Come closer, for my ears are the least of my senses.*

She had the impression that Tecuman was holding his own conversation with his god that she was not permitted to hear. She took a deep breath and one step forward. 'I am here to speak for my – my friend.'

There are no lies in my kingdom, Old Crocodile reprimanded her mildly. *He is no friend. He comes to plead for my blessing but his sister is on my back with many boats, while he flees through my teeth. I have snapped up many fish like this boy, so small I hardly tasted them.*

Maniye opened her mouth, hunting for something she could say about Tecuman. Old Crocodile was right, she did not know him. Before the attack he had been a mask on a throne. After, he had been a burden, brought up for a life of masks and fancy chairs. *He tries,* she thought, because Tecuman had not just stood on his privilege and made demands. He was working so very hard to overcome his own limitations, but he was no hunter, and never would be.

Well . . . ? Old Crocodile prompted, and she saw he was closer to her than before, though she was sure he had not moved.

'He . . .' Abruptly her mind was blank, and she reached desperately for something, anything. *Serpent, help me,* but the Serpent had already brought her here, and whether that was a good thing or not remained to be seen. *Wolf . . .* but Wolf worked his followers like iron, to make them strong. He did not *help*.

'Asmander,' she got out.

Hmm? Old Crocodile shifted again, an idle movement that still brought his jaws closer to her.

'Asmander loves him,' she said. 'Asmander, your Champion, he'd die for Tecuman. And I don't know him, you're right. He's no friend of mine, just some River boy, but I know Asmander. If Asmander values him so highly then he must be worth something. Worth giving a chance to.'

Old Crocodile blinked lazily and gave that croak of a laugh again. *Asmander betrayed you, did he not?*

No point asking a god how he knew anything. 'No,' she told that gleaming eye. 'He remained loyal to Tecuman. He was never mine.'

Without warning, Old Crocodile was in motion, and her whole world was full of the gape of those jaws, enough to swallow the sun. She fell back with a cry, landing between the Champion's paws as it snarled its tiny threat into the depths of hungry darkness that made up Old Crocodile's throat.

Then with a surge of water the god was returning to its lake, laughing at her. The displaced waves washed over her, and with a start she was back in the ruin of the Stranglers, flailing out and being helped up by Moon Eye.

'What was *that*?' Tiamesh asked, plainly unimpressed by the whole business. Maniye clutched for that sense of the down-to-earth. She did not relish being in the company of gods. She did not like their sense of humour.

207

'Tecuman,' she said, and looked for him, afraid Therumit would already have a knife in him or a cord around his neck. Instead, the youth was standing up, stepping back from the priestess, and there was a definite new pride in him, just as she had seen in the Godsland. Whatever had passed between him and Old Crocodile – and whether or not anything Maniye had done had helped – it had ended well for him.

'Name me,' he addressed the old priestess.

Therumit regarded him through narrowed eyes and said nothing.

'Name me,' Tecuman insisted. 'Speak the judgement of Old Crocodile.'

But Maniye did not like the way Therumit stood, the way she looked at the boy.

'I had thought,' the priestess said softly, 'that the estuary would swallow you.'

'And now you see the truth,' Tecuman told her. He was practically strutting, chest thrown out and head high. The tension all around them was tightening and tightening, but the Kasra was blind to it. 'Old Crocodile has seen that I will be a great Kasra.'

'What he has seen is potential.' Therumit abruptly seemed old, like Hesprec had been old when the Wolves had taken him and thrown him in the pit. 'But Tecumet holds the river. We tried to give you the Sun River Nation, but my kin in Atahlan were stronger, in the end . . .'

She sat on a spur of rubble, seeming exhausted, and Tecuman rose to approach her. 'But I passed the test. I will be Kasra.' Maniye saw him hesitate. 'You . . . thought I'd fail.'

Therumit nodded tiredly. 'Of course. Because Tecumet has the river and Tsokawan. I wanted to have been *wrong*.' Her eyes flashed angrily as she looked up at him, and all the wretched cultists around them shivered and shifted. 'You think this is about who rules the river? There is far more at stake than that. You could have been our Kasra, guided by us, to achieve what we need to achieve.' Her claw-like hands shook, clutching at air. 'I am afraid your sister will be Kasra.'

'But Old Crocodile—'

'Old Crocodile must bend to Serpent sometimes. And the Nation needs one Kasra. It should have been you, for you were ours as your sister never will be. But it will be her, and so the world has no use for you any more.'

Maniye was Stepping even as the priestess said the words. She saw the flash of the knife's obsidian blade as Therumit cut up at Tecuman's throat. The point bit his chin and gouged up his cheek as he fell back. Then she had him by the throat with one gnarled hand, and the knife had come back for another strike.

Maniye lunged forwards, but the wasted starvelings all around were dropping down on her with knives and clubs, with rocks or their bare hands. She charged into them, and they were weak and broke beneath her feet, but she felt she had run into thick mud: even torn open they were clinging to her. She felt their dull blades, their nails, the bite of their teeth. Furious, she shook herself, sending them slamming into the crumbling walls or arcing out into that sunken central pool, But there were more of them, like a filthy tide running down the walls. She heard Moon Eye's voice lifted in a dirge as he leapt past her, bloody hatchet leaving a red wake behind it.

Therumit was fighting to get her blade into her victim. She had gashed his shoulder, but he struggled and twisted in her grip, somehow without striking at her or using his young strength to break her grasp. Then Tiamesh was there, sliding as a wolf between the legs of the throng and then leaping up, ripping the priestess's crooked fingers from the boy's throat, holding back the knife.

The knife-hand became a serpent's head with stone-shard teeth; the arm became the long, coiling loops of its body. Therumit melted into the shape of the Serpent and lashed her coils about Tiamesh's body and neck. As the huntress struggled with the choking loops, Therumit's head drew back, hanging above her like a hawk, and then struck, sinking her fangs into the wolf woman's arm. Tiamesh gave out a high, shocked cry and fell back, the weight of the snake pouring off her.

Tecuman had backed up, but now a handful of the Strangler cultists had him in their grip. And there was Therumit, human once more, stalking towards him with the knife in her hand.

Maniye was awash with cultists. They clung to her pelt, they rode her back, they snarled her limbs and filled her mouth with their flesh. Under her feet they were crocodiles and the slippery bodies of toads and lizards. She saw Moon Eye fighting, human still, and lurched towards him, dragging her coat of bodies. She got her jaws into the arm of one opponent and flung the wretched man away with a toss of her head. Moon Eye finished the other, and then he was rushing for Therumit, virtually walking on the backs of the cult to get there.

The priestess turned and smiled like a death's head. What she said did not reach Maniye's ears, but Moon Eye stopped dead and started shaking, the cords of his neck standing out, his hands crooked into claws. The angry spirit was suddenly in him, filling his body, leaking from him at every joint. Moon Eye's mouth opened and the spirit howled and cried through his lips, spitting blood where he had chewed at his tongue.

He turned to face Maniye, and she would have preferred that whatever looked out through his eyes did not know her. It knew her as its jailer, though, and Moon Eye ran for her, snarling, a man for two steps and then a wolf, its jaws running with foam and its eyes wild.

Beyond him, Therumit nodded, as at a job well done, and turned back to her main business of opening Tecuman's throat.

Maniye pushed forwards, because by now the cultists were fewer – or perhaps tired, and growing more cautious. She swatted a pair that were determined to get in her way, and then Moon Eye was leaping for her throat. She shied from him, taking him on her shoulder so that he rolled off her, leapt up and tried to lay open her flank. Twisting away again, she became a tiger long enough to cuff him across the muzzle, then a wolf, hoping the familiarity of the shape would bring him back to himself.

The angry spirit was riding him harder than ever before, though. His jaws gaped for her no matter what shape she owned, and he was a far larger wolf than she was. He almost had her in that moment, tearing her ear and snapping close to her eyes. And Tecuman—!

Maniye cursed all of the south and Stepped to the Champion's shape again. Even as she loomed over him, Moon Eye was still trying to kill her, but she got his struggling body between her teeth, shook him hard and threw him across the ruin.

Now . . .

Therumit had her back to Maniye, bloodied knife in one hand. Was she too late? But there was no dead Kasra at her feet, only a trio of cultists that had been ripped open with broad, sweeping strikes. And there, up two tiers of overgrown stone from the priestess, there was the youth. Between him and Therumit was Asmander.

He was Stepped: his Running Lizard shape with its sickle-clawed feet and dagger-tooth grin, crouched as if to spring any moment. Therumit stared up at him, hand tight about the hilt of her knife.

And, between her and Maniye, Tiamesh lay shaking, clutching her swollen, blackened hand, weeping with pain.

Maniye roared and thundered towards Therumit, willing to live with a curse if it let her crush the old woman's bones in her jaws.

The voice of Asmander sang out, though: 'No, Many Tracks! No!' There was such urgency in his tone he stopped her, practically within arm's reach of the priestess.

'She is of the Serpent,' Asmander, human now, insisted. 'You cannot harm her. You must not.'

Maniye snarled at him, waiting for the Champion to urge her on. Her souls were oddly uncertain, though, milling about inside her. Therumit seemed almost an extension of this broken place and its power. Maniye wondered if the Stranglers had ever really gone away, in those years.

With no more cultists assailing her, she took her human shape and knelt by Tiamesh. 'If she dies—'

'She will die.' Therumit's expression was one of disgust at all the world. 'One of many, when this sunders the Nation. All for the life of a *boy*.' Then she was gone, just a mud-brown serpent like a whip, slithering over the dead cultists and down towards the water.

Maniye held Tiamesh, who shivered in her arms, her breath coming fast and shallow. 'Step,' she whispered. 'Step, and let your soul free. Do not die human in this place.' She bent her head until her forehead touched the stricken woman's. 'I name you Strikes at Serpents. You are a true huntress of the Wolf.'

Tiamesh – Strikes at Serpents – gasped, and Maniye felt the human body in her arms shift and shrink and become the sleek, grey-furred wolf, and die.

'I am sorry.'

She looked up to see Asmander and Tecuman descending. To her surprise, it was the latter who had spoken and his face had real sorrow on it. Warriors died for their chiefs the world over, but a good chief mourned it. Maniye gave him a single nod, his due.

Those cultists who lived had fled, dragging off some of their own dead and wounded, for whatever rites the Stranglers practised. Across at the far side of the ruin, a burly Wolf man hugged himself and rocked, beating his forehead against his knees.

'Moon Eye!' Maniye called, holding her breath to see what would look up, out of the man's eyes. When he lifted his head, though, only the man was there, the angry spirit banished once more.

212

21

Grey Herald spent a day and night in prayer, seeking the Owl in the shadows cast by his fire. In the north he would have watched clouds beneath the moon but, here on the Plains, the sky was a clear canvas of stars.

A band of Wild Dogs found him, a good score of them off to raid a neighbour, but they offered him no harm. They marked their faces with ash from his fire and left him food and drink, speaking not a word.

The day after, he slept, Stepped and huddled in a nook of the rock, out of reach of the fierce sun. When night fell, he was ready. Night was the time of the Owl and the Bat.

Looking up at the heights of the mesa, Grey Herald wondered about that. Owl was respected in the Eyrie, but in the stories he brought madness and the death of children on silent wings. Owl wore the face of the enemy. And for all the respect of the Riverlands, the north had plenty of bad stories of Serpent's deceit.

The Plainsmen came to the mesa only for dark purposes. *What is it about those three brothers, that they are things of fear? Did the fight mark them, or was it that only the grimmest warriors could stand in the face of the Plague People?*

He had no answers. He Stepped and spread his wings, beating up into the still night air. The moon was a curved blade overhead, more than enough light to bathe the whole world in

213

silver for his eyes. His ears tracked every movement in the grasslands around him: scorpion and jerboa, mongoose and snake.

Above him, the mesa was a gap in the stars. The moon would not go there. He swooped closer, almost brushing the craggy, pockmarked rock with his feathers. Whatever ban lay there, it was not for him. He had a claim of kinship, brother to brother.

He looped before the vacant cave mouths. They opened onto thin air, yet he could see the work of human hands there. There had been carvings once, too high for any wingless admirer. He could just make out great figures standing in oddly formal postures, offering up illegible objects, faces worn to blankness by the centuries. Whatever message might have been left here for him, it was lost.

So he chose a cave and soared in, Stepping with a knife in his hand as he landed, for his owl eyes had seen the faintest touch of light from within. He crept as a man, stopped to listen and stare as owl, Stepping back and forth with a stealth that came easily to all his people. The cave twisted and turned, as though those who had mined it out had been mad. *Or serpents*. The thought made his skin crawl, for all he knew that Serpent was his brother, too. *Would Serpent remember me, if I met his mute brothers here within the earth?*

But the firelight was strong enough for human eyes to make out now, and he pressed forwards, sometimes walking, sometimes forcing his body through narrows where he felt the stone pressing on him. Leading with his knife.

At last he burst forth into an open chamber where a fire blazed, and where the curved sweep of the wall was punctuated with statues of attenuated men, each in its own alcove, their arms folded across their chests. The fire was set behind an altar which would once have cast the whole room in the shadow of its stone wings, but they had cracked and shattered on the floor long ago. The dancing light played across the long faces of the statues, their withered lips and sunken eyes. Its motion gave them a surrogate life and banished the stone pallor of their hollow cheeks.

Grey Herald would have studied them further, but he was not alone there. Before the fire and the altar was the last breed of man the Owl would have expected: tan skin, flat features; a northerner, just like Herald himself. He was not young, though he was strong-framed still. His face was lined and scarred, his hair gummed into short spines with red henna, grey at the temples. His chest and arms were bare and Herald saw a curious, branching design across them, like spiky frost or a tree with a thousand jagged branches. It was pale as a scar against the man's brown skin.

Grey Herald had made no sound, but abruptly the stranger was looking at him. He smiled, but the look in his eyes was as broken as shattered ice.

'Welcome!' he called. 'Welcome, brother! I am Storm Born, once of the Swift Backs.'

'I am Grey Herald of the Owl. And you are a Wolf no longer?'

The broken pieces behind Storm Born's eyes moved a little further apart. 'I am He Who Wakes the Sleepers, Brother Owl, and you are come just in time.'

★★★

Maniye and the others left the ruins of the Strangler temple as swiftly as they could. Moon Eye had Tiamesh's wolf corpse over his shoulders, and Maniye stalked beside him as the Champion, senses alive for the return of the cultists. Asmander was ahead, practically leading Tecuman by the hand.

The ruins fell away behind them, the stubs and mounds of whatever greater complex the ancient cult had raised, and time had cast down. By the time the night was drawing on, the place was little more than a bad dream.

When they stopped to camp, Maniye realized they would not be able to give Tiamesh's remains the Wolf's farewell. Lighting a little fire for warmth was hard enough. There was just not enough that would burn.

'Her soul is already hunting other lands,' Moon Eye said, as if hearing her thoughts. 'She will know we mean no disrespect.' His voice was heavy with guilt and sorrow, for all there was nothing he could have done. Therumit had taken him so effortlessly, cast the angry spirit into him with no more than a look, and probably steered him to the temple as well. In her heart Maniye had always known the Serpent's chosen were magicians, despite Hesprec's denials.

'What would you do with a fallen comrade?' she asked Asmander.

And so the River Champion found a swifter-flowing channel, and they built a raft of reeds and sodden wood, laying Tiamesh upon it, curled a little as though sleeping. Then they all watched as the current took her away, deeper into the estuary, perhaps to become the due of Old Crocodile's mute brothers, perhaps to pass into the sea.

'You raised a warband,' Asmander told her softly. 'This is what it is to lead.'

Maniye nodded, and then put all of her concentration into making a tiny fire for them, shrugging off any offers of help.

'Asa,' she heard Tecuman say, and then he and Asmander were embracing fiercely. She stopped to watch that, seeing in that single clasp the whole history of their friendship. She still did not know the Tecuman that Asmander valued so much, but here was the truth of what she had claimed to Old Crocodile.

'The carrion bird sent me,' Asmander said, still holding the Kasra to him. 'I hoped it was no omen. I trusted to the Serpent, to bring me to you. And . . . other things.' A muscle twitched in his face, and at last he stepped back, staring at Tecuman as though expecting him to melt away. 'I swore I would find you or your body.'

'My sister sent men to kill me,' Tecuman told him, sounding dazed. 'I cannot believe it. How has she grown so hard?'

Asmander shook his head. 'I was with her right before I heard the watch-horns. I was speaking with her. There was no warning . . .' I always thought, if it was someone I'd known as long as I knew her, surely I would see if she had turned. But no. I am blind, Teca. Forgive me.'

The Kasra grinned suddenly, a smile Maniye hadn't seen on him before. It seemed to give as much light as her fire. 'Forgive? You brought me your northerners, Asa. They got me away from the killers in my chamber when any of my own people could have been a traitor. My two Champions have both earned their keep. When I return to Tsokawan and take back my seat, you shall be rewarded.'

He seemed so certain and so joyous. To voice the doubts that crowded her mouth would have been cruel. There was a look on Asmander's face that suggested he thought the same thing.

He took first watch and she sat beside him, seeing the darkness of the estuary come alive beyond their firelight: insects and fish and fungi all brandishing their little torches to compete with the stars.

'The Serpent led you to us, truly?' Maniye asked him.

'You doubt it?'

'The Serpent brought us to that Strangling place, but not a friendly serpent. Your god has many heads.'

'These things are known,' Asmander agreed. 'Also, I . . .'

'What?' She glanced at him and found him smothering a smile.

'I flew.'

She stared, then remembered. 'The winged Champion, the . . . like a lizard bat.'

'I flew,' he repeated, nodding. 'I never dared it in your cold country. But I flew. I saw the mouth of that ruin from the air, and I *knew*, somehow.'

Maniye wanted to ask: *What was it like?* But she knew the answer would have been trite, or else profound beyond her ability to grasp it. Meaningless either way.

★

217

In the morning Moon Eye, who had taken last watch, thought there had been hunters out there during the night.

'You should have woken us,' Maniye chided him.

'I was ready,' he insisted. But they could see he was still ashamed, and clearly wanted a chance to prove himself once more.

'They have followed me, I think,' Asmander said softly. 'When I was on the ground, I had a sense that I was tracked, followed. I was like a great kite, blundering in the sky. Many eyes might have seen me and walked in my shadow.'

Maniye didn't understand his 'kite' but the meaning was clear. 'All the way from Tsokawan?'

He frowned. 'I can't think it. But if there were hunters, they could be all through the estuary by now. Or perhaps more of the Strangler cult.'

'But between us and where we need to go.'

'Lying in wait, or gone elsewhere for easier prey?' Asmander agreed. 'We can't know.'

'You want to hunt them,' Maniye observed. 'My souls want the same, but we are few.'

Asmander nodded. 'It may yet become necessary, but for now let's make the best time we can and hope to race them to Tsokawan.'

'You know the path?'

'Enough.'

They made the best speed they could, the four of them, trusting to Asmander to take the lead. Maniye wondered how much he had really flown. Hesprec had given him his new soul, his new shape, but it had been more for shock than anything else. Flying was a hard-learned skill.

Has he been practising? How would he go about teaching himself to fly? *Start by jumping off small things.* She couldn't keep in the laugh that brought. As she was the Champion it came out as a barking *Huff!* that echoed out into the spaces of the estuary.

218

Asmander looked round sharply, but if he knew she was laughing at him, his face did not admit it.

Perhaps the body knows. She had been clumsy in her own Champion's shape at first, too big in a world grown small. Her new limbs had taught her how to use them. Perhaps it was the same even with wings.

Moon Eye growled deep in his throat, pausing, bunched to leap over a channel to the next dry island. Asmander Stepped into his Champion's fighting lizard shape, head raised. Between them, Tecuman clenched and unclenched his fists.

Maniye took a deep draught of the air. There was something disagreeable on it, beyond the myriad scents of the place itself, which she had grown used to: some spoor that was new, and yet familiar.

Asmander Stepped back to pull at Tecuman's arm, and then they had increased their pace. The hunters were unseen, but they were close.

They stayed to dry land as much as possible in the hope it would give them human enemies to outrun. Every pool and stream could hide a foe, every crocodile could be a soldier of Tecumet. *And what else?* Some of the killers at Tsokawan had not been River Lords, after all. How far was the reach of the girl-Kasra when it came to finding knives to do her work?

By noon, she was beginning to feel the noose tightening. She had seen glimpses of human forms – not attacking, but keeping pace. Big men, all of them; paler than Asmander's people. Men with a look Maniye recognized.

Asmander had seen it too. 'The Dragon.'

'Where do they fit?'

'Wherever they fit, it is unwillingly.' Asmander looked tense and drawn, but she sensed an undercurrent of excitement in him that was the Champion making its desires known. And she knew what Champions wanted: an enemy to fight.

'They're for your boy, or his sister?'

Tecuman put in, 'Since they were subjugated, of course the

219

Dragon are loyal subjects of the Sun River Nation and the Day-break Throne,' but he said it bitterly. 'The Dragon will fight for whoever it suits them. Or for themselves. They have always chafed at our hand.'

'I count at least a dozen,' Moon Eye remarked. 'Let me slow them.'

'No,' Maniye said quickly.

'No,' Asmander agreed. 'It will be me.'

'We stay together.'

He shook his head. 'I'm fastest, remember?'

'Doesn't help if they don't chase you.'

His smile was full of an ugly kind of longing. 'I know the Dragon. I fought them back when life was simple.' At her doubting expression he added, 'And if they don't follow me, you turn and fight, and we'll crack them between us.'

'Just us two?'

'Us two Champions.'

Hanging back from the others, Asmander felt them slip ahead of him through the estuary's twisting channels. The trees around him were full of enemies.

He could not fight Tecumet, and he had not yet been given the chance to face her Champions. And so: this. He would shed some blood, for in this service only were the Dragon happy to oblige.

He Stepped into his fighting shape and went hunting, making a wide sweep across the path Tecuman and the others had taken. If they would face him, good; if they fled, he would chase.

He caught glimpses of them in brief flashes: broad-shouldered, sallow men with scarred cheeks and arms, with clothes of shark-skin and goat-hide. They would be armed with weapons of wood and flint and greenstone, but mostly with their lizard shapes, all hooked claws and whip tails and festering bites.

They did not rush to attack him when he made himself known. He kept moving, driving them away, winning Tecuman more distance, and yet the fight he wanted didn't come. He had no sense that they feared him, but they knew him. And as he hunted, he got a clearer idea of their numbers: twenty, thirty? More than twenty. A large warband of the Dragon this far into the estuary would not just be idly roaming.

Then they were no longer fleeing him. Turning a corner he saw they had come together to face him. And he had been wrong about the numbers. He was face to face with a loose mob of at least forty warriors. They held to their human forms for now and looked at him with surly dislike. Though he screeched at them, and though they had the numbers to bring him down, they made no move to attack him.

And at last they parted, left and right, to show him their leader: a burly old Dragon with a greenstone *meret* and a serrated shark-tooth knife, tortoiseshell bracers gleaming on his forearms. Asmander took a deep breath, feeling himself torn between two wildly different reactions. He wanted to go clasp the man by the forearms. He wanted to attack.

But in the end, he owed the Dragon this much, and so he Stepped.

'Venat,' he named the man.

The old pirate nodded. 'Don't suppose you're Asman yet?'

'My father lives.'

'Shame.' Venat spat, and then walked through the unruly ranks of his men, looking Asmander up and down. 'You cut a shape in the air that I remember. Who else, I asked myself, would be flopping through the air like a fish on the sand?'

'You've come a long way from the isles of the Black Teeth,' Asmander noted evenly.

'Is that my fault?' Venat raised an eyebrow. 'The Kasra of the Sun River Nation calls all his, all her warriors to come do battle against themselves. Even the Dragon.'

'And you are known for your obedience,' Asmander said sharply.

Venat grinned. 'We come where the fight is.'

'And what will you do when you reach it?' Asmander asked him. Venat was almost to him now, pausing just out of reach of his opponent's strike, though not of the Champion's leap should Asmander try it.

'Follow our souls.' Venat studied the youth before him. 'They say the boy-Kasra took a walk one night and got lost.'

'Who says?'

'Some longmouth soldiers who were our guests the other night. And I asked myself, who is it that was a great friend of the boy? And then we saw your shadow in the sky. My men were asking what the girl might give us, if we found her brother's head out in the estuary.'

Asmander nodded, feeling his heart speed in readiness, his breath tighten in his chest. The Champion was looking out through his eyes, so close he could feel it as a pressure against the inside of his skull. 'So,' was all he could say. He could see Venat's warband tense, ready to make a fight of it, as far as any one man could offer them that much fight.

Venat shook his head abruptly. 'Look at you, thinking too much, just like before.' And the old pirate crossed the remaining distance between them, swift and unexpected, and clapped Asmander on the shoulder. The move was so unexpected that he forgot to Step.

Asmander's heart stuttered but the Champion was calm, even a little disappointed; it had read the situation better than he.

'So you're all loyal followers of the Kasra now, are you?' What a triumph that would be, to sweep Tecuman back to power on the back of the Dragon. But he knew that was not what was happening here. The Dragon was never so tractable.

'Perhaps, tomorrow's tomorrow, we'll be hunting your boy for real,' Venat said, without acrimony. 'But you and I, we have history, Son of Asman. You made me serve you. You dragged me to places so cold I thought my cock would fall off. And then you gave me back to myself. Right before a fight, too.' The old pirate grinned. 'You have any idea what an insult that is? "Here's a big fight brewing, so walk away"?' He laughed, but his eyes never left Asmander's face. 'Share our fire, tonight. Your boy and the northerners too.'

'And will we wake with the same number of throats we bedded down with? What does the Dragon swear by?'

'The Dragon?' Venat asked, highly amused. 'Nothing, ever. But I swear by my name, may I lose it again if I wrong you this night and day.'

Asmander nodded. 'That is enough.'

22

The hunter known as Nine Teeth of the Many Mouths had gone to the Tiger camp two days after Stag Taker's death at the hands of Aritchaka. Nine Teeth was younger than the dead man, and wiser, too. He challenged one of the Tiger men and killed him in the fighting circle, though he lost an ear, and none could say whether he would see out of his left eye again. To the Many Mouths it was a great victory. To the Tiger, who valued the fighting prowess of their menfolk little, it was an insult: as if one of their warriors had gone to a Wolf camp and called out a hearth-wife.

That same day, one of Aritchaka's priestesses went to the camp of the Many Mouths and called out one of their younger hunters – probably the first she saw, by Loud Thunder's reckoning. They had fought, and it had been a close thing, but the woman had ten years of fight over her opponent and had cut him down and walked away making jokes about a wolf pelt for her cloak. Loud Thunder had braced himself for all-out war between the Tiger and the Wolf tribes, but as always he had been left stumbling along behind events.

A warrior of the Moon Eaters had been challenged and killed by a hunter of the Winter Runners because of some feud that went back two generations, the details of which even the winner seemed unsure of.

A woman of the Boar – stocky and short and nothing so

much to look at – had challenged two brothers, one after another, for taking her children for the Wolf's jaws. She had killed them, too, heedless of hurt and with a savagery that had silenced everyone there. Then the third brother had attacked her at night in a furious rage. Loud Thunder had come in time to intervene and separate them – though he had the mark of fangs and tusks in his hide before he succeeded. That fight went to the circle, then, at the Boar woman's insistence, and she gutted the third brother and trampled his body into the dirt. What name she had been born with, Thunder didn't know, but they called her Ash Maker now because the hearth of the three brothers was cold and abandoned.

One of the Eyriemen had challenged a huntress of the Lean Backs – over no more slight, Loud Thunder thought, than he believed he could win. He had died a hawk, and she had crawled her way out of the circle to die a wolf, three body-lengths outside its bounds.

And Mother looked at Loud Thunder with a frown. She did not need to say anything. Her disappointment was a crushing weight on his shoulders. She had trusted him, and this was the result. He had tried to bring the people of the Crown of the World together and here they were, killing each other.

The other Bears sat and scratched and watched indolently as their guests shed each other's blood. Thunder wondered when one of them would decide to join in. After all, who could face a bear in that small space, and live? The only thing that kept his people out of the fighting was how lazy they were. But the scent of blood was exciting them. It would come.

Loud Thunder knew he needed to talk to them all – he needed to bring their leaders together and tell them: *This is not the way.* And every time he saw Yellow Claw, the Eyrie Champion was smirking at him, palpably enjoying his discomfort.

It was a terrible confession for a son of the Bear, but he wanted someone to talk to. He wondered if this was a disease he had caught from Maniye and Hesprec, when they had wintered with him. *No. I was born with the seeds of it.* He had been one of a warband once, roving the plains and seeking trouble. *Broken Axe, Peace Speaker and the rest . . . And with all this solitary living since, I've been fooling myself, haven't I?*

He could not speak to Mother or any of his kin. He could perhaps speak to Two Heads and his mate, but the Coyote talked to everyone. Give them your words and who knew where they would end up? Loud Thunder sat on a rock out in the wan sun, and thought until his head hurt.

The next day he went to Kailovela because he couldn't help it.

Yellow Claw was off making trouble somewhere, undermining everything Loud Thunder was trying to do. Thunder was glad, though – glad the man held such a reservoir of spite for all the world, glad he cared nothing for his mate save to own her.

Loud Thunder could feel fondness inside him like a sickness. It had touched him when he had first set eyes on her, and each time he thought of her, it crept through his body that much more. He knew that no good could come of it. He knew that she did not look on him with the same eyes. How could she, shackled and claimed and passed from hand to hand? Loud Thunder was uncomfortably aware of being just another warrior who came muscling into her life, to stare and covet.

Yet his thoughts were traitors. His dreams were wild, troubled tangles of her bare skin, her long hair. He dreamt of her laughter, even though he had never heard it. He had wanted women like this when he was young. When he had gone raiding across the Plains with Broken Axe and the rest there had been women, sometimes. He had felt that need like a weakness in him, though they'd always had to approach him first before anything came of it. He had been shy as a youth. He felt little better now.

But he called, of course, to see the hollow creature, the hungry spirit. That was what he told the Owl priestess Seven Mending. He knew in his heart he was breaking his bond as a

226

host each time he came to her tent. He was walking a path that could lead nowhere good.

She should have a hunter's name, for what she is, Loud Thunder considered, and he made that his opening gambit as he sat at her hearth. Kailovela watched him, wary as always. 'The women of the Eyrie have no such names. We can never accomplish a thing worth the naming.'

Loud Thunder supposed he could have guessed. 'What if I name you?' he asked with desperate jollity.

Her expression did not change. 'Then I would carry your name.'

Thunder felt stupid again, and properly so. 'Would you . . .' He almost asked her to give herself a name, but that would have been to pile foolishness on top of foolishness. 'I'm sorry,' he muttered. He wasn't sure what in particular he was sorry for. The list seemed large.

'I have a problem,' he told her.

That fugitive smile flickered briefly. 'You are the greatest son of the Bear. What could trouble you?'

'This nonsense.'

'Your nonsense?'

He nodded heavily. 'It's all going wrong. Every little disagreement since my great-grandfather's day is turned into an excuse to open throats. And every open throat vomits out another three feuds. By the time people leave there will be no one left to go. And I'm sorry. Because this is a Bear problem and you have enough Hawk problems of your own.'

'Perhaps a problem that is not mine is like fresh air to me,' she said carefully. 'Why did you create this "nonsense", Loud Thunder? What was the point of it?'

'Because there is some dreadful fate coming,' he told her with a sidelong glance at the spirit, 'and we need to fight it together. But how can I ask them to forget all their griefs and angers? I sometimes think the whole Crown of the World is built on little hates, that if you dug into the mountains you'd find grudge piled on grudge to hold the sky up. I think tomorrow I will hear that some Wolf's right arm has challenged his left and ripped him in half.'

Kailovela nodded thoughtfully – and she *was* thinking, he could see. He glanced at the hollow spirit, expecting to see it crouched at the wall of the tent, staring hatefully at him. Instead it was busy with something. It had a charred stick from an old fire and was drawing on the leather like a child. The strangeness of the designs intrigued him. There was nothing there he could recognize, no human figures, no beasts, just little twisted knots, as though whatever pictures she drew had contracted in agony into little thorned claws. There was something unpleasantly hypnotic about the design. Loud Thunder shuddered and looked away.

'Feuds and grudges divide people,' Kailovela said softly.

Thunder grunted his agreement.

'They also unite them,' she pointed out. 'You just need so big a feud that everyone is on the same side of it.'

'I have nothing so big as that. Just a few priests muttering warnings of what is to come. And when it comes, that will be too late. Mother asked me for this *now*, and what have I given her? The blood of strong hunters shed for no reason.'

Her little smile was back. It gave him an untoward amount of joy.

'You have one thing big enough to stand the hate of everyone. You have yourself.'

Thunder blinked at her, desperate to have mistaken her. Her gaze was steady, though. Even as he tried to deny it, he knew she was right.

Leaving the tent, he cast one glance back at the crude sketch of the hollow spirit. From this vantage, it looked to him like an expanding cloud of voracious flying things blotting out the sky, here to devour everything like a plague.

He went to his own people first, some half-dozen who were large and strong, and he made them his messengers. They did not

228

want to stir themselves for him. Some he cowed with Mother's name, others he wrestled and cuffed and bellowed at until doing what he wanted was easier than not. He had them go to each of the tribes: some to the Tiger, some to the Eyrie, several to Deer and Boar and Wolf, whose various tribes were spread all about. Each brought word from their host, Loud Thunder: that he called on their best, their strongest. Some he named; with others, he let them choose or fight for the honour, for no doubt they would think it an honour.

They came at sunset to his fire – a grand enough fire that he had made himself, taking ten nights' worth of wood and piling it up in intricate layers, so it would burn well and long. He lost himself in the task because it was something he did well, and it was simple, and wouldn't argue with him or do stupid things.

Then he waited.

First arrived two who were not summoned, but he was glad of them: the two Coyote who were everywhere these days, and most of all at Mother's hearth. No doubt Mother would hear news of this from them, when Loud Thunder himself neglected to tell her. *Well that saves me worrying about how she'll hear it.*

The rest came in separately, each with a handful of friends to make sure this was no trap of their enemies. The friends stayed outside the reach of Thunder's firelight, but they would hear every word, and that was for the best.

The Wolf came in, each tribe alone. The Winter Runners and Swift Backs had sent broad-shouldered warriors in iron coats. They left their weapons with their friends, but they walked like men who claimed the blood-red sunset as their own kill.

The Many Mouths sent a woman, also in iron and looking more dangerous than the men. The Moon Eaters sent an old priest, and Loud Thunder respected that more. He was Icefoot, and he had a face like a mountainside and a mane of white hair. His cloak was bearskin, which was a boast of sorts.

And there were the others: the Boar woman, Ash Maker, and a couple more of her people who were known as fighters –

though they gave Ash Maker room, and none was keen to sit close to her. There was a long, lean man of the Deer, grey-haired and hollow-cheeked, whom they said had killed Tiger and Wolf with a bow, from such a distance that it had been day where he stood and night for his enemies. And, though that was plainly nothing but fancy, Thunder well believed he was a dangerous man.

And there was Aritchaka, because she was by far the most dangerous of the Tiger, and because the Tiger were united behind her in a way no other tribe could boast. And there was Yellow Claw; who else?

Loud Thunder stood with the fire at his back and glowered at them, hoping his face showed them every nuance of his resentment. 'You know me twice over,' he told them flatly. 'You know me as Loud Thunder, son of the Bear. You know me as your host, whose word called you all to this place, to test yourself against each other. You know why I called you here.'

'Why don't you tell us again, O great host?' Yellow Claw asked, laughter in his voice.

Loud Thunder did not acknowledge him, though his words answered the question. 'My Mother has seen a terror falling on us. Your priests, each of them, has seen some part of this terror, and they have come here and spoken with each other or with Mother. At all of your hearths, the Wise begin to understand how afraid they should be. You all know a man of the Seal came here – so far from the sea! – to tell of the shadow his people had fallen under, and those of you who do not see the omens behind it are fools.'

'The Seal have lived in the sea's teeth forever,' Yellow Claw put in. 'Small wonder they're mad. One man's fears, one woman's bad dreams, these are leaves that grow every year and are gone by winter.' The Champion shook his head in disgust. 'Let children fear stories.'

'Children indeed,' Loud Thunder echoed. 'I thought I had called men, women, to be my guests here. Men and women with

230

true hunter's eyes that see to the horizon, not just as far as their own grievances. And yet I find children who cannot keep themselves from fighting each other.' He rounded on Ash Maker even as the Boar woman drew breath, 'Yes, you were wronged. Yes, every tribe here has empty places at one hearth or another, and can point across to some other fire where a killer or a thief sits. But this is not the place.'

'But you've made it the place,' Yellow Claw drawled. 'And you knew it would be. At the Stone Place we told you but you would not listen. Who is the child, then?'

Loud Thunder took a deep breath, knowing the chasm that was at his feet. 'I am your host,' he told them all. 'Any challenge amongst you that ends in death or maiming shall be a challenge to me. And I shall answer. Do you think I've watched all this foolishness and not wanted to be a fool myself? Well then, if you have those who would challenge the Bear, let them come to me. If you have those who will make the wrongs done to them so very grand, let them know that I shall come to them, and I'll not be refused.'

'You are our host,' someone said – one of the Wolves, he thought.

'And this is hospitality in the Bear's Shadow,' he pronounced. 'Race, wrestle, fight like the Tigers do, amongst themselves – where one winner and one loser still walk away. But I shall follow the scent of any who does harm to any of my guests, in the circle or out.'

He watched them, locking eyes with any who would meet his gaze. He stared down bitter Ash Maker and the Deer tribe archer, he glowered at the Wolves, seeing the old Moon Eater priest nod slowly. He glared into the still, cool face of Aritchaka. He saw them adjust their understandings in the face of this new Loud Thunder.

But Yellow Claw snorted. 'You cannot make the rivers flow back to the mountains. You cannot keep the snow in the clouds. You cannot change the ways of men.'

Loud Thunder took a deep breath. 'Some men, perhaps,' and then, as Yellow Claw started to make some other jibe, 'One man, perhaps. I will start with you.'

He could sense the sudden alarm in the two Coyote, who had sat and listened without movement or comment until now. He felt the whole gathering shift about him, all those warriors and hunters and leaders wondering if they had heard him correctly.

'I call you out, Yellow Claw. I draw you from my side like a thorn. Leave the Bear's Shadow tonight or tomorrow you and I shall meet.'

'You called the Eyrie here, Loud Thunder.' Yellow Claw's humour was all gone. The smoke and the firelight seemed to ripple along the vanes of half-seen wings about him: a man larger than life, holder of a terrible, ancient soul. 'Do you want me to take my people off again? Can you do without us?'

Of course, that would be simplest. And of course Loud Thunder had no idea whether the loss of the Eyrie would doom things. But that was not in his mind. His mind was given over to Yellow Claw's mate. At heart, he was as false and irresponsible as the rest of them.

'Do you think they would go, at your call?' he asked Yellow Claw. 'I have seen much of the Owl at Mother's hearth. They know the terror is upon us. They do not waste their blood and their strength in fools' challenges. They leave that to men like you, and if you go, they will not miss you.'

Probably the Eyrie would all go if Yellow Claw demanded, but now it didn't matter. Now it was an insult, a personal barb to get under the man's skin. Yellow Claw couldn't back down without shaming himself. Loud Thunder considered how he had chosen his words, how calm he was about it, and wondered what he had become.

And also, whether he could best the Champion of the Eyrie.

23

They spent that night at the hearth of the Dragon.

Maniye decided to stay awake from dusk till dawn. She was unsure how many warriors Venat led, but it was at least two score and they were never still. Bands of them were constantly strolling off indolently, joking and laughing. Others would be returning, laden with supplies, often stolen barrels and sacks. The Dragon plainly did not care where it found its meals.

When she first came to their fire she could sense many eyes on her. The sons of the Dragon were all big men, ugly and well armed – or else they were low-slung, pebble-skinned lizards with reeking jaws. When she stood before them at first, she was prey – she saw it in their eyes no matter what Venat might have told them. Only when she loomed over them as the Champion of the north did they give her any respect. Even then, she sensed that more than one of them wanted to challenge her, just because she was something new and fighting was how the Dragon tested the world.

Moon Eye was similarly wary of them, but he was of a size with most of them and they gave him space from the start. By the end of the night, he had thrown a couple of them, and one of them – by no means the biggest – had thrown him. Maniye waited for the angry spirit to light on him but either it was still licking its wounds or it was invisible against the wildness of the Dragon.

Most of all, she watched Tecuman. He sat very still, very straight-backed, and she could almost see the robe and mask there, so fiercely was he conjuring them in his mind. In the midst of these savage and unruly men, his one defence was to be Kasra, to sit there as if he were truly their lord and master.

After eating and drinking, Maniye allowed herself to relax just a little, though whether these raiders cared anything for guest-right was another matter. She sat by the fire and talked with Asmander and Venat: there were some days in the Crown of the World that belonged to the three of them and no others. Somehow it was all fond remembrance with Venat, no matter who else's shame or pain he might be raking up. He kept talking about it long after she would have expected him to have run out of things to say – and hadn't he been a thrall chafing at his collar all that time? She remembered him as a sour, surly monster of a man, constantly ready to plunge a knife into Asmander. Watching him now, she wondered if she somehow remembered it all wrong. The old pirate talked about those days as if he pined for them.

Later that night she settled down by Tecuman's side as the Dragon went to their rest one by one, or else sloped off into the estuary to hunt. She lay awake, listening to them grumble and scuffle and snarl at each other, and at the edge of her hearing were Venat and Asmander, still distantly jibing at each other, trying to work out where they stood now the world had moved on.

They left the Dragon camp with the dawn, before most of the warriors there were even awake. Only Venat had watched them go, wordless, but with eyes fixed on Asmander.

'So, did your . . . Venat, did he say how we can get to . . .' Maniye ground her teeth, because she couldn't remember how the name of the southern fortress went.

'My Venat told me much about the path ahead, yes,' the River Champion confirmed.

234

'He wants to kill you,' Maniye stated, with utter conviction.

'He wants to fight me,' Asmander corrected her without looking back. 'But that is how the Dragon greets his friends and his family. Fighting is like breathing to him.'

'He hates you because he was your thrall.'

'Probably.' Asmander sounded cheerful about it. 'Or he could hate me for no reason. That also is the Dragon's path. It is a wonder there are any left.'

'No people could be as bad as you say.'

'Oh, worse, much worse.' Now he did look back, his smile brilliant. 'You northerners think you're so fierce! They say Dragon tore his way out of the egg before his mother laid it.'

'Who was his mother?' asked Maniye, baffled.

Asmander shrugged. 'The sky, I think. There are no stars for the Dragon. Instead, they say all the darkness where the stars aren't is the Dragon's right.'

'They say a lot of things. And I don't trust you when you're this happy about something.'

At that, he stopped and turned, weighing her up with his gaze. '*Do* you trust me?'

Maniye glanced sidelong at Moon Eye, her only ally within arm's reach. 'I don't know.'

'I wouldn't blame you not to.'

'I don't care if you blame me or not.' Maniye scowled at him. 'But I trust you to do right by the Kasra. So as long as I'm helping him too, I don't need to worry about you.'

Asmander's face softened a little and he nodded. 'Good.'

'I want to trust you too, Asa.' Tecuman stepped between Maniye and Moon Eye.

The River Champion looked at him blankly. 'Of course.'

'I remember you and my sister, and your friendship,' Tecuman observed. 'We three were always together, were we not?'

'Teca . . .'

The boy-Kasra blinked rapidly. 'Sometimes we ganged up on

you, and sometimes you and I would tease her, or you and she would mock me. Which is it now, Teca?'

Asmander stared at him. 'I'm here for you, Teca. I brought the northerners for you. How could you . . . ?'

'Where are you leading us? We're leaving Tsokawan behind.'

Asmander rubbed at his face. 'Venat . . . he has seen your sister's soldiers. They're everywhere between us and Tsokawan, he said. They know your only chance is to get into the fortress where people are loyal to you. Although I'm sure Esumit and her people are working on their minds even now.'

'Yes,' Tecuman said flatly. 'Yes, they will be swallowing my support, right now as we speak. My one chance to seize my destiny is to rule from Tsokawan, to rally the people of the estuary against Atahlan. To drive my sister so far back up the river that she must concede the throne to me.' Abruptly his voice was on fire with his need for it. Here was a youth who had been taught nothing but that he would be Kasra. And of course Tecumet would have been taught the same.

Madness. She wanted to shout at them, to ask what sort of a way this was to run anything? And yet she had seen only a small piece of the Sun River Nation. It was large, and full of people. She had seen the farmland stretching off down both banks of the river, and clustered in great swathes about the estuary itself. She had seen the magnificent flotilla of boats Tecumet had brought to threaten her brother, more soldiers than the Winter Runners had people. A nation of strength that had lasted many generations. And yet now, when Hesprec said the world needed such strength most, it was crumbling.

'So tell me why we are not travelling to Tsokawan,' Tecuman said, after a moment's fighting for calm. 'If you say that you have given up on my throne and seek only to save my life, Asa, then know that to live is not enough. Old Crocodile has tested me. I am to be Kasra. Only I.'

'Tsokawan is not your only chance, Teca,' Asmander told him softly. 'That is just what your sister thinks.'

236

'Where else, then?' Tecuman demanded. 'You'll go to that girl of yours from the Laughing Men, and have her rally the Plains tribes in my name? Or will we all spend a year in the north and come back with even more Iron Wolves? I don't have that long, Asa!'

'The north is far,' Asmander admitted. 'But the Bluegreen Reach is near.'

'Your father . . .'

'Is probably still in Tsokawan speaking on your behalf. But our home is close. We have soldiers, servants, strong walls. Nothing Venat said made me think your sister had her eyes on my home.'

'She might. She knows it.' Tecuman's face twisted. 'We played there many times . . .'

'I have no better path.' Asmander spread his hands wide. 'Teca, we are running out of thread.'

'If she's there, we'll see boats on the river,' Maniye put in. 'And Asmander can go first to speak with his people.'

'Once we're safe there, we can send messengers to Tsokawan – peasants, fishermen, people who won't be marked. We can send word to Many Tracks' warband, to the other Serpents, to anyone we trust,' Asmander pressed. 'Teca, please, if we head for Tsokawan we'll have to shed blood for every step, and half of it ours.'

Tecuman grimaced, looking past his shoulder at something – Maniye guessed it was the path to Tsokawan, although how he could know where the place lay she had no idea. The idea of putting so much as a hand's span of further distance between himself and the throne plainly ate at him, but at last he nodded.

24

A serpent needs precious little to live on in the estuary. Hesprec found a satchel and took some cloth and some flints, a jar of oil, some dried fish. She took a staff of pale wood, specifically because it lent her a little of the authority she had grown used to in age, and because, two lives ago, she had practised some amusing tricks involving Stepping with a staff. Who knew when such trifles would come in useful again?

And she took a pouch of gold. It was old Asman's and he was not greatly happy to see it go, especially since his son had danced away from Tsokawan without permission or warning. Hesprec was of the Serpent, though. She had lived a dozen lives, taught a hundred teachers, sat in judgement on clan chiefs and peasants alike. If she said she needed gold, then gold she would have.

'And isn't that the problem?' she told herself, after parting company with Asmander's father. The Riverlanders knew that the Serpent priests had made the Sun River Nation what it was, not by force and conquest but by wisdom. Wisdom brought from the Oldest Kingdom, which had fallen under the Pale Shadow. That lost place, whence all lore and wisdom had come . . . Hesprec felt the familiar sadness just thinking of it, though she had only heard of it from those far older than she.

But because of that heritage, those who spoke for the Serpent were listened to. So: she was ready to take up Matsur's offer, but still she hesitated. Such uncertainty, in one accounted so wise! And yet she felt that she had reached a place where wisdom ran thin. *All that travelling, only to find home such a strange place.*

She had not liked what she had heard behind Matsur's words or seen behind his eyes. It was as though a disease had lurked there. And yet Matsur was of the Serpent, her brother through the ages. He too had lived many lives, learned and studied across the generations. If he said he had found some great salvation, surely she should trust him.

Save that Matsur did not trust the Serpent. Matsur had not gone up the river to Atahlan and brought his great discovery before all the priests there. Matsur and Therumit and some small handful of priests here in the estuary had a secret they did not trust their siblings with.

But they trust me.

And if I wish to tell this secret to the world, what will they do to me? What secret can possibly be so terrible as to breed this subterfuge? All we have built . . . Just a fragment of a thought, but it encapsulated all her fears. Since they had come, refugees, to the River, the people of the Serpent had tried to build something lasting here. They had taken the feuding tribes of the River Lords and made them into one people. They had taught that people how to farm, to write, to make and keep laws. They had grown their surrogate kingdom, and each tribe who joined the Sun River Nation had prospered, even if they had given up something of themselves to do so.

A work of centuries, and now . . . Two Kasra jostling buttocks for one throne. But for Matsur that was only a means to a mysterious end. He needed influence over Tecuman because . . . what . . . ?

If only Maniye was here. I could use a Champion.

So Hesprec wound her way down to the buried, windowless rooms beneath Tsokawan, where the walls sweated swamp water and the servants conspired, and there she bowed her head until

239

it touched the dank stone of the floor, and sought the guidance of her buried god.

'It's time now. It's happening. She's alone.' A hunched black bird at the window become a hunched, painted man: Feeds on Rags.

The Coyote girl lifted her head from her paws and stared at him. She had been lounging in the strip of sunlight the window cast, but now she was in his shadow. She Stepped unwillingly. 'Shouldn't you be watching her then?'

Feeds on Rags fidgeted in the stone slot of the window. 'I don't know what to do.'

'Doesn't normally stop you from doing anything.' But he was already gone. She stood and went to the window, seeing him feathering to another opening lower down. The window was small, but she was smaller; she twisted through it easily. She could always climb – the despair of her parents from the age of four. She had been climbing rocks when the raiders had found her parents' camp when she was eight, and made an orphan of her. Sometimes even Coyotes died.

She scrambled down, and slipped inside to Feeds on Rags, who was hopping from foot to foot in that way he had, when he was so full of bad ideas he could burst. Sathewe liked Feeds on Rags, because he was an adult with a Name, and yet he was still a child. He laughed at what she found funny. He trusted her to do things, even things she couldn't do. He didn't ignore her for being young. Many Tracks was like that, too, except Many Tracks didn't laugh much.

He took her through the snake-twisty paths of the River People's stone house until they were below the ground, and there he pointed out which little room the Serpent priestess girl had gone to.

'So what do we do?' the Crow asked her, rolling his eyes.

'Tell Takes Iron, if that's what he wants.' She yawned. 'This is why you take me from the sun?'

'Many Tracks won't like it. She loves the Snake priestess.

More than she loves Takes Iron, that's a truth. I won't do it. I won't tell him.'

'I thought you were scared of Takes Iron,' she whispered. For herself, she only knew fear in the moment the blade descended on her. Once the threat was past, she forgot.

Feeds on Rags' eyes rolled, each in a separate half of his face. 'That old growler?'

'I saw you when he barked at you. Half your feathers fell out,' she jibed at him. 'If you don't do what he says, he'll roast and eat you. And if you do, Many Tracks will do the same.'

The Crow bared his teeth and hopped from foot to foot again, wringing his hands. 'What do I do?' he demanded.

She didn't know, but he was an adult asking her for advice, so she thought she had to say something. 'Many Tracks isn't here,' she pointed out. 'Takes Iron is.'

That decided it. 'You stay here and watch her,' Feeds on Rags told her with a sickly grin. 'I'll go find the growler.'

He Stepped in a flurry of black wings and was gone.

Kalameshli Takes Iron came at their call, and then sent the pair of them away. He would use them, Coyote and Crow, but he could not rely on them. They were not Wolf.

They were forever prying their snout and beak into matters that did not concern them, meaning they were perfect spies. But keeping mouths shut was not a strength of theirs. He had bound them to silence and threatened them with a blazing death in the Wolf's jaws if they spoke to anyone. By his estimation that gave him perhaps until noon.

With these weak tools . . .

But here he was in the dim rush-lit chambers beneath the Rivermen's stone hall, and although the sound of other humans echoed to him from all directions, his wolf nose told him no others were close. Only the scent of the Serpent girl was real and immediate to him.

He prowled forward with a hunter's careful tread, Stepping

241

so that his claws barely scratched at the stone. The dagger he had brought with him gave his fangs an iron sheen. The Serpent priests no doubt had all manner of tricks and spells, but iron was the Wolf's magic. Kalameshli knew and trusted iron like an old friend.

The Serpent had her hands to the wall, her covered head bowed. The flickering lamplight moved and danced, so that for a moment Kalameshli saw the room around them coursing with scales within the stonework. He shook his head and they were gone. Standing in the doorway to this bare little room, he Stepped to his human form: old, but still strong – stronger than this slender girl.

Hesprec lifted her head. 'Well, you're here at last.'

Kalameshli froze, eyes narrow, then decided it didn't matter. Let her die with foreknowledge or in ignorance. In fact, let her know whose hand cut the head off the serpent. That would make the act sweeter.

'Your two scouts are not very subtle,' the girl went on, hands still palm-flat to the walls. 'There's little that moves in the Serpent's domain that he does not know.'

Kalameshli changed his grip on the dagger. He had been considering a strike into her ribs, but she was so much smaller than he was, a downward strike seemed surer.

She turned to face him. He knew that a shout from her would bring help – not in time to save her, but in time to catch him bloody-handed at the deed. He had already weighed that risk. In the end he knew what was important. The north needed its Champion. It did not need an old Wolf priest who had broken his vows.

Hesprec was smiling a little, and he saw her shift her footing to a wider stance. To his astonishment he saw she was going to make a fight of it. He Stepped as he darted forwards, hoping the swiftness of his wolf shape would pin her so he could get his blade in at his leisure. Even as he moved, though, she was a snake, a thin ribbon that slithered between his feet. He snapped at her vanishing tail and then wheeled furiously, snarling. She was waiting for him, and in that space of a heartbeat she was far larger. The serpent that reared up to threaten him seemed to brush the ceiling, her coils filling the room. She had fangs a finger-length long, dripping with venom.

Fear lanced Kalameshli, but he had struck those fangs out once, in the north. He could do it again. He Stepped as he lunged forwards, one hand grasping the serpent's body, the other striking at her head. She threw a heavy loop about him, trying to trap him, but he climbed up the rough ladder of her body, using her length against her, trying to drive his iron into her. Always she swayed aside, fangs bared but not daring to strike. The moment those teeth sank into him was the moment he would find her head with his blade, and no poison was so swift that it would keep him from hacking it off.

She slung another coil at him, trying to tangle his arms, but he ducked away, breathing harshly. A backswing of the dagger caught her but just skittered off her scales. She seemed to fill the room. Everywhere he looked there were patterned loops of her sliding past each other, melting away when he tried to open them up.

She struck at his eyes, but it was a feint. Kalameshli fell back, tripping over a link of her body, finding his wolf shape as he fell so that he landed on four feet. He got his teeth into her then, a shallow gash along her body before he had to skip aside from the grasp of her coils. He backed away from her, snarling, and she gave him space, the upper reaches of her body winding half-way up the wall so she could stare down at him.

He leapt at her, straight into her teeth, but even as he did she had shrunk down to a tiny thread of a thing and he jarred himself against the wall, whirling to find her a human girl again, standing in the doorway with escape at her back. And yet *not running from him*, not even when he Stepped and loomed over her, dagger in hand. He raged inside: she should fear him; she should cower. But behind that rage was despair. He felt coils tightening about him even though he could not see them. He had attacked the Serpent in its lair, and it had known of his coming. He was surrounded by her god. He was far from home.

'I know why you bear a knife, Takes Iron,' she told him softly.

His grip tightened on the weapon's hilt. 'I am the north,' he grated. 'I am winter. I am the Wolf.' He wanted to lunge at her then, but those invisible coils held him back. It would be like striking at mist, he knew. He could stab and cut all day, all night, all year; the serpent's coils were endless.

'And you are Maniye's father, and you worry,' she told him.

Takes Iron hissed through his teeth. 'I am *not* . . .' he started. But he was, of course. He had hidden it, lied to Akrit Stone River, denied it even in the teeth of the Wolf, but he was the man who had sired Maniye Many Tracks. He felt tears pricking his eyes, fighting to escape: shame, frustration, anger. 'You cannot take her for your Serpent,' he spat. 'She belongs to the Wolf – to the Crown of the World. You cannot take her from me!'

'Kalameshli Takes Iron,' she named him, and he felt another sightless coil loop about him. 'I cannot take her from you. That is not the Serpent's way. Look around you at the River Lords: have they turned their back on Old Crocodile? They have not. Have the Milk Tear and the Hidden People and the Salt Eaters and all the estuary folk forgotten their gods, just because they have heard the Serpent's word? The Serpent runs below all things. The Serpent sets himself above none. Takes Iron, I am not your enemy.'

She spoke so solemnly, all those grave words falling from the mouth of a girl who seemed younger even than his daughter. His knuckles whitened about the dagger. 'She loves you.' Words he had not meant to say, squeezed from him by the Serpent's grip.

Hesprec took a deep breath. 'If you seek a father's love from her, Takes Iron, then I am not what stands in your way. Likewise a priest's respect. My blood will not carry you to any of these things, it will only wash you further from her.'

Now. Stab her while she talks! But he was held paralysed by her words.

Hesprec took a deep breath. 'You took my fangs with your hammer,' she recalled, touching her bright white teeth with her tongue as if to show him how little he had ever really accomplished. 'You kept me in your pit and you would have burned me if you could. Later, you beat me and hung me by my wrists, and you had another fire ready for me. All these wrongs I could bring before the Serpent and the Kasra. But I let them go, Takes Iron. I open my hands and they blow away.'

'Weakness,' he snarled.

'It is not weakness that makes my friends stronger.'

'I am no friend of yours or your Serpent!'

'And yet you are the father of my friend,' she told him. 'Should I not respect you for that? And you are a priest in your own land, and I should respect you for that, as I respect the Wolf even standing in the shadow of his jaws.' She shrugged. 'And I need your help.'

Kalameshli stared at her. There was nothing she could have said that could have thrown him more.

'You know why I was in the Crown of the World,' she told him patiently. 'You know the doom I saw here on the river is seen by your northern priests as well. And . . . more than that, I need your eyes.'

'What do you mean?' Kalameshli felt calmer now, the dagger still a comforting weight in his hand. *And yet you are the father of my friend.* Somehow that had got through to him, when nothing else could. Perhaps it was simply that illusion of seniority she allowed him. He had been left with so little, even that concession meant something.

'I am going into the estuary to meet with my kin,' she explained. 'They tell me they have some great discovery that I must know. And yet . . . and yet I fear, Takes Iron. I fear what they have discovered. I fear to go alone.' She smiled sadly. 'I have known these people for lifetimes upon lifetimes, and now they seem like strangers to me. So I would be glad of another priest, of another god. I would value your advice and your company.'

Kalameshli stared at her, pop-eyed. 'I . . .' He showed her the dagger, as though she might have overlooked it in the fight.

'I know,' Hesprec told him. 'I would fight for Maniye too, if there was a need. But where I stand with her, and where you stand, are two different places.'

Takes Iron felt something drawn out of him, as though he had been stabbed long ago – as long as Maniye's birth perhaps – and never realized the blade was still in him, keeping the wound open. He sagged and almost fell. Hate was flowing from him as though Hesprec had lanced a boil.

'You want me to go with you?'

'I ask your help, as one priest to another.'

I was ready to die. He had told himself it was for the Wolf or for Maniye, but it had been for himself, because he had been walled in, trapped in the dark where he could see no other way out. Now, with Hesprec's words, there was a path at his feet, and he felt it led to the sun.

He nodded. He did not trust himself to words, but he put the dagger away.

Standing before Spear Catcher and the rest of the warband felt strange, as though he had become an imposter. Kalameshli could see their eyes flicking between him and the diminutive Serpent girl beside him.

'I am going on a journey,' he told them all. 'Spear Catcher, you lead until I or Many Tracks return.'

'Takes Iron, what journey?' Spear Catcher asked. 'How long? What must we do?'

Must I explain everything? Kalameshli wondered. But that was why he could overawe Spear Catcher so easily. The man preferred others to make the decisions. *If my decisions had left me with a face like yours, perhaps I'd think the same.*

'Some few days, three perhaps,' Kalameshli laid out patiently. 'I . . .' How to say this, when he barely understood it himself? 'I go to see the secrets of the Serpent, to take their wisdom.' It sounded fierce enough to satisfy them.

'Let me come with you,' Spear Catcher offered. 'Let all of us come.'

Hesprec shook her head slightly but left the talking to him.

'I know their watchers and their guards could not stop you,' Takes Iron told the man, 'but once those walls are kicked down, there's no rebuilding them. Let them think we're tame dogs for now. But be ready. If I come, or if I send the Crow with the word, then let nothing keep you penned here. Before then, give them no warning, you understand?'

'Of course.' And most of the warband were nodding now, happy with the prospect of flexing their muscles sometime soon, but willing to let Kalameshli stalk ahead and flush out the quarry first.

25

Loud Thunder expected Mother to send for him the next day. He sat at his own fire, apart from all others, and waited for one of his people to cast a shadow over him, or else for the sly slink of the Coyotes. Nobody came. If Mother knew what he had done – and surely she did – then she was leaving him to his own stupidity.

His dogs whined and danced anxiously about him as he fed them breakfast. 'So,' he said to them. 'You care if I live or die then. If only because who else will feed you, if I'm gone?'

'I will.' And here were the Coyote after all, both of them. Two Heads Talking stopped just the right distance from Thunder's fire, waiting until the Bear jerked his head at them, inviting them closer.

'They won't be the only ones who miss you.' Two Heads sat down, making a great show of how old and tired his bones were. Though probably he'd be off quick enough if Thunder were to roar at him.

'If you've come to tell me how stupid I am, I can do that myself,' the Bear told him gruffly.

'Not us.'

'No words from Mother?'

Two Heads Talking shrugged. 'The Mother of the Bear can find better messengers.'

Loud Thunder rumbled doubtfully, deep in his chest.

'How will you fight him?' Quiet When Loud asked in her smallest voice.

'Don't know.' Loud Thunder had twice the strength of the Eyrie Champion, but he couldn't fly or even match the man's speed on the ground. Yellow Claw was a testament to the fact that being a braggart didn't mean you weren't a warrior. 'You're wise, you two. Have you come to tell me some secret weak spot he has, some clever way to defeat him?'

The Coyote exchanged glances. 'We wouldn't know of such things,' Two Heads confirmed.

'Didn't think so. Why are you here, then? I've no breakfast for you. The dogs have had it.'

'Because you're very alone,' Quiet When Loud told him. 'We see you: your own people won't face you, and you have no one else. But you're doing what needs to be done.'

Loud Thunder snorted at that. 'Fighting Yellow Claw?'

'Yes.'

He blinked at them both. In the front of his mind, on the tip of his tongue: *But it's because I want his wife, who I cannot have even if I kill him. There's no point to any of it. It was a stupid challenge.* But there was no acknowledgement of any of that in their faces. They seemed to think this was all a good idea.

'He has spoiled your hunt at every turn,' Two Heads remarked sadly. 'Wherever you have gone, whatever words you have spoken, Yellow Claw's shadow has fallen there and he has said bitter things about what a fool Loud Thunder is, what fools his hosts are, what fools all of us are. Wherever you've tried to sow peace, he's grown up like a nettle. Everyone wonders you've left it so long.'

Loud Thunder stared at him. *I had no idea.* Should he say that? What would Two Heads think, then?

Except he didn't even know what the Coyote thought *now*, really. They were too clever by half, the Wolf's little siblings, who had to live by their cunning because they were not strong. Did Two Heads believe what he was saying? He would have spent

249

the night walking from fire to fire, because Coyote travelled everywhere and was everyone's guest. What stories had these two been telling all night, about why Loud Thunder did what he did?

When he left his fire to shamble towards the circle, people looked at him differently. He was just Loud Thunder, wearing his grease-hardened armour of fleeces, his copper-headed axe over his shoulder, his dogs at his heels. But people stared as though he was on fire.

Some of them just wanted to be entertained by a little more blood, he knew. His own people watched him with the sort of interest they would give a pot of honey or a string of fish. Of his guests, there were a few who hated Yellow Claw, who grinned and nodded at Loud Thunder as though he was doing this for their personal benefit. There were many more who feared him for it. *Who is next, they're thinking,* he thought to himself. *And will everyone just leave, if I kill Yellow Claw? Will they leave if he kills me? I don't think I thought this through . . .*

If he pulled the wings off Yellow Claw then he would go straight for the Eyrie's camp. He would find Kailovela at her fire, and he would take her away from there. He would find some quiet place for the two of them, and he would unlace the halter of hair from her neck and she . . . she would be grateful . . . probably she would be grateful. In his mind she was a comforting weight in his arms, clinging to him as he rescued her from tormentors that he tried to forget were her own people. In his mind she was not kicking and yelling at him, trying to prise loose the iron grip of his huge hands.

Loud Thunder stopped, feeling sick. *Too late for sensible thoughts now. You made it so Yellow Claw can't back down. Neither can you.*

He had been looking mostly at his feet as he shuffled along, but his dogs growled low to warn him and he looked up to see the Owl, Seven Mending, standing right in his way. She did not look pleased. She might be no great friend of Yellow Claw, but she was Eyrie, and probably she knew why Loud Thunder was digging this hole for himself. *Owls see more than the rest of us, especially of dark things.* She stared past him, but she was in his way. It was a challenge, of sorts. *Explain yourself. Mend what you have broken.*

Loud Thunder heaved a great sigh. *I never had the words for that sort of thing.* Patiently, ridiculously, he detoured around her, still at his slow, sleep-walking pace. He sensed the fury of her attention on him with every step, for all she never looked at him. *What's one more enemy?*

There was a crowd gathered at the circle ahead. He felt his own approach slow as he heard the murmur and buzz of their speculation. At last he had brought the Crown of the World together. Every tribe was represented there. They wanted to see their host kill his troublesome guest or the other way round. Most of them wouldn't care which.

Loud Thunder knelt by his dogs and leashed them, one after another. Two Heads Talking was still at his heels so he handed the traces to the Coyote. 'They will want to help,' he explained. Then he lumbered into the circle; just one step, enough to cross its boundary and commit himself. He shrugged the axe from his shoulder and set it head-down, resting a hand on its butt. The talk of spectators passed back and forth across him but he paid it no heed.

'Where is Yellow Claw?' He looked about the circle, seeing none of the Hawk, none of the Eyrie at all save some Owls. *Did they just go?* A stab of panic. *Did they take* her *with them?*

Then a piercing screech cut across the sky, followed by the shadow of vast wings. Yellow Claw dropped straight into the circle, landing in its centre and stepping back, curved bronze knives in his hands. All around, the warriors of the Hawk were stooping down to land, shouldering others out of the way, raucous and hungry for blood.

'You called, I came,' Yellow Claw announced. He was wearing

a cuirass of bones with thorns woven amongst them, the same armour on his forearms and shins. More thorns were in a circlet about his brow, and all these would jut like barbs from his feathers when he was Stepped. He had picked Loud Thunder for a grappler and would make him pay for trying it.

Thunder took a deep breath, but his heart was hammering already. Part of his mind was racing about the inside of his skull, calling, *Is she watching? Is she somewhere seeing this?* It was not a thought that would help him win.

Standing at last in front of Yellow Claw, he abruptly realized he did not want to lose, as though he had never really thought about it before. He would suffer surely – humiliation and pain before the whole Crown of the World. Before Kailovela.

With a great roar he whirled his axe up in a sweep that seemed to take up all the circle, charging so as to drive his enemy before him like chaff. Yellow Claw leapt up – and just kept on going, a talon raking Loud Thunder's cheek as he passed overhead. He landed almost exactly where Thunder had started off, laughing.

'Your circle is set in the earth, son of the Bear!' he sneered. 'Be sure you don't stumble out of it.'

Thunder rounded on him and hacked again, another artless, bludgeoning strike that would have turned the man to broken bones and offal if it had landed. Again Yellow Claw easily vaulted it – a beat of wings overhead and then he was behind again, leaving a second shallow red line in Thunder's skin.

'There is no circle in the sky,' he pointed out, grinning. 'I have everywhere between the horizons.'

Thunder went for him again, but he kept the axe moving, turning the crude strike into a pattern of sharp copper in the air, looping the weighty head so that it followed Yellow Claw up. This time there was no return strike, and for a second the great eagle was fumbling in the air, fighting to keep clear of Thunder's swing. Then the bird dropped behind him – the beat of its wings buffeted him, barbed feathers raking his skin. The momentum of the axe cut into his options, making him predictable. He did not even realize Claw had Stepped until the knife drove in. He felt the stab of pain below his shoulder blade and dragged the axe round, but Claw was already sliding sideways out of his reach. His armour had taken some of the force, but he could feel blood slicking down his back. Each blow like that would slow him until his enemy could find his throat or his eyes.

Yellow Claw still had his damnable smile. 'I have the soul of a Champion,' he reminded the world proudly. 'Will you not Step now, Son of the Bear, so your own soul may pass on easily?' Behind his words was the panicked growling of Thunder's dogs, desperate to go help their master. No matter the rest of the world, they had faith in him. That gave him strength.

Thunder Stepped, throwing himself forwards even as he did so, bulking out into a bear that seemed to consume the whole circle. Charging with the speed that everyone forgot bears could call on, he had a moment's satisfied glimpse of Yellow Claw's face – caught off guard midway through his own blather. The man was still too fast for him: one of the Eyrieman's feet actually got purchase on Thunder's neck as he leapt up, and then the wings were out again and he was screeching fury. Thunder bellowed right back. He reared up – twice the height of a man, and his hooked copper claws reaching even further. Yellow Claw's own talons threatened his eyes and gouged furrows in his muzzle. His vast wings boomed about Thunder like thunder itself as he rose up.

The tips of two claws caught at the eagle's leg and hooked in the scales there, just for a moment. Thunder threw all his weight behind them, desperate for leverage, fighting the colossal strength of the sky that was drawing Yellow Claw away from him. The eagle skewed across the circle, battling madly against him, and Thunder became a man, his claws a fist that caught and held. The bear was stronger but the man was strong enough, and he hauled Yellow Claw out of the sky and smashed him on the ground.

That was the idea, anyway – his enemy Stepped as well, landing on his hands and one foot. Thunder still heard half the breath whoosh out of him, but then Yellow Claw had kicked him in the face and got free. One of the bronze knives lanced him in the thigh, coming up under his armour and spilling more of his blood. The axe was useless, his enemy too close.

Loud Thunder backhanded the Eyrieman with all his strength, feeling his knuckles connect with satisfying force against the man's skull, spinning him away. Yellow Claw rolled over, almost out of the circle, before stumbling to his feet, shaking his head. His nose was broken and his own teeth had laid his cheek open from the inside. His face was awash with blood.

He Stepped again, but one second too late. Loud Thunder, axe forgotten, had the eagle in his grasp, one wing and one leg. The free talon ripped through his armour and scored deep lines across his chest. Then Yellow Claw was a man again, driving his knife down at his enemy's neck. Thunder shrugged aside, taking the blow across his shoulder, and slammed the Eyrieman into the ground, hearing ribs crack. Then he was a bear again, clawed forefeet grinding down on his prey, feeling the thorns tear at his skin, the talons of the bird, the blade of the man.

And he roared like all the world was falling down around them, just a single thunderous sound until Yellow Claw was still and frozen beneath him, human eyes wide and no more clever words.

Thunder stared down at him and felt the Bear at his back, driving him on. He opened his jaws wide and lunged, taking Yellow Claw's head between them. His enemy Stepped then, fighting him once more, but the eagle's beak could not reach him, and he had its fragile skull between his teeth.

If I kill him, I can take her. The thought rushed through him with each pulse of his pounding heart. *It's no more than Yellow Claw did, to claim her in the first place. She'll be glad of it. She'll thank me. She'll be grateful.*

Yellow Claw had gone still again, waiting. One twitch of

Thunder's jaws and his souls – the Eyrieman and the Champion that rode him – would be seeking new bodies far from here. *And good riddance.*

But that thought – *it's no more than Yellow Claw did* – was in him like one of those bronze knives, working its way deeper and deeper. Had Kailovela been grateful to be freed from her last mate by the Eyrie Champion? No, she had not.

But I will be kind to her. I'm not like him.

The sickness he had felt earlier was back. Part of him was still raging: *Kill the bastard and she's yours!* But he let go his hold and shambled back, blinking about him as though surprised to find himself there. Then he had Stepped and gone to get his axe, but not with any intention of putting it to use.

Yellow Claw Stepped too, one arm about his ribs, his cuirass smashed to fragments and his chest studded with his own thorns. His face was worse. Heal as he might, he would never be so handsome again. He spat something – some combination of mangled words and teeth – but Thunder shook his head.

'Anyone calling him the winner?' he growled. He hadn't meant it as a joke but some of them laughed anyway. 'Get him where I can't see him,' he snapped, and a couple of the bolder Eyriemen darted in and dragged their Champion away, too hastily to be gentle. Thunder scanned the crowd until he found that one Owl priestess. She nodded once, as though at some inner thought, and turned away. The anger he had seen on her face beforehand was gone. Apparently he had done the right thing.

He left the circle with a tired, foot-dragging tread and let Two Heads Talking and Quiet When Loud tend to his many wounds.

He had that night to rest in. He felt he'd shaken the others enough that nobody would try anything before dawn. When the dawn came, though, he made sure he was on his feet and being seen, limping between the camps with Yoff, Yaff and Husker trotting at his heels. He felt plenty of eyes on him: eyes that were

255

sizing him up, guessing at his wounds, wondering if he was in a position to enforce his new regime.

Some had left: a few Wolves, a handful of Tigers. There were no abandoned fires, though, no missing tribes. Later he realized that, in putting them all in the shadow of his axe, he was protecting them from each other. The thought was less than satisfactory. *Perhaps I only protect the wrongdoers from the wronged.* Too late to think of that, though. The thing was done.

He sensed someone before him and looked up, expecting the Owl priestess come to castigate him, or Yellow Claw, miraculously healed and ready for another bout. It was Ash Maker, though – the Boar woman who had been such a terror. She stood with arms by her sides, big hands curled into fists, staring at him. He waited for it: if anyone would test him, it would be her. For a long time she faced him, and he imagined everyone around them holding their breath.

Come on, then. The dogs sat attentively, not sure what was going on, but scenting the tension. They did not growl at Ash Maker, which was vexing. *Don't know why I keep them around.*

Then the Boar woman snorted and Stepped, becoming by far the most evil-looking sow he had ever seen, bristle-spined and with tusks made for eviscerating. She trotted off without a backwards glance. *Not today, then.*

He lurched on, feeling the wound in his leg stretch and tighten. Other than letting himself be seen, he wasn't sure where he was going. The Eyriemen's camp was like a little coal in his mind but he would not look at it. Not to see *her.* Not to regret leaving his enemy alive.

Instead, he stared straight ahead, looking east, past the last fires and off towards the mountainous horizon. There, in the rugged country where the rocks had no more caves for his people to claim, where none of his new guests had chosen to camp, he saw a great cloaked figure, a woman almost his own size, and made larger still by the great fur cloak settled on her shoulders, with her grey hair unbound and rippling in the breeze. *Mother.*

He hobbled over to her, wondering what had brought her out with the sunrise when she would sleep till noon half the time. She did not look at him, though: her eyes were fixed on another figure, approaching from the east.

It was a bear, a large one, and hurt. It dragged its paws and swayed as it walked, exhaustion in every muscle. He was far too slow to recognize Lone Mountain. With a curse he had Stepped and was lumbering forwards, the dogs yaffing and yoffing behind him. He loped towards his returning cousin, heart leaping. *He's alive! What did he find? What can he tell us?*

Closer, he saw that one of Lone Mountain's haunches was stiff and spiky with blood. The approaching bear's steps were uncertain and the slope of the ground made Lone Mountain weave like a drunk man. He was thin, too, the swag belly on him hollowed out, his skin hanging off him. He had been dragging his wound a long way over the mountain passes.

Loud Thunder Stepped, calling, 'Lone Mountain! Cousin! Let me help you!'

The bear slowed and swayed, shaking his head and growling uncertainly.

'Come,' Thunder addressed him. 'Give me your arm, I shall give you my shoulder. There is a fire waiting for you, a meal, wise heads for your hurts.'

But the bear that was Lone Mountain just stared at him dumbly, making a querulous noise in his throat. He shied away from Thunder and moaned strangely, a sound like nothing heard from either bear or man.

Somewhere behind those wounded animal eyes, was there some trapped spark wrestling for lost language to describe what had happened to it? Lone Mountain lurched away and continued his painful progress towards Mother. Nothing in his course suggested he knew his kinsman at all.

26

When Hesprec presented herself before Matsur, Kalameshli could see the other Serpent priestess was less than happy she wasn't alone. The Wolf grinned to himself at that. He might be allies with Hesprec for now but it was for Maniye only; he owed nothing to this other Snake.

'This is a matter for the Serpent alone.' Matsur was obviously trying to draw Hesprec off to speak to her somewhere else, but she wasn't going.

'I have been to the Crown of the World. I have brought back the wisdom of the north. I bring the gift of that counsel to our gathering.'

'You cannot think that this man will understand—'

'That will be frustrating for him. It will not harm you.'

'Hesprec—'

She hissed, holding a slender finger up. 'Matsur, I shall follow your path into the estuary, but not alone.'

The other Serpent paused, and the expression on his face was one Kalameshli recognized. He had dealt with other Wolf priests over many years. They served the same god, and so they could speak their secrets and trade the wolf-wood and the iron. And yet they served different tribes, and the children of the Wolf were often at odds. A brother priest could yet be an enemy, just as in any family.

Matsur was aghast at the implication that he might mean

harm to Hesprec. Aghast, and yet unable to come out and deny the possibility of it. The Serpent were divided too, just as Hesprec had feared. It made Kalameshli like them more.

'Or I stay here and contemplate the paths of the earth,' Hesprec offered blithely. 'Or perhaps venture upriver to Atahlan and speak to the priests there. Perhaps I don't need to see this wonder of yours.'

'He will regret what he learns,' Matsur said in a defeated voice.

'A moment ago he would not understand,' Hesprec noted. 'I am eager to know which of these truths we might encounter.'

So they trekked out into the estuary, following dry paths that were invisible until Matsur trod them. Kalameshli went Stepped, trying to sift through the wealth of unfamiliar scents and sounds for something he knew. Was Maniye still out here, dodging the soldiers of the girl-Kasra? No word had come to Tsokawan. Either she was still shepherding the useless River boy about with her, or some fate had befallen her. Surely otherwise she would have come back to her people.

He managed to murmur a question to Hesprec, when they stopped for the night. Matsur had chosen a hump of land breaking through the brackish waters like the back of a turtle, and was busy setting a fire. Hesprec shrugged. 'Perhaps whoever we meet will have heard something,' she suggested, without much faith.

Stepped again, Kalameshli kept his own watch until the moon was high, after which he hoped the Wolf of the north would keep an eye open on his account. He faced into the darkness, the fire at his back, and the Serpents talked in whispers behind him. Probably Hesprec knew how sharp the ears of a wolf were. Possibly her kinsman did not.

'I come home to find nothing where I left it,' Hesprec complained, 'including my family. What has happened to you all? It's like a disease has you.'

'A plague,' Matsur echoed, weighting the word. The shadows

of old, old stories seemed to gather beyond the firelight. 'The estuary was always the touchstone for how well we had built along the river. Go to Atahlan – you'll find them without a worry, save for the succession. But here, we can see it all unravelling.'

'These things are known: we built on sand when we built here,' Hesprec commented.

'Those things were never known enough. When it was clear we had no chosen Kasra, the doubts crept in here. Each of the tribes still remembers the way they were before they became part of the Nation. Some fall away from us because their gods pull them. Others remember how dark those days were, how bloody. They grasp for any kind of security. Give them a Kasra and a united Serpent and they're happy. Take those away and you're taking away the walls of their world. They look outwards and see only the dark.'

'So swiftly . . . ?'

'You've been collecting your prophecies of doom for a long time,' Matsur noted. 'Every priest and wise man in the estuary has seen some sharp edge of that doom. A great fear has been eating into them, and now they have nothing to shelter behind. All the old dark ideas are still out there, if you open your mind to them. They say the Rat cult is in some of the villages. The Strangling Men . . . Worse things. They wield the knife because they fear it's either that or be cut.'

Soon after, Kalameshli scented Coyote and Crow, and knew that his two unreliable scouts had at least not forgotten their work. With them close by he consented to sleep, laying his head on his paws and trying to ignore the constant buzz and whine and croak that was the estuary at night. He felt a long way from home. As he was drifting, Matsur spoke again, words that Kalameshli took in, but could not make much of.

'What if we were wrong, at the start?' the Serpent man murmured. 'What if all this was a grand mistake?'

'All this?' Hesprec asked, sounding puzzled.

'The Nation, the Kasra, all we built. What if we should never have left?'

'You're mad,' the girl Serpent said promptly. 'The Pale Shadow came.'

'Neither you nor I was there,' Matsur whispered, on the very edge of Kalameshli's hearing. 'There is none left now, who knows. What if we had been better to stay, and endure the shadow?'

But Hesprec snapped, 'I trust to the wisdom of those who were there. I trust to the choices they made.'

'The wise have open minds,' Matsur replied, and that was the last he said that Kalameshli could hear.

The next day, Matsur was complaining about a dog that had got at his pack and eaten his food, and Kalameshli laughed to himself at the daring of the little Coyote girl. And at her soft tread, too, for she had woken none of them.

After that, they made a swift pace, following paths Matsur knew. Kalameshli held to his wolf shape most of the time: it possessed strength his ageing human bones had lost. He trailed along after the two Serpents, close enough to see where they trod but still hanging back a little. He could almost fool himself that he was stalking them.

The fragrance of the estuary was chaotic – a hundred unfamiliar plants and animals. By late that day he had grown used enough to it that his nose recognized a familiar taint, and he straightened up into his human shape. 'There is death ahead,' he called.

Beyond Hesprec, Matsur frowned. 'Therumit should be close, now.'

'Then she may not be as you expect,' Kalameshli stated. 'I smell decay, dead men.'

They hurried on, and ahead of them the murk between the trees became not more trees but stone laid on stone. There was a great ruin here, half sunk in the swamp, and Kalameshli

261

reckoned it would have challenged Tsokawan when it was in its prime. By now the stink of rot was enough that he didn't need to Step to scent it, and Matsur's movements were swifter as he clambered over fallen stones to get inside.

Within, the sight that met them stilled them all. There were corpses there, a good half dozen at least: starved-looking men and women, River People and some other tribes Kalameshli didn't know. They had been dead just as long as his nose had told him, and the creatures of the estuary were busy taking the flesh off their bones. He saw long saw-backed lizards, crocodiles, vultures and hawks all glutting themselves, and the air was thick with great black flies.

There was one living woman there to greet them, though, seated across the hollow sunken space of the ruins. Although she was only perched on fallen masonry, she seemed enthroned there like the boy-Kasra had been at Tsokawan, the carrion around her as her court. It was the old Serpent woman whom Kalameshli had glimpsed at the fortress. She was withered, bleached pale as Hesprec had once been, but there was a definite power to her. *Not someone to cross.*

'Therumit,' Hesprec named her. 'What is this?' She spread her hands. 'I see weals on their necks. You brought me here to show me the Stranglers have sprung up again?'

The old woman laughed hollowly, the sound cutting through the murmur of the flies. 'We are the Stranglers. The Serpent has many heads. Wherever the people of the estuary turn, in their doubt, they find us.'

'But this is not it,' Matsur broke in. 'Therumit, Hesprec has come here to learn our secret.'

'Has she indeed?' the ancient Snake asked. 'And does she think she's ready?'

'*She* awaits this secret of yours,' Hesprec said sharply. 'Before knowing it, how can *she* judge it?'

'Hesprec is respected in Atahlan,' Matsur argued. 'More than

262

you or I. We've been too many lives here in the estuary. They've forgotten us.'

Therumit's eyes flashed fire at that. *We will remind them soon enough.* The thought was carved on her face. Kalameshli found himself liking her a little, despite himself. She stood abruptly. Her white robe was streaked with grime and dried gore, and flies crawled all over it. Even so, she carried herself like more of a ruler than the boy-Kasra ever had.

'Come then, old friend. See how the world has turned behind your back. And what is this you've brought with you?'

'I am Takes Iron of the Winter Runners,' Kalameshli told her flatly, meeting that lancing gaze. 'I speak for the Wolf.'

Matsur tensed, ready to be reprimanded, but Therumit just nodded. Then she turned away, progressing across the face of the ruin, stepping over a corpse and moving an over-inquisitive reptile with a nudge of her toe.

Kalameshli bent low to Hesprec's ear, his eyes never leaving the old woman's back. 'Does madness come to the Serpent as to other men?'

Hesprec made no answer, but there was a tautness to her face that said the answer was, at least, not a straight 'no'. Matsur was behind them, his tread nervous. Kalameshli reckoned he could Step and be at his throat if needed. The woman was the dangerous one.

Then Therumit stopped, one thin, pale hand raised. 'You have travelled, Hesprec. You have seen many lands and ways. You have not seen this. You will not want to have seen it. None of us did, at first. We wasted much time, spilled needless blood. But know that whatever rage and horror you feel, it has been felt before. You must see past it.'

Hesprec made a noncommittal noise, and then drew a sharp breath because there were newcomers standing beyond Therumit, as though they had arisen from the shadows. Two were warriors, a big woman and a larger man, broad-shouldered and dark, but not River People. They wore helms made from tiger

263

skulls, it seemed to Kalameshli, and blotchy, spotted pelts across one shoulder. In their hands were flat clubs studded with fangs of stone. The central figure, the master to these minions, was robed and hooded, with something weirdly insubstantial about it – as though Kalameshli could look right through it if he squinted hard enough. Then Kalameshli became aware of movement – first above, at the ruin's rim, and then all around them. He barked out a warning and had his knife in his hand even as there were bodies raining down on them.

They were more starvelings in rags, wild-eyed estuary people with raw welts at their throats – Takes Iron knew it for the mark of some initiation that had bitten deep into them. They dropped on him and Hesprec and he was fighting immediately, his iron edge cutting at hands and arms, paring them away even as they reached for him. Then there were too many hands, and he Stepped, his smaller wolf shape slipping from their grasp, chewing at anything that got in his way. He could hear Hesprec's yell become a furious hiss, but at that moment he could only worry about himself. He snapped and snarled, ripped at hamstrings and savaged fingers, but there were too many of them, a forest of legs wherever he turned, his pelt seized and tugged from every direction. The grasp of their hands fumbling at his back, his limbs, his throat. Abruptly he was a man again, a pair of thin arms clasping his neck. He drove his knife backwards and his attacker fell away. Another tried to take the man's place, but there was a new wolf snarling at his feet – no, not a wolf, a coyote.

Kalameshli's wild gaze caught the moment when Hesprec was forced into her human shape – one moment a snake as thick as his thigh, fangs dripping venom as it lashed around, the next just a dark girl held by many hands. Sathewe was still dashing through the mob of attackers, snapping at their legs, making so much commotion that they must have thought a whole pack was at their heels.

He saw the flurry of dark wings even as he got his knife into

264

the face of another River man, losing it as it wedged in his victim's eyesocket and was hauled from his failing grip. 'Go!' he howled at the sky. 'Do what I told you!'

Feeds on Rags was human for a second, crouched above him on a broken pillar, eyes panicked. He might have done anything in that moment, but against all odds the Crow followed orders. He Stepped, swerving to avoid a flung stone, and then he was away in a flurry of black feathers.

Hands reached round Kalameshli, arms hooking his throat and limbs. He fought, but they were gripping him tight, together forming a single constricting body squeezing him, squeezing the fight and the life out of him.

Feeds on Rags' wings fought with the thick damp air. His mind was in fragments. Sathewe was behind. He'd led her into trouble *again*, and this time – this time it was trouble that even the old growler Takes Iron couldn't fight.

He heard her scream – not pain but utter terror – a sound she'd never made before. She never met anything that scared her much at all. Sick through his whole body, Feeds on Rags soared above the trees of the estuary, above its mud and water-gleam and secrets. He could see the tall shadow of Tsokawan through the mist. He was going to rouse the warband, and they would answer, if they had to gnaw their way out of the River People's innards to do it.

27

Afterwards, Shyri was never quite certain what old Asman knew, what he guessed, or whether the man was a magician whose manipulation of the world was so effortless as to be invisible.

At the time she took it for a bad sign that Asman and his people took to their boats at night, and abandoned Tsokawan. True, more and more of Tecumet's people had been creeping in as Tecuman's support evaporated. Thus far, Esumit the Serpent had ensured no knives were drawn, but anyone who was still against Tecumet was getting nasty looks, and everyone knew Asman was Tecuman's chief counsellor.

So he had gone rather than risk a knife coming for him, as it had come for Tecuman, and Shyri had been hard pressed to find a boat she could manage, to follow after. She assumed this was what Asmander would want her to do, and she was curious as to what Asman might be up to, which was a more compelling reason. Perhaps the old man had an army hidden somewhere upriver. Perhaps he was going to come back and spring some masterful trap to destroy Tecumet and her warriors. Everyone went on about how cunning Asman was.

And yet, at the same time, it did look a great deal as though he was just running away. When his boat docked, it was only at a big farm on the fringes of the estuary. There was a village there, of the flat-roofed mud buildings of River Lords, and beyond that there was a big house. It wasn't much compared to the stone spires of Tsokawan, but it was the biggest thing in sight, painted white to throw back the sunlight, and surrounded by a sort of tame estuary, greenery kept under careful control. Beyond it stretched fields and fields, knitted together by a lacework of silver channels cut from the river.

Asman and his retinue had outpaced Shyri there, but the old man must be in the big house with his servants. There were some guards about – River Lord spearmen on the bank and the boundaries, plus some suspiciously vigilant crocodiles in the water. Not an army, though. Not enough to take Tsokawan or fend off a determined assault by Tecumet's forces.

Shyri didn't rush in; she had a bad history with that tactic. Instead she went to the estuary and watched for some time, hoping that Asman's grand plan would somehow reveal itself to her. It didn't. She glimpsed the man sometimes in his gardens or briefing his guards, but mostly he stayed out of sight behind his walls, whilst a steady trickle of his people went in and out. Perhaps he was organizing a grand assault; perhaps this was just how things were run when the master was home.

At last, that night, boredom got the better of her and she crept out of the trees and played dodge-the-guards until she was in the fields. The River Lords kept to their human shapes on land, at least, and a hyena saw better under the moon than any man who ever lived. She counted their patrols and slunk in with her belly to the ground.

She had seen that the farmers used the same tracks over and over. Some parts of the land were crawling with them each morning, growing grapes and yams and the barley they made bread and beer out of. Other parts were left for the weeds. She found herself a little den hidden in the tall grass, and rid the world of a handful of mice while she waited for dawn.

Her nose told her something was up before the rest of her realized. Sunrise had begun to lighten the sea but the great dark wedge of the estuary cast a long shadow over Asman's estate. Just enough time, then, for a latecomer spy to creep in. Her nose had picked up a scent that wasn't man and wasn't Old Crocodile, but still one she knew. It was the smell of Asmander's fighting shape.

Of course there were more Champions on the river than Asmander, and so she tailed the stalking creature cautiously for a while – didn't Tecumet have some girl who could pull the same trick, after all? But her nose had made its mind up: Asmander for sure.

When she appeared almost under his feet, he nearly went for her, but she wouldn't have minded that. She trusted that she could skip aside for long enough, and the pained expression he wore when he Stepped made it all worthwhile.

'You?' he demanded, crouching low in the long grass.

'Always so unhappy to see me,' she noted. 'Also, you are terrible at being quiet. And at listening. I was following you for—'

'What are you doing here?' Asmander hissed.

'Watching.'

'Watching what? I told you to—'

'I don't do what you tell me,' she snapped. 'Watching your father.'

He blinked. 'He's here?'

'No. I can see really, really far away.'

He frowned blankly at her. 'That's wit on the Plains, is it?'

'Perhaps I should go back there.'

Now he had a hand to his forehead as though trying to stop it popping open. She had forgotten how satisfying annoying him was.

'Tell me,' he asked, and she relented and laid out what had happened.

He had thought the house might have been taken by Tecumet, hence creeping about on his own doorstep. Now he stood and rolled his shoulders like a man going into battle. 'I will tell my father to ready the house for guests,' he decided.

★

268

Asmander had hoped to have the Bluegreen Reach estate to himself. In his plan, his father had still been in Tsokawan shoring up Tecuman's claim to the throne. To find the man already here was unwelcome. It made Asmander just a piece in someone else's game once more.

Asman received them in the big central courtyard of the house, open to the sky. He made a great show of greeting Tecuman, bowing before him, calling him Kasra. Servants were sent scurrying off to fetch anything the boy might need after his ordeal. The best chamber in the house was prepared for him. The two Wolves were consigned to smaller quarters with less ceremony.

Next Asman turned his gaze on his son, and it was narrow. Asmander stood there and bore it, just as he had so many times.

'Word will get to Tecumet that he's here,' Asman noted. 'Did you think of that?'

'We couldn't just hide in the estuary. Worse things hunt there than Tecumet's people,' Asmander reported calmly. 'Why . . . ?'

'I left Tsokawan because I could see the tide going out. I wasn't the first. The clans loyal to your boy are falling back to their estates. Tecumet hasn't made a hard move against us, but everyone can see it coming. And some of them bowed the knee to her, of course. The weak ones. At Tsokawan, her eyes were on me every moment. I couldn't send people to look for the boy. From here, I can.'

'And now you don't need to.'

Asman stared at him coldly. 'Yes, by all means let us celebrate your decisions. Tecuman is here at the Bluegreen Reach. The world is saved.'

Asmander fought down a spark of anger with the ease of long experience. 'He lives.'

'He doesn't rule. He needs his people to rally to him. Tsokawan is the place for that—'

'Let them rally here. Let us gather every weapon we can and

269

take the river back from them.' Even saying it, Asmander felt it was foolishness, but he had no other way to turn.

Asman gave a great sigh. 'You'd raise our banners and go to war, would you? With whatever rabble you can muster?'

'For the true Kasra.'

'For your friend.'

'Yes.'

'You were friends with the girl, too, remember?'

'Yes, but the priests say—'

'These things are known: the Serpent has many heads.' Asman grimaced in disgust. 'Our clan has only one. However we act, it must end with the Bluegreen Reach riding high on the tide. That means no banners and no battles unless we can be sure we'll win. I despair of our clan's decline the moment you take my name.'

Asmander stared at him mulishly.

'I will send you to Tecumet once more,' Asman decided. 'You can at least learn what her plans are, and if this goes badly perhaps she will remember you as a friend again.'

'No,' Asmander declared.

Asman blinked, and then repeated, in exactly the same tone, 'I will send you to—'

'No.' Asmander stood his ground. 'Not again. I stay here.' He could feel the Champion within him, rising close to the surface, looking for a fight. Asman stared at him long and hard, and Asmander braced himself, but at last his father shook his head sourly.

'Well then, stay out from underfoot while I find a way to restore the boy and save the fortunes of our clan. Because if all you're for is fighting, then you're no use to me at all.' Asman bared his teeth in annoyance. 'You will never understand how hard I have worked for your future,' he told his son, and flicked his fingers in dismissal.

★

270

After that, Asmander checked that the two Wolves were being looked after – they had been stowed in cramped servants' rooms without much courtesy, but they were being fed and that seemed to be enough for them. Then he went to Tecuman, who was in the grand guest chamber in the south wing. The boy-Kasra had musicians there, and servants in case he needed anything, and food and wine. His eyes smiled at Asmander, though he kept the rest of his face solemn – a mask to replace the one he had left at Tsokawan. Asmander wanted to send everyone else out and just talk, reassure his friend that all would be well. He wanted to take Tecuman's hands and swear his loyalty again. He wanted them to be as they were when they were children. But he just bowed and stepped out of the room. Tecuman needed to remember what it was to be Kasra.

Instead, Asmander went to find Shyri. She had not been part of his triumphal entrance, despite her demands to see how his father treated him. He had found a hut for her at the edge of the village and made her a guest of the family there. Word would get to Asman eventually but probably not soon. Asmander decided that he wanted at least one pair of eyes that was his and his alone.

'Just watch,' he told her. She rolled her eyes, but she would do it.

Beyond the Bluegreen Reach the estuary was busy. In the shadow of its canopy, armed men were gathering in loose-knit bands, spread out from shadow to shadow. They kept no fires, and for once they were quiet and sober. They'd get to bloody their teeth soon enough, and that thought was enough to keep them in line for now.

The Black Teeth warriors, Venat's warband, had followed in Asmander's footsteps.

Venat himself went from group to group, slapping down arguments before they could get inconveniently loud, tasting their eagerness. They had come all the way from the islands with only a handful of dead longmouth soldiers and a few plundered swamp villages to keep them happy. Much longer and he wouldn't be able to hold on to them.

And they don't call the River Lords 'Patient Ones' for nothing. All that waiting and talking! It was Venat's good luck to find the one amongst them who was up for some action. Izel, Tecumet's Champion, had been a brooding, grim presence at his shoulder all the way to the Bluegreen Reach. Sometimes she had been in her human form, and just sulked and scowled and snarled at any of his people who tried their luck with her. More often she had taken her fighting shape, that stalking lizard that would always make Venat think of Asmander. Hers was darker, maybe a little larger, but there was that same lethal elegance about her. Of course that hadn't stopped one of his warriors from bothering her, but Venat had plenty more, and he wasn't going to shed a tear when someone got the stupid cut out of them the hard way.

Now they were stopped and in that fragile moment when his people were actually showing a little discipline. *These things are known: the Dragon's teeth all line up right before he bites, and only then.* Izel had been off somewhere, making contact with her masters. Now she was back and he had located her to make sure she was going to get her plan in motion, whatever it was, before his men got bored. But here she was, human again and walking straight for him no matter how many of his people were in the way. And they gave her room, too. *They've learned something! Who'd have believed it?*

'You know what you're doing now?' he asked her, facing her down. The problem with people like Izel and Venat was that neither would give ground so they ended up staring at one another a lot. 'Or did we just come to see how the harvest's going to be this year?'

'There are a lot of these estates about the estuary edge,' Izel told him. 'Most of Tecuman's supporters come from these lands.'

Venat made sure his expression told her just how interested he was in all of that.

'You were cast out from your people, before Asmander tamed you.' She said her fellow Champion's name with such hate that it almost took the sting from the rest. 'You were a pirate. You struck from the estuary at places like this.'

'These things are known.'

'So have your men do what they're good at. Have them start fires down the river after dark – on any estate but this one. Have them take what they want. Give me a night of flames and screaming.'

'But not here.'

'No. And not you. You stay here with me. I have a use for you.'

Venat found that he was not even slightly tempted to make a lascivious reply. He knew Izel was loyal to the girl-Kasra, but beyond that he couldn't imagine the woman having a single fond feeling for any living thing.

Still, these were orders that his men would like, and it would give them something to do. And if Izel's intention for him involved turning him into a corpse, he reckoned he could take her. He knew how Champions fought. Given where he was and who was around, it seemed possible the morning might see quite a few dead Champions.

28

Sathewe screamed, twisting and writhing as she tried to pull herself from the robed figure's grip. A hand pale as snow had her about the wrist, and she did not Step, but cried out and convulsed as though the touch was ice to her.

'Release her!' Takes Iron snapped. For all that he was held by a dozen scar-necked wretches, there must have been some authority left in his voice. The white hand flicked open and the Coyote girl dropped to the floor, sitting down hard and clutching her arm. Kalameshli almost expected there to be rotten black marks, like frostbite, where those fingers had touched.

Hesprec, as much a prisoner as he was, had retained her dignity. 'I am not impressed with your hospitality, Therumit. Perhaps you might explain . . .' and then she faltered to a halt, as the pale hand had reached up to cast the cowl back.

The woman revealed was pale and fair and utterly alien. Her features were sharp and thin, her eyes like ice. Nothing about her admitted to a kinship with her guards or any people Kalameshli had ever seen, north or south. She should have been unnatural, but she was beautiful, and that – Takes Iron decided – was part of her magic, a glamour about her that had nothing to do with the way she actually looked. But still, he felt there was something insubstantial about her, as though some vital part of her was missing, in a way his eyes could not detect.

'What is this?' Hesprec hissed flatly.

'She has come as an emissary,' Matsur put in. 'Not to threaten or to harm. Her . . . people wish to talk.'

'I find it difficult to hear any words when I am a prisoner,' Hesprec snapped. 'Captivity sounds loud in my ears.'

'As does the sound of your own voice, always,' Therumit remarked acidly. 'I will have your promise, first. That you will stay and listen.'

Hesprec stared at the pale creature, and Takes Iron saw fear in her that she had not shown when she was to be given to the jaws of the Wolf. Therumit's gaze was on him, next. 'And you, Iron Wolf. As you are a priest, swear that you shall keep the peace.'

'What is it?' he demanded, glowering at the emissary.

'I am Galethea, man of the north. My people have been guests of the Serpent long ago.' The pale woman's words were strangely spoken, hard to follow.

Kalameshli and Hesprec shared a tense glance, and the Serpent girl shuddered and nodded. 'Act like a host, and I shall behave as your guest,' Kalameshli told Therumit sourly, and the old woman made a brief gesture. The cultists released them both and stepped back, crouching about the stones and staring fearfully at . . . at everything, Takes Iron thought. At Therumit most of all, but the whole world seemed to make them flinch. Without their numbers, they had nothing.

He scowled at the nearest of them, making them back away, and then found himself a piece of ruin to sit on, because he was old and the air was hot and close; let these southerners and their emissary stand up and argue. Sathewe crept over to him on coyote paws and crouched at his feet. Hesprec was making a great business of tugging her robe into place and resettling her headscarf.

'If you wish us to be civilized in all things, then let us be so,' Therumit stated, as though asking to be free of the hands of the cultists was some bizarre affected luxury. 'Make a fire,' she instructed the cringing creatures around them, who scrambled to obey. The old Serpent priestess looked at them, face to face. 'I make you all my guests,' she stated, allowing for no refusal.

Kalameshli watched the neck-branded servants get some semblance of a fire going, nothing that he would dignify by the name of 'hearth'. The three Serpents and the pale woman took places about it, with much hesitation and many narrow looks. He remained on his stone, slightly further from the flames, one hand resting lightly on Sathewe's head.

The thin wretches melted away into the shadows again, and nobody drew attention to the corpses strewn around them, the flies and the stench and the carrion creatures. This, apparently, was 'civilized'.

'So,' Hesprec started. 'How long?'

'They first came two years before the Kasra died,' Matsur stated.

For just a little stick of a girl, Hesprec had an old priestess's glower. 'And why would you invite our old enemy to share your fire?' she asked.

'Because of you, sister,' Therumit stated. 'Because you and the other doomsayers had shown us all that the world was ending.'

'And we thought it must be *them*, when they first sent the Jaguar to bring word,' Matsur put in. 'Of course we did. But they came with the same warnings. Hesprec, even the *Pale Shadow* fear this doom.'

Kalameshli shook his head, a little. This was some Serpent tale not told in the north. Catching his movement, Hesprec sighed, rubbing at her face as though trying to smudge off the rainbow scale tattoos here. The quiet stretched out between them, something none of the Serpents seemed willing to break.

'The pale one, she has no soul.' Kalameshli dropped the words into that silence and watched the still waters break. 'What is she, that she has no soul?'

'They are our enemies,' Hesprec observed, obviously not ready for this Galethea to lay down any truths just yet. 'Let me tell you a story, man of the Wolf. After we came across the sea, the children of the Serpent joined with the Jaguar to build a new home for themselves, rich and good with all the secrets of the lands-that-had-been. And for generations, the people of that kingdom wanted for nothing, and the earth sprang with life at their touch, and they made a city to rival dreams.

'Then there came to their shores a new people, saying they were long-lost kin who had fled the Plague but become lost upon the seas. And we were grand and prosperous and open-handed, and they were beautiful and had many diversions and pleasures, and we welcomed them as long-lost family. They could not Step, for they said they had been cut off from their gods. We thought they would learn. They were bright and merry, and soon every lord and lady of our city had one to whisper secrets in their ear, and the chiefs of the Jaguar took pale men and women to mate. Soon we could not live without them, for all they had their own secret speech and took no totems, and had no souls. We thought they would learn. But we were the ignorant, in that city.

'And then one day we found the city was no longer ours, and the Jaguar no longer our friends, and everything we had was taken from us by these guests, who had told us they were friends. And so those of us who lived came north to the River.'

'And all we have built here is but a whisper of the Oldest Kingdom,' Matsur said reverently. 'A whisper and a dream.'

Kalameshli shook his head again. *I'd like to see them try that with the Wolf.*

Hesprec fixed the Pale Shadow woman with a keen eye. 'Convince me that you're not our enemy.'

The pale creature had waited through all of this, eyes flicking between the speakers. Kalameshli had a strange sense that she was working hard to follow the words – there was something to her look like dogs he had seen in other tribes, that understood a little human speech but not enough.

277

'You are the Seer,' Galethea pronounced. 'You watch the storm that is coming.'

Hesprec nodded impatiently.

'We have seen what is coming. We understand it more than you. Yes, we are your enemy, but the Plague People are both our enemies. That is why I am here. We offer our help, against the enemy that is coming.'

'And they offer more than that,' Matsur put in.

'Too little help is worse than none,' Hesprec decided. 'Why is yours so great a gift?'

'Because we know the enemy as you cannot.'

Hesprec made a show of being unimpressed, but Kalameshli saw the tension in her. 'There is a tale from the years after the fall of the Oldest Kingdom,' she said slowly. 'It is denied by many because of how foolish it makes us look. It says that the Pale Shadow were not fleeing the Plague after all. They were one and the same.'

Hesprec looked sharply at Galethea. If she was expecting protestations and denials, she was disappointed. Galethea's face was composed, still radiating that awful beauty that seemed to come from that soulless hollowness within her, which Kalameshli felt with his being rather than saw with his eyes. 'This was many generations ago,' she said, and seeing that Hesprec would not relent, 'but it is true. We were of the Families once, but they fell upon each other once you were gone, for that is the nature of people everywhere. So we fled, and most of us died upon the sea, but some few came to you, and you took us in.'

'And you repaid that.'

'I speak only truths at this fire. You were friends to us, and we were foes to you, but now a greater enemy has come, and we would be friends again. Because the Families will devour everything and remake these lands in their own image. And we will be cast down, and you . . . where will you run? You have no more world to flee to.'

Hesprec appeared to digest this, and Kalameshli bent low

and murmured in Sathewe's ear, so the coyote crept off amongst the bodies for him. Then Hesprec clapped her hands together sharply – they all jumped – and put on a bright smile. 'Well,' she remarked. 'I see now why none of this was taken to our siblings at Atahlan. Sharing a bed with the Pale Shadow?'

'Hesprec, you have been preaching doom for years,' Matsur insisted. 'Will you turn away any help, now?'

Hesprec stared from him to Therumit. 'You take this creature's prophecies so much more seriously than mine? Or is it that you have been here in the estuary so long that you fear you are forgotten, and this is a secret that makes you important again?'

Therumit's face twitched at the criticism, but Matsur was rushing on.

'There's more,' he insisted. 'Hesprec, you *know* us. Of course we were suspicious. Galethea is not their first emissary – the first two met worse ends because we feared to trust them. But then we thought of your warnings, and . . . they have an offer for us. They . . . they give us our world back.'

'This is our world.'

'What we have built here on the River?' Matsur threw up his hands. 'This makeshift imitation? Where we must work every day to stop everything coming apart, stone from stone? We have laboured lifetimes over this and all we have made is—'

'A whisper and a dream, yes,' finished Hesprec. 'Such is the world.'

'But it's not how it was,' Matsur insisted. 'They will give us back our Oldest Kingdom, Hesprec, if we will only share it with them. We won't have to scrape and struggle any more.'

Hesprec stared at him until at last Galethea's weirdly accented voice broke in. 'We will listen,' the Pale Shadow woman said. 'You will speak of the Serpent and we will listen. Is that not your way?' And the hollowness inside her came into her voice, a dreadful empty yearning. 'We want to have souls. We want what you have.'

279

'You have always wanted that,' Hesprec said darkly. She was leaning forwards, narrowed eyes fixed on the pale woman.

'Teach us,' said Galethea. 'Come back to your kingdom. Teach us, and learn from us. With our combined knowledge, we can fight our enemies.'

Takes Iron decided things had gone far enough. There was magic here, but none that the Wolf would like the scent of. He could see it working on the Serpent girl, word by word. He felt it in the air, so that when he tried to speak, it forced his voice back down his throat. It left him helpless in the face of this terrible, cold creature.

'Hesprec,' Therumit said. 'Go to Atahlan and speak for us. Tell them the dooms you've seen. Tell them that we need allies, no matter how unlikely. Tell them we can have our rightful place back. For it may be the River cannot be saved. It may be the world cannot be saved. But our Kingdom . . .'

Then a cold nose touched Kalameshli's hand, and Sathewe was there. In her jaws was his iron knife and he took it gratefully, not as a weapon but as a token of his god. The Wolf's strength flowed into him and he shrugged off the magic that the pale woman was weaving. He knew nothing of any Oldest Kingdom or Pale Shadow, but this pale creature made his hackles rise. Therumit was venomous and mad; Matsur blinded by what he wanted to believe. The Wolf was calling for him to rise up and open throats. And yet sometimes a priest needed tact. They were surrounded by the servants of the Snake, and even though they were weak, there were many of them.

So he stood and put on his best priestly manner, stern and forbidding. It was the face he used to scare children into obedience, to cow proud hunters into listening to him. 'All this talk,' he told them, and saw from all their faces that his opinion was unwelcome. Nonetheless, he pressed on. 'All this talk gives me a thirst, and my hosts have offered no drink. All this talk makes me hungry, and my hosts offer no food. This talk tires me, and your hearth is not restful.' The Serpents were staring at him, even Hesprec, and the pale woman most of all.

'I am Takes Iron of the Winter Runners,' he told them. 'We do not have Kasras or Old Kingdoms where I come from but we are good hosts to those we take as guests. So: I will leave your fire now, for I see I am not welcome, since you offer your guests nothing but words, which are dry in the mouth. I will return to the fortress on the river and seek food and drink and rest there. Hesprec, I charge you as my first host to take me there, for the paths of this place are strange to me.'

Hesprec drew breath to speak, and in that moment Kalameshli had no idea which way she might go, but Matsur broke in, protesting, 'This is not your place. You cannot understand the importance of what we speak of here.' He drew himself up, measuring himself against Takes Iron. 'We have lived many lives—'

'As have I,' Kalameshli told him. 'Wolf, and man, and wolf again. I know you Snakes are different. I have seen this one with an old face. But if you have lived many lives, where is your hospitality? The least pup of the Wolves knows things the oldest Serpent has forgotten.' And he was surprised at the rush of sour joy it gave him to say so: that there was this one stick he could beat them with.

'We are remiss,' Hesprec stated. She sounded reluctant, but she was speaking words Kalameshli wanted to hear. 'I shall guide my guest back to Tsokawan.'

'Hesprec—' Matsur started, but it was Therumit that Takes Iron was keeping an eye on.

'Go,' the old Serpent priestess said, 'but take our words with you. The knowledge will burrow into you as it has into us, that we can have it all *back*. So go, Hesprec Essen Skese. Travel as you might, your mind will not go far.'

Hesprec was standing by then, turning away from her kin with a troubled look. She pulled in her shoulders as though the gaze of Galethea was ice on her back.

★

They travelled into the night, putting distance between themselves and those sunken ruins. Hesprec said little, steering them a different way to the path they had taken before. Even so, when they made their camp at last, they were not left alone. Sathewe barked out a challenge, and then Matsur was there, looking grave and angry and anxious, all at once. He was plainly waiting for Hesprec to go and take counsel with him, but she gestured pointedly at their meagre fire. 'It's cold in the Crown of the World, Matsur.'

'What is your meaning?' he asked.

'Perhaps this is why they understand the importance of things we take for granted, like the hospitality of a fire. If you've yet more words to spend, bring them to our little hearth here. Be our guest, and behave as befits one.'

Matsur would only hover at the edge of the firelight. 'I want to know that you will not discount our words.'

'I want to know why you think I'm so important,' Hesprec remarked drily. 'I'm more used to being laughed out of Atahlan than listened to.'

'You underestimate your reputation.'

Hesprec sighed. 'I have known you and Therumit for many, many years. You are neither of you fools. My mind has been fed many meats it doesn't like the taste of, Matsur. Let me digest.'

It seemed the Serpent priest would raise some new objection, or that he would come to their fire after all, but after an uncertain moment he was gone, nothing but a snake slithering away into the dark. Hesprec sighed and settled back. 'Sometimes the path of the Serpent is a knot that is hard to unpick,' she observed. 'The trail of the Wolf is straight and simple in comparison.'

Kalameshli frowned, then realized there was a compliment in there, if he could dig down to it. He nodded stiffly. 'I suppose you will back the girl now, if these others back the boy?'

'Hmm?' The Serpent cocked an eyebrow at him.

'They want the boy to rule because he will do what they

want, and they want this alliance with these shadow creatures,' Kalameshli observed. 'So you will back the girl.'

'I back nobody,' Hesprec said, and she was thoughtful as she stared into the fire. Kalameshli remembered Therumit's parting words and knew that, amongst the Serpents, nothing was ever simple. Whatever aid or offer Galethea had been hinting at, it had been too fine for Wolf ears, but there were hooks in Hesprec still. He was willing to bet the Serpent girl would dream of that Oldest Kingdom when she slept, and perhaps a promised return to it. For himself, he decided that nothing good could ever come of such things.

29

Within Mother's cave, the great weight that was Lone Mountain shuddered with each breath. His eyes stared out at them without recognition. Even for his cousin, his rival, Loud Thunder, there was nothing.

Of all the people of the Bear, he knew only Mother. He had stumbled and lurched to her and put the huge blunt wedge of his head under her hand. The sound Lone Mountain had made then had turned Loud Thunder's stomach and broken his heart. He never wanted to hear that much pain and grief in one quiet sound again.

Mother had taken the limping bear to her cave, and there she had boiled herbs and made poultices, and sent for another hearth-wife of the Bear who was well known for her lore. Then the two of them had hunched together over the wounded animal. She had sent for Two Heads Talking and Quiet When Loud, and Seven Mending as well. They had spoken in low, worried voices, tried this herb and that, and all the time Lone Mountain's flanks had shuddered with each hard-won breath.

Loud Thunder sat at the entrance to Mother's cave with a heart like a stone, and waited, feeling each wheezing sigh tear something within him. Then Mother called out that he must fetch Icefoot of the Moon Eaters, and Thunder thought that could only mean death, for what medicine did a Wolf know that all the Bear and Owl and Coyote did not?

But he shambled out, feeling his own hurts as meagre things compared to the injury Mountain had taken. He fetched the white-haired bearskin priest who had watched him challenge Yellow Claw. When he heard that Mother of the Bear had requested him, the old man asked no questions.

After examining and then cleaning the wound, Icefoot took out the iron knife that was sacred to the Wolf, whetted its edge, and held it in the fire. When it glowed the fire's red back at him, he put it to Lone Mountain's haunch and cut. The huge bear screamed, another sound Thunder never wished to hear. He was called in to hold his cousin down – he and Mother and the hearth-wife, leaning all their strength to hold Mountain as still as they could while Icefoot cut, and cursed, and cut again, running his knife into and out of the fire between forays at Mountain's corrupted flesh.

And at last – after decades of struggle, it seemed to Thunder – he cried out in triumph and drew something from the wound, casting it to the cave's floor, where it rang and danced and was still.

Lone Mountain convulsed massively, and Thunder wasn't sure whether it was relief, or whether he was dying even so. His shuddering breath caught, held, then resumed as before. There was no sudden recovery.

While Quiet When Loud took his place at the wound with water and poultice and needle, Icefoot approached the thing he had dug from Lone Mountain's haunch. He had tongs with him, part of his priest's tools, and he lifted the token up and washed it clean of blood and pus. He sniffed at it, then laid it on the ground again and Stepped, bringing his wolf nose close then snatching it away. His face was grim when he resumed his human shape.

'Iron,' he said hollowly. 'Not iron as the Wolf knows it, but some cousin to that iron. What happened to him?'

But Lone Mountain was answering no questions, and nobody else could speak for him.

Thunder had sat at the mouth of Mother's cave for a long time before a voice brought him out of his solitude. Many had gathered, waiting for word. Everyone knew Lone Mountain was back and where he had returned from. Suddenly the whole squabbling pack of them had come together in full understanding of the Bear's purpose here. There was a threat to the east, beyond the mountains. There was a terror that had come from the sea.

Perhaps I didn't need to maul Yellow Claw after all.

They kept sending emissaries asking for news. His storm-cloud visage turned them all away. Lone Mountain was not ready to die, that was all Thunder knew. His body lived, and just as well, for none could say what might happen to his soul if he passed on in this state. What Mother guessed, beyond that, she kept with all her other secrets. Or perhaps even she had reached the far shores of her knowledge.

Then there was a light step near the cave mouth and he glowered up through red eyes. But it was her. Kailovela had come down from the Eyrie camp with a cloak of feathers about her shoulders, and alone. He had never seen her alone before.

'What . . . ?' he grunted. Speech came slowly to him, as though he was going the same way as Lone Mountain. She knelt down facing him, every bit the demure Eyriewoman. Except she was here without an escort, not even the Owls to watch her.

'You didn't bring the . . .' One of Thunder's hands made a vague, low gesture. *The little spirit.*

Kailovela shook her head. 'She's leashed. She cannot go anywhere.'

She sounded bitter. Thunder's eyes strayed to her own halter, the rope of hair about her neck. A leap of intuition told him she was here because Yellow Claw was hurt and in no position to keep an eye on his mate.

'How is your friend?' she asked, and he told her what little he knew. Hope leapt in him and he asked, 'Can you heal him?' She shone in his eyes, as though her face caught and threw back more of the sun than anyone else's. He would have believed anything of her.

But she just shook her head again. 'I'm sorry. I am no magician, Loud Thunder. Or, if I am, it's a magic that's done me no good.'

Still, he had her go into the cave – heedless of Mother's stare – and lay a hand on the slow-heaving flank of Lone Mountain. There was no miraculous cure, no sudden release to human shape. Just a sad Eyriewoman with a bowed head, and an injured bear.

Mother came to him that night, kicking him as he slumbered, a bear himself, at her doorstep. He started awake, growling, then bit back the snarl as he saw who it was. Mother was old – long past the age that most Stepped for the last time and walked off into the wilds. She was strong, though, and straight-backed. The years had piled up on her shoulders and she had borne them.

Now she stood over him, her knotted staff in her hand and a suspicious look on her face as he pushed himself tiredly to his clawed feet.

'We walk,' Mother told him. 'Don't Step. Just listen.' She sounded angry – with him, with the world, who could say? She sounded tired, too. Not just the weariness with everyone's stupidity that she usually projected, but real bone-deep exhaustion. She had not had a moment's rest since Lone Mountain returned. She strode out, cloak swirling like her own piece of night, and he padded heavily after her, into the darkness that held sway between all the fires of their guests.

'Nobody wants to see their prophecies come true,' Mother said shortly, or at least she said it out to the dark and the stars, and Thunder caught the words as he shambled along behind her. 'That Snake priestess, the one who changed, she must be feeling the knife even more than me. But we were all right. This one time, every halfwit priest and fortune teller in the Crown of the World saw it coming, some piece of it.' She came to a great stone and sat down gratefully, her eyes still on the sky. Loud Thunder settled at her feet and she put a hand on his back, digging her fingers into his pelt.

'Lone Mountain cannot come back to us,' she told him, and when his skin shivered she said, 'Yes, I know. You would have gone in his stead if you could. And then I would be speaking to him, and you'd be lying there.'

Thunder shuddered again and growled, deep in his throat.

'We need to fetch him back,' Mother told him. 'Someone must go to him and show him the way home.'

She was not asking him; she was not telling him. But then she seldom had to, to make her wishes fact. That Mother wanted something was enough, amongst the Bear. He lifted his head and looked at her sidelong, to let her know he understood.

'We will have more moon tomorrow,' she decided. 'Not enough moon, really, but I can't wait until it's full. He's drifting further from us. Soon enough he'll not know even me. So I'll show you the way. You'll go and find him, or . . .' Her voice shivered, and she did not finish the sentence. 'If any gods owe you favours, now's the time to go to their fire and beg their help.'

Morning's light didn't make any of this look rosier for him. *I preferred it when it was just fighting Yellow Claw.* Loud Thunder sat shivering at his fire, wondering how he could possibly prepare himself for such a journey. *I don't know where I'm going, but it's nowhere I ever travelled before.*

He wondered if any gods did think of him fondly. It seemed unlikely. The Bear mostly liked not being bothered: a big, lazy god prone to fierce rages when disturbed, and who brought howling winds and snowstorms down off the mountains. Loud Thunder was his son, but the Bear had no favoured children. Perhaps he might listen to Mother, perhaps not even to her.

Of the rest, Thunder felt he had been putting the backs of all the gods well and truly up. He had dragged their warring children to his hearth, and forbidden them to act out their

288

vengeances. The Wolf and the Tiger were hardly going to thank him for standing between them, after all.

Still, he went to Gnarl Hide, the Boar who had brought him a gift of honey, and he let the old man paint his face with ash and red earth. Gnarl Hide wore a tusked mask and danced before his fire while the Boar children made a racket with hollow sticks and pipes, until the air about Loud Thunder was so full of sound that he thought he heard a deeper squealing behind it all as the Boar heard his people. Gnarl Hide asked for him to endure, to find strength when all strength was gone.

Then he went to Icefoot, the Moon Eater priest. He brought a goat, and the Wolf had a stone altar that was a rough shadow of his god's jaws. They gave the goat to the fire, and ate of its flesh after, and Icefoot thought long and hard about what the Wolf might give to a Bear who must hunt.

'May your senses be keen,' he said. 'Find your quarry, and find your way home.'

With the stink of the Wolf's fires still on him, Thunder went to the Tiger camp and Aritchaka. In the depths of a cave they built their own fire, fanning the smoke until Thunder's eyes watered and his throat burned, and the patterns of red light and dark shadow on stone shifted and stalked about him, growling softly. Aritchaka named him for the Tiger, and begged that his feet be sure and the dark be his friend.

He knew none of the Deer but he came to their fire anyway, and a lean old man donned antlers and danced, and told him he would be swifter than the wind. Two Heads Talking shared a meal with him, of food taken slyly from the camps of other tribes, and asked for Coyote to grant him wisdom.

And then he went to the camp of the Eyriemen.

They were not pleased to see him. The warriors of the Hawk stood as he approached, and there were weapons in many hands. Loud Thunder ignored them. The Owl watched him narrowly as well, but he shrugged off their stares and their fear-painted faces. He went to Kailovela and told her what he must

289

do. She sat in her tent with the spirit creature. She was mending Yellow Claw's armour, he saw, while the man himself lay at the next hearth under the care of the Eyrie's healers.

'I cannot help you,' Kailovela told him simply. 'The Hawk will not listen to me. The Hawk listens only to men. Go speak to the Owl.'

Loud Thunder said nothing.

'Why are you here?' she asked him.

He had been waiting for the question. He had wanted to say something dramatic about the way she lit his world, that she was a brand bringing heat and fire to him whenever he saw her. But the words choked in his throat and he wished he had Stepped, so he had an excuse for saying nothing at all. He wanted to ask if she felt this same thing for him, and he said nothing because he did not want to hear the answer.

At last he said, 'What can I do for you?'

Kailovela blinked. 'Have you not come seeking something from the Eyrie?'

'Not the Eyrie. You. What can I do for you?' Each word was as hard to get out as a stone.

She said nothing, and that gave him a weird connection with her. Both of them were full of words they could not say. And he knew what she wanted. It wasn't what he *hoped* she would want, but it was something he could understand.

'Give me your blessing,' he said abruptly.

'I have no blessing. I am not a priestess.'

But he just looked at her, huge and heavy and mournful, until she leant forwards and laid a hand on him, on his shoulder first, and then against the line of his jaw, fingers losing themselves in his beard.

'Come back to us,' she told him. It was enough.

By then the day was almost done. The west was gaping to receive the sun. The night hung over his head like a boulder. The various blessings and benedictions he had received seemed flimsy and fragile, things that even a breeze might shred. He felt

290

the evening chill coming on – he, a man of the Bear, who laughed at winter. Only where Kailovela's hand had rested still felt warm.

He realized he had one god yet, who might owe him some small favour. It was not a god he would mention to Mother. He felt that he was creeping behind Bear's own back, to make the plea, but then Bear slept most of the time. The north was full of stories about how Coyote went to Bear's cave and stole all manner of things, even the sun, once, when Bear had taken it from the sky, so Loud Thunder asked Coyote to help him with this little piece of sacrilege, and he went into the cave where the Tigers had lit their fire. In the darkness there, beneath the earth and with the ashes warm beneath his feet, he closed his eyes and waited.

In the utter darkness within his head, he hunted something that did not even belong in the Crown of the World. Except he had been told that this divinity was everywhere, beneath all lands, beneath all gods. He remembered tales told at his hearth over winter by a pale old man from far away.

Serpent, he asked the darkness, *help me find my path.*

And he waited, although night would be claiming the sky outside, and Mother would be looking for him. He waited until the quiet and the darkness honed his senses; until he knew himself surrounded by an endless vastness of earth and stone, riddled with caves and cracks and tunnels, with great echoing chasms, buried seas, secret dark vistas never seen by mortal eyes.

Beneath his feet, he imagined the crumbling flakes of ash and burned wood were scales. His closed eyes tricked him, seeing a faint sheen of rainbow running ahead of him, a path leading over the hills of a country he had never seen.

Serpent, guide me.

Loud Thunder stepped out of the cave, seeing that the moon was just pulling itself free of the mountains. Mother would be waiting for him. It was time.

30

'It was like when we were children,' Tecuman said excitedly. He was wearing one of Asman's best robes – too loose for him, but the servants had taken it in until a little of the regal had returned to him. 'Adventures, Asa. Terrible things!'

Asmander leant against the wall and watched him, smiling a little because he couldn't help it. 'Terrible things,' he echoed. 'You're eager to go back, then?'

Tecuman, who had been looking at himself in the polished bronze of a mirror, turned suddenly. 'I will be the Kasra of the estuary as well as Atahlan. Why has this division occurred? Not just because the Serpent cannot choose between my sister and me, but because the estuary is too far from the Daybreak Throne, and my father never went downriver to show his face there. The Kasra is too distant and the estuary is too large. That's why we're breaking the Nation in half.'

Asmander nodded. It was more insight than he'd have expected from his friend. 'Will you load the Daybreak Throne onto a boat?'

'I might,' the boy-Kasra said. An odd look came onto his face. 'If I could have met with Tecumet . . . Couldn't we *both* have ruled, somehow? Opposite ends of the land, two bodies but a single heart. And you could be Champion for both of us, and tell us when we were being stupid, just like old times.'

'Perhaps there's still time.' A sudden rush of emotion – the pure stuff of childhood – rose in Asmander and he fought it down. 'I spoke to her, before . . . all this. She—'

'She didn't seem like someone who would have her brother murdered?' Tecuman asked sharply.

'Teca, she didn't.'

'She had bad counsel, perhaps.' Tecuman touched his own face, as if seeing who he was becoming. 'I don't want to have to kill her.'

'I know.'

A hard look at the mirror. 'But I will, if I must. We can't go on like this. If it's the only way . . .'

'I know.'

Tecuman looked back at him. 'And would you do it, if I gave the order?'

Asmander let out a long breath. 'These things are known. But it would hurt to hear that order.'

'Would the Iron Wolf hesitate, if I spoke it to her?'

'In the Crown of the World they hunt each other, and the land and the weather hunt all of them. She'd do it.' Perhaps Asmander exaggerated the savagery of the north, but he did not want to open Tecumet's throat. Even if she had given the order to kill her brother, he did not want to be part of Tecuman's reply.

Tecuman nodded and opened his lips slightly, and what his next words might have been, Asmander would never know. Perhaps they would have been that order, after all. But a servant scuffed to a halt outside the room, breathless and with news that old Asman wished to speak to his son.

When he arrived, his father had a dozen peasants arrayed before him, men and women from the farms that ran along the river's banks. Some were injured, all looked frightened. Asman himself looked profoundly displeased with his son, but that was not unexpected.

Asmander said nothing. His father would let him know when it was his turn to speak.

'So, you came out of the estuary, you came home,' Asman said.

No questions yet, so Asmander remained silent.

'How simple a path, in the end: no obstacles can keep a son from his father's hearth.'

Still silent.

'No obstacles worth mentioning?'

Only a slight lift in his father's sharp tone, but a question nonetheless. Asmander thought about the Strangler cult, about fighting against a Serpent priest. He met his father's gaze and managed to look as though he was thinking about nothing at all.

'Of course, why would you mention an old acquaintance to your father?' Asman hissed. 'Why would you say, "I met my slave in the estuary. He had a warband"?'

'Venat?'

'Your *slave*, until you were fool enough to free him. The most dangerous pirate in a generation. *Here*, with a Dragon *warband*, and you didn't think it might warrant a mention?'

Asmander looked at the miserable, soot-stained peasants, whose presence now took on an entirely different meaning. 'What has happened?'

'Your slave has been setting fires down the river, drawing a bright line that leads from the estuary towards *here*.'

He wouldn't. But of course he would. Venat had given him one night of truce, and no promises. Old Asman was waiting, staring at him. Asmander blinked. *Tecuman,* he thought, thinking of a blood-mad warband of the Dragon coming here, setting fire to the house he was born in, opening throats in their search for . . .

'He was not under Tecumet's orders, when we met.' He flinched from his father's look. 'Yes, we met. We shared a fire. For old time's sake, one night.'

'Who said anything about Tecumet?' Asman asked him

294

sharply. 'Your slave never needed anyone's orders to burn and kill.'

'Stop calling him that.'

'Your *slave*,' Asman repeated, stepping closer. Asmander could feel the Champion rising up inside him close to his skin, looking for a way out. It was something he could never tell his father: how much the Champion hated him.

'He was never my slave.'

'If you made him more than a slave in your mind, then that is your error. Those fires are your making, and all the blood he will shed. And he is not razing villages on his way towards us because of *Tecumet*. He is doing it because of you.' Asman shook his head in exasperation. 'At last you have what you have always wanted. This is all *you*, Asmander.'

Asmander jabbed a hand at the peasants. 'You think all this is just him sending me a message?'

'In the only language the Dragon knows,' Asman agreed.

'Then I will go and meet him. I will . . .' *Open his throat.* But what would that achieve, really? 'I will make him ours. I will have him bow the knee to Tecuman.' The thought of Venat willingly bowing the knee to anyone was ludicrous.

'Make him your slave again.'

'I will make him an ally. That's better than a slave.'

'Not for the Dragon. The Dragon forget their allies.' Asman shook his head. 'But you'll have to learn that with the edge of the blade and not the flat, as usual. You never could be taught. Go, then. Go pay good coin for a slave's services. You'll take some of the house guard.'

'I will go alone.'

'Asmander—' Amazing how Asman could make a name so like his own into a curse.

'How will I win his respect, hiding behind our soldiers? I will go alone.'

For a long moment Asman looked at him, eyes hooded and showing no feelings. 'You are my eldest son. That you have not been the son I would have chosen, we both know, but you're my heir.'

'Sentiment, Father?'

'No, but I have invested much in you, that you constantly attempt to cast away. Well, so be it. Your sister, your brother, they are fostered out to other clans, winning allies and learning the skills of the court. If need be I will rest my hopes on one of them. But you – you were placed with the Kasra's own children. And you have spent every moment squandering what I have built for you.'

It was a tirade Asmander had heard before. The familiarity was almost comforting. 'I will succeed for our clan. I shall win the Dragon.'

Asman shrugged, a tiny shift of his shoulders consigning everything Asmander might or might not accomplish into irrelevance. 'Be thankful you have a father who sees past the horizon,' was all he said.

Shyri crept up on him when he was at the river's edge, slinking among the evening shadows until she could have leapt on his back, he was so absorbed in his thinking. Instead, and impressed at her own restraint, she just let out a little heckle, giving him the chance to contain his surprise.

'Look who comes to blight my day still further,' he observed, but – she thought – fondly.

'Where are we going?' she asked him.

His face closed down immediately. 'Nowhere together. I go to hunt. I've already cut away all the burdens my father would foist on me. And now you.'

'A burden, is it, Longmouth?' She kept her tone light.

For a long moment he stared at her – he was the image of his father when he was like that. Then something broke inside him. 'I go to find Venat. To make him my follower again. Or if not, he and I will fight.'

'No change there, then,' she tried, but his face was all wounds,

296

right then. *They'll fight for the last time.* 'So let me come. Talk or fight, I can help.'

'Just me and him,' Asmander told her flatly. 'Just as it was before. You . . .'

'Stay here and watch your useless father and your big ugly house and your idiot Kasra boy,' she said. 'Or perhaps I'll go. I'll cross the river and head home.' *Wherever that even is from here.* 'Or maybe I'll go to that girl-Kasra and tell her what I know.'

'What do you know?' Again, she guessed he didn't realize just how like his father he was, when he spoke like that. He was so much the centre of his own world, he didn't think twice about dismissing anyone else.

Abruptly she felt she was on a leash, twisting and turning, tied to him, to his stupid family and country and boy-ruler. She could feel her Hyena soul gnawing at the tether, captivity anathema to it. And yet here she was.

'Go into the Dragon's jaws, then,' she said bitterly. 'Go get your tail chewed off. It's all you deserve.'

'Yes,' he admitted, in that infuriating way of his, and then he seemed to see her properly for the first time and put a hand on her bare shoulder. 'You are a good friend, Shyri. You deserve better.'

'Yes, yes I do.' And she felt that leash tighten a notch, because without that last valediction she might just have gone – she told herself – but now . . .

I'll watch for you, she wanted to say, but the words would have tasted like bile in her mouth. Inside her, the Hyena was raging, *How dare you let this longmouth use you?*

Then Asmander had slipped into the river, Stepping as he went so that a lazy flick of his long ridged tail sent him gliding away, no more than a ripple to tell of his presence. Even as a crocodile he had a fluid grace to him. Feeling frustrated and angry at herself and generally hard done by, Shyri Stepped herself and skulked back to her stand of trees.

Shortly after, the noise started. Out beyond the boundaries of

the estate she heard whoops and yells, and sometimes a rhyth-
mic stamping and chanting, some sort of war-song. There were
fires, too – nothing that crossed onto old Asman's farmland, but
the attackers out in the dark were surely working themselves up
to it. Shyri decided it was none of her business. She devoted her
time to not thinking about how Asmander was doing.

The ruckus had not gone unnoticed within the house. Soon
enough there were soldiers piling out, stalking the grounds
and roving the boundaries. Mostly they were longmouth men
and women in dark scaly armour, carrying stone-toothed spears
and *maccans*. Shyri saw a big wolf amongst them, and a tiger.
Whoever the attackers were, the Dragon or Tecumet's people,
they were going right into the jaws of the north if they tried it.

With the defenders eyeing the boundaries, she found she
could slink about the estate quite freely. It pleased her to imagine
herself an enemy, able to wreak whatever mischief she wanted
because of all that noise. What might she do . . . ? Poison their
wells and steal their food, like a true Plains raider. There was so
much yapping and yipping going on that she might get away
with anything . . .

Or someone else might.

Something in the back of her mind had been nagging at her,
something about the *shape* of this, the direction of the yelling
and the fires, the gaps . . . She quickened her pace and loped
swiftly through the tall grass of the farmland, Stepping to look
out over it. There was a man there, on the edge of the fields, but
far from the noise and display. A big man. She knew him.

That he might kill her for discovering him was in her mind,
but if he tried it, she would trust to her swiftness and make him
regret it. Because it was her nature, she circled around him,
hoping to come up behind him as she had with Asmander. He
was keeping his ears open, though, looking as she came close.

'You, then.' He sounded disappointed. She was getting a lot
of that.

298

'You-then, yourself,' she snapped. 'Aren't you supposed to be somewhere else?'

Venat shrugged. 'I'm the Fire Dragon the Rivermen scare their children with, girl. I can be everywhere.'

'I thought you were just servant to a stupid boy.' She put so much venom in that last word that the actual insult to Venat was lost entirely.

'What's he done now?'

'He's racing up and down the river looking for you, like a fool.' She sniggered. 'That's funny. He's chasing all about desperate to fight you or . . . and here you are. I found you.'

He shifted, and she Stepped instantly, waiting for the blade to come out. Instead he sat down, looking . . . to her hyena eyes he looked old and tired and unhappy. He had looked more cheerful as Asmander's thrall. She resumed her human form, stepping a little closer, like a game of Bait-Old-Crocodile. 'Why are you here?'

'Politics.'

She laughed uncertainly. 'What's that, now?'

'River politics. I should just have gone and burned a village or two. That's what we *do*, isn't it? The Dragon. And then whoever's Kasra would have sent some spears, and we'd have a fight. And probably there would be another war over the islands, once we'd burned enough huts and broken enough spears. That's what happened all the other times.'

Shyri shrugged. 'Sounds fair to me. So why the fires and the shouting, and you're not out there burning stuff?'

He shook his head. 'I just came to see. I'm . . . *waiting*. She said to wait, and I'd find out what I needed to do. So this is what it's come to. Waiting.'

'You've changed.'

'I've *tried*. Because I didn't just want to be . . . the same stupid old Dragon, who it never ends well for. But . . .'

That nagging voice in her mind had its teeth in her again, snarling and pulling. Abruptly she was dancing away from him.

'Is this . . . you're here to . . .' *Distract me*, she'd been about to say, but who cared about *her* in all this? Without another word to him she was Stepped and pelting away, heading for the big house.

She paused when she reached it, for there were guards at the door, and she had forgotten for a moment that she was Asmander's secret. Nobody on the river was going to welcome one of the Laughing Men to their hearth. She kept to the evening dark, skulking and sneaking, looking up at the high small windows. Most of the house was dark along this side. One window alone showed a glimmer of lamplight. She judged it auspicious for a stealthy entry. *This must be the servants' quarters*, she decided. Probably old Asman didn't waste his wealth on letting his lessers see what they were doing.

The windows were high and covered with fretted grilles. She reckoned she would fit through one with a little force and some judiciously broken wood. She Stepped back to human and took a run-up, kicking off and reaching so that one hand found the sill. With a single convulsive twitch she pulled herself in so that her toes found the cracks between mud bricks and she hung there, taking a deep breath for the work ahead.

Breaking into Asmander's house felt good, she could not deny it.

The grille over the window was more hole than wood. She examined it, saw that with a little knife work she could loosen it, and prepared to do so, mindful of the lit window in the next room. There were voices, two servants discussing their day, no doubt. *Keep talking, shout a bit even*. But she was curious. Who did these voices belong to, the only servants in the house to warrant lamplight? Clinging there, she looked across to the next window and reckoned she could make it if she stretched.

One precarious moment later, and she was peering into the lit room. It was a big one, and she saw she'd been wrong: no servants here, unless old Asman was a softer touch than she took him for. There were bright hangings on the walls – gold in them, even – and a fine bed and other heavy, impractical furniture, all of it heavily worked and carved in that way the Rivermen had, who couldn't leave things alone.

She saw a youth – Asmander's age, maybe. A moment later she realized this *was* the youth who had come in with Asmander and the two northerners. Which meant that he was . . . She blinked. Seeing the Kasra of the Sun River Nation in nothing but a loincloth was an education. He was so *thin*. Who was he talking to? The Kasra had a woman in there, which she supposed was no surprise, She was outside Shyri's view, but she had a strong voice – familiar, a little. *Someone I've heard before.*

The idea of spying on the Kasra's bed games was enormously appealing, although Shyri hoped they got down to things quickly because her fingers were cramping.

'I'd let myself hope,' Tecuman was saying. He sounded tense and nervous, which she thought was amusing. *Call yourself the Great High Crocodile, you're still ruled by your little Serpent.* Then he said, 'I thought someone else might have sent them, but now you're here,' and Shyri didn't understand that.

The unseen woman said, 'Perhaps this is just for me.' *She* certainly sounded like she was enjoying herself.

'Why?' Tecuman asked. Shyri was just thinking, *If you're as skinny as that, don't question your luck.*

'Because I've hated you for a long time,' the woman said flatly.

Shyri twitched. *Wait, what . . . ?*

'You and Asmander filled my life with scorn,' the woman explained. 'No great clan, no great wealth, but the Champion chose me. And you could never live with that.'

'Tecumet mocked you too,' Tecuman said.

'But after, she would come to me and call me sister. She was kind to me, of all of you. Even though I was Champion, no other in your father's palace would look at me twice. I would always be a servant to them.'

301

'Did my sister send you?' Tecuman asked. That tremor in his voice was not from amorous nerves, she realized belatedly.

'You'll never know,' the woman said, and Shyri had a name in her mind at last. It was Izel, the fighting woman who'd been sent from the boy's sister, to guard her people in Tsokawan. Shyri's blood ran cold. She clung to the wall with the nails of one hand as she tried to slide out her knife.

'Aren't you going to run?' Izel asked softly.

Tecuman took a deep breath, even as Shyri was wondering how quickly she could get the grille off the window.

'No,' he said. 'I've tried running. Asmander showed me sometimes you must fight.' And he stooped, and there was a *maccan* in his hands, the wooden blade with stone teeth. He raised the weapon in a way that must have shown Izel clearly he didn't know how to use it.

Shyri made her choice. She did not ask herself why the boy mattered to her. It was enough that he was in danger. Izel laughed again, and then a hyena shattered the window grille into fragments and rammed into her shoulder. The woman cursed, stumbling back into the wall. Shyri was on two human feet already, shoving her along the side of the bed and then ripping a tapestry down on top of her.

She saw Tecuman raise his *maccan* awkwardly and yelled at him to run. The real panic in her voice sent the weapon spilling from his hands and he dashed out of the room. Shyri had seen the shape beneath the tapestry change abruptly into something with more than enough claws and teeth to finish both of them. She had always wondered what it would be like to fight Asmander in his Champion shape. Now she decided she didn't want to know after all. Even as one of Izel's sickle claws caught in the heavy tapestry and started to cut it open, she snatched up a finely carved chair – probably worth her weight in gold – and smashed it over the recumbent Champion.

It would not stop Izel. It might not even slow her. She did not stay around to see the results but was running after Tecuman in

302

the next heartbeat. She caught up with the boy quickly, because he was a terrible runner as well as a terrible fighter. 'Where are your people?' she demanded, but of course they were outside waiting to fend off the Dragon. 'Where are the servants, even?' She had no idea what servants did when they had no tasks. Was there a storeroom for them somewhere in the cellars?

Even as they broke out into the entrance hall, a stocky man in a pale robe walked out in front of her, his hands out and soldiers at his back: old Asman, the master of the house. His eyes widened as he saw a Plains girl apparently abducting the Kasra, and she scrabbled to a halt right in front of him, keenly aware of the spears of the soldiers.

'I'm Asmander's friend! I came with him from the north! You saw me in Tsokawan!' she yelled at him. 'There's a madwoman trying to kill your Kasra! Send your soldiers to his room! No, keep them here—!'

Old Asman looked at her quite calmly. Perhaps River Lord chiefs were used to humouring the mad. Shyri waited for Tecuman to back her up but he was too busy wheezing for breath, and besides, old Asman was focused entirely on her.

'Just go to his room,' Shyri insisted. 'I swear on my mother, Tecumet's Champion is after your boy!'

'He's not been my boy for a while,' Asman said conversationally, and then the razor-sharp flint of his knife blade entered her side.

31

'Surely they have woken,' Grey Herald said. 'The Plains people tell tales of their wings.' *Of their appetites*, he almost added.

Storm Born smiled, exactly as though he had heard those unspoken words. 'It is not they who wake, but the memory of them. They send out nightmares and feed on the fear they spread, but they do not move.'

'I saw a man who slept in the shadow of this place. He was drained of blood at dawn,' Grey Herald insisted.

The Wolf chuckled. 'So terrible, those nightmares. But it's not nightmares we need. We must wake them, Brother Owl.'

Grey Herald regarded him doubtfully. 'Why is this your task? You're a long way from home for a man with no wings.'

Storm Born's broken-shard smile only widened. 'Brother, I was a fool once, before I became a priest. I was a man too quick to take up the knife against my kin, and they cast me out. The Wolf was in me like an angry spirit. When I was young, he struck a hole in my mind, so he could go in and out of me as he willed. He made me mad, sometimes. Or perhaps it was the storm,' tracing his fingers down the branching scars of his bare chest. 'Storm Born,' speaking his own name with reverence. 'No man ever earned a name as I did. Touched by the sky! Touched by destiny. I left the jaws of the Wolf and came south with a warband, looking for the pieces of myself that were missing, you understand?' His smile was full of razor edges. 'We had such times. We fought for the Plains people, and against them. We heard their tales, but I heard more than the others. I heard a voice calling me through that hole in my mind.'

'And you came here,' Grey Herald finished.

'At last I did, at last. After much hunting and listening, and some blood. I followed the sound of their wings. And I have kept my fire here, and waited for the time. I have followed their marks in the stone, the pictures they left of themselves. I have learned their rituals in my dreams. It is only you I have been waiting for.' And then he had paused, with a childlike vulnerability in his face. 'It *is* time, isn't it?'

You are a broken thing, Grey Herald thought. 'You know the way?'

'It is the only thing I am certain of.'

'Then it is time,' Herald agreed, and knew he was going to regret it.

There followed days of work, rituals and tasks that Storm Born insisted were necessary. They had cleared the floor of the altar chamber of years of dust, scrubbing and scraping until a great tangled maze of channels was revealed, an inch-deep labyrinth incised into the stone, which led the eye around and around, inexorably trapping the gaze until the watcher was brought to the centre. There were long spaces of silence before the altar. There were stories told over the fire with a ritual solemnity – but little of what Storm Born spoke made sense, and Grey Herald himself had only the Three Brothers stories he had grown up with. Apparently they were enough, though. At other times, when Herald was supposed to be sleeping, Storm Born would polish and sharpen certain implements, ancient tools of bronze that were finely made and very, very sharp.

All the while the petrified gaze of the Bat was on them. Herald looked up into their withered faces, a people utterly unlike any he had ever known. He examined their sharp features, their deep-set eyes and the pointed ears folded back against their skulls. Most of all he saw the sharp teeth their shrivelled lips could not hide.

The channels of the maze that led him ever inwards led out as well. Each of those stony husks had a runnel leading to its alcove. Herald wondered if this carving had even been here, when Storm Born had first arrived, or whether the man's madness had driven him to grind out this pattern as he waited for his brother from the north to arrive. *I must not think of it as madness.* For though the lost Wolf was clearly no longer master of his own mind, Grey Herald believed something else was. Some whispering dream had crept in by that invisible hole the man had spoken of, and taken up its seat in his skull.

The Bat knows its people must wake. That was all he could cling to. *Whatever happens, this is the right thing.*

'They came into my head,' Storm Born said later. He had lit a fire before the altar and was feeding it handfuls of grass. It was not a ritual act, Grey Herald thought, so much as nervous fidgeting; a man on the threshold of something he could not take back. 'When the others went back north, I was left here with the voices in my head.'

The chamber was silent, save for the fire and Storm Born's ragged voice. To him it was full of whispering, Grey Herald guessed. Those desiccated corpses all around were speaking into the broken space within the man's skull. Grey Herald believed many things, but right then he could not believe wholeheartedly that there was anything here to wake. Were there really wings in the night to terrify the Plains people, or just stories to scare their children? Surely Storm Born's madness was enough to weave all this out of no more than scraps.

'So what comes now?' he demanded. 'We have followed your rituals. We have cleaned and prayed and lit fires and painted red and white men on your walls. And now we're here, with your fire, and your altar.' And Herald jabbed two fingers at the bowl-like concavity that Storm Born's scraping and scrubbing had unearthed there. 'And everything about us is dead. More dead than anything I have ever known. And so I'm waiting, because I know what your next move will be. I have seen the blood-channels on the floor and the knife you think is hidden in your belt is plain to me.'

Storm Born started, guilty as any man Grey Herald ever knew. 'What are you saying?'

'Blood is at the heart of all the Bat stories the Plains people tell.'

Storm Born blinked furiously. 'Are you saying you don't *want* to give of yourself to bring the Bat into the world?'

Grey Herald stared at him levelly. 'I have only one life. I will spend my blood on destiny if I must, but not on madness.'

'Why did they send you to me?' Storm Born asked hollowly, sounding betrayed. He left the fire and went to one of the withered statues, or bodies – they seemed stone to Grey Herald, and yet far too finely worked to ever be the craft of human hands. 'You speak so clear to me, can you not put a word in his ear? What am I *for* if not to bring you into being?' His voice had died away to a whisper, trembling with uncertainty. He took the iron knife from his belt and threw it ringing onto the floor.

'Tell me what they say.' Grey Herald stepped closer, warily. The fire sent light and shadow dancing over the drawn stone face. For a moment he thought it had opened its eyes.

Storm Born shook his head and said something that was swallowed by the statue's alcove, and Herald drew closer despite himself, almost close enough to touch the man's shoulder.

'The jaws of the Wolf need no knives,' the madman repeated. Then he Stepped and turned and went for Herald's throat.

He nearly took it, too, bowling the Owl over, slathering and foaming. His jaws locked on Herald's upraised arm and worried it savagely, slicing him open from wrist halfway to elbow. Then Herald had Stepped into a huge Owl, driving the talons of one foot into the wolf's head, tearing across one staring, insane eye.

He was free, but he was battering about the cave ceiling, and the way out of the cave – which should have been so clear – was hidden from him. Storm Born had Stepped, his face running with blood, one socket just gore and ruin, but he had his knife back, and the cave was low enough that he would be able to put it in Herald just by reaching up.

Grey Herald swooped on him, but flurried away when the knife rose to meet him. He Stepped himself, feeling the weakness of his wounded arm, taking out the bronze of his own knife. He was younger but Storm Born was mad, and losing an eye didn't seem to have bothered him.

There was no way out of the cave without a fight. It was not that the Wolf stood before the exit, it was that some power had taken the exit away. His eyes could not find the opening, nor his mind conceive of it. The price of its return was plain enough.

The two of them clashed, each man grappling for the other's knife-hand. Herald's slick hand fumbled its hold and Storm Born stabbed him in the shoulder. He yelled and Stepped for just a moment, beating at the man's face with his wings and then ripping a gash in the Wolf's tattooed chest with his beak. Then he was human again and ducking low, even as Storm Born drove the knife deeper, as though trying to force it all the way from shoulder to heart.

Herald took hold of the Wolf's leg and threw him, almost one-handed. Storm Born landed hard on his back, the breath vomiting out of him. That was the time to finish the fight, but the effort left the Owl priest weak and dizzy. He staggered away, the darkness and the fire spinning about him, each movement grating the knife against his shoulder.

He was going to lose, he realized. It would be his blood flowing down the channels to those long-dead figures. Whether or not it would achieve anything, he knew what every sacrifice knew: he did not want to go. No matter the Owl, no matter the world, he did not want to die.

A wolf again, Storm Born howled and came for him. Grey Herald tried to dodge aside, but the stone beneath him was already slippery with blood and he fell. The wolf skidded past him in a skittering of claws, and when he came back, Grey Herald stabbed him in the side, dragging his blade along the beast's ribs and laying open his grey hide. Storm Born snarled and snapped at him, bloodying the back of his hand, but the Wolf was slower too. The wounds were beginning to overwhelm even the madness in him.

But he wasn't giving up. Back he came, ravening for Herald's throat, and the Owl Stepped once more, lurching into the air and leaving Storm Born with a mouthful of feathers. Herald faltered and fought with the close, smoky air, even as the wolf below him jumped, jaws agape, and then fell back and staggered sideways, whining.

Below him, Storm Born was at the heart of the pattern, and the channels gleamed darkly, throwing back the firelight like jewels. He watched the creep of blood – his blood, Storm Born's blood, as it touched the first of the parched statues.

Those shrivelled eyes did not open, but a shudder ran through the stony substance of the figure and it shattered, so dry and rigid that the very moment of waking was too much for it. It exploded into shards and dust and was gone.

Storm Born let out a howl of pure loss and then he was a man again, running from statue to statue, babbling desperate pleas, scrabbling at the bloody floor, and each time too late. The blood touched each stiff icon in turn, and it came apart, tearing and splintering into pieces.

Grey Herald dropped to the ground and Stepped, holding his shoulder. His own blade was lost somewhere, but on the ground was Storm Born's iron. He took it up, determined to make an end of this for better or for worse. The fight had gone out of the Wolf. He knelt in the centre of the room, sobbing, shielding his ravaged face from the fire. Simple enough for Grey Herald to kick him over and kneel on his back. Simple enough to lift the knife.

Storm Born didn't even struggle. 'End it,' he choked out.

Grey Herald's arm wanted to. His muscles twitched and strained to force the issue. Probably the man would die soon from his wounds anyway. Possibly they both would. But stripped of his murderous intent, what was left of Storm Born? A man who had believed. A man who had been faithful.

Grey Herald wanted no ghosts to burden him. Even the weight of one might be too much. He sighed and tried to stand, but ended up sitting beside the Wolf, his breath shuddering in his chest.

Except it was not in his chest that the air shuddered. The sound came again, and both men froze, sitting there in a maze of their own blood. Another beat resonated about the chamber, then another. They came from outside, the sound of them thundering into the cave mouths and funnelling into the shrine.

Grey Herald said, 'Wings,' but by then they were no longer alone. People were filing in from that winding entrance. Or, beings that looked like people. Not the shrivelled husks that had guarded this place for centuries, but a dozen who might have been those cadavers' great-great-grandchildren. Smooth faces of an alien caste, gaunt and hollow-eyed but living and young; men and women of another time, another race, skin like yellowed bone and teeth like needles. They stood in a ring around the battered men as though they had arisen from the shadow and the smoke and the blood itself.

One of them was a lean woman who stood a head taller than anyone Herald knew except for the Bear. She smiled at them both, and spoke, her words strangely slanted. Only after some thought did Herald understand, 'Blood is spilt, yet two men live. What a strange thing to wake to. Is this a merciful age, then?'

'No.' Grey Herald sucked in a harsh breath, feeling the presence of the Bat Society people like the night against his skin. Were they truly here, or was this a dream born of ritual and blood loss. He could barely even recollect why he had travelled so far to call them up. He looked down and met Storm Born's torn-up gaze, seeing the madness there, but beyond it the

310

despair. The Wolf had given far more than he to see this moment, and even Storm Born could not tell truth from vision. Grey Herald felt the moment tilt on a knife edge, trembling.

The great enemy was coming. The end of the world was here. If not now, then when should these gaunt people be woken, and what would be too great a cost to have them at the Owl's side in the final fight?

Storm Born shuddered; the seeds of attack were in that movement but they would never grow again. Nonetheless, Grey Herald took it as his example. The iron dagger fell ringing to the ground and he was an owl again, the great sweep of his wings filling the chamber as he dropped claws-first onto Storm Born's scarred chest, rending and rending with his beak until the man had at last stopped moving, and the Bat Society had all the blood they could possibly want.

And as they gathered close, truly real now, nothing of the dream about them, he Stepped and sat down heavily, letting them dabble their long fingers in the ruin he had made.

'Mercy is not what we need,' he told them heavily. 'If it were, we would not have called on you.'

***

Feeds on Rags battered through the air in a flurry of dark wings. He did not stop or slow, not for the heat, not even for the hawk which swooped on him and veered off at the last moment, finding him larger than it had thought.

His flight was a straight line to Tsokawan, and he thundered in at a window, darting and diving about the interior. Rivermen servants scattered or chased after him, yelling, but he had no time for them. He had charted a course all across the estuary but now he could not find his way within the maze of rooms and passageways. At last he was reduced to running about the place on his human feet, shouting out for Spear Catcher until one of the Wolves heard and hailed him.

They thought it was just him playing the fool as usual. When he tried to gabble the story to them, his words got twisted and

311

they looked around for Sathewe and said he was tricking them again. Then they walked away and he had to trail after them, gasping and wheezing over his repeated warnings, until Spear Catcher himself cuffed him and shouted at him to go away.

It was when that did not get rid of him that the warband began to take him seriously and something of his panic communicated itself to them. They sat him down and he explained where they had gone, what had been done: the Serpents, Sathewe's scream. Takes Iron and Maniye's Snake friend were captives. Only Feeds on Rags was free to find help.

There was a little talk then, but only a little. Wolves were not given much to debate. That the masters of Tsokawan did not want them just running off was no great secret. Thus far they had been given good food and attentive servants, but the northerners felt this could change very quickly. In particular it would change if Spear Catcher announced his intention of leading the warband off into the estuary to look for their priest.

So: no announcements would be made.

One of the younger warriors suggested they creep out in ones and twos. All very well, Spear Catcher considered, save for whoever got trapped inside when their hosts saw what was up. 'Let the Snakes look to creeping,' he decided. 'All of you, put on your armour, take up your weapons and Step. We go out all together and in iron, and let's see if any of them want to get in our way. We stop for nobody.'

The other Wolves set to it immediately – those with iron pelts shrugged into them, and the rest trusted to their hides and bronze scales, whatever protection they had. The iron-wearers would go first, and if there were spears or arrows they would trust to the Wolf's metal to protect them.

The Rivermen did want their Iron Wolves, Feeds on Rags thought, calmer now that he had delivered his message. The effort of holding himself to his task over such a distance had worn him out. At last Spear Catcher nodded to him. 'You, keep

312

in the middle of us. Fly as soon as we're out under the sky. Show us where to go.'

It was not exactly praise, but it was belonging. Sometimes that was enough. Feeds on Rags Stepped and dug his clawed toes into the coat of a wolf as the pack streamed out of their quarters, scattering curious servants and leaving a trail of chaos in their wake. Somewhere in Tsokawan men were shouting the alarm, but the wolves were running now and they would be gone from the fortress before any answer could be made.

When they reached the edge of the estuary, where the ground got marshy and the farmland gave way to the gradual encroachment of trees, they slowed a little. Feeds on Rags swung back to them and cawed raucously, and Spear Catcher Stepped to speak with him.

'Easy for you in the air, but there's no path for us,' he pointed out.

The Crow shifted to human shape as well. 'Keep to where the tree roots are,' he suggested. 'It's dry there. I will come back for you, over and over. I'll fly up to see, then I'll fly back down.'

'How far to where they were?' Spear Catcher asked him.

'Far.' Feeds on Rags shrugged. 'Not so far. Tomorrow.'

Spear Catcher grimaced, but reckoned he had no real choice. 'Just don't forget about us.'

Then there was nothing for it but to pass under the trees' shadow; to trust to the shifting ground and endure the heat and the flies. The warband was more used to the hot southern sun by now, but the air of the estuary seemed more than half water. *You'd think, with all their craftiness, they'd have done something about it.* But the place was probably a perfect delight if you were a crocodile half the time.

Some of the Rivermen did try to get in the Wolves' way, but half-heartedly, never daring to make a fight of it. Spear Catcher didn't know whether they were from Tsokawan or from the other lot, the girl-Kasra's people, or just regular raiders or brigands.

Groups of southerners in armour kept showing up with their stone-headed spears, and they called out challenges or formed a line across the warband's path. Probably they had laws against ravening bands of wolves charging about their places.

Each time, the warband faced off against the soldiers, often outnumbered two to one. They kept to their beast forms so that the enemy couldn't see who had iron on them and who only bronze. Nobody Stepped, they just snapped and snarled and threatened. And each time, instead of standing firm and drawing blood, the River Lords backed off. Spear Catcher thought it was cowardice at first, but after a while he realized it was confusion. The land around them was at war with itself. The soldiers couldn't know where they stood with these foreigners. Probably there were bands of Plains raiders daily crossing the border to set things on fire, and nobody was standing up to them because they were all looking to that Daybreak Throne, or whatever they called it.

Takes Iron had called for them and, in the absence of Many Tracks, it was the priest's voice that set the pack in motion. Spear Catcher didn't hesitate in carrying out his duty: he fully believed that the Wolf's ire would find him even here if he betrayed the old priest.

This was his time, Spear Catcher knew. Many Tracks was off guarding the boy-Kasra, along with Moon Eye – their strongest warrior when he was in his right mind. Takes Iron was in danger, and so was Many Tracks' Serpent friend, and it came down to old Spear Catcher to make up for a lifetime of failures, small and large.

So thinking, he led the warband at a fierce pace, a rushing column of grey wolves winding between the trees, scrabbling and leaping from root to root, from island to island. The beasts of the estuary got out of their way, crocodiles slithering off the banks into the water, birds raising a racket of clattering wings as they leapt into the air. Spear Catcher's mouth was open as he

314

panted in the heat, but inside he was grinning like a young hunter.

Only when the dark came did he falter and call for them to make camp. It was a very different dark they had in the estuary, peopled with all the wrong sounds and smells, and the going had been treacherous even during the day. Spear Catcher weighed his new-found heroism, and then conferred with Amelak, his wife, always the keeper of his common sense. That done, he had the warband set watches to wait out the night.

The call came from Feeds on Rags at dawn. The Crow had been scouting in the first grey light but now he dropped amongst them shouting that they must be ready, rousing the warband to furious motion. They faced out all ways into the murk of the estuary. Spear Catcher braced himself, ready to test the iron of his hide against anything the south might throw at him.

When he saw what was coming, though, it was the one confrontation he had not prepared for. No soldiers, no reptile jaws, no great force of southerners to break against the iron bastion of the Wolves. Just one of their own: Takes Iron's lean grey shape slipping through the trees ahead, with a little coyote skipping at his heels. Sathewe had a makeshift sling looped about her body, and Spear Catcher saw the narrow head of a serpent lift from it and taste the air.

'Um . . .' Feeds on Rags said awkwardly. Spear Catcher glared at him, feeling as though the Crow and the world had conspired to make a fool of him.

Takes Iron Stepped, the years falling back on him as he took human shape. And if there was magic here on the River, this was it, because Spear Catcher had not been blind to what Takes Iron thought of the Serpent – of *this* Serpent in particular. When the two of them walked the estuary together, it seemed certain only one would return. But here they were, if not as friends, then at least as priests together. And whatever they had been doing, plainly that was priest business that Spear Catcher could not begin to guess at.

'I think it is time we found a missing friend of ours,' Hesprec said. 'There should be a Champion and a Kasra loose in the estuary, but I have had my belly to the earth and felt no tremor of them.'

'Does your magic tell you where they have gone?' Spear Catcher asked.

'The magic of knowing who else went to find them, and where his family dwells,' Hesprec agreed. 'But knowing is more than half of any magic. We need the river, and we need a boat.'

At last Takes Iron turned to Spear Catcher – and the rebuke didn't come, wonder of wonders. Instead, he nodded. 'It's good you're here. Knowing Many Tracks, we'll have need of you all.'

32

Loud Thunder knew he was in Mother's cave; that he sat at her hearth as she spoke to him of the Godsland, the far unreal country where gods came from and souls went. He knew the darkness about him was only night and the shadow of a stone roof. It was her words that turned the leaping of the firelight against his closed lids into a sky scattered with moving stars.

He knew his hand was on Lone Mountain's slow-heaving flank, but the laborious breathing of his kinsman had become a great far wind that blew about the mountains and chasms of this place, forever and forever. Some part of him knew that it wasn't real, pictures put behind his eyes by Mother's words. The rest of him understood it was very real indeed, and that he was unprepared for it.

Maniye walked here. She had spoken of it to him, in the lowered tones of one imparting a secret. He had been the one who was injured then, and she had come across all the Crown of the World to make sure he would live, because that was Maniye Many Tracks: a good friend.

Armed with that thought, he ventured forth into the night landscape of the gods. Maniye had spoken of hills, and on each hill a god; of Wolves and Tigers and all manner of beasts. Perhaps the Bear lived in a different part of the Godsland, or perhaps it was different when his children visited him. The land around was snow-laden, the drifts past his knees. The keening

317

wind howled with a terrible patience. Above him, the stars moved like fish in the sky, and he remembered what Maniye had said. *Like they were looking for a way in.*

He wondered if he should Step, but the Bear was his soul, the part of him that would travel here before it found a new body. What would happen if he became no more than his soul in this place? The complexity of the thought hurt his head. He remained on human feet and set out hunting.

When he climbed up, he saw the Godsland stretching out on all sides: crags and black rocks and white snow. There was no bear-shape here, mortal or divine. He was utterly alone.

Inside his head he seemed to hear a voice, mocking, despairing, sniggering at the big, stupid Bear. *Is this truly a thing you need help with? How do you ever feed yourself? When is it easiest to find your dinner than when the snow lies over the earth and tells you where every foot has fallen?*

It was Quiet When Loud's sly teasing. And thinking about it, he remembered of course Lone Mountain had gone this way before him. So where were his tracks? As if the very thought brought them into being, he saw the prints of a bear, of a size to match his own soul's shape, uneven where it tried to keep its weight off one rear leg.

Even as he was hastening along the trail a convulsion went through the Godsland, as though the very world around him resented his prying. The wind was whipping fresh snow past him, flurrying down to fill those deep tracks and hide where Lone Mountain had gone. He set out at a swift walk, but that would not be enough. His kinsman's trail was already being swallowed up. He broke into a run, forcing his way through the snow, fast enough that he almost felt he was tripping on top of it, rushing along the trail before he lost it. The wind plucked at him, the ground clawed at his feet, but he let nothing slow him. He tore across the rugged terrain of the Godsland and, if the gods were there, they stayed out of his way.

The trail led higher, up amidst the jagged black crags that

curved overhead like claws. The sky was busy above, the lights beating angrily against whatever barrier held them in their place, swallowed by the snow and then revealed again. Loud Thunder just ran until the snow outpaced him and erased all trace of where his cousin had gone. He stopped then, chest heaving for breath. All around him the dark stone rose, sharp and hostile. The air was a flurrying swirl of white that stung his eyes.

He took a deep breath, in through his nose. Past the snow and the darkness there was something: a scent he had been born into the shadow of. A bear was close, and in this terrible place who else might that animal be?

He was about to call out, but some intuition told him he might attract the attention of other things than his cousin. This was no land for human voices. And besides, he could not know if his cousin would just flee his kin until he was nothing but the bear.

So Loud Thunder took another deep breath, filling his nose with the scent of bear, and he crept forwards, letting his nose guide him, hands and feet finding holds and niches in the dark. Setting his shoulders against the wind, he let the cold and the weariness slough away from him, put off until such time as he could afford to indulge them.

And there was Lone Mountain, past the next crag and on the far side of a narrow crack in the earth. The great bear paced and shook his head, tried to sit but stumbled, flinching from the pain. His haunch was blackened and eaten away, seething with tiny, skittering things that Loud Thunder could not quite make out.

Lone Mountain rose up to his full height and bellowed mournfully at the sky, begging for help, for some release from his pain. Loud Thunder looked up, and further up, following his cousin's maddened gaze to the high peaks, he saw the Bear. The Bear was the mountains. The Bear was the landscape surrounding them. Thunder understood why this land was so different to what had met Maniye. The storm and the jagged land were the

Bear's fury, a god driven to rage because it could not help its injured son.

Lone Mountain's pleading bellow sounded again, but the very substance of the land seemed to shrink away from him. Whatever had touched him had driven a wedge between him and his god.

Loud Thunder took three quick steps and jumped the chasm, coming to a skidding halt and dragging at his cousin's attention. If he had hoped for a joyous reunion he was disappointed. Lone Mountain stared at him through mad eyes, the man lost deep inside the wounded bear.

All his life Thunder had been the biggest, strongest son of the strongest people. Standing as a man, before Lone Mountain's bear, he understood what it was like to be everyone else. The huge beast roared a warning at him. Mountain's flank seethed with illness that mirrored the agitated stars above. Thunder put out a hand, as he would to a dog. 'You know me,' he said softly. 'Come on, cousin. You may not like me but you know me.'

A shudder went through the bear. It remained on its hind legs, towering above him, but its anger shrunk to a confused whimper. Thunder took another step into its shadow, reaching out with his open hand, speaking whatever came into his head in a comforting tone.

'Remember when we were boys, and there was the pike in Hook Lake. They said it was bigger than two men. They said it had a soul, that if it lived another generation we'd find a Pike people living on the shore there, remember that? I'd let it be, if it was me, but you wanted to be the one who caught it. You and me on that raft we made, letting a line down, night after night?'

His hand advanced. He could feel the bristling touch of Mountain's pelt at his finger ends.

'And then one night something took your bait, and I held on to you and you held on to the raft and we got pulled all over Hook Lake, screaming like babes. Or perhaps that was just me.'

He reached further, waiting for the contact that might reach the man within the beast's shape. As his fingers touched, a shock of images lashed through Thunder's head like a lightning strike. He saw a bluff swathed in walls of white, a Tiger huntress, terrible people with empty human shapes – an emptiness he had seen before.

Thunder sprang back with a yell, and Lone Mountain dropped to all fours and raged at him, snarling right into his face, fangs bared. He was only just holding himself back, Thunder could see. Thunder was a big man, but a man's shape would not survive a single blow from Mountain's paw. He had two choices now: flee and fail, or fight.

He had been putting it off but he called on his soul now, and let it take him, bulking out into his own bear, tall as Lone Mountain and even broader, the greatest of his Mother's children. Now, when Mountain bellowed he bellowed right back, growling and showing his teeth and standing tall, trying to cow the other bear by sheer presence.

Lone Mountain had never been a man to back down, though, and he was driven by pain. In moments the roaring and posturing became an attack, his great claws raking at Thunder, who came back at him just as fiercely.

He and Mountain had never really got on.

They battered at each other, chewed each other's pelts, shoved and shunted and then broke apart and roared again, and always with the crumbling edge of the chasm yawning for them. Thunder dropped down and shook his head. The touch of Lone Mountain had a poison in it, as though what festered in him was leaping from him like fleas. Moments of pain and fear coated Mountain's claws. Thunder's mind was full of seal faces that had once been Seal faces. He saw empty villages, heard again the stories of what had been worked upon the bodies.

He rushed forward, even so, making the contest one of sheer brute force. It had always been like this between them: each of them showing they were better, until they had become grown men, and life had given Thunder all that Mountain wanted, and nothing that Thunder would actually have chosen for himself.

Loud Thunder felt the pieces of Mountain's mind lance him like bees. He saw the hollow people; he saw the grey man with white eyes like the mask the Owls wore; he felt Mountain's terror and saw the Tiger huntress's end, unmade by the sheer presence of the Plague People.

The Plague People with their white shadow walls. He had heard all this before, but he took the fear and made it into anger, which was more useful to him. He made it into strength, even as the sickening touch of the injured bear was sapping him. Bear strength was something of the moment, and if it was not enough then a bear would go elsewhere, because bears never wanted anything quite enough to work that hard at it. From within him, Loud Thunder found a new kind of strength, the strength that comes in the moment before death and cares nothing for pain or fear. He smashed and gnawed at his cousin, forcing him back, bludgeoning the other bear unmercifully until Lone Mountain fell away, even his madness beaten into submission. He dropped and ducked his head and then lurched over onto his side, and Loud Thunder followed up, roaring and roaring into the other bear's face, bellowing out wordless volumes of spit and noise and stinking breath.

And he almost lost himself then. He was a bear in the Bear's far country, which was no place for humans. How much easier – how much *better* – to stay a bear and never go back. Human life had always bewildered him, after all. He had never liked the company even of his own kind. Why not stay?

There was a terrible poison in the world. His head was full of all that Lone Mountain had seen. How much easier not to go back and face it? After all, as the Plague People spread out from the coast, more and more of the Bear would come here in pain and terror. He could help them return to their god. He could free them, as he was freeing Lone Mountain. They would be reborn as bears, if never again to be men.

But there was a voice in his mind, a faint and distant voice, and it said, *Come back to us.*

Stepping to his human shape was the hardest thing he had ever done, but he did it. He made his great claws into human arms, and threw them about the beaten bulk of Lone Mountain. He held his cousin tight until he felt the bear flesh shift and diminish, and become only a man. A hollow-faced, sick man, but his cousin nonetheless. Thunder named him, and saw recognition in Mountain's eyes. He had broken the Plague People curse. The wound was just a wound.

Thunder took a deep breath and released his kinsman, and the two of them stared at one another. He had hoped that, with this victory, the land around him would calm itself: the snow ceasing, the crags becoming something less edged and vicious. The Bear was slow to change, though. The Godsland loomed jagged and angry on all sides.

Lone Mountain's hoarse voice reached him. 'Where is home, from here?'

All the tracks were gone, and his nose, which had brought him here, would not lead him out again. He could not even find his own trail. And yet he stood, that stubborn strength still in him. He helped Lone Mountain to his feet, putting the man's arm over his shoulders and taking half his weight. The land around them was black rock and white snow, but somehow his eyes had seen a shimmer of colour, as though something long and sinuous was moving, just close enough to the surface for him to detect it. It stretched a long winding way, he knew. There would be no simple awakening.

But he knew the path and, now he had won back the mind of his cousin, the rest would be just a matter of plodding forwards. That was something he could do.

And later – an age later in his own mind – Thunder opened his eyes at his Mother's hearth, and looked down at Lone Mountain, his cousin: thin, drawn and hurt, but breathing, and human.

Looking up, he met his Mother's eyes, expecting no more than a brief nod: he had done as he was told, for once. A lack of disappointment was high praise, from her. Her eyes were on him, though.

'What have you learned?' she asked.

'Enough.' His mind was still raw with what Lone Mountain had seen. 'I know where they are. I have seen them. Everything you feared is true.'

He could not sit still. The knowledge was making his mind crawl. He lurched to his feet, shivering.

'And what?' Mother asked him.

'And I know what must be done, and I'll do it,' he told her. 'I know what all this was for. I know why you chose me.'

At last something of her usual manner returned to her. 'It could have been another,' she told him tartly. *However big you think you are, you're still a child to me.* But then she gave a grudging nod. No words, but he knew he'd done well.

Striding out into the night, he thought of all of it – calling the tribes here, facing them down, fighting Yellow Claw. All of it had seemed such a fumbling business at the time. But Mother had known. Mother had chosen him because his mistakes would turn out to be right all along.

He found the two Coyote at their fire and forced himself to sit there until Quiet When Loud woke. She regarded him warily, but she could see on his face he had done what he set out to do.

'You must go to every hearth, you and your mate,' he told her. 'Bring them all, the priests, the chiefs and hunters. All who came to show how strong and fast and clever they are. We have a journey to make and a war to bring.' The words were cold on his lips. They were all on the brink of something terrible.

33

Asmander had chased fires up and down the river for half the night. He had found the Dragon's tracks and its work: burned fields, slaughtered goats and dogs, dead men and women who had been unwise enough to try and fight them. Everywhere he went, they had already departed though. He had seen them only as fleeting shadows. The Dragon was not even raiding properly. Plunder took time, and the Dragon was just racing back and forth with Asmander in pursuit. Then the messengers came, desperate and wild-eyed, calling him back to the Bluegreen Reach. They would not say what had occurred, but when he arrived at the docks he saw the banners raised there: ochre cloth with the blind white eye, blind so that old enemies would not see the soul as it departed, or hinder its rebirth. It was a blessing reserved for the great, for the lord of a household.

He had thought it was his father's death, when he stepped ashore. His heart had been lighter for it. But there was old Asman striding to the jetty with his judging look on a face grey with pain. One hand was bandaged halfway to the elbow.

'What has happened?' Asmander demanded.

'Your slave,' his father told him flatly. 'He came looking for you. You failed to catch him.'

Asmander had questions, but the chief answer was already there, waiting for him to accept it. A great lord was dead and old Asman yet lived. He tried to ask the question but the words lodged in his throat. His father nodded tiredly, his confirmation equally unspoken, yet unmistakable.

'We have sent to Tsokawan for a priest,' Asman went on. There were no insults, no more recriminations, just a tired recital. Every word struck like an arrow even so.

'Where were our guards?' Asmander demanded, meaning, *Where was I?*

'Some in the house, who saw nothing. Some who had gone out to defend the estate.'

'Where was Many Tracks?' meaning, *Where was I?*

Old Asman turned and stalked back towards the house. 'When the Dragon started fires and threatened an attack, she went to meet them,' he threw over his shoulder. Still the final judgement hung over Asmander, unspoken.

'None was with him to defend him?' Asmander demanded, meaning just the same.

Without looking back, old Asman held up his wrapped hand with a grunt of pain, and at last let the sword fall. 'Where were you?'

Asmander could have shouted that his father had seen him off and blessed his night foray. He could have complained that he was one man and could be only in one place. He could have cried that it wasn't fair until his throat burned. But the truth was he had been betrayed. By a man he had hoped might be his friend, but was only a man who had once been his slave. He had failed his brother, his Kasra.

Now his father stopped, with the lights of the house gleaming on him. 'I have not sent men after the murderer yet,' the old man said softly. 'But it is long past time the pirate's throat was opened. If you had not been so soft, he would have died long before, and none of this would have happened.' Still that slow, weary tone, no venom in it but the words hurt like razors.

'I will kill him,' Asmander swore, hearing his own voice shake.

'Are you sure you will not make him an ally? Are you sure

326

you will not share his hearth and be his mate?' and at last the
venom was back, and Asmander welcomed it.

'I will kill him,' Asmander repeated. 'I will tear his corpse into
ten parts and scatter it from here to Atahlan.'

'Just kill him,' old Asman suggested. 'He was a weakness in
you from the moment you spared him. Rid the world and yourself of him, and then return and I will tell you what must happen
next.'

There were men who had seen which way Venat had gone,
who would show Asmander the trail. He followed them with the
Champion scratching at the inside of him, eager to get out.
What happened elsewhere on the estate, he had no eyes for.

★★★

Old Asman's blood was in her mouth, but Shyri's own blood
was all down her side and she felt the exchange had not been
worth it. When she had pelted out of the big house, she had
been human still and dragging the boy with her, even as Asman's
soldiers clustered around him. Now she was a hyena, limping
along as best she could towards the forested edge of the estate
with Tecuman outpacing her and coming back for her. The old
bastard's knife had cut her up. Old Asman might not have been
a warrior but she'd bet he'd put the blade in more than once
when words alone hadn't carried the day for him.

She paused, looking about her and trying to get her bearings.
The blood was still running down her side and she felt the
wound like a weight trying to drag her to the ground. She didn't
yet know what sort of wound it would be: the kind that would
kill her by slowing her down, or the kind that would finish her
off without outside help. Right now she was just concentrating
on keeping moving. The Hyena didn't lie down and give up, not
ever. The Hyena's destiny was to rule the world over a mountain
of corpses. She kept telling herself that her own corpse wasn't a
part of that picture.

And the boy – she had pressed her knife into his hand, but
without any faith that he could make good use of it. He had no

swift shape to shift to and his human feet sent him stumbling all over in the dark. He must be leaving a trail a blind hunter could follow. Shyri cursed herself for getting involved. *I never did know when to keep out of things.*

She was amazed Izel hadn't caught them already. She knew how fast Asmander could go on his lizard legs, and surely the woman was no slower. At last she summoned the strength to Step, trusting her soul to her faith that she would not die just yet. The shift of shape sent agony stabbing through her and she lost her breath, the words bottled as she tried to cope with it.

'Come on,' hissed Tecuman, plucking at her arm, and she slapped at him angrily. *There, I've struck the Kasra! If I'm going to be killed by the River Lords it might as well be for something real.* The thought made her feel better and she hissed a laugh through her teeth. 'Where are we going?' she got out.

She saw the whites of his eyes go wide. 'Where were *you* going?' he demanded.

'Away, mostly,' she replied. 'Your land, your people, your bastard old men with knives. You lead for a change.'

'But I don't know anywhere,' Tecuman said, voice trembling. 'Asman has betrayed me, Therumit wanted to kill me, and the Dragon is out there.'

'The Dragon's the least of it,' Shyri told him, but of course they'd brought him up on stories of the terrifying Dragon raiders, and he was nine parts fear of everything right then. 'Come on, boy! I shed my blood for you. Do something for me.' Abruptly she sat down, though she hadn't intended to. Her head was spinning and she tasted vomit at the back of her throat. No more words. She Stepped, drinking deep of Hyena's bloody-mindedness. *Oh, I am not going to die of this. Not of an old man with a little stone knife. Not of a little running about in the dark. Not me.*

'Come on,' Tecuman said again, and she forced herself up onto four legs and began the journey to the treeline, because it was dark and sheltered there, and that seemed a better place to be than out in the open.

She cast a glance behind, seeing the lights of the big house, and not as distant as she'd have liked. No swift-onrushing reptile shape, though; no Izel. And then she heard the voice from ahead of them, the little titter of mirth. Every child of the Laughing Men did her best to avoid that final moment when only her enemies had something to laugh about.

She slowed, baring her teeth. Izel was not behind them. Izel and her swift-clawed feet had skipped around in front of them, and not broken a sweat in doing so, Shyri would wager. The woman stood there on human feet, stone knives in her hands. Her teeth flashed white as she grinned.

'O Kasra,' she said. 'This is no road for you. Do you not know the night is full of Dragons?'

'I do not believe my sister sent you.'

Izel took a graceful step forwards, plainly enjoying every moment. 'The Kasra speaks. Do his words shake the world? No? Then perhaps you were never meant to sit upon the Daybreak Throne. Perhaps you are only a scared little boy.'

Shyri growled savagely, though the sound came out as little more than a whine. Izel barely spared her a glance, focusing purely on the boy. *I will make you regret that. Just come closer.* But Izel did come closer, and Shyri readjusted how close she'd have to come before any regretting might happen.

To her utter shock, Tecuman stepped forward until he stood beside her. One hand touched her tawny mane and the other jabbed the knife towards Izel. 'I will die as a warrior dies,' he said, his voice thin and unsteady.

'I will tell you how you will die,' Izel stated, almost in knife range, almost in range of Shyri's jaws, dancing at the very edge of their reach and fully aware of it. 'You will die at the hands of the Dragon, everyone will say. Their chief, who was Asmander's slave, he will murder you. He already has, in fact – about an hour ago. And Asmander will go and fight him, and perhaps his

329

slave will open his throat, or perhaps he will become a man at last and kill his slave. For his father hates that old slave of his, more than life itself.'

Shyri thought of Venat, waiting out in the trees. Of course they'd guide Asmander right to him. Would there be accusations and denials? It would not matter, not with Asmander grieving his dead friend. So, they would fight, as they had been itching to all the time she had known them. Then one of them would die and the world would be a poorer place.

'And old Asman thinks his victorious son will come back to him, purged of all the impure thoughts that slave put in him. But he's wrong. If that slave doesn't do the job, then I shall. And when you are dead, O Kasra, and he is dead, there shall be none left who once mocked a poor girl from the fields for being Champion.'

'I will fight you,' Tecuman quavered, but his voice died entirely because Izel had finally Stepped, having wrung every drop of amusement out of this situation. She came forward, killing claws held delicately up to keep their edges sharp. Shyri took a deep breath.

She laughed. There was nothing in the world like the cackle of a hyena. Even here and now, weak and bloodied and facing a Champion, she could laugh, and it gave Izel pause despite herself. It was a laugh that said, *I know something you don't.*

For that crucial heartbeat, Izel did not spring, and then the night was rushing in on all of them, as something big enough to eclipse the stars thundered from the darkness and slammed the River Champion away. Izel's human nose and ears had not been keen enough, but Shyri had scented tiger in the grass. It was good to have something to laugh about.

What had come barrelling towards Izel was no tiger, of course: it was the Champion of the Crown of the World. *And Hyena had a hand in the making of that.* Izel rounded on her attacker, screeching, and met Maniye's jaws head on. The huge beast just bellowed at her, a roar that seemed to call down thunder from the sky. Izel could have no knowledge of what the monster was, save that a Champion's soul rode it. She feinted, trying even then to get round to kill Tecuman, but Shyri snapped at her, and there was a wolf alongside her, dark and snarling, fending the lizard off. Then Maniye was rearing up like a bear, swiping with her forelegs. Izel screeched again, but a moment later she was gone.

Shyri Stepped, gasping with the pain. 'Get the boy away. She'll come back with soldiers. Asman's betrayed us all.' She lost sight of the world for a moment with the strain of forcing the words out, and then she was looking into Maniye's concerned face.

'You're hurt,' the Wolf girl saw.

'I'll live. Get the boy—'

'No,' Tecuman said. 'We have to save Asa.'

Who the plague is Asa? But he must mean Asmander. For a moment Shyri couldn't remember what it was about Asmander, but then the knowledge returned to her like a blow. 'Ah no, he's off to fight Venat, the idiot.'

'Where?' Maniye demanded, and of course Tecuman didn't know, but Shyri did.

'Be your . . . your thing that you are.' She let Maniye pull her up. 'Carry me.' If she hadn't felt so very, very bad the idea of riding a Champion would have made her laugh. She looked at the other wolf, who had become a big northerner, one of Maniye's people. 'Your man here needs to get the boy out. You carry me. I'll show you Asmander or his corpse.'

34

For once Loud Thunder had no difficulties finding his audience. For once it wasn't him trekking from fire to fire with his requests. From the moment he left Mother's cave, there had been eyes on him. That evening he went to the fighting circle, built up a windbreak of stones and banked a fire against it. He cooked some fish Two Heads found for him, and he made a fuss of his dogs and he waited, taking comfort from mundane things.

They came to him, gathering about the edge of the circle. Each time he looked for a face, he saw it there. Gnarl Hide, Ash Maker, Icefoot, Aritchaka, the two Coyote, even the Owl priestess Seven Mending. Priests and hearth-keepers, hunters and chiefs, they all came to the circle and waited. Everyone had heard what he had done and everyone had come to hear what he had discovered. All save one. Kailovela was not free to walk where she wanted, of course. Hers was the one face missing. So: he would go tell her all. She was the one person he would stir himself to visit.

Nobody there loved him. Even the Bear were mostly indifferent to him – he was the war leader Mother had set over them, and they resented it.

Everyone knew Loud Thunder, strongest of the sons of the Bear. He had gone to places only priests knew the ways of. He had accomplished something beyond mundane men. He had fetched his cousin from the shores of death. He had defeated the poison of the Plague People.

The Plague People. He heard the name on many lips as he sat there. The oldest enemy, whom their ancestors had only been able to flee by putting the sea between them. Except the sea was no longer enough.

He finished his fish, made sure his dogs were fed. He stood and turned slowly, seeing the multitude gathered about him.

'My cousin crossed the mountains to the sea,' he told them. 'I have heard what he has to tell. I have seen what his eyes saw. What you fear, it's true, and worse than true. A blight has come to us. It takes the shape of people, but they have nothing inside them, no souls. They have consumed whole tribes of the Seal: killed them and unmade them. The mere sight of them is terrifying, and that fear becomes a weapon in their hand that they use to sever you from yourself.'

It was eerie, to have so very many around him, and so silent.

'But they are not many. They are not a great plague yet. Those of you who have seen a Seal village know they are small, and this plague has set its tents about just one such. They have put up walls of white shadow and made the place their own, but it is a small place, still. Next year it may be larger, or many such places. The warnings that have come to the wise in dreams have given us the chance to fall upon them and drive them back into the sea.'

The silence persisted after he had finished, when he would rather have heard a rising murmur of excitement and determination. None of them would admit it, but they were scared. At last the old Boar priest Gnarl Hide coughed and said, 'If they truly are the Plague People, we cannot fight them. Our ancestors could only flee them.'

'And where will you flee?' Loud Thunder asked him. 'We have lost one world to them already. How many more worlds do you have that we can go to?'

'Let them have the land sunward of the mountains, then,' said

333

one of the Deer, always readiest to avoid a fight. 'I weep for the Seal, but they are not my kin.'

'Why should they limit themselves?'

'Why should they not? Who will teach them the passes through the mountains?' the Deer persisted. 'You do not know they will come. But, if you fight them, then for sure they'll come.'

'Because the Seal are our kin.' It was Two Heads Talking who broke in. He hunched his shoulders a little under the collected stares of all those assembled. 'When Coyote goes to war, you listen,' he added, a saying many there knew. Coyote only bloodied his teeth when he had nowhere else to go. 'The Seal are our kin, because we are all kin compared to the Plague People,' Two Heads said simply. Beside him, Quiet When Loud leant into him and cradled her belly, all the humour gone from her.

'What do the Coyote know?' a Wolf growled.

'We know to listen. We listen to everyone,' Two Heads replied. 'What say the Owl, am I right?'

Seven Mending nodded. She didn't look happy about being roped into the debate, but Two Heads Talking drew the words out of her as though they were on a cord. 'Our ancestors stayed to fight the Plague People, to hold them until the fire and the sea cut them away from these lands. They are not us. They have no souls, just hunger within them. They are no part of our world. I would be this Coyote's twin before I was the most distant family of the Plague People.'

Loud Thunder looked at them, seeing each unwilling to speak, and at last he remembered the other thing that had happened, that Lone Mountain had told him of, or that he had seen in his cousin's mind – he found it hard to separate which was which.

'They bleed,' he told them all.

A long, slow moment of thought passed.

'Lone Mountain saw them bleed. There was a Tiger huntress with him there. She gave her life so we could know they bleed.

Red blood like us, for all they are not us. And they are not many. And they will not look for us to come to them in force.' *And I hope I'm right in saying that.* It was time for him to become what Mother had always planned for him. It was time to be war leader, not just of the Bear but of all the Crown of the World.

'I will go and fight the Plague People,' he told them. 'I will take my people. We are the strongest warriors in the world. If we must go alone, then we will go alone. If we go alone and die, you will remember when the Plague is at your hearths, eating your food and slaying your warriors. You will remember that you had a chance to drive them into the sea, and that you chose to turn your backs. Who will come with me across the mountains? Who will bring their wisdom and their speed, their arrows, their bronze and their wolf-iron? Who will bring fire and axes and destroy our enemies before they grow strong?'

There was a gap into which his words fell, and for a moment he thought it was bottomless. But at last there came an echo back: a woman's voice.

'I will come.' It was the Boar woman, vengeful Ash Maker. 'You won't let me kill Wolves. So I will come with you and kill your enemies instead.' She stepped into the fighting circle and looked about at the rest with scorn: just a stocky woman of middle years, but nobody could meet her gaze.

'The Owl will stand with you.' Their priestess stepped forward too. 'We had hoped never to hear the call again, but we know our duty.' Her voice shook a little and her hands were twisted together. Then Aritchaka and two of the Wolves stepped in at the same time, freezing to glower at each other with mutual suspicion. The Tiger priestess faced them down and snarled, 'It is our lands they will come to, if they cross the mountains. We will fight.'

'The Swift Backs also,' snapped a Wolf, as though Aritchaka meant it all as a personal insult.

'The Many Mouths,' said the woman beside him. Then she shrugged, as though wondering what had put her up to it.

'The Winter Runners!' Another warrior had stepped forward. 'The Winter Runners, the Champion's own pack stand with you!' And then they were coming in all together, each trying to drown out the last: Boar, Deer, Hawk, old Icefoot of the Moon Eaters, until the fighting circle was packed with them.

This is what she saw, Loud Thunder told himself. If Mother had trodden before him in her mind, he could at least pretend he knew he was doing the right thing.

'Gather your supplies,' he told them all. 'My people will give up what they can,' *or I shall have words with them,* 'but you each know what you lack. Make yourselves ready for a cold journey. Archers, fill your quivers; warriors, sharpen your blades. And those of you who are wiser than I, go tell the gods what we are about, for the Plague People are their enemies too.' A sudden revelation struck him and his mouth went on with the words before he could stop it: 'I have seen the Godsland, and I have seen the lights that throng the sky trying to find a way in. The Plague People are not just here to devour us; their very presence drives out our souls and our gods and everything that we are. So if you are wise, send your words up to the gods and call them to arms as well.' *Because we will need all the help we can get.*

He let them return to their hearths, talking amongst themselves about what they would need and where it might come from. He watched old enemies go, not quite shoulder to shoulder, but at least facing in the same direction. Looking to the east, he almost expected dawn to be breaking over the mountains, but of course the night was yet young.

'That was a fine speech,' said Two Heads Talking, at his elbow.

'Thank you for being at my back.'

The Coyote shrugged. 'We are all selfish, Thunder. I will have a daughter come the spring. If I save the world, even a little, it is for her.'

'A daughter?'

336

'Quiet When Loud says so.'

Loud Thunder found the thought made him less happy to fight, not more. It was a reminder of how very fragile everything was. And a reminder, of course, that he could be selfish too.

'Will you be with us, over the mountains?' he asked.

'What man would I be, to whip up all the others and then not go?' Two Heads asked him, and then grinned. 'And I'll come back with you when we've won.'

'You see that in the future then?'

The Coyote shrugged. 'Takes more than two heads to know the future.'

Thunder left him. That sense of the fragile was everywhere around him: his people, the other tribes, the very land itself seemed brittle. *What will be left if we fail? Even if we succeed, the Plague People know where our shores are. How long can we keep them away? What if this is where the end starts?* A desolating sense of everything he and his people had ever known rushing away into darkness. *So we must hold on to what matters to us, as long as we can.* And with that thought he was striding for the Eyrie camp, imagining himself trampling custom and propriety under his feet.

They did not stop him when he went to Kailovela's tent. He felt their eyes on him, the Owl especially, but none was fool enough to stand in his way. She was lying beneath her furs when he came in, sitting up hurriedly when she saw her visitor. Across the tent from her the little hollow spirit glowered and scowled – and he knew it, of course. Those Lone Mountain had seen had not been small, like this, but they had been just as soulless. How this little flying Plague-girl had been caught by the Eyriemen, he had no idea. As to what they would do with it . . . He had some thoughts, but that was for later.

'Kailovela.' He sat heavily beside her.

'They say you went to the gods for your cousin's soul,' she murmured, staring into his face as though she could read the story there.

337

'Something like that. And now we go to war. All of the Crown of the World goes to war against *her* people.' A jerk of his head indicated the little creature tethered across the tent.

'She has no people.'

'Some other tribe of her people perhaps. We're going to destroy them. And when we come back . . .'

She watched him carefully. If there was an expression on her face there was at least some dread in it. She had heard this before, probably even from Yellow Claw.

'I will come back for you,' Thunder forced out. 'For you. Because I can't do otherwise.'

'And if I am in the Eyrie again by the time you return?'

'Then I will go to the Eyrie.'

Her jaw twitched. Her expression resolved into sheer frustration: with him, with the world. He read there, *I thought you were different*, but perhaps that was just him. Perhaps she hadn't really thought he was different, after all.

'I'm not—' He wanted to say *like them*, but he couldn't get the lie out. Instead he just muttered, 'I'm sorry. I was lost as soon as I saw you.'

'Yellow Claw blamed me,' she told him bitterly. 'When he took me, when he killed the man who had taken me before, he said it was my fault, that I had driven him to it.'

'That's not what I mean.'

'Do you even know what you mean?'

Her sad gaze, at last, drove him out of the tent. And there he met Yellow Claw, who had surely heard every word. The Eyrie Champion was still in a bad way, but he was standing, perhaps by sheer will. He glared pure hate at the Bear before him – or perhaps it was hate at the woman in the tent, and Thunder was just standing in the way.

Touch her and I'll kill you. But Thunder couldn't get the words out. He was too snared in his own motives to make the threat.

At last the Champion stated flatly. 'When you go to war . . .'

Thunder waited, fists clenched.

338

'I will be with you,' Yellow Claw finished, each word dripping venom. 'I am the Champion of the Eyrie. I will fight.'

Thunder stared at him. *I gave you a beating, little man. You shouldn't even be standing up.* But *something* was holding the Eyrieman together. The invisible wings of his Champion soul were folded about him, giving him strength.

'And when we return, we will fight again, and you will kill me, or I will kill you,' Yellow Claw promised. 'Because she is mine. And she will be mine until I am dead.'

Looking at him, looking past the transient majesty of his mantle, Loud Thunder felt pity for Yellow Claw and for himself. *This is what I'll become. When I claim Kailovela I will be no better than this.*

The night was advanced by then, the moon high, but he could hear the urgent murmur of voices from many fires, still. He'd given everyone a lot to think about. And sleep was far from him too. Sleep was a next-door country to the Godsland, and he had no great wish to travel near those borders so soon.

So he went and sat beside Lone Mountain in Mother's cave. His cousin breathed still, and Mother said he would live and grow strong again, but Loud Thunder sat there for a long time, staring at the walls as though the cracks and contours there were a map of a land he would be forced to travel to, one day soon.

Probably he dozed a little, but he woke when Mountain woke breathlessly, fighting with the air, gasping as though drowning. Thunder put a hand out, and met his cousin's anguished stare without flinching. He had seen what those eyes had seen. He understood.

'You're safe,' he said gruffly. 'Stop making a fuss. You'll wake Mother.'

He saw Mountain mouth the word 'safe', and for a moment the man was still back there, still on the wrong side of the mountains before the white walls of the Plague People. Then knowledge came to him, a remembrance of who and where he was, and he relaxed.

'I don't need you here,' Mountain said. His voice was just a husk of itself.

Thunder shrugged. 'Am I here for you? I just didn't want to have to make my own fire.' He wanted to say, *We're going to war. We're going to destroy them.* But even that might bring the bad memories back, so fresh. So he just sat there until dawn, watching Lone Mountain drift in and out of healing sleep, and tried to think about nothing at all.

A warband needed many things: food, weapons, hides, sleds. Some of these things the Bear had, others needed finding, making, mending. It seemed that, among their guests, there was always someone professing to be an expert. There were those who could hunt and gather, those who went down into the lowlands to cut wood, those who stitched or carved, fletched or cooked. And there were others, priests mostly, who could plan and keep tallies and say, 'We need more,' or 'Enough.' And over the next few days the balance of their counts slowly shifted from 'More' to 'Enough', until there were more and more men and women standing idle while the last few finished their work.

On the third day, just as Loud Thunder realized there were no more obstacles to keep him from setting out, a new batch of supplies arrived from an unexpected direction. Padding into the Bear's Shadow came some two dozen Tigers from the Shining Halls, all warriors armed and armoured in bronze, with a half-dozen horses drawing their supplies. Loud Thunder had not thought about sending for reinforcements, but the Tiger lands were nearer than most and plainly Aritchaka had the foresight he lacked. But that was not all: almost on their heels came a score of Swift Back hunters, the closest of the Wolf tribes, and there was a moment when the old war between the Tiger and the Wolf was nearly rekindled there and then. Loud Thunder intervened, however, and his voice and his shadow were large enough to keep the old enemies separate.

Now they had another forty fighters to bring against the

Plague People, and there was nothing left undone, and so Loud Thunder called them all, all the warriors of the Crown of the World. *They will tell stories of this*, he thought, proud for a moment, but then, *What kind of stories, though? Sad ones, probably.* They were all looking expectantly at him. That was the worst part. All those eyes, all that hope. It made him want to shout at them and tell them to go home.

But instead he raised his axe high. There should have been more grand words, but he had exhausted his supply with his speech before, so he just Stepped and lumbered off, his dogs and their sled trotting after him. Would any of them even follow him, after all this?

But he couldn't fool himself. The ground was busy with clawed feet and hooves, and winged shadows passed overhead as the Eyriemen took flight. He had them at his back for now, all of them forged to his purpose. The great host of the Crown of the World was heading for the mountain passes, coursing in a long, snaking column of furred backs: grey, brown, dappled and striped. Under the eyes of their loved ones, their mates, their families they ran, swift and fierce and unified, the Hand of Thunder, a warband such as the world had never seen.

35

Asmander didn't think too much about how neat were the directions he had been given: how they took him past the borders of his family estate, but not so very far. They were just tools for his use. Right now he was in no position to consider how conveniently they had been placed within his reach.

Because of course Venat was the most notorious pirate of the estuary. They whispered about him and his warband to scare children. He was the Dragon incarnate; he was a monster. And he *had* been a monster, but Asmander had looked on him and recognized something monstrous within himself, that the man called out to.

Those years ago he and his father and their soldiers had come upon Venat's warband, finding them drunk and sleeping, and it had been a hard fight nonetheless. Asmander had been Champion for mere months, still finding the fit of the new soul within him. It had been his first true fight in that shape. He had been raw, but swift and fierce and *right*. Venat had been wrong, but he had been strong and savage. And magnificent. Asmander had never fought, before or since, as he had fought that day. The Champion had come alive within him, like a new sun driving away all the brooding clouds that shadowed him. That was why he had argued so fiercely for Venat's life. As he could not have the man as an eternal adversary, he had settled for having him as a companion. Not a slave. Never a slave. That was why he had freed him in the north.

He had indulged himself and the Champion's own drives and desires. He had cast aside loyalty to his father and his clan, to the Kasra and the Sun River Nation. He had done these things because he wanted to, and because they had made him fleetingly happy. And of course there was a price, just like in the stories. The price was the life of his old childhood friend and his Kasra.

Father always despaired of my choices, Asmander knew. *Now I see he was right to.*

And Venat was ready for him, when he arrived. Of course he was. The Dragon told the same stories as Old Crocodile. He knew how this went. He had been sitting at a meagre fire with the carcass of a goat nearby – already sheared and shredded by lizard teeth. He was wearing his sharkskin vest and his tortoise-shell bracers, and he had his greenstone *meret* ready to hand, the bladed stone club that was sharp as flint and harder than metal.

They stared at each other, old comrades, old enemies.

'I thought they'd send you. I thought this was what it was all about,' Venat said heavily. There was less glee in him than Asmander had expected. No gloating about Tecuman's death, just . . . resignation. It was disconcerting.

'Did you think they'd let you live?' he demanded.

Venat stared at him. 'I knew it would be *you*,' he repeated. 'Your father wanted you to kill me back before. He's wanted it ever since. Was that the first time you bucked him?'

'My father was right,' Asmander stated.

Venat stared at him, and Asmander was surprised to see an expression of real sadness touch his face briefly. 'That's how it is, then?' he asked.

What did you expect? There was something off about this whole encounter. Venat was not playing his role properly. *Revel in what you've done, will you? Make this easier for me!*

'I am my father's son,' he insisted.

'That's a narrow shirt to wear,' Venat told him. 'How small a man you'll have to become, to fit it.' He kicked his fire, scattering the sticks and ashes of it. No guests, no hosts here, just two warriors.

'When you gave me back my name,' the Dragon said, 'you kept something of me. Some part of me: my skin didn't fit properly, when it was gone. I went to my people and made myself the big man amongst them, like I'd always wanted. But it wasn't enough. I came back to the River with my people because, with those pieces of me gone, I couldn't be happy just being what I had been. But look at you, you're friends with your father and so you've come to gift me back those pieces of me you no longer need. And that's good. One of us can go and be content with what we are, when this is done. Just one.'

'Just one,' agreed Asmander, feeling the Champion rising up within him, sharpening its claws. But then the words burst from him: 'Is that why you did it?'

Venat's face showed no understanding of what he meant. For a moment he wavered, wondering . . . but perhaps it was just that, to the Dragon, opening the throat of a Kasra was no great matter. Asmander Stepped and sprang forward in his fighting shape, feet first, sickle-claws raised high.

He should have been ready for Venat's own Stepping – dropping low as a black-scaled lizard and darting beneath Asmander's leap. The stone-hard whip of his tail lashed the Champion across his ribs and he landed awkwardly, claws digging in for purchase. He turned swiftly, right into Venat's open jaws. Even a few scratches from those festering teeth would start to slow him, he knew. He Stepped again, getting one arm under Venat's chin and fending him away. The Dragon's hook-clawed forelimb raked down his chest, ripping into his padded cuirass and grating against the stones sewn there. Asmander twisted out from under him, lashing at the lizard's back with his *maccan* and feeling the solid contact. Then he kept running, putting distance between them, Stepping back to the Champion as he turned.

Venat stood there, human, rolling his broad shoulders. There was a slight smile on his face, despite the blow he'd just taken. If Asmander had Stepped to a human shape, he might have matched it. He hated Venat for what the man had done. But the Champion and Asmander's own soul loved him.

He stalked forwards, no great leap this time: he wasn't going to catch the old pirate off guard. *So do something different.* They circled as he closed the distance, the Dragon waiting for him to commit himself before choosing what form to meet him in. So Asmander became a crocodile, lunging forwards into the low-slung shape and scything at Venat's ankles with his long jaws. Then he was human again, so that the reptile's jagged teeth became the stone shards of the *maccan* sweeping up at the Dragon's belly. Venat cursed, hopping backwards off balance, his own strike going over Asmander's head. In that moment, the boy almost had him. The *maccan* ripped open the sharkskin but only scored the skin beneath, and then Venat was a lizard once more, falling onto four feet and pitching forwards, jaws closing a finger's breadth from his enemy's leg. Asmander became the Champion, leaping on the lizard's back to drive his claws in, feeling the saw-edged scales cut him back. For a second he had his enemy pinned, but Venat was an old warrior and he Stepped back to human shape in a twisting shudder that threw Asmander off him.

The pirate scrambled to his feet, breathing heavily. He had taken a few hard strikes, nothing to end the fight but enough to wear away at even his endurance. Asmander looked into his face and saw an acknowledgement that Venat was facing a younger and swifter man than he would ever be again.

'This is good,' the Dragon announced to the world. 'Tell me you don't think this is good.'

This is good, but Asmander held to his Champion's shape so that the treacherous words couldn't escape him. *All good things end.*

He leapt again, not straight at the man but to bring himself beside his enemy, where he could rake with his claws. Venat caught him a blow on his scaled shoulder that drew a shallow line of blood, even as he fell back from the Champion's talons. Then he was in and grappling, big human frame against the Champion's strength. Asmander ripped with his foreclaws, abruptly too close to bring his feet or fangs to bear, feeling the vice-grip of the old pirate's arms about him. He smacked the side of his jaws against the Dragon's skull without loosening that hold, feeling his ribs and spine creak against the pressure. Venat cried out, part triumph, part pain, teeth bared.

Asmander reached inside him and found the one shape he'd not fought in yet: the great leather-winged creature Hesprec had gifted him with. It was not strong, but it was shaped entirely differently to the Champion and when he Stepped, he exploded from the man's grasp, the force of his wings battering Venat to the ground. Then – in the air – he was the Champion driving down, slamming his bladed feet into his enemy, forcing the old pirate's breath from him, ready to finish what had been started years before at the camp of Venat's raiders.

There was a voice shouting at him, he realized. He paused just a heartbeat: Shyri's voice yelling at him to stop. But she was a Plains creature and what did they know? Venat twisted, but every move drove Asmander's claws into him. His *meret* had flown from his hand when he was knocked down. It lay out of reach but in his sight. He stared up into Asmander's jaws and snarled, defiant to the last.

Then a great wave of sound, like thunder or the breaking of mountains, rolled over them, sending Asmander leaping back from his quarry, snarling and hissing at this new challenge. For it was a challenge, unmistakably: a challenge between Champions.

For a moment he did not recognize the beast that stood before him, overshadowing him and Venat both: a mountain of hair and muscle, hulking and monstrous, with Shyri sitting atop it, leaning forward across the matted hill of its shoulders.

But then he knew it and knew he had brought the creature to his home, and he Stepped so he could name it. 'Maniye?'

Venat had squirmed out from between them and reclaimed his blade, Asmander noted.

'Ask him!' Shyri demanded. 'Ask him if he killed your boy!'

Asmander stared at her blankly. 'I don't need to. And who trusts the words of the Dragon?'

'Well he didn't,' she spat. 'You asked me to keep watch? Well I did.' And only then did he register the blood on her, how ashen she looked.

'I . . .' *But Venat killed Tecuman. My father said so. My father, with his hand bloodied by Venat's teeth . . . the flag . . .* The teeth of the Dragon were a terror, but there were other teeth in the world . . . Treacherous thoughts began to raise their voices in his mind. He looked at Venat, and saw the old pirate as baffled as he was.

'Tell me,' he demanded, and then, because of her expression, 'I should have come to find you. I am sorry. Please tell me.'

'Just come with us,' Shyri hissed at him. 'Just stop your talking and come with us. Tecuman was alive when we left him to save you two idiots from each other, but he might not be now. We need to get back before the Champion girl finds him!'

At that point Asmander gave up on any thought of controlling his own destiny. When Maniye turned and rushed back the way she had come, still swift and soft-footed despite her bulk, he ran with her. Venat was left to follow as best he could on human feet.

The forest verge was dark, and the yelling and the fires of the Dragon had gone to trouble other homes. And surely they had been unleashed for no other reason than to cover a crime. But not Venat's crime. That flame burned in him and gave him strength, despite the dawn light that showed he'd been chasing about the river all night. That Tecuman might yet live was fine news to bring swiftness to his feet. That Venat had not betrayed Asmander after all was sweeter still.

347

Maniye drew a straight line between the trees, shouldering through the dense undergrowth, shaking off thorns and vines and tearing up the carpet of ferns in her haste. A brief glance showed Shyri on her back, eyes on the fleeting reptile Asmander had turned himself into in order to keep up. He remembered when she had forced herself into his company back when he was heading north through the Plains on his father's errand. He had come close to killing her then, thinking her an agent of Tecuman's enemies. And now she had saved Tecuman and bloodied his father both. He did not even try to think forwards: what happened when not only Tecumet and the Serpent but even Asmander's own blood turned against Tecuman? What fates awaited a failed claimant for the Kasra's throne, or was there somewhere he might still go for aid?

For a moment, dashing along in Maniye's shadow, Asmander considered bringing Tecuman before the Dragon – going to the islands and fetching an army of raiders to make war on the whole Sun River Nation. He would have Venat backing him, he knew that now. He could burn it all down, every house, every palace. And the Champion's soul leapt at the thought: to reduce centuries of tradition and history to a fight and a fire. How tempting it was!

Then he heard a wolf howl urgently from in front, answered by a screeching cry he knew well, for he had given vent to it many times. Izel was ahead of them, facing off against one of Maniye's people, and that was a fight that could not last long.

36

Tecumet stayed unseen and sheltered until her people had made sure this wasn't some elaborate trap. She had brought plenty of soldiers, and they marched out and made themselves known, ensuring that there were no surprises lurking anywhere. After all, she had been brought here by news of the shedding of royal blood. She had no wish to add to that. What her soldiers would not be discovering was whether it was true. That was not a job she could send someone else to do. She owed it to Tecuman to look on his face herself.

And part of her did not believe it. Part of her thought she might well find him, but with all his blood still in his body. Perhaps this was his way of throwing himself upon her mercy, and giving her the chance to simply banish him. She wondered if she *could* simply banish him. Her advisers would say *No*: even if he himself never entertained another thought towards the Daybreak Throne, others would on his behalf. Anyone could take up Tecuman's cause vicariously to seize the throne. The moment she made a mistake, they would say, *He should have been Kasra*, and there would be more blood, and perhaps some of it would be hers.

Or perhaps it *was* a trap, just not one to be sprung at the dock. Perhaps Tecuman had created the lie of his dead body as bait and old Asman had given his house as the stage for the ambush. Esumit had advised her that she should not go –

the Serpent priestess would instead identify the body. But Tecumet could not let her. *I must see.* She would have to rely on her Champions if there was foul play.

Or her Champion. The Stone Man, Tchoche, was still at her side. Izel was gone. Esumit assured her it was some vital errand. Which raised other possibilities that Tecumet had carefully not asked about.

Now one of her guard returned to the barge to assure her that they had the dock secured. The people of the estate were assembled to greet her as their Kasra, old Asman at their head. It was time.

She had on her war mask with its scowling reptilian features. She wore heavy robes, ornamented with jade, bulky enough that none would see the cuirass she had on beneath. It would not do for the Kasra to seem afraid. She guessed Tecuman would not have had armour on when he died. If he had died.

She walked out into the bright sun, unable to shield her eyes because the Kasra did not need to. The sun was a servant of the Kasra, bringing bounty to the Sun River Nation at her command. Maybe it was only within the loneliness of the mask that she knew the sun went about its business heedless of her wishes. Tecuman was the only person she could have shared these thoughts with. *Tecuman.* She could have enjoyed a rule where all the burdens fell on two pairs of shoulders, she thought. If only . . . If only . . .

Tchoche stepped ashore before her with his customary slouch. He wore his heavy bronze armour, a long hauberk of overlapping plates, a helm and high collar, and he had a metal-shod shield slung over his back. He always moved like an indolent old man, fat and lazy, until it was time to fight. He surveyed the disposition of Tecumet's soldiers and then rolled his armoured shoulders, signalling he was satisfied with arrangements. Around him, the other Stone Men had taken up key positions amongst her guard, polished metal thronging with the touches of the sun. With treachery very much on her mind they were a sobering reminder that, for generations, Kasras had not been able to trust their own people, not quite, not always.

She stepped onto the dock and made her solemn procession until she stood before them all. She inclined her head and set her hands over her breast in an attitude that conveyed the sorrow that was appropriate to a Kasra mourning a brother. It was a thing quite distant from the sorrow she genuinely felt.

Esumit spoke for her, announcing that the Kasra was filled with grief and that, despite the rift that had grown between them, she had loved her brother still. The death of Tecuman had been a tragedy and all the nation would grieve for him. And Tecumet watched out of the mask's eyeholes and knew everyone there thought she had ordered it.

She could not protest her innocence. She could not tell them that she would have done anything to save her brother. She did not even know if it was true. How else would the argument between them ever have been resolved, save by the death of one by assassination, or the deaths of hundreds in war? Was this not, then, the kindest way?

Except if he and I had just sat together, alone, we could have found a middle path, I know it. If there had been no priests and clan heads and hangers-on telling both of us what we must be, we could have been something different.

Old Asman bowed low before her and declared the Kasra welcome to his estate. Nobody mentioned that he had been her brother's most ardent supporter. Somehow that seemed not to matter. Now Asman was inviting the Kasra into his home, and apparently the Kasra was graciously accepting the invitation. The locals were parting, and her guard and Esumit and Tecumet herself were processing towards Asman's home, the House of the Bluegreen Reach.

Tchoche stood close to her, right at her elbow. His honest bulk was comforting. He had been her father's most loyal servant and that loyalty had transferred seamlessly to her. If there

351

was a blade ready for her in that house, it would have to saw through Tchoche's bronze first.

But the treason never came. She entered into the house and there was a feast prepared – she had people who would taste the dishes before her, of course – and Asman was still going on about the dawn of a new age for the nation and how she must, of course, be in Atahlan soon to formally claim the Daybreak Throne unopposed.

Tecumet reached out and touched Esumit's shoulder. Was there a moment of hesitation before the Serpent priestess leant back to hear her words? Was there a brief look of exasperation? But Esumit announced, as instructed, 'The Kasra would view the body of her brother to pay her respects. The Kasra commands Asman of the Bluegreen Reach to guide her to where the body of Tecuman lies.'

This had plainly not been part of anyone's plan. Asman looked as though a lot of grand words remained unsaid in his mouth. Now that Tecumet's orders were out, though, what could he do?

So it was that, with Esumit, Tchoche and Asman, Tecumet was led to the cold cellar where her brother lay. She was braced for the sight, she thought: she expected to see a boy gnawed thin by privation, a terrible expression of betrayal still on his face. She was ready.

She was not ready. The cold cellar was empty. Its condensation-shiny walls glimmered the lamplight back at them, cut only by their own shadows.

She turned slightly, shifting the close view from the mask's eyeholes. There was nowhere a body could be, and yet Asman's face, and Esumit's, did not suggest some corpse-thief had crept in to take it.

Asman bowed, or at least tilted his head. 'The killers took his body, of course. No doubt they practised vile rites on it. It is best that those without believe we hold it here.'

Esumit was nodding, as though that was an entirely reasonable thing to suggest: that the Kasra lie to the whole world about having seen her brother's body. Except of course the lie would slip from *Esumit's* mouth, not her own. It was just everyone would hear it as though Tecumet herself had spoken.

She murmured to Esumit. The priestess frowned and shook her head slightly, a rebuke the Serpent might deliver to the Daybreak Throne from time to time. Tecumet tried again, giving the woman every chance, but still her words remained unsaid, and so she just said them, muffled and hollow from behind the mask. 'Tell me the truth about this death that came to my brother.' Echoing from the close, cold walls, her own voice sounded strange to her.

Esumit went still at this breach of etiquette, but Asman's face remained mobile and smiling. To the priestess he said, 'We would have to have this conversation soon enough, would we not? Events being what they are. In this room, away from the peasants, we can speak openly. My family has always been close to the throne, after all.'

Tecumet gestured impatiently, and at last the Serpent took away the heavy mask, which had grown heavier with each passing moment. 'Speak,' she commanded old Asman. After all, was he not renowned for loving his own voice?

'Your brother is dead,' he announced. 'None doubt this. You are now unchallenged Kasra of the Sun River Nation. It only remains to see how well your subjects will love you for it.'

'How did you come to fail my brother, Asman?' Tecumet demanded. 'Who killed him?'

'Why, you did,' Asman informed her pleasantly.

She stared at him.

'When a usurper sets himself up against the true heir to the Daybreak Throne, that man, that woman, must die. You are that true heir, after all. He died at your hand as much as anyone's.'

'I did not desire my brother's death!' Tecumet said. She felt that, of all of them, only Tchoche, the foreigner, understood her words.

'That is a story you must of course tell the world from Atahlan to the estuary,' Asman agreed, mock-solemnly. *And that will not be believed,* he did not need to add.

'You were my brother's greatest ally,' she accused him.

'On the contrary, you will find I have always been your supporter. That is also a story that shall be told all down the river.' Asman sighed, though still not unhappily. 'What can be said of what happened to your brother in my house? Can I say that wild raiders of the Dragon attacked my estate and slipped past my walls and murdered your brother, for sheer spite? Yes, it can be said, and everyone knows the Dragon. They will believe any tale so long as the Dragon are vile and bloody-handed in it. Or can I say that the Kasra had her Champion kill her brother because he challenged her for the Daybreak Throne? That also has the ring of truth to it.'

'Izel? Where is she?'

Asman's smile was a thin, subtle thing, and yet the more she looked at it, the more monstrous it became. 'She will return as soon as she has finished washing the blood off her claws.'

Tecumet's stomach lurched. 'And what if I tell them it was *you?*' she demanded, and then she had stepped right up to him, glowering right into his face. 'What if I have Tchoche break your bones, old man?'

He was not worried, not in the least. Old Asman held the oar of the world and steered it where he would. 'The world already tells the story of a sister's hate for her brother. It needs no servant of mine to speak the words. For anyone seeking news, that is the first they will come across. And if not, well, many of my people will tell the river that they saw your bodyguard leave bloody footprints across my lands the night your brother died.'

'And you,' Tecumet said to the priestess. 'You knew.'

'Everything, Kasra,' Esumit agreed blandly. 'We fulfil the needs of history.'

'You have painted the Daybreak Throne with blood.'

'Do you imagine it is the first time?' Esumit's tone had echoes

354

of the dozens of lives she had lived, one after another, back down the ages.

'So I must . . . what? Forgive my brother's murder and the suborning of my Champion? Embrace the man who ordered it? Let him tell his lies about the Dragon?' Tecumet demanded.

'As to that,' old Asman broke in smoothly, 'he who serves the Daybreak Throne does so in the knowledge his rewards will be great. If I am called upon to gild events so that the estuary will not speak of fratricide for three generations, such gold must come from somewhere.'

Tecumet could not express, just then, how much she hated him. 'You will barter with your Kasra like a merchant?'

'Yes.' The terrible smile, like Old Crocodile's own, hungry enough to devour the world. 'For I have something to sell: a story that keeps the support of the estuary. Who else has wares such as these?'

She looked to Esumit, but the Serpent priestess was expressionless. If she found old Asman's lack of respect distasteful, none of it showed on her face. *And she has lived a dozen lives, and she has seen it all before.*

'So, you have a price,' she said at last. 'Speak plainly: what?'

★★★

The Wolf warrior was bloodied but he still stood, iron in his hand. Perhaps it was that northern talisman that had warded off Izel, for she stalked back and forth before him, hissing and flexing her claws. Tecuman crouched on the ground at Moon Eye's feet, and in his trembling hand was Shyri's bronze knife.

Asmander saw Izel bunch to spring – his own muscles shivered with anticipation at the sight. He gave out his scream of challenge, outpacing Maniye in a rush, so that the other River Champion leapt clear of Tecuman and the Wolf.

Maniye thundered up behind him but he Stepped and thrust a hand out. 'No! This is my fight! It's always been my fight.'

Izel shifted too, just for a moment, grinning at him. Asmander had seen hate before. The hate of the Dragon, the hate of the

355

Plains, the overflowing lakes of hate the northerners all seemed to have for each other. But Izel put them in her shadow, when it came to hating. Her eyes were like a blade that cut his soul. And he could not deny he had given her cause, in their younger days. She had been the poor girl from the peasant village, the Champion's mistake. He had mocked her, because he had been young and arrogant and a fool.

And now at least I am less young. He opened his mouth to say something – perhaps an apology, what little good it might achieve – and she went for him in that moment, screeching. He Stepped to meet her, claw against claw, and for a moment they were leaping at each other, feinting furiously in the air then falling back down.

He gave her room and they stalked, circling. They had sparred before and he had known then that she wanted to kill him, but they had been bound by the conventions of time and place. Now, nothing held them back.

He sprang, but she twisted sideways, snapping at his neck and swerving aside as his jaws came right back for her. The curved talons of her feet flashed for him. He kicked her hard, knocking her down, but she was up in a moment. She was slightly bigger than he was in this shape, and the Champion burned as bright in her as in him.

They clashed again, and this time neither backed off, so that their initial flurry of strikes turned into a grapple where his jaws cut into her shoulder and hers gnawed away at his, their claws digging for purchase, trying to open each other up. Asmander broke off first, trying to spring back but catching a swipe from her feet as he did so, ending up sprawling on the ground. He jumped up, but Izel had been his shadow, on him before he could regain his feet, slamming him down again. He snapped at her, but she got a clawed foot about his muzzle and forced his head back down.

He Stepped to a crocodile, writhing sinuously but unable to escape her grip. He Stepped to his winged form, which thrashed and flapped helplessly, out of its element. Then she shifted her grip so that her foot was about his throat, and he had only one form left to him, the one he had been born with.

He lashed his *maccan* at her belly but she struck at it with her free foot and came down hard on his wrist. He felt bones grind there. Izel leered down at him, jaws agape. He knew how long she'd been waiting for this – practically ever since they'd met. He could not say she wasn't owed it. He resolved to die with the composure of a Champion, and then to haunt her like the most vindictive ghost the world had ever seen.

Izel shrieked in triumph and Venat cut her head off with a single blow of his *meret*.

Her body collapsed onto him like a bundle of thorned sticks and he fought his way out from beneath it, her claws still gouging him even though the will to kill him was gone. 'What have you done?' he demanded.

Venat looked at his blood-slick stone blade. 'If you can't answer that, I don't know why I bother.'

'But it was my fight! A Champion's fight!'

'I don't give a bent cock about your Champion or your honour.' Venat shrugged cheerfully and went to look at the head where it had fallen, as though considering to what use it might be put.

Shyri went hunting for ants, and then spent a while carefully letting their long-jawed soldiers bite along the line of her wound, before twisting their bodies away. She was left with a neat line of black beads stitching her skin closed. From the appalled looks of the Rivermen, Maniye saw this was obviously a Plains practice alone.

At last, the Laughing Girl looked up and gave them all a hard smile, though her skin was the colour of rust and dried blood. 'Truly,' she remarked, 'the thanks of the Patient Ones are legendary,' and, when Asmander stumbled over his words to thank her, she waved him away. 'I did it to spite your father, not to save your chief. I would have bitten him anyway, for my own amusement.'

Her voice sounded so shaky that Maniye thought she must fall over at any moment. As it was, she Stepped and made a great show of padding about in a circle before lying down, her spotted snout on her paws.

'My father . . . Asmander shook his head.

'Don't look so surprised,' Venat advised. He still held Izel's head. 'You've not had a good word for him since I met you. I preferred *her* father. At least he was honest.'

Maniye scowled at the old pirate, which was like throwing stones at an avalanche. Moon Eye came back then. He had gone padding off to scout, in case there had been a band of spearmen following Izel's trail. He Stepped as he ducked through the trees, and Maniye saw he had news.

'Soldiers?' she asked him, jumping up.

'Boats,' he told them. 'Lots of boats, but most of all the big one. The biggest we saw on the river.'

Tecumet. Maniye did not need to voice the name. Everyone there must have been thinking of it.

'This is it, then.'

Those were just about the first words Tecuman himself had contributed since Izel's death. He left a silence, perhaps hoping someone would spring forward with a grand plan to save him, but they just waited to see what he would do next.

'Old Crocodile tested me,' the boy whispered. 'He found something in me worth sparing. And the Serpent said I would be Kasra. Except even Therumit turned from me in the end. I have lost the estuary clans. I have lost Tsokawan. You here before me are my only followers.'

'Speak for yourself,' Venat scoffed, and Maniye waited for the boy to flinch back, but instead he took the words with a perfect grace. She realized she had never seen him like this: a calm had come to him after the night's attempted murder. Perhaps there was even something regal in his bearing, now it was all too late.

'Asa,' Tecuman said.

'Teca?'

'Are you my Champion?'

'As you are my Kasra.'

'Then you know what you must do,' Tecuman told him. Asmander went very still, and Maniye saw Shyri's head pick up, staring at him. 'Asa, she sent her Champion to have me killed,' Tecuman said, still with that royal calm about him. 'Before then, she sent her assassins into Tsokawan. And you, each and every one of you have had a hand in saving me. But who will be there next time?'

Asmander took a deep breath, and Shyri Stepped and burst out, 'You say the girl's boat is there? I was on that boat! I saw how many spears she has. And your father, he has spears of his own. Will you fight your way into your own house and kill every one of them? Because you'll have to.'

Asmander stared at her and she bared her teeth, so angry that she winced around each word as she spat them out.

'Don't you look at me as if your honour's got you in a hold and you've no choice. Put your back to the River. Come with me to the Plains and let that lizard of yours fight the Lion with me. Bring your boy there, if you must. Let him learn to stitch and mend for us. Don't you tell me you have to go get yourself killed for River honour.'

Asmander shrugged. 'I will go do this one small thing,' he said softly, 'and then we will talk of what comes next.'

'You are so stupid, Longmouth,' Shyri growled.

'Yes,' he agreed earnestly. 'But the Champion is like a rod up my back. I cannot bend as I might want to.'

'A stick up your arse, more like,' corrected Venat. 'Going to go face your father, as well as all those soldiers? Kinslayer, now, are you?'

'These things are known!' Asmander almost shouted at him.

Venat made a great show of shaking his head disappointedly. 'All this talk of honour, and you don't talk about the one who's really wronged, here.' At their blank looks he jabbed a thumb at his broad chest. 'If this had gone off, no doubt old Asman would be telling all the world how I killed the Kasra, before you killed me. Or how I killed the Kasra and then killed you, maybe. Been seven generations since a man of the Dragon went to rest with that kind of blood in his mouth.' He grinned at them. 'I've been robbed of a story they'd be telling to my grandchildren's children. Where's my honour getting satisfied from?'

'What are you talking about?' Asmander demanded.

The old pirate looked at him fondly, a teacher with a slow pupil who would get there in the end. 'You Rivermen, so used to having your Snakes think for you. Just listen, will you?'

And he outlined his plan, and Asmander's face grew longer and longer with every word. At last, when all was said, he blurted out, 'Why? Why would you?'

Venat shrugged. 'Your father is very free with my name. I thought it was time we met again.'

37

Grey, silent wings, almost invisible against a ceiling of cloud. A half-dozen great owls came gliding in from the east, bringing the night sky in their wake.

Loud Thunder had set watchers for them – some handful of the night-eyed Tiger who were grateful to end their vigil. His warband was making camp high in the mountain passes and the day had been bitter. They would exhaust the last of their firewood tonight, despite the warnings of the wise to ration it. Thunder couldn't blame them. He was better suited to the cold high places than most, and last night he had huddled alongside his kin, all bears together trying to husband their warmth until the wan dawn.

Last night the skies had been clear, so that what little warmth the day had gifted them with had fled almost immediately. Tonight the clouds would hold a little in, but those same clouds might be the end of them, heavy with snow. If they were caught by a blizzard in the high passes, then his warband would begin to die, first from cold, then from hunger and each other's knives and teeth.

He looked about him, seeing men and women worn down from a long, cold trek. Word was spreading that the Owls were back, and everyone seemed to take that as the order to stop moving and unpack their tents.

'Nobody camps. Rest and get your strength back, but we

don't stop yet!' Thunder warned those nearest, and then went from band to band of them, repeating his orders. He saw plenty of resentment and rebellion, but nobody challenged him openly, not yet.

Eventually he found Two Heads Talking trotting at his heels, and stopped to let the man Step and be talked at.

'The Owls, any word?'

'They're talking it over,' the Coyote told him. 'You know the Eyrie. They could be caught in a snare and they wouldn't lend you a knife to cut them down. They'll come to you, when they think you've waited enough.'

'I should go to them.'

'Only if you want to wait twice as long,' Two Heads remarked with a crooked smile. 'So we're not stopping?'

'Worried about snow,' Thunder explained.

Two Heads looked up at the sky and grimaced. 'Go all night and you won't stop it snowing. And then if it snows tomorrow you'll lose people all the more, when they're beaten down.'

'You're a priest. Tell me when the snow will come.'

Two Heads Talking shrugged, but then he went off and talked to some of his peers who had an eye for the weather – Icefoot of the Moon Eaters and a Deer tribe woman. Loud Thunder just settled himself on a rock and watched the different pieces of his warband rub roughly against each other. Already he could see the strain. The Wolf tribes were constantly snapping at each other, which stopped them doing anything more serious. The Tiger were staying away from them, but they were abroad at night, stalking between the camps. They said they were keeping eyes open for the enemy but nobody else liked it. Privately, Thunder guessed it was their young huntresses daring one another to push the bounds of safe conduct. All very well, until the Swift Backs woke to find a clumsier-than-usual Tiger at their fire.

And of course the Boar and the Deer were leery of both Tiger and the Wolf, and of his own people . . . The Bear were used to taking what they liked when times were hard. Times hadn't become hard enough for any of that yet, but a day caught in the snow would tip the balance. Loud Thunder didn't fancy having to face down a succession of his own kin with empty bellies, and if he lost just one such fight, the reins holding the warband together would snap. Everyone would be at the throat of everyone else.

So he stirred himself and ambled along from one cluster of warriors to the next, exchanging a few words with their leaders, letting his shadow stretch out so that people remembered why they were there. He let their young hunters boast to him of the revenge they would bring to their enemy. He spoke to their priests and their chiefs of how the talents of their followers might best be employed. These conversations started as a way of reminding each band that he was watching them and showing them that they were valued in turn. After a while, he realized he was speaking of such matters in earnest, though, weighing up what he might do with his Tigers and his Wolves, his Eyriemen, his Boar. He was thinking of them as though they could be given special roles and instructions, and counted upon to carry them out.

That would be fine, he thought. After all, he had the largest warband in the north at his disposal. If they would do what they were told, what could he not accomplish? What enemy could he not beat? He could attack *here* with *these* and while the enemy was dealing with that incursion, he could attack *there* with *those* and catch them unprepared . . .

He thought about the wars between the Tiger and the Wolf. Had there ever been a force this large in that fight? Surely the High Chief of the Wolves and the Queen of the Tigers must have made such choices: lives to throw upon the fire, so the other warriors would have light to fight by . . . Loud Thunder shied away from the thought but he could not quite escape it. It remained caught in his mind like a fish hook.

Two Heads Talking came padding over to him again, Stepping to announce with a shrug, 'Best guess of everyone worth asking is, not tonight. Soon, though. Let people rest while they can, push through it tomorrow if it falls. If we make good time then tomorrow night we'll be in the foothills on the far side. And maybe it won't snow tomorrow either.' The Coyote spread his hands. 'Can everyone who thinks the weather will listen to them set up an altar or send up a prayer? If we're fighting for our gods, then our gods can go howl outside the weather's hearth and get it to hold off another day or two.'

'Unless the gods have sent this weather themselves,' a new voice broke in. The Owl priestess Seven Mending had stepped silently up behind them, her head cocked. The sight of her grey and white mask made Loud Thunder shiver; he had seen the original.

'Come and hear what we have seen,' she invited them, her eyes staring past them at sights unguessed-at.

'Are they there?' Loud Thunder demanded. He had only Lone Mountain's fragmentary memories to vouch for it, after all, and who knew how accurate they were.

'Come and hear, Warbringer,' she told him, and then managed to pin Two Heads with her attention without actually looking at him. 'Go find your wise friends, little ragged man. Bid them come.'

She Stepped and was gone, with the beat of a wingspan broader than Loud Thunder was tall, and yet which made no more sound than a whisper.

'"Little ragged man,"' Two Heads echoed. 'This is what passes amongst the Eyriemen for the respect due to a priest.'

'I prefer your name to mine,' Loud Thunder murmured. 'Do not let them remember me as "Warbringer".'

'No man can say how his children will know him,' the Coyote decided, and then he Stepped to lope off and fetch whoever he counted as his wise friends.

'We travelled up and down the coast before we saw it,' the Owl priestess told them. 'We saw many Seal villages. Some were

364

burned, others held bones picked over by the gull and the crab. Still more had been abandoned, but we could see that those who had dwelt there had at least taken their belongings. However, we found no surviving village of the Seal on all the coast.'

Of course, this was what Loud Thunder had gleaned from Lone Mountain. To hear it from one who had seen it with her own eyes was more chilling still.

'We found dead children,' the Owl added, keeping her voice hard. 'On the beaches, strung out between villages, fresher than the bones. Some had starved, some washed up drowned.'

Her audience – priests and war leaders and scouts, tough men and women who had seen death – stared at her bleakly.

'When the Seal Stepped, the children could not go with them,' the Owl set out. 'Whatever drove the Seal into the sea, it robbed them of the ability to think of their children. We have heard what the Bear saw, when he came to the coast. It is a weapon of the Plague People.' She shook her head, as though trying to order her thoughts. 'It is a fact of the Plague People's very being. They are inimical to us. Even if they had not come to make war on us, their very *difference* is a weapon that unmakes what we are. If we did not have cause to drive them away before now . . .'

'But what of their camp?' the Boar Ash Maker demanded. 'Are they still there?'

'Yes,' the Owl confirmed quickly. 'We overflew it, and we saw a great nest there within their shrouds of white. There was a beast in the water that they had called up, which had a hide of overlapping scales. There were lights that knew no fire, but turned their place from night to day. The homes of the Seal were being torn down to make way for their own dwellings.'

'How many?' one of the Wolves asked.

'At least two score.'

'That is not so many,' Ash Maker stated contemptuously.

'Believe me, it is enough,' the Owl told her. 'If the very air they breathe out is poison to us, it is enough. We have heard they can strike with invisible arrows that mean death and corruption. We have heard they can drive the soul mad, trap it within a shape. How many do you think they need?'

'Are you saying we can't fight them?' Loud Thunder asked.

'I am saying we must fight them,' the Owl said. 'I am saying we must not underestimate them . . .' Her voice trailed off. Her eyes were looking past all of them, at nothing anyone else could see. 'Who is here?' she asked – little more than a whisper but they all heard it. '*What* is here?'

Axes and knives were in hand even as she asked it. There was a confused murmur that had the seeds of panic in it, everyone imagining that if they could spy on the Plague People, so their enemies might spy on them. Wolves and tigers were abruptly rushing off into the night, bears and boars dashing back and forth, and still nobody could find someone to fight. Much longer, and they would fight each other.

'Hold,' bellowed Loud Thunder, and his voice echoed from the rocks above. 'Hold still!'

Seven Mending was walking between them, the crowd melting away before her. She had a hand half outstretched, and Loud Thunder followed its line until he saw . . .

'Who is that?' He squinted, seeing a lone figure standing out in the dark: a broad-shouldered man, his features hidden by the darkness. When the priestess passed by, Thunder fell into step beside her, ready to Step the moment the intruder revealed himself as a foe.

Just one: have the Plague People sent an emissary?

But it was no invader from across the sea. It was a man of the Owl, looking haggard and weary.

'Grey Herald?' Seven Mending named him. 'How can you be here?'

'Because I found what I was seeking,' Grey Herald told her. 'I know what you are about, and I have brought help.'

'Friends?' Loud Thunder asked, but the Owl man shook his head.

Then there were more dark wings above, but not Owl wings. Great vanes of skin, as far from tip to tip as two men, and the light shining through their translucence to silhouette their stretched and skeletal fingers. With a sound like rags flapping in the wind, the Bat descended, Stepping as they landed into tall lean men and women with fierce eyes. There was something burning in them, a hunger that made Loud Thunder take a step back, lest their very presence draw something vital from him.

'Not friends,' Grey Herald said. 'But help. We need that more than friends.'

38

A night of doing what they did best had left the raiders of the Dragon strewn up and down the river on both banks. Some would doubtless be caught by soldiers of the River Lords – or just mobs of enraged peasants – but they were a resourceful people with a fearsome reputation. Most would shamble back towards the estuary and come together there, ready to take on whatever came next.

Venat found a band of eight who were camped out almost in sight of Tecumet's barge where it was docked. They were half drunk and half hungover, spattered with blood and spilled beer, but he kicked and cursed and cuffed them until they were on their feet. They stared at him with a mutinous dislike which he joyously took as his due.

Standing there with them, he went back and forth about whether he was going to carry out the plan at all. He could just round up his boys and make the most of the raiding before Tecuman finally got his throat cut and Tecumet's forces started to restore order. That would be the Dragon's path. He wondered what Gupmet, the Black Teeth chief, would advise. Would he just sit within the Dragon's stinking jaws and tell Venat to burn it all down?

And what had been burned, last night? How many River throats had been cut, women raped, children eaten? And the River Lords in their big houses would shake their heads and tut, and everyone would say, *It is the Dragon*, and perhaps there would be soldiers on the water heading for the islands to exact vengeance, some day soon. Nobody would be saying, *It was old Asman who brought them here. It was his plan that had the Dragon go mad along the river, all so he could play politics.*

And Venat thought, *We make such a good excuse.*

He smacked one of his less attentive people across the head to lend them a little focus. He might only have one foot in the Dragon's jaws, but old habits died hard.

'Right, you stupid bastards,' he told them. 'We've got jobs, you lot and me.'

They didn't like the sound of that, but he told them what their role would be, and that brought them round. Nothing too strenuous; nothing that would tax them. It wasn't as if he was asking them to *think* or anything. They didn't ask what his job was and he didn't volunteer it.

Soon after, he was standing at the edge of the Bluegreen Reach estate, looking across the fields at the big house where old Asman would be. And the girl-Kasra too, of course. Her barge was taking up all the space at the Bluegreen jetties, and there were other boats out there as well. She would have plenty of people to keep her safe.

But Venat strode towards the house with a thousand children's stories ghosting the air about him. *Nobody is safe from the Dragon*. At his back, his people started up a proper battle-whooping. Nobody could make noise like the Dragon. They beat drums and blew goat horns and whipped their scaled tails against hollow logs. Eight of them sounded like a whole war-band out in the trees.

Venat, still walking, saw the first signs of alarm from the big house. There were soldiers spilling out from it, or appearing on the balcony above the door. He held his hands wide, just in case there was an over-eager archer amongst them. He had his standard with him, that awkward wrapped weight on the end of a long staff.

Behind him, his people really got into their stride, the exercise driving off their hangovers. Two or three ran out from the trees and began doing what the Dragon did, which meant setting things on fire. Venat quickened his pace, because the wind was shifting about and he didn't intend to get burned alive by his own plan. Behind him, the first field – a fallow tangle of dry grass and brush – began to leap with flames.

Venat had heard that when River Lords called at each other's big houses, they sent a servant ahead to tell their hosts how important they were. He thought of the conflagration at his back as his own herald.

The soldiers were piling out now – off the barge and from the house. He kept walking, grinning at them. He saw that hit home: the men from the house knew him, and they would tell the rest. Not just a Dragon, but *this* Dragon. They had a creditable spear fence, but he saw the men at the front try to shuffle back a little as he approached. Old Asman must be watching – Venat reckoned he felt the cold spike of the man's glare. He stopped two feet from the spears and held up his standard for all to see.

'I thank you for the welcome!' he bellowed, the voice he usually reserved for shouting at his own people. 'Good to see you've not forgotten me!' Behind him the flames leapt, and the whoops and yells and drumming conjured an army of mad savages. 'I come to speak for the Dragon!'

At last the master of the house appeared at the balcony. There was no fear on his face, but at the same time he knew *exactly* how many Dragon raiders had come upriver, and he couldn't know they weren't all at Venat's back right then. The order would come sooner or later, but right then old Asman was the most patient of the Patient Ones.

'Why do you come here, pirate?' he called out.

'What? Can a man not come when his Kasra calls? Word came to the islands and the Dragon is here.'

Asman made no comment on the manner of his entrance, nor the events of the night before. He did not have to. Every Riverman there would be thinking, *Call on the Dragon and something will burn.*

'And is this not my house of old?' Venat threw in, because it would madden the old man. 'Did I not sit faithful at the feet of your son?' No answer from Asman, which Venat could hope was because he was about to die of bottled rage.

'And last, I came across a thing of yours. I thought you'd want it back!' he shouted at the balcony. He waved his standard around and then whipped the covering off, thinking, *Now they kill me, if they're going to.*

He could not have hoped for a better reaction. The fires burned, the warriors whooped and thundered, and the staff's end was thrust into the gape-jawed head of a Champion. He saw the whole mass of soldiers shudder at the sight, spears waving and clattering against one another. From old Asman he saw only that the man gripped the balcony rail that much harder with his good hand. It was Izel's head, of course, but the old man had sent his son to finish Venat. Surely for a moment he had thought it was Asmander's.

'I come to speak for the Dragon!' Venat bellowed again. 'Come, take my gift and let me in.'

To kill a messenger was a thing the River Lords didn't like to do. It wouldn't buy him much, but it might stop the old man giving the order to put a hundred spears in him. Venat hoped so; it had been a long night and he didn't feel like fighting that many longmouths in one go. You could have too much of a good thing.

Venat waited, and he reckoned the noise from off in the trees only grew; probably others of his people had been drawn by it. He matched gazes with as many of the River Lord soldiers as he could, seeing each look away in turn.

At last the word came, and the soldiers parted before him, forming a spear-lined road to the door of the big house. Venat had no illusions about the reception he was about to meet. River

Lord traditions aside, nobody was about to treat a Dragon pirate like an honoured guest.

He had one last moment in which he could run away. Perhaps the boy had even done what was necessary already. If their positions had been reversed, Venat would have been in and out in a heartbeat, leaving while the blood was still on his teeth. But Asmander could never do anything simply. Probably he would want to talk about it first, and complain about how unhappy everything made him. So he would need as much time as possible to get it done.

Venat grinned fondly. Inwardly, he apologized to the Dragon, that rapacious god who was surely looking with bitter disappointment on his favoured son.

And so he squared his shoulders, raised his gory standard and marched into the house.

Tecumet had wanted to go out to face the man, when she heard what was going on. Tchoche counselled against it because the Dragon was dangerous, and he could not guard against every stray stone or spear. Esumit argued that the estuary was still not in love with her, and to see the Kasra even flinch from the Dragon would harm her standing. If she should actually be struck or forced to flee, that would be far worse. And Asman had his own reasons, of course. When he heard just which Dragon was coming, a change had gone over him no matter how he tried to hide it. Tecumet thought of the story he was telling, that the Dragon were her brother's murderers. *What might this man tell me that he doesn't want me to hear?*

But by then she had already been respectfully ushered back to the chambers Asman had prepared for her, and shut out of what was going on in her name. There was even a hurried discussion about taking her out to the barge and casting off, but Esumit felt that was too much like fleeing, and besides, the Dragon was almost as swift in the water as Old Crocodile.

So she sat in this room overflowing with finery – the curtains and the hangings and the tapestries surely harvested from across the house to show her how much old Asman esteemed her. She felt as though she was something of delicate clay, packed in straw in case any little shock would break her. She glowered at the Kasra's battle mask where it hung on the wall. It frowned emptily back at her. *I am looking at a truer likeness than a mirror would show me. This is all of me the world will ever see.*

Tchoche was at the door, and she had two servants with her who were plainly out of their wits with fear at the thought of the Dragon. Tchoche was treating matters seriously, and grew more serious still when the door opened a crack and someone murmured news in to him. She saw her Champion's whole bearing change, and his expression when he glanced at her was frightening.

'What is it?' she asked, and had to ask again before she could prise the words from him.

'Izel is dead,' Tchoche reported. 'The Dragon Venat is here with her head.'

Tecumet sat down heavily, oblivious to the wailing of her servants. *And was this the old man's doing? Suborn Izel to kill my brother, suborn the Dragon to kill her. And they will kill him before they let him speak.*

'Go, hold him,' she told Tchoche. 'See he is taken.' Her mind hunted for a way to throw Asman and Esumit off the scent. 'Say he must be executed in Atahlan, given to Old Crocodile in the pit.'

Tchoche obviously didn't like the sound of keeping Venat around a moment longer than necessary, but he was her Champion first and foremost. He nodded and stepped out of the room in a clatter of bronze. She sat back, trembling. Izel was dead. Izel, whom she'd known since childhood. Yes, the woman had taken the fate of the Kasra into her own hands, but she would have sworn at every step that she did it for Tecumet. *You can be too faithful.*

And then an arm was about her throat, the razor edge of a

373

flint blade pressing beneath her chin. A familiar voice hissed in her ear, 'No sound from any of you or I kill her now.'

Asmander. Of course, the world had more than one Champion who was loyal to a fault.

The Champion was baying for blood and Asmander felt his hand tremble, a hair's breadth from cutting Tecumet whether he meant to or not. Venat's plan had been built on the bones of the Dragon: Asmander would creep into his own house, find Tecumet while most of her guards were out facing the threat Venat would whip up, and he would open her throat. Tecuman would be the sole surviving child of Old Tecuman, the Kasra that was. Who would deny him the Daybreak Throne? It was the only way to save his friend, and here was the woman who had plotted his murder. Yet his hand shook and he held the Champion's vicious spirit back.

'Asa,' Tecumet gasped, and a spasm of anger went through him. He felt that the knife was the sole still point that the world revolved around.

'You have no right to call me that,' he hissed in her ear. He was having trouble keeping track of the two servants. They were staring at him wide-eyed, but the longer this went on, the more their fear would ebb. They had Old Crocodile's shape in them, just as Tecumet did. A moment's lapse – of his attention or their judgement – and they would sound the alarm. And then he would have to make that knife move. 'I met with Izel. I know what she was sent to do.'

'And she is dead,' Tecumet observed flatly.

'Yet not the one who sent her.' Asmander was reaching for the righteous anger that had driven him this far. He had a sinking feeling that he had already lost it from the first word he spoke. 'I hold her less guilty than the one she served.'

'Go cut the throat of your father then,' Tecumet told him, with exactly that same still calm that her brother had so recently learned.

374

'Oh, I know he had a hand in it, but I know Izel served you.'

'She loved me.' A single twitch passed through Tecumet's body, a silent tear for dead Izel. 'She served me, but in the end she loved me more.'

'I will not believe you didn't order Teca's death.'

'So he's Teca, but you're not Asa to me? And I'm not Te to you?'

'He didn't send killers after you.' Even as he said it he recognized the absurdity. 'He didn't bring things to this point.'

Something went out of her, such an abrupt change that he thought he'd killed her anyway. He thought it was fear she had lost, at first: that somehow he was already betrayed; that she had a way to dodge his knife. But no, it was caring that had gone. Suddenly Tecumet, Kasra of the Sun River Nation in everyone's eyes but Asmander's and her brother's, did not care about the knife or the hand that held it.

'Everyone will think it,' she told him. 'Even if Izel's part is never known, they'll think I had my own brother killed. Many of the clan chiefs will probably even think the better of me for it. Old Crocodile will forgive a little kinslaying if the river runs clear when the blood's washed away. Your father said his stories of the Dragon will keep the estuary in line, but even if nobody rises up, if nobody ever says it to my face, they'll always think it. And in time the Serpent priests will shed their old memories and remember only Tecumet who slew her brother.'

Asmander thought of how he had gone to Venat and just called the man out, riled up by his father until murder was the only thing in his mind. *And here I am, about to shed blood without raising the very death this all follows from. A death which hasn't happened.*

He knew he should keep it secret. There would be no more assassins sent after a dead man, after all. But he had to know how she would react, and so he leant in close and whispered. 'Izel failed.'

She twitched again, and he grew tired of not seeing her face.

In a swift movement he had her at arm's length, one hand clasped to her throat to prevent her Stepping, the other still holding the knife, which had danced along and never left her skin. One of the servants let out a shrill squeak of fright and they all waited for the inevitable tramping feet, but they didn't come.

Tecumet's eyes were bright with tears. She was searching his just as fiercely, looking for the truth. Finding it, too; he had never been able to lie to her or her brother. He had loved them both too much.

'What now?' she asked him, which was a good question. He could hear a row from within the house. That was Venat's voice shouting, and Tchoche cursing. His stomach sank, and he knew that someone was going to pay dearly for the time being bought.

'You ordered his death.'

'I did not.'

'You sent the killers to Tsokawan, when I was on your barge.'

'Your father's work as well, it must have been.'

'You knew of it. You knew my father would order it, and turned a blind eye.'

'Last night, news came to my barge that Teca was dead in your father's house. That was the first I heard. Asa, you have to go. Get him far away from here. Nobody will know he lives. Take him somewhere he can be happy.'

'There is no such place but on the river.' He knew the words were true as he said them. Even if Tecuman went into exile he would never forget the Daybreak Throne. He would raise an army if he lived, and come back to take his birthright. 'On the barge, you said you'd do anything to have him by your side.' He matched her wary look. 'In this house he said, if only the two of you could meet. So you'll meet, you and he.'

'You can't bring him here.'

'No,' he agreed. He felt a smile trying to take hold of his face, despite everything. 'Terrible things, Te. There's nothing else left to us.'

She would refuse, of course. He felt her tense, knew she would try to break from his hold. Then he would have to kill her or he would be lost, and then Tecuman would lose too. He would discover, in the moments between heartbeats, whether he was Izel's equal in cold murder.

And then that twitch went through her again and she said, 'Then we go quickly, for Tchoche will not permit this, and nor will your father. How did you get in here?'

He stared at her for too long before jerking his head upwards. There was a wooden hatch in the ceiling that led to a cramped space where the servants stored bedclothes, and from there, another to the roof. He had glided in on silent leather wings when the Dragon began their charade out in the fields. He had been hidden in the room before Tecumet was shepherded back to it, to keep her safe.

Now she told her servants to stay silent, though Asmander had little faith in them doing so. He clawed his way up and drew Tecumet up with him, marvelling at her: the woman who had been the girl he knew, and all that growing up in the scant time since her father died.

He had her cling to him, atop the roof, and then he Stepped and cast himself into the wind, letting it belly out his wings. He dropped sharply with her weight on him, but he let the Champion's strong legs take the landing, and then he was human again, watching her reassess him and his many shapes.

Then he was running, hand in hand with Tecumet. It felt so natural, as though they were barefoot children in the gardens of the palace at Atahlan, looking for Tecuman who had hidden himself somewhere. Asmander could feel his heart breaking, because he knew all this was only putting off the moment. He was killing Tecumet more slowly than the knife would have. Yet she ran beside him, because she wanted to see her brother.

And when Tecuman ordered Asmander to kill her, what then?

The thought consumed him so much he almost missed the shouting. Not all the soldiers had been posted at the front of

377

the house, because his father was no fool. Abruptly there were feet on the trail behind him. He risked a glance and saw at least a dozen men of his father's, yelling their heads off as they chased after him.

He felt Tecumet slow; perhaps she wanted to order them to go away, or even come along as an honour guard. But Asmander could not trust his father's people, not a one of them. Not after discovering that his own flesh and blood was at the heart of this rot along the river.

So he just dragged on Tecumet's arm, feeling her pull against him, then give up and hurry along. Like Tecuman, though, she had not needed to run like this in a long time. The trees were close, but the soldiers were gaining. Asmander wished he had a form like Maniye's, that he could just put her on his back and carry her away.

Then there were more soldiers ahead – men who had been scouting for Dragons, perhaps. Asmander veered sharply away from them, but they were already on a path to get between him and cover.

'Asa—' Tecumet got out, but Asmander could only see one way this would go. He let go of her hand and Stepped, letting the Champion out to screech defiance at them. There were close on twenty men with spears and *maccan* swords coming for him. Even the Champion had its limits, but he was prepared to test them.

But he had made his choice now, and the Champion didn't care about odds, so he measured the jump that would take him past those spear-points and into their midst. Then they were shifting, losing their rigid discipline and backing away, the spears starting to waver and shift. Asmander shrieked at them, and abruptly the soldiers were pulling back – a disorderly rout towards the house. He had never dreamt that he cut such a figure.

There was movement at the edges of his vision: shapes padding in on either side. A huge dark bird flapped overhead and came to earth a man with half his face tattooed. There were wolves here, silent and fearsome, and there were men who wore coats of grey metal and carried axes and blades of the same. And in their midst was Maniye Many Tracks, Champion of the north. The Iron Wolves had come at last.

39

They had locked Venat in the cold cellar beneath the big house. Apparently old Asman had not thought to build dedicated cells in his home, but they had found plenty of stout rope and bound him, and put a halter about his neck to keep the Dragon safely confined in his human shape.

Venat tried to work out whether he should be dead by now. Asman hated him as the sun hated the moon, but the old man was shrewd. Possibly he would have swallowed his loathing to keep an extra knife in his belt that he could use against his son. Or not. The man's eyes had bulged like a frog's, the hatred behind them had been so pressing. If ever there was a moment when old Asman acted on the now and not the tomorrow, that was it. But then the Stone Man in all his fancy bronze had said the Kasra girl wanted to kill Venat herself, and that had tipped things enough to give Venat a brief space of extra life.

Soon after they had consigned him to this chill vault, he had heard the ruckus from upstairs. He couldn't catch the words, but hoped it meant Asmander had been a man about things and cut the girl's throat without hesitation. Certainly he could hear the Stone Man mustering a great many soldiers, and they departed in great haste soon after. Were they tracking a regicide? Or had the boy got it all wrong again, and they were just off to catch a fugitive?

Venat could take satisfaction from the thought that Asman's

plans for his son must be in hopeless disarray. *You should never have brought the Dragon into your schemes. We are the death of all your careful tomorrows.* In the quiet of the cellar, he gave rein to the fond thought of recovering the warband, or even bringing a proper army of all the Dragon islands to the River. It was a daydream of burning and pillage. Safe enough to play with such thoughts now he had no chance to put them into action.

He hoped Gupmet lived long as ruler of the Black Teeth, and led their people to some place in the world that didn't involve burning everything down. That was the problem with the Dragon's fire: it consumed its own yesterdays and tomorrows, as well as everyone else's. And the Dragon's warrior swagger just reinforced that heedlessness, so that any who even suggested building something would be cursed and cast out.

Then he heard sandals scuffing on the steps, and the master of the big house himself entered the cellar, a couple of guards at his back in case even ropes and collar could not constrain the Dragon.

Venat made sure he had a big grin on his face to meet them. He turned it on the guards and saw them edge back just a little. He let that smile of his strike sparks off Asman's stony countenance.

'Some days just get worse,' he said conversationally.

'Today will get worse for you, certainly,' Asman said tightly. 'Only the Kasra's word stayed your execution.'

'He got her, did he?' Venat found another inch of grin.

'I should have had you given to Old Crocodile when we first caught you,' Asman told him coldly.

'It's no good indulging your children, they only turn on you,' Venat agreed. 'Only I don't remember it as doting Da giving in to favoured son. The way I remember it, he was Champion and you were scared.'

Asman stared at him and Venat raised a chuckle.

'Magnificent, wasn't he? A bigger man than you, in a way you

381

could never match. I remember your face right then. No wonder you sent him to the north to get killed.'

For a moment Venat thought the man would snap and have his men hoist his prisoner on their spears. Then Asman found a smile of his own. 'But he lived and came back stronger. And I will make him stronger still, though he fights me. Your influence over him is at an end, finally. You have been like a disease that sickened my son.'

'Your son killed the Kasra, old man. You'll make him a big man on the River after that?'

But now it was Asman who was smiling and Venat who felt hate prick at him, for the old man shook his head pityingly. 'You truly think he could do such a thing?'

The little flame of triumph Venat had been trying to kindle was suddenly cold. *Oh, what's the fool done now?*

'You have stirred up a little mud, man of the Dragon,' Asman told him. 'But I am the River. Enjoy your last few hours of life. I plan to make quite the example of you.'

***

Maniye went amongst her people, clasping their forearms and shoulders, feeling the rough iron of their coats, back with her pack. She welcomed Spear Catcher's crooked smile and the effusive attempts of Feeds on Rags to tell her everything all at once: how he had saved Takes Iron, how he had called the warband to arms, how he had flown over all the river there was until he had found her.

Sathewe was there too, weaving in and out of the warriors, a coyote yipping and jumping up on her hind legs, and then a girl hardly less excited. Moon Eye was greeting his comrades, warrior to warrior, and telling of the death of Tiamesh Strikes at Serpents so they knew the woman had died as a hero with a name.

And then there was Takes Iron, standing a little aside from the others, sour and awkward and out of place because he refused to fit in . . . except those hard edges were rubbed smooth a little. Something of the south had got into him.

Hesprec stood beside him and Maniye saw them: two very different gods but one calling. Probably they still didn't like each other – after all, Kalameshli Takes Iron was not a likeable man – but Maniye could see the beginnings of respect.

'Here,' the Wolf priest said curtly, but he had her cuirass of bronze that one of her people had apparently thought to bring. She donned it thankfully, welcoming its weight for the strength it would lend to her hide. They had iron mail for Moon Eye, too – his own hauberk he had been forced to leave behind in the escape from Tsokawan.

And then she turned to that other reunion: two River Lord men, one woman, staring at each other.

'What's this, then?' Kalameshli asked.

'Tecuman, Tecumet,' she explained, and then with a little exasperation at his expression. 'And you know Asmander. We came south with him.'

Takes Iron made a disrespectful noise, as if to say one River Lord was much the same as another, but Hesprec was already edging past them, eavesdropping as subtly as possible, and Maniye Stepped to her wolf shape, which had the better ears.

'I never gave the order,' Tecumet said. Her brother was standing back from her as though fearing that she would finish the work with her own hands. Maniye seemed to see the crocodile in both of them, no less a killer than the wolf or the tiger.

Anger passed back and forth across Tecuman's face like waves blown by the wind, never settling, never quite gone. 'It changes nothing,' he said at last. 'Who sits on the Daybreak Throne, Te? You think, because your people have hunted me this far, that I will just go away?' And he raised a quick hand. 'If it was not your words that sent them, it was your cause. And if I had been at the head of your army, then some follower of mine would have played Izel and tried to cut your throat to please me.'

'Teca . . .'

'I am born within Old Crocodile's jaws,' Tecuman said stubbornly. 'I will not live as an exile. If I am not Kasra, what am I?' He gestured grandly about him at Asmander and the Wolves, the little piece of River that he still controlled. 'Asa, give her your knife.'

Asmander flinched. 'Teca—'

'This is how it ends, is it not? This is what is best for the Nation.' He should have sounded self-pitying, but instead that royal calm was back. His eye lit on Hesprec, and he beckoned her closer. 'You are the Serpent who came back from the north. Know that your kin in Atahlan chose against me, and your kin of the estuary have turned on me.'

'Let us not speak of the Serpent in the estuary,' Hesprec said darkly.

'Will you be witness now? The Daybreak Throne is mine by right of blood. Let my sister take that blood, and take that right.'

Hesprec glanced at Maniye, then at the others. 'Most generous is the host who offers what need not be given,' she murmured. 'Most kind the guest who will not take what the host cannot spare.' Her exasperated look undercut the ritual words. 'I never wanted to get involved in the succession. Prophecies of the end of the world are easier company than chiefs and Kasras. But just now, the Serpent has but the one head and it is mine. So let us sit, the three of us, and talk of the Daybreak Throne, if there are truly no more sensible things to speak of.'

Even as she said the words, Sathewe was darting back amongst the pack, yipping excitedly and then jumping up, waving her arms and full of warnings. 'Soldiers coming from the house!' she got out. 'Feeds says River Lords with spears, many many, and a man of bronze.'

Asmander took out his *maccan*. 'Messenger,' he addressed Hesprec, 'tell me you have a plan.'

'A plan is a grand word for what I have,' Hesprec replied. 'But give me time to speak to the brother and the sister, no other voices, no factions, no politics, and who knows if one will come to me? Go strut and shout and do things warriors do when they don't want to fight.'

Asmander gazed at her levelly. 'There will be blood, Messenger.'

'Then know each drop on either side is a failure.'

The River Champion nodded, and then he was off in the direction Sathewe indicated, running on clawed feet. Maniye Stepped to her own Champion's form and loped after him, knowing the warband were following her lead, a grey tide of wolves rushing silently through the trees.

They came out and met the River Lord soldiers in the fields, and they must have made a fearsome enough show that the southerners did not just fall on them and destroy them. The legend of the Iron Wolves had plainly travelled down the Tsotec's back, and Maniye herself was a fearsome sight. Moon Eye snarled softly at her side, and she glanced around to find that her warband had grown without her asking it. There were men of the Dragon coming from the trees too, a dozen of Venat's own warband slouching up insolently with clubs of stone and shark-tooth. She didn't know whether they had any idea about what was going on, or if they just wanted a fight. They added a very recognizable threat to the mystery of the Iron Wolves.

The soldiers set out a line of spears while the second rank Stepped so that the jaws of crocodiles jutted between the legs of their fellows. It was a fearsome, jagged thing to face, studded with the bronze of the Stone Men, Tecumet's bodyguard. Here were surely all the soldiers from the barge and most of those from the house, forming a great serrated block of men that stretched out on either side. Maniye imagined those spear-lined ranks closing on her little band like Old Crocodile's own teeth.

Asmander had Stepped, standing tall and proud. He took two long strides forward until he stood before the spears and the arrows, spreading his arms wide. 'I am the First Son of Asman!' he called out. 'I am a Champion of the River! I was chosen!'

Maniye watched the soldiers shift uneasily but hold their ground. She had the sense of being on the edge of centuries of accumulated custom and hierarchy that she would never understand: Champions, Kasras, Serpent and Crocodile. She thought of Hesprec's people, who had brought this place about. This must have happened before. How had the long-lived Serpent priests dealt with it then? She had the uneasy feeling that history was not kind to men in Asmander's position.

'Will you not let me in to see my father?' the River Champion cried. 'Will you not bring water for my guests?' and he gestured to the Wolves and the Dragons. In some horrible way Maniye felt he was enjoying himself. The hard things had already happened. It was all over bar the bloodshed.

Then someone was pushing their way forwards through the line: a man with ruddy skin wearing a remarkable weight of shining bronze, a shield half his height on one arm and a wide-bladed sword in his hand. Maniye saw through his indolent act immediately. This was another Champion, from some tribe she knew nothing of.

'First son of Asman, your father has many guests already. Tell your friends they must find other shade for their heads.'

'Tchoche,' Asmander named him. The unfamiliar name sounded like a clearing of the throat to Maniye's ears. 'Will you keep me from my father's house?'

'Ah, now, that's an awkward one,' Tchoche admitted. 'Look, now, you'd bring these guests of yours to your father's door as well, then?'

'I am told my father's house is a dangerous one to venture in alone.'

The bronze Champion grimaced. 'Well, now, well,' he said noncommittally, making a sideways motion of his head that clacked his helm against his high collar. 'Look, now, what's it to be, with you? Your friends there have teeth but we have more.'

'I will go into my father's house with these my guests,' Asmander said flatly.

'And I will have my Kasra back from you,' Tchoche replied. 'And you will kneel before her and beg forgiveness for your acts against the throne, look now, and hope she still has some fondness for you.'

At Asmander's elbow, Maniye Stepped to murmur, 'Could you beat him, if you fought him?'

'These last four years, I could have beaten him. He served the old Kasra since before I was born. He should have gone back to the Stone Kingdom years ago to live out a rich old age.'

'Challenge him,' she said flatly. 'Beat their Champion. Make the fight last.'

Asmander stared at Tchoche. To Maniye it was plain the old man in bronze was waiting for it. 'Challenge him,' she repeated.

'I . . .' Asmander glanced at her, and for just a heartbeat his hard, angry mask was gone. He didn't want to kill this fat old man, she saw. Tchoche was one more fixture of his childhood that the times were stripping away. But either that or there would be a greater fight, and probably Tchoche would die anyway. Certainly a lot of others would. He opened his mouth.

'You,' Maniye called. 'Bronze man. I am Many Tracks, Champion of the Crown of the World.' She strode forth, just a little northern girl in a bronze cuirass. 'Fight me.'

Tchoche glanced from her to Asmander. 'Well, so,' he said. Apparently that passed for agreement.

'This didn't work out so well for the last Champion fight we saw.' It was Shyri; Maniye hadn't even realized the Hyena woman had come, but now she slipped from the midst of the warband. 'It's almost as if nobody really cares about all these rules of yours, once they get in the way.'

'That was Venat,' Asmander said, wrapping up all the world's chaos and anarchy in one name.

'Someone will play Venat here as well,' the Laughing Girl warned, 'if breaking rules means they win.'

Maniye rolled her shoulders and stood forwards. She glanced back once to look at her people: Moon Eye, Takes Iron, Spear Catcher and the rest.

'Well, then,' Tchoche announced. She weighed him with her stare: he looked slow, but his mail was made with a craftsmanship she'd never seen before, and she guessed he was strong. Also, nobody would waste armour like that on a man who couldn't fight. His bronze sword was short and came to a wicked point, and she had no iron to blunt it. The rites to attune to iron were secret and cruel, and Takes Iron had never been her friend, to teach her.

So she Stepped, letting the great bulk of the Champion rise up before the River Lords and their allies, seeing every one of them fall back a step or two save Tchoche himself. She felt her shadow stretch out to fall over them, in the mind of every enemy there, feeding on their fear.

Tchoche had a strange expression on his face. He was not afraid – his own Champion soul would be ravening for the fight – but he seemed almost wistful. She read that look as, *That I have lived to see this day.* He approached her on human feet, walking warily with his shield held before him. His hauberk came down to knee and elbow, where it met greaves and vambraces of the same metal. His helm was strong and simple, lacking fancy crests and ornament where her claws might anchor. But he was a man, a human man, and though he was heavy-set, she dwarfed him. And he had not quite realized her reach or her speed.

She lashed out with a forepaw: he had his shield up as she did but she hooked the edge of it and just slung him sideways, shifting all the weight of his metal and flesh without straining herself.

He went head over heels and came down on animal feet: a stocky, dark beast with silver streaks from snout to ears and down his back. For a moment she was baffled, holding off because Tchoche was nothing but an old badger, a digger in the earth, and what kind of Champion was that?

But it was his people's totem he had fallen back on, not his

Champion. In the first instant, the badger was scrambling for her in a desperate, suicidal charge, but he Stepped again even as he came, his barrel body burlier still, claws longer and fangs sharper, something like a badger, something like a wolf, something like a spitting nightmare.

And when the Champion rode him, Tchoche didn't care how much smaller he was. He flung himself almost into her jaws with a berserk fury, raking at her with all four feet, snarling and snapping and screeching like a mad ghost. He tore lines across her muzzle and shoulder before she got her teeth into one of his legs and flung him off, sending the dark-furred monster end over end away from her. He landed in the midst of his own people, scattering them and biting at them, as though anybody's blood would do now his rage was up. In that moment she felt a shock of recognition. His Champion was the angry spirit that came sometimes to Moon Eye. He had the same blind savagery to him, but he rode it like a man might ride a half-broken horse, just barely in control.

And then he was tearing up the earth towards her, frothing at the mouth in his need to fight her. She fell back before his advance, astonished at what the fat old man had become. But she had picked this fight. She swiped at him again, connecting solidly but feeling the hardness of metal beneath his pelt. He went bowling over but was scrabbling back for her the moment he could dig his claws into the ground, launching himself at her face again.

Even as he was in the air she Stepped, human and crouching low with her knife upraised. She felt the blade grate against him, then briefly rip across softer meat, and then she was a tiger, matching him speed for speed as she turned, batting at him with a paw, baring her fangs. She danced aside as he went for her, Stepped again to drive wolf teeth into him, feeling the bronze she wielded skid off the bronze he wore as she bit down. As he whirled, yammering and mad, she vaulted his back as a woman, driving her knife at his ribs and then landing on the Champion's heavy feet to weather his next onslaught.

Tchoche screeched and howled at her – the sounds went through her body like fear looking for somewhere to roost but she held firm, drawing on the Champion's reserves of strength. His flank was bloody and for a moment he was just holding his ground and trying to cow her, rather than launching another attack. She guessed her flurry of shapes had thrown him, creatures he had never fought before.

Then the angry spirit was back with him but, as he bunched himself to spring, the Rivermen were everywhere around them, driving at her with their spears. Shyri had been right. For a handful of heartbeats she was hard-pressed on all sides, swiping at their spears and shattering them, feeling the stone points break against her own bronze hide yet draw blood in a dozen places. Then her own people were amongst them, and there was sheer chaos and battle everywhere she turned. Her outnumbered wolves danced in and out of the enemy, or ran up their flanks to tear into the archers. Crocodiles snapped and lunged about her feet, so she brought her claws down on their armoured backs. She had no concept of the shape of the battle, no idea who had attacked who.

Asmander cut through the fight to her left, and Tchoche leapt to meet him, screaming and trailing blood. The two southern Champions struck each other and went rolling away, each clawing at the belly of the other. Then a River Lord soldier drove a spear into her side and she rounded on him, snapping the weapon and then going for him with open jaws. He Stepped as she did so, and for a moment his own long ranks of teeth were at her throat, threatening to drag her into her human form. She shook herself massively and threw him off, feeling jagged pain where he had bitten down.

Her people were holding their ground despite the numbers. Their iron was keeping them alive and they were forming up around her. Shyri would say, later, that it was impossible to know who had broken the peace first. The northerners had not trusted the southerners, and the mistrust was entirely reciprocated. Each side had been jostling forward in little steps, ready for the treachery of the other, until someone's nerve had given and everyone had gone for their enemy's throat. Maniye, leader of the warband, wanted to call them back, but Maniye the Champion wanted to fight. All her souls were baying for blood.

Tchoche gave it to her. He had got free of Asmander and tore into her side furiously, hanging there with all claws as he gnawed at her. She twisted about, unable to reach him. The ground around her seemed lined with the jaws of crocodiles, the air brittle with spears, and still the Stone Man Champion was ripping at her.

Then he was gone, torn out of her like a thorn. She whirled to see Tchoche grappling and snarling at a dark wolf who had his jaws in the Champion's hackles, trying to shake the yowling creature as he would a rat. Moon Eye had the rage on him, snapping and ripping, heedless of the ragged red strips Tchoche was gouging in his skin.

She lunged for them to break them apart but had to rear back from the needle points of spears jabbing at her eyes and throat. She swiped at them, smashing some, knowing that Moon Eye couldn't win and her own people must be shedding their blood for her, all around. They had iron hides but the heat would be slowing them by now.

Asmander was suddenly before her, enacting some plan of his own with a handful of the Dragon as his vanguard. They scattered the spearmen and let her through. She came down on the two struggling beasts and got her claws into Tchoche, slinging him away from his prey. Moon Eye lay there, bloody and torn, his sides heaving weakly, and still he snapped at her, the angry spirit knowing no friends.

But she stood over him and defended him, even though he could not recognize her. She stamped at crocodiles and bellowed at men and waited for the tide of the river to roll over her.

391

It never did. Something was happening to the battle. It was coming apart, unseaming itself. Something was passing through the melee and leaving a trail of empty space behind it, that separated the south from the north. Maniye squinted, trying to understand what she was seeing. At first her eyes showed her the colours, a snaking line of rainbow that cut its undulating curves across the ground. The River Lords fell back out of reverence, the Iron Wolves from fear of something venomous. But it could not be the Serpent, not here, in this world and visible to the mortal eye . . .

She blinked and shook her head, and there was no great scaled body there but a girl, a dark-skinned girl with gleaming scale patterns on her forehead and cheeks, moving between the fighters like a dance. Maniye wished later that she could have recalled the steps of that dance, the precise attitudes of body and limb that brought the presence of the Serpent out from the earth to break apart the battle. She never could, though. She only recalled them as beautiful and elegant, human joints and bones used to express something inexpressibly graceful and fluid.

And at last Hesprec had made her round and stood in the midst of all the fighters, and faced them down. She turned one way and then another, and both sides gave way before that keen, clear gaze.

'Look to your wounded,' she told them all. 'Staunch their bleeding. Healers shall come for them and save who can be saved.'

Maniye Stepped back to her human form with a start and looked for Moon Eye. With a jolt of shock she saw one of the enemy had not gone back to the far side of Hesprec's line, for Tchoche was there, his helm and shield thrown down, working frantically to stem Moon Eye's bleeding. Maniye knelt by him and he glanced at her momentarily before returning to his work.

'We will tend him,' she suggested.

'No,' Tchoche told her. 'He's my brother. I saw it in him.'

392

Another brief look, with a bitter smile. 'My people came from the north an age ago. We left our blood behind us. Our blood and our rage.'

'Messenger,' Asmander called hoarsely. 'What has happened?' *Who is dead, he means,* Maniye thought.

Hesprec held her hands up: just a little River girl with a scarf about her head and rainbow tracks on her brow. 'Hear me, all of you,' she called, 'for I am the Serpent!' When she said the words, a ripple went through the soldiers there, as though the earth had shifted beneath them very slightly. She felt it herself, and knew Hesprec's god was rising close to the surface to listen to his little priest give judgement on a nation.

'Hail, the Kasra of the Daybreak Throne!' Hesprec announced, her high voice carrying to every ear. 'Hail Tecumet, may she live a hundred years!'

Maniye's heart jolted and she looked to Asmander immediately. His face was like stone, even as the River soldiers roared their approval and shook their spears at the sky.

'Messenger!' the River Champion barked, as close to disrespect as he had ever come. 'What, then? What of Tecuman?'

Hesprec held her hands up for quiet once again. 'You have all heard the Serpent at Atahlan speak for Tecumet. You know the Serpent of the Tsotec's mouth spoke for Tecuman. And each has mourned that two such paragons were born to a single throne, that such a cruel choice must be made. But I am the third head of the Serpent, and I have come home with learning that my siblings never knew.'

Maniye could only marvel at the utter silence they gave her, in this space which had moments ago been roar and fury. In Hesprec's young voice she heard the old man she had known, and who knew how many others: men, women, old, young, loops of a single serpentine body stretching back through the centuries.

'We face a time of trials, when our nation shall be tested as never before,' Hesprec told them all. 'And why else would two such siblings be born to the palace, but that we would need them both? Tecumet is Kasra, and Tecuman has knelt before her and sworn himself most faithful of her servants. With my own eyes I have seen this, and called for Serpent to bless it. The time of strife is over.'

You cannot just make it so by saying, Maniye thought, but she could almost feel the peace radiating out of this one small River girl. And soon enough, Shyri was leading the brother and the sister both to stand before the host, hand in hand.

'Sometimes,' and Hesprec was at her elbow suddenly, making her jump, 'the best choice is not to make a choice. Enough tugging back and forth between the palace and the estuary. We don't have time for this foolishness.'

'What will your kin say?' Asmander demanded of her.

'Esumit will rejoice that her candidate has won,' Hesprec told him. 'Of Therumit and her faction . . . they will accept my judgement, for their own reasons, and I shall pay the price they will exact.' For a moment, a shadow passed over her and she seemed smaller than before, a girl dwarfed by the authority she tried to wield. Then Asmander was looming and she looked up at him brightly. 'And now, First Son of Asman, I sense you have unfinished matters, and I will keep no son from his father.'

40

They made good time through the passes, and though the sky above was leaden and pregnant with thunder, the snow did not fall. And then, at last, the mountains were behind them.

Ahead of them was the strip of land the Seal had made their lives on, a sloping shelf of shingle between the rise of the mountains and the great black expanse of the sea. None looked on that endless water without a shudder. The sea had always been the door to evil, and the Seal mad to live by it. Now that door had been opened.

They camped hard up on the foothills not long after midday, for everyone was worn down by the pace they had set to get here. The wind off the sea was bitter enough to cut through any layers of fur and hide, but Loud Thunder ordered no fires. He had thought a great deal about what Lone Mountain had seen and said, and spoken much with Two Heads Talking. This was an enemy who seemed inimical in their very nature. To draw their attention would be to invite destruction before the attack could even begin.

He wondered if the Plague People themselves thought – and if so, whether they saw the people of the Crown of the World as enemies at all. *It's been a long time. Do they even remember that they drove our ancestors here? As a people we can recall only a little of the matter and, after all, you remember taking a wound far more than dealing one.*

He thought of the little flying spirit Kailovela kept leashed, how it was hollow inside. *And does it know it's hollow? Do any of them?* Perhaps the Plague People felt that hollowness as a constant hunger that drove them to consume the world. Or perhaps they looked on the true people and saw something bloated with a soul they could not understand.

Or perhaps we are just things to them, in the end.

'Loud Thunder!'

He started from his gloomy reverie to find Yellow Claw standing before him, arrogant as the sun despite his bruises and bandages. 'What, now?' Had the Eyrieman come to challenge him again, to take over leadership of the warband? Loud Thunder could have believed it, save that the Champion was surely not back to his full strength and the fight hadn't gone well for him last time.

'The storm will break soon.'

'The storm's been breaking *soon* for days,' Loud Thunder pointed out. 'Why tell me?'

'I will lead scouts to overfly the Plague People and spy them out.'

Of course the Owl were better placed for that, and could go by night. More importantly, Loud Thunder reckoned the man would go whatever was said, and at least he had the courtesy of announcing his intentions.

'Be nothing more than birds to them,' he warned. 'No foolish tricks or you'll put them on guard, and we'll be lost.'

'Yes, yes,' Yellow Claw snapped. He paused for a moment, other words plainly on his tongue but still behind his teeth.

Thunder could guess they related to Kailovela and the fight, but he had no energy to spare for that. 'Take an Owl with you,' he said. At Yellow Claw's suspicious look he added, 'Unless you'd prefer one of the Bat?'

'They won't come. They'll save themselves for the fight,' the Champion announced haughtily.

Of course, Thunder feared them too. They were strange,

these men and women of the Bat Society. Grey Herald said they had been sleeping many centuries. To them, perhaps, the fight with the Plague People was recent history. Unlike the Owl and the Serpent they had not become just a tribe amongst tribes. They had held to their purpose in spite of time and death, and it had twisted them.

Yellow Claw and his Hawks and Owl took wing long before sunset, and returned before midnight, bone-weary and freezing but without any sign the Plague People had detected them. The word from the Eyriemen was plain: the Plague People were still there. From Yellow Claw's words, they seemed to be building more, their white filmy walls spreading out from the captured Seal village like a wound gone bad.

'And we heard children,' the Eyrie Champion reported. 'Children's voices, crying out.'

Nobody wanted to think much on that.

The next morning he was roused by Two Heads shaking him. He stared blearily at the man, finding darkness all around them.

'Too early,' he muttered, but the Coyote jogged him again. Loud Thunder considered rolling over and squashing him.

'They say it's time,' Two Heads Talking hissed.

'What? Who say? I lead this warband,' Loud Thunder growled. But he was awake now, and hauled himself into a sitting position. 'Is it Yellow Claw? Tell him to put his head in a fire.' He shook himself. 'No, no fires. Tell him to jump in the sea.'

'It's . . . well, a whole pack of them. Some of the Owl, and that Moon Eater priest, Icefoot, and Aritchaka—'

Abruptly Thunder was very awake. 'Together?'

'Shoulder to shoulder,' Two Heads agreed. 'And it's the *others*, too.' And again, he didn't need to name them for Thunder to know.

'What do they say?' he growled, and then, 'No, I'm awake. Let them tell me to my face.' He shrugged a great pelt about his shoulders and straightened his goatskin robe, trying to salvage his dignity before being face to face with the wise.

Two Heads hadn't been exaggerating, either. The Wise were indeed there, all of them, and several that Thunder reckoned owed more allegiance to the Foolish. All around them, the entire camp was on its feet and strapping on armour. He was apparently the last to know. *Or the slowest to wake.*

'Someone tell me something then!' he demanded as he closed with them. He came up short because one of the newcomers was abruptly standing right in front of him. He hadn't seen much of the Bat Society – they hadn't shown themselves to many other than the Owl priests, but here was one, standing tall enough almost to look him in the eye. She was thin, hollow-cheeked, wearing a threadbare robe that glinted with gold in places, but was worn through entirely in others. Her eyes were narrow, half closed, as though even this pre-dawn glimmer was too bright to her.

'I will tell you something, Warbringer,' she told him, because apparently that was his name these days. 'I will tell you of the storm that will break before noon, and of the deep forests that overlook the nest of the Plague People where a hundred warriors might hide. I will tell you of the fury of the winds and the snow that will blanket the homes of our enemies.'

'Nobody will fight in that,' Thunder told her.

Seven Mending spoke up. 'We are the vengeance of the Crown of the World, and our gods have sent this storm to aid us. Do you think these Plague People will find a friend in the weather of our land? Do you think they will watch keenly when the ice is in their eyes? Go now and strike with the storm.'

He looked at the others, those priests and wise women. 'You're agreed, all of you?' They were, and by that time just about the whole warband was ready and waiting for its leader to lead them.

So he sent out Tigers and Owls to go ahead of the pack and scout out the terrain. He gave each tribe its place within the warband. He led them down from the foothills into the forest that hugged the highlands, where there was enough soil for its roots. And before mid-morning, under the grey cast of the heavy sky, they saw the gleam of white walls and heard the low rumbling roar that must be the Plague People's sea beast. In the trees they waited, watching the small figures of the enemy as they crept about their domain like spiders in a web.

The wind grew stronger. It began to shift back and forth from sea to mountain, and then to funnel down the gap between them, so that the Plague People fell back behind their unnatural walls, and Thunder knew the Wise had been right.

The first snow began to fall, not single flakes but fierce flurries that danced and twisted in the air like veils. Thunder stood, knowing all eyes were on him. No words, no speech, no war cry even. They all knew what was at stake, and they knew their place in the fight, if they bothered to keep to it.

He made himself a bear, always the largest and strongest of his kind despite his other failings, and then he was lumbering forwards towards the edge of the trees and the open ground beyond. The rest were flowing after him within a heartbeat: wolves, tigers, boars, deer, men. Overhead the Hawks and the Owls spread their wings, and chasing their shadows came the webbed wings of the Bat Society.

★★★

'If I'm to say anything at all,' Hesprec told Maniye, 'it's that the river has run very murky this last year, and my kin have been raising up a lot of that mud from the bottom.' She shook her head. 'And so I stopped it.'

'Just you?' Maniye asked doubtfully.

They were sitting outside old Asman's house, waiting to see if Asmander's conference with his father would end in murder. Servants had brought out cloth and made shelters for them, and the warband lolled about and lapped at watered beer while the locals watched them warily. Takes Iron was sitting close as well

– closer to Hesprec than Maniye, so that she felt the two of them might take her to task about something any moment.

Hesprec shrugged. 'In Atahlan, they weigh the gold on scales.' She mimed something that see-sawed back and forth. 'Sometimes a little push can set it all swinging, if you know where to put your finger. Being away during all this lets me stand outside the balance and tug as I will. For I came home with all the secrets of the north.' She flashed her white grin at Kalameshli as nobody had dared in all Maniye's years. The old Wolf's mouth twitched.

'But all this . . . it's almost a war,' Maniye struggled. 'Because they were twins? And if one was a year older or younger, nothing?'

Hesprec shook her head. 'The purpose of histories is to instruct and improve. The chroniclers of the Daybreak Throne will have some tidy story that will not touch on Matsur and Therumit's reasons for supporting Tecuman.'

'Or will you tell those to your city Snakes as well?' Kalameshli asked her.

'Hrm.' Hesprec tugged at her shawl and didn't answer.

'What if he will not live with being second?' Maniye asked. 'Tecuman – what if next summer he dreams of being Kasra again?'

Hesprec's grin had gone. 'It is a wise man who knows what worries next year will bring,' she said. 'There are things we have seen that must be answered.' And the Wolf priest nodded sagely, a moment between them that excluded Maniye utterly.

'We'd say, where we come from, if you see a snake, kill it or you'll find it in your bed.' Even old Takes Iron couldn't leave that without a rider. 'You say it differently here, I'd guess.'

Hesprec nodded. Seeing Maniye's aggrieved look she briskly changed the subject. 'Where will the Champion go now?'

It was Maniye's turn to shrug. 'Tecuman does not need us, I think. My people like the food and the servants here, but they are ready to trade them for the cool of home. I don't know, Hesprec. I came here to win a war, but there wasn't one.'

Hesprec pressed her lips together, looking Maniye over as though weighing her for market. 'That's not why you came here.'

'Oh?' Maniye glared at her. 'The Serpent knows that as well, does he?'

'I was not absent when you made the decision,' Hesprec reminded her. 'I remember a girl given gifts she did not know how to use, pulled in all directions by the hopes and fears of the Crown of the World. I remember a child who needed space to become full grown. And you have.'

★★★

'You're still holding on to your anger, I see,' old Asman observed.

As usual, thought Asmander, he was right. He was so smug and satisfied with himself, here in his audience chamber, alone save for his son. *And a dozen guards who'll run in the moment they hear a cry, no doubt.* Asmander wondered if he would – could – do it. Kinslaying left a taint on a soul, after all. It was one of the great sins. Killing a parent, in particular . . . *But it might be worth it.*

'You betrayed Tecuman, who you knelt to. You sent killers after him twice. You stole Tecumet's own Champion for it. Everything you have done has been to spit upon the Daybreak Throne.'

Asman sighed, distressed by his eldest son's obtuseness as always. He sat back on his fine seat, surrounded by his fine hangings in his fine house, and he shook his head over the foolishness of his heir. 'You will have to grow up one day, Asmander. All this running around and having adventures, associating with those beneath you, it must stop. It has locked you into thinking like a child.'

'I think like a Champion.'

Again that sigh. 'That is why you should never have been one. Leave that honour for thugs and foreigners, not for one of

401

the great clans. It was a sour day when that mantle fell on you. If your sister weren't eight years younger I'd be having a much more cordial conversation with her, no doubt.'

'There's no loyalty in you,' Asmander said, sadly.

'My loyalties have never wavered,' his father said sternly. 'They are and always have been to my clan. To you, if you will.'

'I don't want them.'

'And you are far more a fool than the heir I would have wished, but you are what I have to work with. You are here, and of age to be a man, if you'd only act like one. Asmander, they call our people the Patient Ones down the river. It's a virtue you've never possessed.'

'No,' Asmander said. 'I did not come here just to be talked down to and criticized by a murderer. You were Tecuman's. You sent me on an ungodly journey to bring him his Wolves. And when I returned, the first thing you do is send killers to end him?'

'A wise man lets the river carry his boat. Back when the Kasra died it looked like the boy would win. He had the estuary – that's food and resources and warriors of a dozen tribes – and he had loud voices of the Serpent backing him. Atahlan was in confusion; the girl looked weak. And we are an estuary clan, Asmander. If Tecuman came to power on a wave of our support, who would profit? Only the Bluegreen Reach and our allies. The girl's advisers were all Atahlan clans from the wrong end of the river. If she had been named Kasra at the start, where would we have been? When the Serpent was split, it was a sign from Old Crocodile that the time for patience was at an end.' He had been fierce and forthright up to then, but Asmander saw a slight shiftiness in his eyes as he went on, 'And sending my firstborn to find the greatest guard a Kasra ever had, well, it was a sign of loyalty. It bought our clan esteem at Tecuman's court.'

'Did you think perhaps I might not return, and you'd be rid of an inconvenient heir?' Asmander snapped.

'Not for a moment.' The answer was so smooth that Asmander couldn't know.

'Then why . . .' The Champion crooked his fingers into claws, trying to prise apart his father's reasoning. 'Tecuman was here, safe. You could have rallied the clans. He might be on the Daybreak Throne even now.'

'You would prefer Tecumet dead?'

'That she lives is no credit to you. You'd have had her killed just as swiftly if it suited you.'

'I would,' old Asman allowed. 'But when Tecumet brought her army all the way to Tsokawan, she showed herself the stronger. I had to make Tecumet as Kasra work for me.'

'By killing her brother?'

'Whilst she couldn't thank me openly for that, it seemed a good start,' Asmander's father agreed pleasantly. 'Of course your Wolves – the Wolves I had sent you for – got in the way, and then nobody knew what was going on. Tsokawan was on a knife's edge, which is why I returned here in the first place. But then you came through for your family, even though you didn't know it. You brought the boy here and gave me a way to twist the girl's arm about it.'

'Don't make me a part of this.'

'You *are* a part of this,' old Asman retorted. 'You are my son. And Tecumet is Kasra, and we both had our hand in that.'

'And what good has it done you?' Asmander shouted at him. 'It's not as though she'll reward you for it.'

'But she *will* reward me for ensuring what tales the estuary tells about her.' Asman smiled thinly. 'Stories are roguish things, Asmander. The estuary has been told of Kasra Tecuman, and then they have heard how his sister tried to kill him – twice! If he *has* bent the knee, what will they think but that he was forced, and that their duty remains to him. Or they might, if such a story was spread by one who knew all the ears in the estuary. Every estuary tribe that wanted to set down the yoke would say as an excuse that she was no true Kasra. We'd have the Dragon up in arms within a year. But if the Bluegreen Reach, Tecuman's most loyal supporters, show their devotion to Tecumet? Then all will understand that things are as they were meant to be. She might even be able to concentrate on this prophecy of the Serpent that everyone's talking about. That's worth a little gratitude, isn't it?'

'And what baubles will that gratitude buy you or our clan?'

'Tecumet will take you as her mate.'

Asmander's words died inside him and he stared at his father.

'You and she were good friends, growing. Why do you think I worked so hard to place you with the Kasra's children, if I didn't have some such thought in mind?' Asman asked him. 'She has agreed to it – once when she thought her brother dead, once again when he is alive. After all, with you to stand beside them, how much less chance that they'll be at each other's throats within the year. Your eldest shall be the next Kasra – the Clan of the Bluegreen Reach on the Daybreak Throne. And that, you'll find, is worth a little attempted murder.'

'Regicide.'

'Blood all looks the same once it's spilled,' Asman said.

Asmander stood silent for a while, turning the maze over in his mind, looking for a way out. 'You overlook one thing,' he said at last.

'Do I?'

'I will not be a part of your treachery. I would rather break the Daybreak Throne. I would rather return to the cold north.'

'That is the child speaking. It is time you became a man.'

'That is me speaking, Father. Just me.'

'Yes, yes, a last chance to be wilful, to turn down the chance to marry a beautiful woman with all the power in the world. Who, for reasons beyond my comprehension, remembers you fondly.' Asman spread his hands. 'But you will do it. You will do it because your slave sits in my cellar under sentence of death. His death would benefit the Nation greatly. Who tried to kill

404

Tecuman? The Dragon. Who abducted Tecumet? The Dragon. That story will find many a willing ear.'

'You think I—'

'Care? Yes, I think you do. I think that of all your failures of judgement, that is the most unfit for one of your birth and blood. That you took a Dragon criminal as your slave is no great matter. That you took him into your breast as a friend is rank foolishness. That you welcomed him into the closest parts of your heart, reserved for those we love best, that is beyond folly. You cannot spend your love on a man of the Dragon. They know only killing.'

'And we, of course, are so ignorant of that,' Asmander hissed.

'We are civilized men. We kill for civilized reasons. And your Dragon friend will find the death he so richly deserves, and history will know him only as a monster.'

'Perhaps he'd rather die.'

'You want everyone you love to be greater than mortal,' old Asman told him, 'but the Dragon Venat is just a man, and, as I say, all blood is the same when it is spilled.' He sighed. 'Or you can go to Tecumet's bed, and plant heirs in her, and have the world know that she and her brother were never truly enemies, and that Izel, her Champion, acted against her orders when she tried to kill Tecuman. Surely even for you the true path is clear.'

And Asmander said, 'No.'

Asman stared at him, and for the first time a little doubt fluttered behind his face. 'You will do as you're told, or else your brother—'

'My brother is barely ten years old. And even if you had Tecumet promise herself to him, a few years to secure her power and you'll see that promise rot. Because she knows you meant to kill her brother, and although she might need you now, she can never trust you. Plus, she plain doesn't like you, Father. I don't think anybody does. So, just as you had your price to aid her, so I have my price to aid you.'

Old Asman regarded him for four long heartbeats and then

405

said, 'At last you start to think like a man. What is your price, then?'

'It is time you retired.'

Asman went very still.

'Father, you have schemed for many years to bring the Blue-green Reach to pre-eminence on the river. Lo, now you have succeeded! Your firstborn is to sit beside the Kasra. There is no higher honour. So your work is done, is it not? You have held our family's name in your hands for too long. It must be a great burden to you.'

'No.' Old Asman was shaking his head. 'You will need me here while you are in Atahlan.'

'You mistake who needs who. I have laid no grand plans requiring your obedience, Father. I am the tool, and the tool cares not if it is used. But you are the man who must build.'

'Asmander—'

'No.' Just saying that 'no' took years of burden from his shoulders that he had not even realized were pressing him down. 'It is not fit that Kasra Tecumet marries a boy with a child's name. It is time you retired and left the clan to your loving and *obedient* son.'

Old Asman was shaking his head in small motions, his good hand gripping the arm of his chair. 'This is childish defiance,' he croaked out.

'Or I will not be the mate of the Kasra, and your grand-children will not sit in Atahlan. I will go from here to the cellar and kill your guards, and Venat and I will lead all the Dragon up and down the river until every one of your schemes is ash. So that is my price, Father. I will be Tecumet's mate, but I shall be Asman when I give her my vows. And you shall be just Asmaten, the old man who was, and you will retire and seek wisdom in the retreats of the old, with all those others whose days have passed them by, and who have no more trouble in them. That is my price. Tell me it is not too dear.'

406

41

They came in with the storm, and it was like no storm Loud Thunder had ever known.

The wind, which had been coming in chill from the sea, and then milled back and forth along the coast as they assembled under the trees, now turned back upon itself. It howled down from the mountains, riding the steep slopes like a great river the width of the world, wielding claws of snow and ice.

The warband broke from the trees even as the air around them became a blinding whirl of white. Loud Thunder could spare little attention for the forces he nominally led – already some were outpacing him, others falling behind. The clouds overhead were so thick that it felt like night had come to noontime. The whole land was cast under the shadow of something greater than men, greater than gods, as though the Crown of the World itself had woken at last. To Thunder's left and right were only charging shadows: the shapes of boars and wolves, tigers, bears and men.

The open ground between them and the Plague People, over which the enemy might have seen them coming and worked their killing magic, was gone. They broke from the shelter of tree and branch into the teeth of the weather. Thunder felt as though the storm was rolling forward with them, as though their vanguard was the sky itself.

From the edge of the forest they looked upon the white walls of the Plague People. *Pale Shadow People*, he thought, a name from old Serpent stories. The walls were indeed pale shadows, lit from behind by the ghostly radiance of the enemy's flameless lamps, making them a beacon. Nobody could get lost in the storm if they were bringing the fight to the enemy.

Thunder was close before he could see the shadows moving behind those filmy walls. In that first glimpse they were hunched and hurried, just as though they were ordinary people seeking shelter. In the next heartbeat – even as he pounded closer – he saw them start and move more swiftly and he knew that some sentry had given out a warning.

Death began to reach from the white walls. Thunder was barely aware of it, but the air was busy about him as though swift insects cut through the wind. His warriors were dying one by one; picked at random from the onrushing host, they were thrown bloody to the cold ground. But they were almost at the walls now, almost at the gate.

The Plague People had formed a line in that solitary gap in their walls. A handful of Wolves and Deer met them, the swiftest of the swift, trying to overrun them before they were ready. The enemy were armoured and bore spears and swords and rods, but Thunder felt his heart leap as the charge hit home: these were just hollow things. He wanted for them to smash like ice.

Sightless death lanced through the attackers like sleet, and fire as well, snapping and crackling from the Plague People to send Thunder's warriors spinning away, burning and writhing. When the first wave of warriors reached the gate they were too few and fell back almost immediately, gripped by terror. Some were panicked into running, charging back through their comrades, getting in the way. The next wave were already pushing past them, though, rallying them with their sheer presence and numbers as they roared forwards.

He himself came up against the wall and reared up, swiping down with one mighty paw to tear it apart. The substance of it was flimsy enough that he could see the shapes of the Seal dwellings through it, but after it gave beneath his strength, it sprang back, snarling his claws. It was like a clinging mist: he could not break it, he could not tear it. The weapons of his people were getting tangled in it, caught and lost.

He saw more of his people rush the gate but the Plague People were there in strength and many had rods which brought death to any they were directed at. And the stronger the enemy got, the greater was the fear they brought, radiating out of them like a cold even the winter could not overcome.

Then Icefoot, the Moon Eater priest, was dropping down beside Thunder, grinning madly through his beard. He had a stone cupped in his hands – a stone pierced with holes, and Loud Thunder saw there was a fire inside: some magic of the Wolves.

Another pair of Icefoot's people were with him, young men who must be his acolytes, and they had skins of some sharp-smelling liquid that they doused the white wall with, working with a frantic pace. The stuff smelled like fat, like the marshes of the Stone Place.

Icefoot put a hand to his pelt and tugged him back. The priest raised his hands up and called out to the Wolf. 'Lend us your breath, which is the breath of the forge!' he cried, and opened up his stone so that the sparks of the fire came out and scattered across the white wall.

Despite the wind, despite the snow, fire leapt there at once. Thunder almost thought he saw the smoke describe the Wolf's very jaws, gaping open to gift them with this bounty. The stuff the Plague People built in shrivelled away, so that a new gate was gaping before them, and Loud Thunder knew it was his time.

He roared a bear's great bellow to tell his followers the way was open, and then he was through, bursting out into the narrow spaces between the enemy's white walls and falling upon the side of the gate guardians like a great hammer.

He had a moment to feel that fear, the vast *wrongness* of the

409

enemy reaching out to strangle his soul within him, to make him not a son of the Bear, but just a bear, speechless and unchanging. It slowed him, even though he had seen it in Lone Mountain's mind and tried to brace against it. All around him his people were flinching away and falling back. He saw the light of thought guttering in their eyes. In that heartbeat they were not warriors of the Wolf, not huntresses of the Tiger, but wolves and tigers, wild and panicked and without understanding.

Then the shadow of broad-webbed wings fell over them, and there was a sound that Thunder felt with his chest and not his ears, a vibration loud enough to blot out the storm, yet something that he never heard before. It shivered through him and the white walls sang discordant notes with its passing, but its effect on the Plague People was astonishing. Thunder was looking into their eyes in that moment, and he saw an unreasoning fear twist every face. The sound went into them and resounded in the emptiness it found there, and they broke.

He went after them unthinkingly, and that might have been the end of him except that a dozen more struck the enemy alongside him. And then more, a tide of hair and claws and teeth that ripped past the Plague People's iron armour to open up every soft part of them, exposing their hollowness to the angry sky. He saw that fear turned back upon the enemy, at which many of them threw down their weapons and fled, or sprang into the sky on shimmering wings. Others stood to fight, but they were beset on all sides and dragged down, a dozen sets of jaws to tear each of them limb from limb. Lone Mountain's recollection had been right: they bled just like men. The hollowness within them melted away when he tore them open, leaving just dead flesh behind.

But the inside of the Plague camp was a maze. The white walls stretched between every available anchor-point and the flameless light cast shadows through it all, so that every direction seemed wrong. Even though the warband was within the gates now, the silent death still cut through them, picking out

410

individuals and striking them down. The Plague People darted and flitted overhead, pointing and killing. *Everywhere is a new gate they can hold*, Loud Thunder thought, hurling himself forward. He found the wreckage of a Seal hut and had a sudden revelation. The white walls did not stand on their own, any more than a cloak of hide might. With more time he might have tried to root out where the walls were stretched from, but the air about him was thick with mounting panic. When he called, it was only his strength that answered.

He put his back to the wall of the hut and pushed, feeling the resistance as the walls about it snapped taut. He hunkered down lower, tearing into the earth, digging at the foundations. A moment later a Boar was there, rooting deeper, her snout a pale mask: Ash Maker. She squealed shrilly, and more of her people came, ripping up the wooden posts as though they were saplings in a forest.

Thunder felt the moment that the uneven pull of the walls began to shift the whole hut sideways, the wrecked wood of it collapsing inwards. He Stepped, half climbed the sloping side even as it fell, and leapt over, swinging his axe. The first handful of Plague People fled, but then their warriors were coming, from the earth and from the air. The warband that had come with him shuddered back and he felt the moment balance on a knife-edge.

The soundless keening of the Bat Society rent the air again, though, throwing the hollow creatures into confusion, and Thunder charged them, overrunning them, leaping up to snag them out of the air with bear claws. Abruptly the entire enemy camp was fleeing towards the sea with the ravening warband in pursuit.

Loud Thunder paused to regain his breath and see what was where. There were more flames in the Plague People camp now – and surely this was Icefoot running about setting fires like a mad spirit, because when the cold lamps fell they smashed like ice and the light spiralled away like fireflies. There were warriors

411

rushing on all sides, tearing down the white walls, killing the hollow people wherever they could. And death was still reaching for them, from anywhere the Plague People turned to make a stand. Thunder saw a stag spring over a fallen wall and then drop, collapsing in a sudden tangle of limbs with a hole ripped in him. He saw dead tigers and wolves who had never seen the enemy that killed them, and dead men and women too. There would be plenty of ghosts haunting this place.

He growled and stirred himself into motion again, but some sound or scent held him, that his conscious mind had not acknowledged. There was a Seal hut nearby, complete enough to hold his gaze. The Plague People had torn down much of the rest, save posts and pillars that they had strung their walls from, but this . . . why was this one untouched?

It was aflame – the fire leaping about one side and running up the eaves and the roof. The pale shadows the Plague People had strung there shrivelled and sprang back. Loud Thunder stared into the dark of the doorway, flecked with embers and crossed by drifting lines of smoke. He saw eyes, huddled shapes smaller than human. His mind went to the creature Kailovela was warden of and he lumbered forwards, waiting for his battle-rage.

But his rage would not come, held back by that part of him that had drawn his eye there in the first place, until he was looming outside the doorway of the hut, staring in and seeing a dozen pairs of eyes staring back out at him. Wide, terrified, *young*. Seal children from the look of them. The thought of what use the Plague People might have had for them set his insides squirming.

He Stepped. 'Come on, out, now!' he barked, but they seemed as afraid of him as of everything else around them. At last, though, one stepped forward, a child who must surely have been old enough to Step, with a ragged mop of hair and an expression so surly he couldn't tell if it were boy or girl. The child stood before its younger peers practically snarling at Loud Thunder, daring the huge man to make a move.

Thunder wondered for a moment if he should just reach in and grab the child and be done with it. There was such a weight of antagonism in that glower he judged it more trouble than it was worth. Instead he took a flint knife from his belt and threw it at the child-youth's feet. 'Save yourselves,' he said.

The youth's eyes flicked sideways to something past the doorframe and Thunder's blood ran cold. He took a step, then another, watching. With a swift lunge the youth snatched up the knife and snapped some order, and the rest of the children were running past him, the older carrying the younger, terrified, wearing the strange, flimsy clothes he had seen on the Plague People.

The youth with the knife came out last. At the doorway he stopped, looking once again at whoever – whatever – stood there waiting. Then he fled the hut, joining the huddle of children outside, standing over them as though ready to fight the storm itself.

Thunder could hear the fighting going on closer to the sea. They would need him. But he had to know. He took a deep breath, and then put all his bear strength into a swipe that tore away half the wall of the hut.

There was a scream and he saw a woman falling back from him. Not a woman: one of the hollow enemy, pale like ice and threatening him with nothing more than a knife. He reared up, bellowing, and something monstrous scuttled forward to threaten him back: a many-legged, chitinous thing with glistening black fangs.

He Stepped, because tackling the thing with his axe was preferable to letting it latch onto his flesh, but the Seal youth was yelling at him and punching him. Thunder rounded, axe still between him and the monster. 'No!' the youth was shouting. 'No!'

He thought about how the hollow woman must have been standing, ready to attack him as he came through the door. If

413

she had wanted to harm the children she could have killed them long before Thunder arrived. He could not quite believe she had been protecting them, but his rage was ebbing, and he decided there were other fights that didn't pose as many questions.

He yelled at the Seals to go, told them there were people beyond the walls who would find them warmth and food, and he turned to go, pushing onwards towards the sea.

Loud Thunder looked back once: the hollow woman and her monster had disappeared.

He had expected to find the surviving Plague People trapped and desperate at the bluff's end, throwing themselves into the waves to avoid the vengeance of the Crown of the World. But of course he saw them ascending on shimmering wings as though they were truly spirits. The fall had no terror for them, and they had help coming.

Out on the sea, the great bulk of their sea monster was roaring like a thousand lions, shuddering the air with its voice. It was armoured in large sheets of metal, Thunder saw, and there were more Plague People standing atop it. It was not a monster. It was a boat that sounded as though huge beasts were being tortured within it.

The Plague People's warriors had formed a line at the edge of the bluff for the rest of them to hide behind. Thunder saw the first charge of his warriors even as he arrived, but the invisible death of the enemy cut them down, spearing holes through them, ripping their bodies and their souls. His followers fell back and he saw the Plague People gather themselves, looking out to that howling metal boat as it neared. It was tall enough that it would meet the bluff, he saw. Would they merely flee onto it, 'or would a great torrent of new warriors vomit forth onto the land and kill every one of Thunder's people?

Is this where the wise would give up and run? But he had none of the Wise close by to ask, and if they ran they might never stop running.

But it was hard. It was not just death, it was the terrible fear and wrongness of the enemy. Now they had turned to fight he felt it again, seething in the air strong enough to fight off the storm. He feared them because he had seen what their touch could do, and that fear gave them power over his soul. He felt their fingers crook into it, to crush and suppress what he was. To just rush out there into their faces terrified him far more than death.

But he was Warbringer, Loud Thunder, greatest of the sons of the Bear. So he gathered himself, knowing he must rush into that rain of death and trust to his luck and the gods, because if he did not do it, who would?

Ash Maker did. Her white-faced form bolted from the lines, and another score of Boar with her, already moving at top speed when they outstripped the rest of the warband. Their tusks gleamed even in the dull storm-light as they lowered their heads to gore.

Loud Thunder was moving the moment he saw her, because he felt as though his moment was being stolen, even if it was the moment of his death. When Thunder went, they all followed after. Abruptly there was a great tide of pelts and teeth, of axes and arrows flooding towards the embattled Plague People.

And the death lanced through them, heedless of who it touched. The Boars shouldered the brunt of it. Thunder saw a dozen of them at least drop. Ash Maker was still rushing forwards, though her bristling hide was bloody. She reached the lines first and tore open two of the enemy before her strength gave way and she fell. The front line of Plague People had resorted to spears and blades and were fighting furiously, nothing at their backs but their people and the sea. They had armour that was proof against claws, weapons that carved into the strongest hide, slowing only against the iron of the Wolves. But they were few, and the Crown of the World was angry.

Loud Thunder smashed into a metal-bound body hard enough that the creature inside the armour broke and bled. The great roaring boat was at the bluff, and with a shock of relief he saw that the Plague People who were not fighting were fleeing to it, either flying or just jumping the gap like any normal man or woman might. With a jolt he thought, *hearth-keepers*, just as those who fought and died beneath his claws were the hunters.

He stopped, letting the tide of the fight wash back and forth past him. He tried to see them differently. Hollow they were, and bloody-handed. They had butchered the Seal; they were different in their very substance. The air was loud with their weird cackle and gibber of their voices, sounds that echoed back and forth between them almost like real words.

At the metal boat's front, watching over the fleeing Plague People, a man with a grey face and white eyes, like the Owl's painting, stared at Loud Thunder with a malice as old as the world. *That* one knew, Thunder decided. That one knew all about being an enemy.

Then the boat was drawn backwards in the water without oar or sail. An over-keen Tiger huntress jumped the widening gap and was struck down the moment she did. The last of the Plague People on the land tried to take wing – a couple made it to their kin, one took an arrow in the eye, and the last was caught by Yellow Claw even as she ascended, ripped open by that cruel beak. Around him the Bat Society wheeled, their soundless shrieks shivering the sky and making the Plague People cower.

But the grey-faced man was pointing at them, and Loud Thunder's hide bristled at the thought of what magic he must be calling up. One of the huge web-winged bats faltered in the air and then spun down, scything into the sea's chill waters, and the rest pulled away, higher and higher, and then recoiling back from the clouds as though the metal boat had some reflection there to fright them. They scattered and then flurried back down to the warband below. Yellow Claw Stepped briefly, his face twisted with thwarted rage, and then he was the eagle once more, about to launch out towards the boat.

Loud Thunder had not realized what some small and buried part of him had been wishing, until he saw Yellow Claw spread his wings once more. Only when he felt that piece of him leap and rejoice did he recognize that he could be as petty as that. So he ran forwards and bellowed at that huge eagle, seeing the Champion falter in the air. And he Stepped and reached, catching a taloned leg and fighting the beat of the man's wings. Perhaps he would not have been able to stay Yellow Claw even so, but the Eyrieman was still weak from their previous fight. He dropped and became a man, knives flashing at Thunder's face. The Bear cuffed him, though, knocking him down. Looking at the Eyrieman's hate-filled countenance, Thunder thought he should have let the man go and get killed. Would that not have fed his own soul, to have Kailovela's mate dead? But it was for that reason he had acted. Otherwise he would have gone back to her with the fact of his pettiness, and she would have seen it.

The Plague People's boat was drawing further and further from shore, and at last Loud Thunder's people began to cheer and exult, dancing on the bluff edge as their enemies fled from them, back to the great expanse of sea that had cast them forth. Loud Thunder felt a touch at his elbow, and saw Two Heads Talking there, but the Coyote was not celebrating. Instead, he was looking up at the clouds.

The storm was clearing now, its work done, but the skies still held a burden. Loud Thunder saw the remaining Bat Society darting away, seeking haven on land now the sun was out to blind them. Or perhaps they were fleeing something else.

Something hung far up in the sky, as though challenging the sun. It moved with slow menace, like a shark in deep waters. From far off, Loud Thunder thought he heard its voice, akin to the tortured rumble of the metal boat, as it turned and coasted away. It did not shadow the boat's retreat, but lazily turned and drifted landwards, until the clouds hid it once more. When the

417

sunlight had caught it, it had gleamed in colours of black and gold.

Nothing was over. Loud Thunder had brought the war, but not the war's end.

42

'I'll go back to Where the Fords Meet,' Maniye decided.

'And then to the Crown of the World,' Kalameshli added.

'If so, it'll be no sooner for you making up my mind for me,' she warned him. She wasn't sure where she was with him, now. Something had thawed, and she wouldn't have thought it possible. Hesprec had changed him, worked him into a new shape that fit the hand more easily, even though he was all Wolf's iron.

'The warband has been blooded,' he observed. Hesprec watched them both through unblinking eyes. Out on the river, the boats were massing: all the vessels that Tecumet had brought with her, crammed with her servants and soldiers and advisers.

'A little.' Perhaps the Plains would have new trouble for them to get into. It was what the Plains were for, or so said everyone except the people who actually lived there.

'The north needs you,' Kalameshli noted.

'And what do *I* need?'

'The Wolf's true blessing.'

She rounded on him, feeling him trying to take possession of her again, but then she understood. 'Iron.'

'You heard the words the Serpent speaks. A terrible thing is coming to all the world. So you will need the Wolf to guard you. You will need the rite of Iron.' All his pomp and slyness was gone from him. She found herself nodding, feeling her younger self reeling at the reconciliation.

The thought of Where the Fords Meet was a bittersweet one. She knew Kalameshli was right: they would not stay long there. But perhaps a certain hand-son of the Horse Society might be heading north. She found that absence had not smothered her fondness for Alladai. Yes, well past time they were away from the River.

Not that all of them would be going. Moon Eye had not known how to speak to her about it, but she had been able to speak for him. Yes, he would stay here because Tchoche knew the angry spirit like a brother. The priests of the Stone Men could build cages for it, inside the mind, so that Moon Eye would be able to let it out and send it back whenever he wished. Tchoche was calling him Brother and Blood of Champions. Her comrade would be well looked after.

A horn sounded out across the river. All of Tecumet's people were aboard now, out of the House of the Bluegreen Reach. Tecumet was back on her barge, and Tecuman and Asman with her – young Asman, as they were calling the youth who had been Asmander. Maniye would never understand southerners and their names. One lone figure stood at the dock, watching the River Lord boatmen prepare to cast off. Maniye drifted over to her.

'I'd thought you were going with him.'

Shyri gave her a look without expression. 'Why? Am I his dog?'

'I thought he'd asked you.'

'Maybe he did. What did he think? That I would sit at the foot of his bed while he and his Riverwoman fumbled at each other?'

'I don't think he knew what he thought. I don't think he ever does.'

That raised the slightest smile on Shyri's face. She was still carrying herself gingerly, the mark of Old Asman's dagger-blow in every movement. 'I am of the Laughing Men. We go where we wish. We pay no heed to the words of arrogant River Lord boys.' The need to believe it was in each word but they rang hollow nonetheless.

'Come with us.'

'Back north?' Shyri asked her, wrinkling her nose. 'Cold place, Many Tracks.'

Maniye shrugged. 'Come and wrestle the men of the Crown of the World and teach them lessons.'

'Asmander told you about that, did he?' Shyri grinned at the memory.

'Venat did.'

The grin died. 'Maybe I will,' and the Laughing Girl took a few steps back from the edge of the dock. The barge was just beginning to move now, its crew shoving at the dockside with poles to get it into the river, and oars being unshipped all down its length: against the current, all the way to Atahlan.

Shyri looked from Maniye to the boat, watching the gulf of water slowly widen, bunching to run and jump after it, and then relaxing. Maniye waited, knowing nothing she said would alter what might happen. The choice was Shyri's to make.

On the barge's deck, Tecuman sat and stared out over the water. He was wearing robes befitting a high-ranking clansman rather than the rough garb of an estuary peasant, and the change made him seem smaller for some reason.

He glanced up, sensing Asmander's gaze on him. 'You wonder if I have second thoughts now, Asa.'

Asman – Young Asman – said nothing.

'Would your father have married you to me, do you think, if he'd found me the stronger?' Tecuman grinned faintly. 'But you're to be my brother in truth now, as you always were in here.' He tapped his chest. 'If the day comes when I decide I must be Kasra, I will be raising my hand against you as well as Te. And if she decides she cannot share the River with me, then she, too, sets herself against you. If the Serpent's knot holds, it will be because of you. Do you think Hesprec foresaw that?'

'These things are known: Serpent only tells half a story.'
Asman shrugged.

The barge was starting to pull away from the dock, its sail snapping taut as it caught the wind. Tecuman smiled again. 'I will never have to wear that mask and that robe, and have your father put words into my mouth. The Daybreak Throne is the only cage people are desperate to cram themselves in. Well: they will not cage me in it now.' He cocked his head towards the awning at the rear of the deck. 'Speaking of which . . .'

Asman followed his gaze and knew he was right. Time to go to the woman he would marry.

Behind the cloth walls, Tecumet had divested herself of that mask and the ritual robes: just a slender River Lord girl, surely too young to sway the might of the Sun River Nation.

'It's not like they think,' she said, 'being Kasra.'

Asman watched her silently as she dropped onto the piled furs and cushions that were her bed.

'When people look at the Daybreak Throne,' Tecumet went on, 'they see the sun, and who can sway the sun? The sun gives warmth and light, and everyone knows the course of the sun is inviolable. You live your life by its movements. You can't reach up and pluck down the sun.

'But when you wear the mask and sit on the throne, you find there are a hundred strings dragging the sun about the sky,' she explained. 'It only looks as though it cuts a straight course. There are the Serpent, who can't be ignored because they're wise and old. There are the clan chiefs who can't be ignored because they have a hundred ways of causing trouble that aren't quite disobedience. There are the estuary tribes, who give us half our food and don't like us. There are the Stone Kingdoms who always want something – and now they have their own Stone Serpents it's hard to say no, because they dress up each demand as wisdom. You can't make everyone happy, but everyone expects you to.'

Asman regarded her. They'd had little chance to be together

422

since the fight, save when he stood beside her and swore his devotion, as a clan chief and the future Kasrani, as he would be.

'What are you thinking?' she asked him. Without the mask he saw again the girl he had grown up with, whom he had loved along with her brother.

'Terrible things,' he replied.

'Wait until you hear what warnings Hesprec Essen Skese brings.'

'I've heard them.' He shrugged. 'Probably she's right. The world is full of terrible things.'

'Asmander—' She stopped herself. 'Asman.'

'Tecumet.' Asa and Te; Asmander and Tecuma; Asman and Tecumet. They were both grown up now, as in control of their own destinies as anyone ever was, which is to say, not at all. 'You know I'm here because my father promised me. Because he can't be happy being just a great clan chief. He had to have more for his family.' He scowled suddenly. 'You know my heart is split.'

'It always was.' Before he could correct her, she added, 'And you do not just mean my brother. I know. I do not ask for all of your heart. It is enough that you are no longer my enemy. Do not let your other loves make you my enemy.' Kasras had fallen out with their Kasranis before.

It was the warning that melted him. He had always valued people who pushed against him. They gave his life shape. 'If I was your enemy, I wouldn't be here talking. I'd fight. I'm not my father. I have more souls than faces.'

Tecumet thought about that. 'Your father will find a way to Atahlan sooner or later, you know.'

'I think not.'

'He is not a man to live out his last days in thought and reading. If not him, then he will suborn others to speak for him. Clan chiefs will come with his words in their mouth.'

Asman shook his head. 'I have friends who are proof against his words.'

'Then keep them close.'

Asman had to smile at that. 'Soon enough.'

***

Asmaten, as old Asman was now, awaited news of the coronation from his spies. The retreat his son had sent him to was neither near the capital nor close to his old haunts of power by the estuary. But that would not stop him getting word. Already he had begun to influence the other anchorites in the retreat: they might all be old men but they had their weaknesses, wants and foibles. He would make them his creatures and twist them to his purpose soon enough. He had lived his whole life like that. His son was a fool to think he would just shuffle into retirement and fade away. And foolish to think of him as an enemy, too. All Asmaten's plots and schemes were to further the power of his family, after all. Couldn't he see that?

True, he had not always been his son's friend. Until recently, he had thought the world might be simpler if he were not lumbered with a firstborn so blind to matters political. His first son had always been a boy far too fond of tales and heroes. If the Champion had not lit on him, then he might have been salvaged, but that had made him inflexible, simple-minded.

Asmaten told himself that he had known his son would return victorious from the cruel north, but that was only because he was just as capable of lying to himself as he was to everyone else.

Yet now, his first son had become a valuable piece in the game at last. Despite his great disrespect to his father, he had done his familial duty. It just remained for Asmaten to keep smoothing his way, peopling Atahlan with those sympathetic to his cause – and perhaps creating the odd accident here or there for rivals or enemies. Such matters could be arranged easily enough from a retreat once he had taken control of it, and had messengers speeding back and forth along the river as he wished. It was a shame that young Asman would never be the cunning man old Asman had been, but he would always have his father watching over him. Whether he liked it or not.

His cell was still quite bare: a pallet bed, a chest for the simple, homely clothes he was supposed to wear. That would change, too. The retreats had rules about fine living, but Asmaten was a man who made rules, not meekly followed them.

A shadow fell on him through the door of his cell and he stood, squaring his shoulders in anticipation of breaking down another of his fellow anchorites. He had a lot of work ahead of him before he restored himself to the heart of the world. The figure in the doorway was far too broad of shoulder to be one of the old men of the retreat, though. Asmaten froze, staring into the long, lantern-jawed face of the Dragon, Venat.

The old pirate smiled. 'Comfy, eh? I never got these places, myself. When a man's too old to stick the knife in, it's time he takes his final Step and goes away. But you River Lords, you make things easy for yourselves. Too many of you grow old.'

Asmaten took a deep breath. 'Son of the Dragon,' he started, as imperiously as he had ever spoken, 'do not think that I don't know what you want.'

'What does the Dragon ever want?' Venat asked lazily.

'You've more ambition than the other Dragon. You'd see your people become something more than just the River's dark joke.'

The old pirate nodded thoughtfully. 'It's crossed my mind.'

'Then listen to me, because I'm the only one who can bring about such a thing. If you will let me.'

'Last I heard, you were telling everyone I murdered the Kasra,' Venat pointed out.

'And the river flows on, and here we are now. Where we can help each other. Son of the Dragon, I can give you what you want.'

Venat considered this. 'I reckon so.' He shrugged. 'I've a message from your son first, though.'

'He's made you his messenger?'

'I offered.' The Dragon shook his head disgustedly. 'You've got me half-tame already, you people. He says: you win.'

Asmaten stared at him, feeling a sudden leap of hope.

'You've made him like you, after all,' Venat explained, grinning. He drew out his *meret*, the greenstone blade gleaming. 'And as to what I want, old man, I want to go back to young Asman with some good news about his father, and there's only one thing I could say about you that'd bring a smile to him.'

***

The Kasrani wore a simple white robe to be married, weighted down with jewellery at neck and wrists that was heavy and constricting. The tale went that a Kasra of old had allowed his mate to arrive Stepped, and had married the wrong crocodile. The belt was the worst, formed of linked squares of precious stone: jade, chalcedony, amethyst, greenstone. It weighed so much that young Asman was terrified it would slip from his hips and shatter on the marble floor before the pit.

Old Crocodile's pit stood in the square before the Kasra's palace, its stepped sides descending to a pool in a way that now reminded him of the Strangler ruin out in the estuary. The pool was linked to the Tsotec's flow, and the crocodiles knew to gather there on certain days when the priests or the courts of justice were in session.

Tecumet was coming to him. She dragged her scaled belly up the tiers of stone, her jaws still smeared with blood. He had not seen her Stepped for a long time; the priests had painted her back with designs of blue and green and red that meant the river and the land and the sun. That was the only way he knew which of the beasts in the pit was coming to marry him. When she Stepped, he was no wiser. The regalia of her office hid every inch of her.

The High Priest of Old Crocodile, his own face hidden within its gape-jawed mask, gave his sonorous blessings. The man had been old when Asman was a child here, long overdue to Step one last time and go to the river. There were a handful of priests of estuary gods there as well, Toad and Turtle and Heron, each permitted a few heartbeats to call the benevolence of their totems. Nothing for the Dragon, of course, but then weddings usually went more smoothly without the kind of blessings the Dragon brought.

Next came the Serpent, a delegation of a dozen of them with Esumit at their head. Asman kept his face carefully neutral, because when his father had made plans to decide who sat on the Daybreak Throne, Esumit Aras Talien had been at his elbow. Still, the Serpent's road was a crooked one. Perhaps she had done what she must, to bring this moment about.

Then there was one final Serpent, Hesprec Essen Skese. The diminutive figure spared him a brief smile as she skipped through the proper words and every eye was upon her: the Serpent who had returned from the north; the priest who had stopped the war.

At last it was time for the clan chiefs and their delegates to kneel, one after another, with gifts and ever more effusive declarations of loyalty. The ceremony would drag on and on, and Asman wondered how Tecumet could stand the weight of the mask and robe. There was only one declaration he was interested in, and that came first.

Tecuman stood before his sister and his friend, and everyone must have seen him hesitate just for a moment. Probably he even gained for it; who wouldn't have, on the cliff-edge of all their ambitions?

But he Stepped and laid his long, scaled body before Tecumet, who set her foot on his back for a moment to show she accepted his fealty. When he had given place for the first of the clan chiefs, Tecuman Stepped back and his eyes met Asman's. There was a smile there, a private one between the two of them. *Terrible things*, he mouthed. Asman did his best not to grin back, because apparently it was unseemly for the Kasrani to show himself happy on his wedding day.

★

After all the speeches, and then the feast, and then the entertainment – the dancers, the fighters, the Stone Men songs – Hesprec slipped away. The other Serpents were leaving too, Stepping and sliding off into cracks and holes until they gathered in their own temple in the city, where no others went.

There, Hesprec told them what she had found in the north. It was the confirmation of all the fears that had sent her there in the first place. The threat to the Sun River Nation, fear of which had driven such a scrabble over the throne, was greater than they could have guessed. It was a threat to the world, from the endless ice all the way to the banks of the Tsotec.

She came close to telling them what other forces were stirring in the world; what she had met in the estuary, and the invitation it had given. In the end she decided those revelations could wait for another day. They would only divide what she was desperately trying to unite.

And at the day's end, Tecumet Kasra and her new Kasrani retired to the palace, and at last the servants took away the robes and the mask and left just the woman, weary and sweating.

Her look at Asman was shy, a little fearful. The ceremony was done but the demands of tradition were still upon them. Neither of them had thought about this moment. Not so long ago he had held a knife to her throat. She was Kasra now, not the girl he remembered from childhood. The boy she knew had been chosen by the Champion, had gone to the north and returned changed, just like Hesprec. And his heart was measured out like sand: a handful for her, a handful for her brother, a handful elsewhere.

But when the servants had disrobed her, he slipped out of his own garments, removing all the priceless clutter with relief. He took her in his arms and she saw that he was happy at last, because all the things he valued were friends at last. He might not love her to the exclusion of all else, but right then he loved her enough.

They were still awake past midnight when the commotion outside drew them from their bed to the window. There were guards chasing back and forth in the courtyard, and what they chased was sometimes a great black bird and sometimes a man with half his face painted, yelling like a madman that something terrible had happened.

43

Mother was watching for them, when the warband returned. Loud Thunder saw her standing, high on a crag and silhouetted against the sky, eyes turned towards the mountain passes. She stood and observed the ragged column as it tracked back into the Shadow of the Bear and then she Stepped into her heavy, slouching other shape and shambled away, satisfied.

She would have seen that there were fewer who returned than had marched out. The invisible death of the Plague People had left many wolf corpses, many dead tigers, boar, deer, even bear. Most had died Stepped, their souls able to flee the terror of the enemy and seek a new birth. Their human bodies the warband had brought back, so the priests could release their ghosts from their human flesh.

But the mood was high as the warband returned. Yes, the enemy had been terrible, but they had *won*. A great blow had been struck against the most ancient enemy of all people. Except Loud Thunder was not sure just how much of a blow it was. He guessed at least half the Plague People had died, who had made their home in that place, but there had not been so many. All that ruin they had made of the coast, of the Seal, and there had barely been three score of them. And the thing the oldest stories were sure of, no matter who told them, was that the Plague People had been a *plague*. They had been a swarm on the land, devouring everything – men, women, beasts, even thoughts. Everything that was not *theirs*.

'Perhaps these were all that were left,' Two Heads murmured, when Thunder mentioned the thought. 'Perhaps they starved, when we escaped them.' But he did not believe his own words. Loud Thunder kept thinking about the great metal boat that *someone* had fashioned, and of the flying thing like a black and gold moon. The war was not over.

But most of his warband were happy and willing to celebrate. Wolf and Tiger and Boar and the rest had fought side by side. That was *his* victory; that was what Mother had wanted from him. Against all odds he had delivered it.

When Thunder went to see him, Lone Mountain was awake and looking stronger. The Bear was coming back to him, all that slow strength and endurance. Thunder tried to make the story of the battle a tale of heroes but his cousin must have heard the doubt behind every word.

Later he went to find the Seal children. Most were asleep, worn out from the long march. They had become mascots of the warband's victory. They would not lack for hearths and food. The eldest was awake. Thunder found the youth sitting by a fire, tapping carefully at the flint blade of a knife. The work was good, and the Bear was about to ask who had taught those skills, but there would be little happiness in the answer, he guessed.

'Do you have a name?' he asked.

The youth looked up angrily – the youth did everything angrily – and Thunder guessed she was a girl, though the anger was writ so large in her that it was hard to tell. Everything else seemed secondary.

'No,' she told him, and went back to the knife. 'Not yet.'

Thunder grimaced. 'Not a hunter's name yet, no, but—'

'Look at me.' She glowered into his face.

She was tiny; he could have tucked her into his sleeve. Still, against that unyielding glare he took a step back. 'What did they do to you?'

431

'When they came from the sea the adults feared them, and the fear made them Step. And they couldn't Step back. The fear was too much. But you're nodding. You know everything, then. You don't need me.'

'I know some things. Far from everything.' Thunder sat down cautiously, the fire between them.

'We couldn't Step, so they took us. They thought we were their children.'

Loud Thunder frowned, baffled.

'My soul came to me when I was with them. It came to me and told me to be a Seal and be with my family. But it couldn't reach me. The sea people drove it away. So I am like them. I grew up and never got my soul.' She examined her knife blade.

'You're not like them,' Thunder tried awkwardly. The sharp gaze of the Seal girl spitted him, refusing to be talked down to or fooled.

'I like you, War Bringer Bear,' she told him.

'Don't call me that.'

'It is not for the war you brought that I like you. One among the Plague People took care of us. You spared her.'

'I . . .' Thunder considered his brief glimpse of the pale woman and her grotesque attendant.

'She was going to teach us to be Plague People,' the Seal child went on in a singsong voice. 'Perhaps I will have to go back to her, to learn.'

'You can't,' Thunder said flatly. 'She's gone. They've all gone. And if they're elsewhere, then we'll find them there and make them go. There's no place for them here.'

The girl stared at him, nameless expressions passing over her face. 'But there must be. Or there's no place for me, either . . .' She tried a smile, and the sight of it had Thunder backing nervously away. She couldn't have been more than thirteen years old.

And then there was Mother waiting for him, lurking in her cave. But he wasn't ready for her yet.

Instead, he marched off towards the Eyrie camp. His stride was swift and determined, because otherwise he would change his mind. They watched him: Owl eyes and Hawk eyes, and probably the cold eyes of the Bat Society from wherever they were hiding. Yellow Claw was there too, hating so much it felt like a knife at the Bear's neck. But when Thunder turned to stare at him, the Eyrie Champion would not meet his gaze. When Thunder approached him, he gave ground. That loathing made it like walking on flints to go near him, but Thunder would not give him peace and would not stop advancing until Yellow Claw at last had to lift his head and face his enemy.

'I beat you in the circle,' Thunder told him. 'Fight me again, why don't you? I am here. Fight me now, kill me if you can. You are the Champion, aren't you? Have I beaten you enough, or not?'

He watched the currents of pride and fear and shame tug at Yellow Claw's face as the man tried to raise the courage. Perhaps he had gone about the fires of the Eyrie and told them some story of how he would face Loud Thunder and kill him, once the Plague People were defeated. Thunder was giving the lie to that story now. And Thunder waited, as a Bear can wait, until Yellow Claw shuddered and turned away.

'I'm taking her,' he announced to all the Eyriemen. 'I, Loud Thunder, take her, as Yellow Claw took her from her mate before.' And he waited for the Owl to protest, or some Hawk hunter to plant a spear in his back. None of it came. He let the hate of all the Eyrie wash over him like a fire, and he was not burned. None of them stood in his way when he ducked into Kailovela's tent.

The look she gave him when he entered was not one to welcome the returning conqueror.

'You heard all that, of course,' he said softly.

She nodded wordlessly.

'Hrm.' Thunder look a deep breath, ready to say important

433

things, but apparently there was more small talk before he could build to it. 'They call me Warbringer, you hear that?'

Kailovela nodded mutely. Behind her, the little hollow creature watched with bright, crafty eyes.

'I led us to war. We won. I even brought most of us back. Right now, I get what I ask for. Before they forget or I lose a battle, or Mother slaps me for getting above myself. What I want, I get, if I ask for it.' Again that silent nod. Her eyes were very frightened and the sight of that made him sick.

'You know I want you. I can't bury the thought deep enough it doesn't shine out of me. I've never known someone like you. I can't even say *why*, but you're right there, in my head.' So easy, to make it something she was doing to him, to make her deserve what she got. But he knew his own head, empty as it usually was. He knew nothing grew there without him planting the seed himself. 'There is a cabin and a cave, straight south from here,' he told her. 'Two, maybe four days' walk, or whatever that is when you're a bird. Beside a lake that's curved like a bear claw. You understand? A clearing, and a house of wood that's built into the earth.'

She stared at him blankly.

'Fly south of here, towards the edge of the Bear's lands. It's my home. It's quiet, I don't like people much. I don't know . . . with the child.' He made a stifled gesture at her swollen belly. 'But it's there. And they won't let me go back to it. So it's yours. There's food there, firewood, shelter.' He took a deep breath. 'And I can't promise I won't turn up there, because I have never felt about anyone the way I do, when I think of you. But if you tell me to go, I'll go. I promise. First of all I want you to be free. To fly.'

'I can't . . .' and her words dried up because he had a knife out. With a sudden lunge he had her by the hair, and then he was sawing through it determinedly as she held herself still as stone, eyes closed.

He nicked her twice, and cut his own thumb, but then all of

a sudden her hair was ragged and short, and he had unwound it from her neck and cast the severed length away. 'Stay if you want. With me,' he said, 'or with your people or with anyone. But if you will go, that is a place you can go.'

He stood, giving her space, putting the knife away. He had one job left, and his eyes turned to the hateful little creature that crouched at the back of the tent. Kailovela stared at him, and when he hunched down to advance on it, she put a hand on his arm.

'Please . . .'

'You like being its keeper?'

'Please, she . . . there's no harm in her.'

Loud Thunder nodded bleakly. 'And you talk to her.'

'What?' But Kailovela's surprise was a little late, a little forced. She had been with the creature long enough.

'I heard them, its kind. I heard them with their sounds, like words. I know they speak. So you and she, you know her sounds, a little? She knows yours?'

'Only a little,' Kailovela breathed.

'Good. So I have a message for her. Tell her, as best you can. Make her understand.'

He lunged out again and caught the hollow woman's leash, yanking her close to him, the knife flashing out to hack through it so he could drag the creature out into the sunlight. She buzzed and darted at the end of its cord, ephemeral wings glinting, half there, half not. Then he gave the line a yank and dragged her down again.

Kailovela had come out, blinking in the sun, a hand touching her bare neck, the other cradling the burden of her stomach.

'Tell it,' Loud Thunder said, 'that its people are not welcome here. This isn't their land. Tell it we killed its kin where they landed, and we'll kill them again where we find them. Tell them to go back to the old lands. Tell them this time we're not running.'

Kailovela stared at him, and then at all of them, her kin

435

who had let their Champion cage her. She opened her mouth for some rebuke, but then the change surged through her after being denied so long, and she Stepped into a pale-winged hawk, wings clapping as she ascended. Thunder released the cord, and the hollow woman was following her, with the impossible flight of her people. They circled each other, some wordless communion, and then they were heading south, the two of them. Loud Thunder felt the angry eyes of the Eyrie on him, but none of them gave chase, and he found he didn't care what they thought.

44

Travelling the Plains with Shyri was a joy. She knew a hundred ways to find food and the meaning of every scent. Once she led the warband in a raid against a lion kill, driving the mute beasts off with whoops and clashing metal and stealing the aurochs' calf they had brought down. When they camped, she had a story about every Plains tribe, every one setting the warband roaring with laughter at the subject's expense. Despite her wound she grinned harder and laughed louder than any of them. Kalameshli never warmed to her, of course, but the rest adopted her as *their* Plains woman, and Maniye knew they would defend her as they would each other.

Only when the band had settled in to sleep did the other Shyri come out. Maniye only saw it because she was watching for it. Once the wolves had stretched themselves out about the fire and the sentries padded off a little into the darkness to keep watch, Shyri would put her back to the flames and stare out at the Plains stars. They were much like the stars Maniye knew, but they had different names and shapes, and following them would lead to different places.

Maniye sat herself down, not right next to the Laughing Girl, but within arm's reach, waiting to see if she got a scowl for it. Shyri just cocked an eye at her and said, 'You don't know.'

'So tell me,' Maniye invited.

'You think it's him that's got me like this. It's just strange to be home after so long.' Shyri waited for Maniye to call her a liar and scowled when she didn't. 'What do you know, anyway?'

Maniye shrugged. 'Was it because he had the Champion in him?'

'No. It was nothing about him. He was too proud, and always needing something, and he had too many moods. A man like that is too much hard work.' In the moonlight her eyes glinted. 'Let him make that Riverwoman unhappy with his demands. Let her always be there to save him.'

She was plainly waiting to be disagreed with, but Maniye just sat there quietly, surprised by how much the woman had already said. Abruptly a shrill cackle sounded from out across the grassland and she jumped.

'Hyena is laughing at me,' Shyri told her sourly. 'I have been a poor daughter to her since that River boy crossed my path.' And then, 'I should just have made him fight me. That is how you get a hook into that one.' She scowled disgustedly up at the moon, and then turned a sharp eye on Maniye. 'What about you?'

'And Asmander?' Maniye gaped at her.

'You and your Horse boy. You think I don't see that?'

Maniye let herself grin. 'I will not be unhappy if Alladai son of Ganris is at Where the Fords Meet.'

'Go to him and take him,' Shyri said bluntly. 'Nothing good comes of waiting.'

The thought sped Maniye's heart a little. She remembered how she had been before they came to Tsokawan, breathless and shy every time she saw him. Now she weighed Shyri's words and knew they were good advice. Wolf and Horse would never share a roof, but perhaps they might share a night.

By Shyri's best guess they would make Where the Fords Meet before dusk the next day, and Maniye set a swift pace for the warband, letting Shyri ride her Champion shape when the Laughing Girl's wound tired her. More than once they saw

438

Plains people watching them, but the wolf pack was more than any Lion or Plains Dog raiders felt like challenging.

It was soon after midday that they began to see the horses.

First it was just a handful running through the grass in the distance, then some lone individuals, then a whole herd, and Maniye did not know whether this was usual on the Plains. Shyri tugged at her pelt, though, and then stood up on her back, toes digging in for balance as she scanned the horizon.

Maniye waited until she had jumped down and then Stepped. 'What is it?'

'There weren't all these horses running wild when we were here last,' Shyri pointed out.

'The Plains has wild horses, doesn't it?'

'Not the size of those,' Shyri said. 'These are the herds of the Horse.'

Maniye stood still as she considered the implications. She knew the Horse grazed their herds out on the Plains, beyond the marshes of Where the Fords Meet. They guarded them well, and no other tribe could master the beasts to ride anyway. Attacking the herds was a poor choice for a raider. But then everyone said the Plains people were always fighting.

'Maybe the Lion?' Shyri said doubtfully. 'They never liked the Horse much.'

They pressed on towards Where the Fords Meet, seeing more horses and expecting each band of them to Step as they approached, for them to become men of the Horse out to round up their scattered beasts. The animals avoided them, though, plunging away through the grassland wild-eyed, flanks foaming with sweat. Or else they came near and reared and screamed and bucked before charging off, as though trying to communicate some terrible warning. By now the warband was becoming uneasy, and even Shyri had no explanations.

Maniye called Feeds on Rags to her. 'You go see,' she said.

He strutted a bit at the responsibility, then took to the air on his wide black wings. The warband continued on its way, and soon after they saw the Lions. There were enough of them that the warband stopped and crouched low, unwilling to provoke a confrontation. As the beasts passed, though, Maniye could see they were not out to bring trouble to anyone. There were thirty or forty of the beasts in all, and many were laden, slung with packs and baskets in a way that would have been comical in other circumstances. Others bore copper-skinned children on their backs, and some of the women walked on human feet and carried babies as well as spears and bows. Shyri stared and stared, and when she Stepped there was no ready joke about the Lion on her lips. She looked afraid.

'Should we go ask them?' Maniye prompted.

Shyri shook her head, which turned into a shiver through her whole body. 'What do the Lion know about anything?' she whispered.

'Wings,' Spear Catcher said, at Maniye's elbow. 'Feeds is back.'

The Crow dropped into the middle of them, Stepping as he touched the ground. He stared at them all out of the mad eye in the painted half of his face.

'Tell us,' Maniye directed him.

'There is a mist over Where the Fords Meet.' Feeds on Rags' voice jumped and stuttered as though he could barely force real words out. 'A solid mist.'

Spear Catcher cuffed him. 'Talk sense.'

The Crow flinched. 'A white fog between the buildings. It was growing as I watched. I kept my distance, yes I did – so high they did not see me.'

'They? The Horse?' Maniye demanded.

'No Horse,' Feeds said. 'Not a one of the Horse did I see. But there were men there, or things that walked like men, and other things that crawled. I daredn't go close to see more, not on my own, but Where the Fords Meet is not a Horse place any more.'

'Then where are the Horse?' Maniye demanded, but nobody there had any answers. She looked around her, trying to open her head wide enough to understand what was going on, but then Kalameshli stepped forward and pinned the Crow with his gaze.

'A mist,' he pronounced. 'A pale shadow?'

'Yes, that is it, exactly,' Feeds on Rags agreed.

The Wolf priest's face closed like a trap.

'What is it?' Maniye pressed.

'A thing the Serpent spoke of.' And to her surprise there was no condemnation of the south in his voice. 'Will you still travel to Where the Fords Meet?'

Maniye nodded. 'I want to see this thing.'

'Yes,' Kalameshli agreed, to her surprise. Whatever it was that the Serpent had spoken of, it went beyond rivalries between gods.

They saw more horses as they drew closer; some seemed to be mad. One even attacked them, rushing into the centre of the warband and striking out with its hooves, screaming in a way Maniye had never heard before until the pack brought it down. In Maniye's mind its blood seemed to carry a sour taste of rot and ghosts.

Where the Fords Meet was just as Feeds had said. They could see strands and sheets of white strung around the Horse huts and creeping out along the walkways. There were human figures there, no more than a hundred, but they were not people as Maniye knew them. It was not the clothes, not the skin, nor – as the warband crept closer – was it the alien tools they carried or the strange sound of their voices. They carried an absence within them, hungry enough to consume the world and not be sated.

And as the Horse Society had kept its herds, so these new-comers had their own beasts. They were bulbous-bodied monsters with many eyes and skittering legs, from the size of a hand to half the size of a man, and they seethed at the edges of the white walls and spun and spun, building a fortress from nothing and shrouding all the places of the Horse in white.

Kalameshli told them then: 'The Serpent have an old fear they call the Pale Shadow. It took their first land from them. I have seen these Pale Shadow, and they are like these empty men here. But the Pale Shadow themselves have an old fear, and it is our oldest fear too. The Pale Shadow fear their brothers from over the sea who are the Plague People. They came to the Serpent because they knew the Plague was coming.'

The warband milled and whined at the name, and Maniye felt her own souls, Tiger and Wolf, tremble at the thought. She remembered hearing the tale of the Plague, and her ancestors' escape from it: Grey Herald had whispered it in her ear. She wanted to tell Takes Iron that he was a foolish old man and these could not be the ancient enemy. The words would have been weak as smoke, though. She knew he was right.

She looked out at those advancing white walls, woven into existence with frightening speed by the Plague People's many-legged beasts. Did any of the Horse survive in there, slaves or food for the invaders?

She thought of Alladai.

Maniye's band were at the damp land of the marsh's edge by now, where the walkways of the Horse began. To approach on those paths would put them in full view of the new masters of Where the Fords Meet. The wolves were no great swimmers, despite their experiences along the river.

Tigers could swim, though. The water was second nature to her.

'I will go,' she told her people. 'Stay here within the grass, and stay unseen.'

'No,' Kalameshli began, but she shook her head firmly, and became the tiger he could never abide, slipping away to pad softly over the soft ground, each footprint filling with water and being swallowed even as she left it.

She was halfway towards the closest of the walls when she realized she was not alone after all. A little coyote was creeping along in her tiger's shadow, and overhead a pair of dark wings circled. She turned and glowered at Sathewe, but held her peace. Where the Fords Meet was eerily quiet, no birdsong, no frogs, and the chirr of crickets seemed a sinister sound when it was heard on its own. The stutters of the Plague People voices were unnaturally clear, the muscles down her spine twitching every time she heard them. She could not order the girl back without being heard.

She crept closer, step by step, letting her body flow sinuously between clumps of grass and wiry bushes, belly to the water. She was close enough to watch the spiders extending the closest wall. All around her the shimmering silk was springing up like a fungus.

There were Plague People coming: a handful of them with some many-legged thing dragging a post ripped from a Horse hut. She saw how they would set it up as an anchor for their white walls, and began to shift backwards. There had been something hanging in the air about her all this time, but only with the arrival of the empty people did she realize it was fear. Not rational fear, but something that reached deep into her and clutched at her souls. The hunger in these creatures began to gnaw at her, even though they had not seen her.

Sathewe crept forwards another few steps, but her ears were back and her tail between her legs. Maniye had never seen her scared before. She nudged the coyote urgently, feeling that all-enshrouding fear began to leach into her, a deeper shadow beyond the pale shadow of the walls.

The empty people had got their post down, and their creature was rooting in the soft earth for them. Maniye stared at them, frozen. They were very close: pale men in banded armour, like humans to her eyes but hollow to her soul, the absence within them sharp-edged as broken ice.

Sathewe took another step, and they saw her. They saw Maniye. That cloud of fear about them focused like an eye and the awful wrongness of them tore into her, driving her souls before it like a storm scatters birds.

443

For a moment she had lost herself. She was just the tiger, yowling and snarling at them as they raised their hands in threat. Everything that was Maniye Many Tracks was being driven from her.

Then the Champion rose inside her, furious in its outrage, and she Stepped into its shape, swelling until the empty creatures were in her shadow and their digging beast fled in a rattle of limbs. She roared at them, seeing their hollow faces react in shock. Fire flared from their hands but only singed her coat. She beat one down with a single sweep of her paw, grabbed Sathewe's thin body in her jaws and fled. When she reached the warband she did not stop, and they followed her in a winding trail through the grassland until they had put a good distance between themselves and the place that had been Where the Fords Meet.

When they were far enough from danger, she set down Sathewe and Stepped, shivering at the memory of what she had felt. They waited for the Coyote girl to take her human form too, but the little animal just whined and stared at them with wide, mute eyes. Feeds on Rags landed and talked to her, and she sniffed his hand and seemed to know him, but they never saw her human face.

Maniye had been ready to shout at Feeds on Rags. She knew it must have been his idea to follow her, and Sathewe would always do as he suggested. Watching his increasing desperation, as he spoke more and more words that Sathewe could plainly not understand, she knew she did not need to. He had lived up to his true name once again: Feeds on Dreams. Now it was Sathewe's dreams he had eaten. He was his own punishment.

They moved further from Where the Fords Meet, and this time they were seeking Plains men. They found them, too – word of what had happened to the Horse had begun to spread. The scouts of many tribes were coming to see. They met Lion and Boar, Plains Dog and Shyri's Laughing Men, even one

444

sinewy huntress of the Leopard. To each they gave their warning of what lay ahead, to be heeded or ignored.

Maniye called Feeds on Rags to her and gave him his task. If he wished to redeem himself, he must fly to the great city on the river and find Hesprec. The long-foretold doom was here.

And, after he had flapped off south-west with his warnings, Kalameshli came to her.

'We must find somewhere we can be still,' he told her. 'Some Plains village where they will let us be. If this thing has come to all the world, as Hesprec said, then you will need to come into your birthright. You will need the Wolf's iron.'

***

When Feeds on Rags had finished, the silence lengthened until it seemed nobody would dare speak again. His head twitched back and forth, one eye and then the other passing over his listeners, until at last both were fixed on one face only. Slowly, the attention of everyone gathered before the Kasra's throne was drawn to the small form of Hesprec Essen Skese.

'Yes,' she told them. 'Yes, this is the start of it. This thing that has come to the Horse, it's come to all of us: Plains, River, even the cold north. Gone is the time for infighting and factions. Send Tecuman to the estuary – they know him there. Have him warn them of what sits on their border; tell them to give any refugees all aid. Send word to them to bring their wise and their strong. Send emissaries to every Plains tribe who will speak to us and beg them to do the same. This Crow must return to his mistress, and she must take word to the Crown of the World. The Plague People have found us, and we must face them before they consume this land as they did the last.'

Tecumet sat very still on her throne, but Hesprec thought she saw the Kasra's hands tremble. The very day after her investment, the very day after her marriage, she had become the woman who would save or lose the Nation and the world.

Soon after, the orders were going out. Horse messengers from their embassy in Atahlan were galloping north; a swift boat

445

was skimming Tecuman along the waters of the Tsotec. Feeds on Rags had eaten and drunk, and was spreading his wings for Maniye Many Tracks and her warband.

And Hesprec was left with her thoughts in the vaulted halls of the palace, waiting.

She would never know if the old woman had some fore-knowledge vouchsafed her, or whether she had just trailed Hesprec all the way to Atahlan like a lost dog. Certainly Therumit would never admit to the latter, and so Hesprec didn't ask. Either way, when she turned she found the slender shadow of the old priestess waiting for her.

'I suppose you heard all of that, then?' Hesprec wondered which nook had sheltered the slender snake Therumit would have become.

The old woman nodded impatiently. 'And?' she snapped.

Hesprec felt she was at the edge of a precipice. She sought for Serpent's guidance: *Surely this cannot be what you intend?* But Therumit was as old and wise in the ways of their god as she was – and twice as suspicious – and she had been convinced.

That meeting out in the estuary had planted a terrible seed in Hesprec's heart. She had always been the traveller, the seeker of knowledge in far-flung places. Yet there was one place, looming so large in the Serpent's memory, she thought she would never see. It was a terrible reason for so dangerous a journey, and yet it itched at the inside of her mind and would not be stilled.

'Very well then,' she said at last. 'Let us hope the Pale Shadow understand guest-right; let us hope they have some way of fighting their kin. We shall go to our Old Kingdom, and see what they have left of it.'

extracts reading groups

competitions books new

discounts extracts

competitions

books new events reading groups

extracts discounts

events books

extracts

new titles reading groups

interviews

events extracts

discounts

new books events

events new

discounts extracts discounts

www.panmacmillan.com

extracts events reading groups

competitions books extracts new

Acknowledgements

As usual, much thanks to my agent, Simon;
to my editor Bella and everyone at Tor;
and especially to my wife Annie.